PRAISE FOR THE HOLLOWS

"*The Hollows* is much more than a murder mystery. It weaves racial integration, labor organizing in the Appalachian coal mines, Prohibition, and women's rights throughout the narrative."

—Associated Press

"Readers will find Montgomery's storytelling prowess in full bloom. Enjoy."

—*Dayton Daily News*

"A skillfully told murder mystery that features a rich array of characters and a sophisticated portrayal of a small town grappling with its own racist past and ongoing conflicted present." —*Kirkus Reviews*

"Skilled storyteller Montgomery takes up the issue of racial prejudice as it existed in that place and time in this historical mystery that shines with its strong and appealing female characters." —*Booklist*

"Realistic characters complement a great sense of place. Montgomery does an admirable job of portraying brave women such as Lily who must become the support of their families in the face of their own grief after their husbands' deaths." —*Publishers Weekly*

"Colorful Appalachian dialect and details of geography and nature add to a well-crafted mystery . . . *The Hollows* [is] dynamic historical fiction as well as a riveting mystery." —Shelf Awareness

"*The Hollows* is a finely crafted, exciting page-turner and is highly recommended for readers of historical mysteries and anyone interested in novels of strong and empowered women." —Historical Novel Society

"Beautifully written, poetic, and full of fascinating historical detail, Montgomery masterfully portrays the strength of the brave women who became the pillars and support of their families in the face of their own grief after losing their husbands." —CrimeReads

"Montgomery has written another suspenseful mystery full of atmosphere and surprising historical details. The characters' emotional struggles don't overshadow the action but actually help to deepen the historical elements of the story while adding a palpable urgency to the mystery."

—Criminal Element

"Remarkable . . . memorable and vivid. My best advice: dive into these wonderful novels. It's an immersive and beautiful experience."

—Aunt Agatha's

"This character-based mystery has a strong and intriguing plot, a well-written narrative with vivid characters that are authentic to its time and place . . . perceptions of working women and treatment of mental illness are fittingly intertwined into this powerful story."   —*Fresh Fiction*

"With a seemingly effortless touch, Montgomery manages to deftly weave together believable characters, dark historical truths, and an enthralling mystery in *The Hollows*. The result is genuinely mysterious and utterly satisfying."   —Greer Macallister,
author of *Woman 99* and *The Magician's Lie*

PRAISE FOR THE WIDOWS

"Montgomery's debut features two tough-as-nails, strong-willed women whose empathy leaves a lasting impression. A simultaneous examination of women's rights, coal mining, Prohibition, and Appalachian life, this is a fantastic choice for historical fiction fans."

—*Library Journal* (starred review)

"Beautifully plotted and filled with believable characters, *The Widows* explores an era and an area struggling to be a part of the modern twentieth century, yet constantly pulled backward to its unsettled past . . . the launch of this series shows much potential."   —Associated Press

"[An] engaging debut . . . Vivid historical details, an intriguing mystery, and strong female characters."   —*Kirkus Reviews*

"Deeply felt . . . the feisty female protagonists do their real-life foremothers proud."   —*Publishers Weekly*

"Remarkable . . . [Montgomery's] writing is brisk, yet it lingers long enough to indulge readers with beautiful prose along the way."   —*BookPage*

"Set when coal was king and the Pinkertons its strikebreakers, *The Widows* is a gripping, beautifully written novel about two women avenging the murder of the man they both loved."

—Hallie Ephron, *New York Times* bestselling
author of *You'll Never Know, Dear*

"*The Widows* is the story of a community in crisis . . . Jess Montgomery's gorgeous writing can be just as dark and terrifying as a subterranean cave when the candle is snuffed out, but her prose can just as easily lead you to the surface for a gasp of air and a glimpse of blinding, beautiful sunlight. This is a powerful novel: a tale of loss, greed, and violence, and the story of two powerful women who refuse to stand down."

—Wiley Cash, *New York Times* bestselling
author of *The Last Ballad, A Land More Kind than Home,*
and *This Dark Road to Mercy*

"In the hard-luck, homespun, Appalachian town of Kinship, Ohio, in 1924, two strong women become unlikely comrades to solve a murder in this flinty, heartfelt mystery that sings of hawks and history, of coal mines and the urgent fight for social justice."

—Julia Keller, Pulitzer Prize–winning author of *Bone on Bone*

"Two women, a murdered husband, and the secret life he lived. Set in Appalachian Ohio coal country in 1924, *The Widows* kept me on the edge of my seat. Jess Montgomery is a masterful storyteller. This is a novel about courage and the good hearts of women, and it builds, almost unbearably, to its stunning end."

—Lee Martin, author of the
Pulitzer Prize finalist *The Bright Forever*

"With compassion and skill, Jess Montgomery deftly smashes stereotypes and puts a human face on the cost of coal mining in 1924 Appalachian Ohio. Rich with historical details, yet fast paced, *The Widows* revolves around a murder investigation. But it was the vivid voices of Lily Ross and Marvena Whitcomb that completely captivated my heart and kept me reading long into the night."

—Ann Weisgarber, author of *The Personal History of Rachel Dupree*

"Pulling back the curtain on a time and place where women's roles were too often overlooked, *The Widows* is full of characters who surprise those who underestimate them. A rich, empowering, and satisfying read."

—Jessica Strawser, author of *Not That I Could Tell*

ALSO BY JESS MONTGOMERY

THE WIDOWS

JESS MONTGOMERY
THE HOLLOWS

MINOTAUR BOOKS

NEW YORK

To Janice, My Mother-in-Law,
Who Once Wrote to Our Daughter:
*"It is impossible for a woman to learn too much,
dream too big, or live too joyously!"*

Published in the United States by Minotaur Books, an imprint of St. Martin's Publishing Group

THE HOLLOWS. Copyright © 2019 by Sharon Short. All rights reserved. Printed in the United States of America. For information, address St. Martin's Publishing Group, 120 Broadway, New York, NY 10271.

www.minotaurbooks.com

The Library of Congress has cataloged the hardcover edition as follows:

Names: Montgomery, Jess, author.
Title: The hollows : a novel / Jess Montgomery.
Description: First Edition. | New York : Minotaur Books, 2020. | Series: The kinship series; 2
Identifiers: LCCN 2019035901 | ISBN 9781250184542 (hardcover) | ISBN 9781250184559 (ebook)
Subjects: LCSH: Spirits—Fiction. | GSAFD: Mystery fiction.
Classification: LCC PS3613.O54858 H65 2020 | DDC 813/.6—dc23
LC record available at https://lccn.loc.gov/2019035901

ISBN 978-1-250-78169-7 (trade paperback)

Our books may be purchased in bulk for promotional, educational, or business use. Please contact your local bookseller or the Macmillan Corporate and Premium Sales Department at 1-800-221-7945, extension 5442, or by email at MacmillanSpecialMarkets@macmillan.com.

First Minotaur Books Trade Paperback Edition: 2021

10 9 8 7 6 5 4 3 2 1

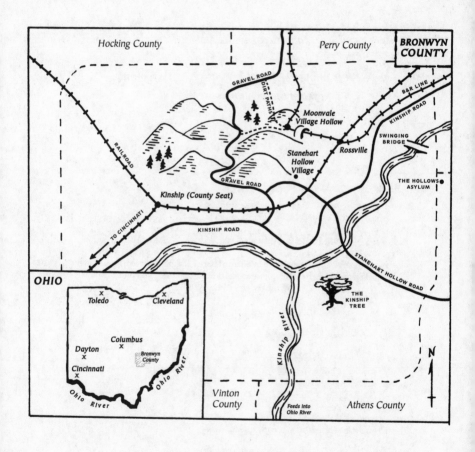

PROLOGUE

Tuesday, September 21, 1926—9:12 p.m.

For near on ten miles, the old woman walks without ceasing.

The full moon ladles light into the deep, clear night. The light trickles between trees—some already bereft of leaves—to softly pool in spots along her path.

The path her daddy had taught her.

She follows it now as then, harkening to his whisper welling up from seventy years past, and as she does, her hips and knees unstiffen into sprightliness. At each milestone—across the swinging bridge, past a large boulder tumbled down from the ridge countless ages ago—her breath and heart quicken, not so much from physical effort as from the excitement of the path springing back to life. At herself springing back to a younger life. Years and places and people fall away as if the path forgives her for forgetting it, as if it has always remembered her, has patiently awaited her return, knowing she would at last remember it, too, and come back to it.

Knowing it would, in the end, claim her.

There—a natural spring bubbles up, guarded by a stone well.

There—the Friends meeting house, its simple angled roof cutting a wedge out of the moon. *We have allies there, but we only stop if truly desperate; it is too obvious a place.* She gasps. Daddy's whisper, scholarly and somber and smoky from his pipe, is no longer within her but beside her, and she turns to look at him.

In the spare second it takes to see he's not there, she stumbles for the first time since escaping, comes to herself, to momentary full awareness of who she is now: an old woman, shivering in her thin nightgown and robe, her bare feet wrapped in cleaning rags she'd managed to sneak aside, clutching her daddy's gold compass, the only item she'd kept from childhood. Except—*oh!* Her jagged fingernails—only recently neat and polished—dig into the palm of her hand, find that she's clutching nothing.

Perhaps she'd dropped the compass. Or perhaps she hadn't brought it with her. Of late, it's become so hard to know what's real, what's not.

For some time, people and moments and events—living and dead, past and present—have been raveling free of one another, like pieces in a patch quilt whose connecting stitches have broken, the pieces all still there but floating separately, randomly, in her mind.

Then she spots the wild pawpaw tree. *Oh!* It's still here, this tree she'd loved to visit in the fall as a child.

No, she loves visiting now, for isn't she a child?

She twirls—or tries to, for she also loved dancing as a child—and the resultant stumble brings her back to her elderly self. But she stares up with gratitude at the tree. Then she reaches for the just-now ripe fruit, the sight and touch of which sets her mouth to watering and her stomach to grumbling.

After her quick meal, beyond the tree, she spots the rock face and the pile of boulders. On the other side of the rock face is the cave, where they should be waiting for her. John, Garnet, and the baby. . . . Her heart races; her pulse thrums; the patch quilt pieces tumble and tangle.

No. They're not there yet. She's making this trek to *find* them. Warn them. Save them.

Hurry, her daddy whispers.

And so she keeps on, taking hidden ways, not stopping when far-off coyote calls pierce the close-up chittering of crickets and katydids, or even at a whiff of woodsmoke from a cabin, the scent stirring a longing for home and food and rest.

Finally, by instinct borne of long and deeply buried memory, she turns up a rise and at last comes upon the train track.

With her first step onto the crushed stone ballast between the wood ties, she cries out. Her feet are already gashed and swollen from her flight through the woods. Pain rattles up her legs to her hips. Her next step is onto a wood tie—easier on the bottoms of her feet than the ballast, but the ties are set too far apart for her to set her pace to them.

She settles for walking as lightly as she can on the ballast, quick dancer steps, as if her calves and feet remember their time onstage, even if her mind does not.

Except . . . a flash of memory of dancing shoes. Then of sturdy walking shoes, from recent days. Why wouldn't Mama let her have her shoes?

No, it wasn't Mama who took her shoes—

No matter. She will distract herself by counting each step. After a while, she no longer feels the crushed stone lacerating her feet, the cramps in her calf muscles, the spasming in her hips and back.

She no longer deftly leaps forward. She simply walks, walks, walks without ceasing.

Until she comes upon the Moonvale Hollow Tunnel.

The tunnel is made of stones quarried and hewn from a nearby hollow. Trees grow on the earth mounded over its flat top. Moonlight skims the trees and drips generously enough to create the illusion of another full moon awaiting on the other side.

The old woman stops. Halting brings awareness of pain and her legs tremble, give way, and she falls to her knees. She cries out—now as then, old woman and young girl, one and the same. A realization flickers—she has been seeing this tunnel her whole life, shimmering out of the corner of her right eye, like a misaligned stereograph slide.

In this moment, the actual sight of the tunnel is a gut punch.

Still, she must go in, through the darkness, to the moon on the other side. She rises shakily. She wants to move forward but for a moment forgets how to walk. There—a flicker of movement in the corner of her left eye. A twig, snapping.

And so for a moment, the old woman gazes to her left, into the thicket.

Stillness. Darkness. Silence. Nothing.

She looks back to the maw of the Moonvale Hollow Tunnel.

There—her father.

He hangs by his neck from a rope lashed around the trunk of a tree growing on top of the earth-covered tunnel, his body a dark silhouette over the light on the other side of the tunnel, the light brighter now and filling the whole opening, and his body shifts back and forth, a flutter's worth of movement.

A piercing wail. Not her scream, not yet. The wailing grows along with the light behind him, and only as that light grows to claim her father's image, to take him from her again, does she cry out for him.

Time, that cruel trickster, freezes her to the spot.

Someone grabs her. Drags her from the track, from the growing light and noise, from her father. She struggles to wriggle free but only manages to twist enough to see the side of the man's face.

John!

No—the shiny, taut scar from earlobe to dimpled chin, the houndstooth-checked cap—these are not John's. Yet in his countenance of concern, the alarm in his kind gaze, she sees him after all. *John.*

And she relaxes into his grasp as he pulls her to safety into the woods.

This time, this time, she'd found him soon enough.

CHAPTER 1

≫

LILY

Tuesday, September 21—11:10 p.m.

As promised, a man with a mule-drawn cart waits a mile or so from the turnoff onto Moonvale Hollow Road. Lily Ross spots them in her headlights as she eases around a sharp turn.

She pulls off to the side, relieved to come to a stop. Ever since turning off from Kinship Road, her Model T rattled in protest at ruts and jags, wheels jittery on dirt and gravel at her initial fifteen-miles-per-hour speed. She'd had to slow to ten. No use losing a tire.

Now as she stops, she sees the man—young, early twenties, one hand on the mule's lead, the other thumbing his overall strap. Lily turns off her automobile, picks up her flashlight, opens her door. She steps out carefully, her sight needing a moment to adjust to the moonlit night.

When it does, she notes the man gaping at her. Then grinning slowly. He can't see, or maybe can't read, "Bronwyn County Sheriff" emblazoned on the door.

As she slips her key ring into her skirt pocket—she's recently added pockets to all of her skirts and dresses, even her Sunday dress—she briefly pulls back her jacket and touches her revolver, holstered around her waist. Then she reaches back in her vehicle, grabs the sheet she thought at the last moment to bring with her, and tucks it under her arm. She shuts the door, turns on her flashlight, shines it directly at the young man. He's still grinning. Must not have noticed the revolver.

"Ma'am, you need some help?"

She turns the flashlight onto her sheriff's star pinned to her lapel. She takes a deep breath, notes the loamy dryness of the autumn air. *Good.* Rain would only disturb the body she has come for, the area around it. She hopes to see both as intact as possible. She turns her flashlight back on the young man.

He's no longer grinning.

"My apologies, ma'am, Sheriff, no one done told me—"

"You work for the B and R Railroad?"

The young man straightens with pride. "Flagman. In training."

Lily nods, steps forward toward the mule and cart, waiting at the head of the dirt path that actually leads to Moonvale Hollow Village.

"Don't know how clean the straw bales in back are; if I'da known—"

The mule fusses as Lily approaches. She pats the flank of the poor beast. More than likely tired out from a day's work, and now called into service at night.

Lily, too, is bone weary after a long day.

Just an hour earlier, she had been tempted to ignore the knock at her door—probably Missy Ranklin again, given to coming late at night to complain about her husband, Ralf, but never willing to file formal charges.

On the off chance Missy might actually file a complaint that Lily could follow up on, Lily had answered her door. Instead of mousy Missy, a telegraph delivery boy greeted her. Lily's hand had trembled as she reached for the thin slip of paper. The last telegram she'd received, just over a year before, had been from the powerful Cincinnati attorney, business mogul, and big-time bootlegger George Vogel; that telegram brought a cryptic message Lily had deciphered quickly enough: an offering to expel those responsible for her husband's death from the region.

This telegram, though, was from the deputy stationmaster for the B&R Railroad line in Moonvale Hollow Village: someone had fallen from the top of the Moonvale Hollow Tunnel onto the train as it headed east to west. A B&R Railroad man would meet her on Moonvale Hollow Road by the narrow dirt path that led to the village: population one hundred souls—depending on the ebb and flow of birth and death—existing only to serve as a rail switching yard and depot, and inaccessible by automobile. Folks can get in and out only by train, mule, or foot.

She'd tipped the telegraph boy a dime to go fetch her closest friend, Hildy Lee Cooper, who lived a few doors down from the sheriff's house. Hildy, who also worked as the jail mistress, could always be relied upon to come stay with Lily's children—seven-year-old Jolene and five-year-old Micah—when duty sometimes called Lily away of an evening.

A few minutes later, the boy was back—neither Hildy nor Hildy's mother was at the Cooper house. Lily spared a moment's worth of surprise to wonder where the two could be, so late at night—but the more pressing matter was the dead person along the rail line in Moonvale Hollow Village. Two more dimes sent the telegraph boy back out to fetch Lily's own mama, residing at the end of the street.

After he left again, in the scant time it took Lily to put water on the stove to boil, rush upstairs to change into one of her older dresses and work boots, and then hurry down again, Mama was letting herself and Caleb Jr.—Mama's change-of-life baby, same age as Lily's son—into the kitchen through the mudroom door.

Lily gave her little brother a quick hug and then tucked him in under a quilt on the parlor's settee. She retrieved her notebook and pencil from the rolltop desk, pulled open the top drawer to grab her flashlight, then hurried back to the kitchen. As Mama finished making the coffee, Lily got her revolver and sheriff's star from the top of the pie safe. While Mama poured Lily a cup of coffee, Lily explained, "I've been called out to investigate an accident on the rail line in Moonvale Hollow Village."

Mama's eyes widened; both knew of the remote village, the source of ghost stories children told one another, but neither had ever visited. There'd been no reason. The village had been founded by Adam Dyer just before the Civil War, on land his family had passed down generation-to-generation, the original claim given in lieu of cash as recompense for serving in the Revolutionary War. Two generations of Dyers had hardscrabble farmed the ornery land, riddled with hollows and ridges, until coal companies needed a quick shortcut through the area from points east to a bigger depot from which they could go to Cincinnati and Columbus. Cleverly, Adam Dyer leased out his land for a rail line—only wide enough for one track—and Moonvale Hollow became a remote village. Dyers had always been synonymous with Moonvale Hollow.

Until, of late, Perry Dyer—Lily's opponent for the role of sheriff in the upcoming election. Perry, sole heir of the rail lease rights and village property, had moved with his wife, Margaret, into Kinship a year before, shortly after Perry's father died. Talk was that Margaret had a strong preference for big-town life and, with her father-in-law gone, she could finally have her way. Perry, who'd opened a hunting supply store in Kinship, had pounced on the opportunity to run against Lily this fall. His editorial in the *Kinship Daily Courier,* which had only recently become a daily, another sign of the area's growing prosperity, made clear his position: he knew the county inside out, even the most remote pockets, and though Lily's tenure as appointed sheriff was a quaint novelty, it was time for a real sheriff to take office. Meaning, a male sheriff.

Lily said, "I'm sure this investigation will go quickly. Just a matter of some official paperwork with the rail company."

Mama had looked relieved, said, "Good—you have the meeting first thing tomorrow morning to prepare for the debate with Perry Dyer, and the Woman's Club meeting coming up, and don't forget you need to get your pie into the county fair—"

Lily groaned.

"So you're running for sheriff in your own right." Mama cast a pointed glance at the top of the pie safe, from whence Lily had just grabbed her revolver and badge. Pushed to the back of the top was a red glass dish in which nested Lily's old best-in-show county fair pie ribbons, once a point of pride, now gathering dust. "They still want to know you're a woman."

"According to Perry Dyer, that's not a favorable asset."

"Well, worse'n a woman in a man's role is a woman who acts too much like a man."

An argument Mama had made, years before, when Daddy had taken tomboy Lily on hunting and fishing expeditions. Lily gave Mama a reassuring smile. Mama had, after all, come quickly, dragging herself and Caleb Jr. out of bed and down to Lily's home—the county sheriff's house. As Mama did, every time Lily asked.

Even so, with her work and all the tedious campaign tasks necessary for election for a full four-year term in her own right as sheriff, Lily barely had time to bake and cook for her own children. She didn't want to bake a damned pie for a contest. But she knew Mama was right, so she would—later. Right then, she gulped the strong boiled coffee, knowing she'd need it to stay alert for her drive to the designated meeting spot, and the investigation to follow.

Now, at the mule cart, Lily hoists herself up and sits on the driver's bench. The mule heaves forward, but Lily pulls gently back on the reins. She looks at the young man, still gaping at her.

"You planning to drive us there, or walk behind?"

He glances over his shoulder, winces. He's holding his right shoulder tight to his collar. He looks back at her nervously. "Anyone else comin'?"

Lily bites her lip to stifle her sigh. It is, after all, 1926 and in the big cities—from what she reads in the newspapers, anyway—standards have relaxed, but here in rural Ohio, it's still improper for an unmarried man and woman to be alone together.

"Son," she says, though at twenty-eight she's barely older than he, "like it or not, I'm the sheriff of Bronwyn County." She'd been appointed a year and a half before to serve in her deceased husband's stead, then won a special election last November. "I can question you while you drive us, or I can drive myself, and ask you later when you catch up on foot—and delay further your train getting back to running. I can reckon what your boss would prefer."

The flagman in training hesitates, but as she lifts the reins he hoists himself into the cart, plops on the driver's bench, and grabs the leads from her.

A few jolting steps forward and they're down the path, ducking so their heads won't knock into a broken, dangling limb of an oak. Overhead, tree limbs clutch one another, forming a tunnel of branch and leaf. Meager moonlight sifts onto their path, wide enough for the cart and mule. Lily glances over her shoulder. Already, she cannot see the dangling limb, or the rutted road where she left her automobile.

It's cooler on the path, the dense forest exhaling the last of summer's warmth while inhaling the coming winter. The quietness of night thickens, clinging to trunks like lichen. An owl hoots from a distance yet sounds as if it's beside her. Another animal—raccoon or fox or bobcat—rustles in the thicket.

Out of the corner of her eye, something shimmers. A young boy. He dashes merrily, chasing something. A ball or a dog. Suddenly he disappears. Lily rubs her eyes, reprimands herself: She's not really seeing a child. She's just tired. Should have had more coffee.

Yet her temples pound, and she fights the urge to gasp for air.

She glances at her driver. He stares ahead, placidly. He starts whistling, off-key. Irksome, but it covers the sound of her nervous gasp. With her next inhale, she steadies her breath, focuses on the odors of the mule, the hay bales, the musk of the forest, finding comfort in their earthiness. She exhales slowly.

Then she asks, "You came from Moonvale on this path?"

The man startles. Lily smiles a little. Perhaps whistling is his cover for uneasiness.

He nods. "Widest and easiest path in or out of Moonvale, south toward Kinship, so I was told. There are other paths. Anyway, this rig belongs to a villager. The engineer laid claim to it for to fetch you. There's another path like this 'un, but toward Athens. That's it, other'n walking trails only the locals'd know."

The way he draws out his vowels tells Lily he's from Appalachia, but not her part of it. Farther south, she reckons.

"Where are you from to begin with?"

"Logan County. Kentucky."

Coal-mining territory. "You're not working the mines there?"

He straightens, a mix of pride and defensiveness, winces again. That shoulder. "I did, but I got out—work for real money, real job, not company scrip!" He glances at her, wary and apologetic. "I reckon you're not from coal—"

"My daddy's people were," Lily says, meaning her father's father. "He got out. He ran the grocery in Kinship."

"That sounds right nice."

"Yes." No need to say Daddy had died alongside a union organizer and the common-law husband of her friend Marvena Whitcomb, trying to rescue miners from a cave-in, two years ago. On an autumn night, like this one. Lily clears her throat. "What can you tell me? All I know is someone fell from the top of the Moonvale Hollow Tunnel."

He stiffens. "I was told to meet the sheriff, ma'am. Bring him—you—to the scene."

"You didn't see what happened?"

"No, ma'am. I was dozing in the crew car."

"How'd you hurt your shoulder?"

The flagman stares ahead into the darkness.

"I hope the injury doesn't get in the way of your training. Send you back home."

He inhales sharply at the notion.

"Course, in that case, it would be good to have an official record of the injury not being your fault. You'd have time off, to heal up? Working for a real company, and all?"

For a long moment, the only sounds come from the forest—another owl cry. The chittering of crickets. A nearby stream.

The young man clears his throat. "Train stopped, all of a sudden. I got thrown out of my bunk. Hit the floor."

"So the train was going fast?"

"No faster'n usual."

There's a tight defensiveness to his tone. Lily asks gently, "What's usual?"

"Coming out of the tunnel, maybe twenty miles an hour, and the brakemen would be fixing to slow her down before crossing another trestle bridge into the village."

"But you were asleep before the train stopped."

"Yep."

So he would not know whether the train was going its usual speed.

"What did you do after the train stopped?"

"Well, me and the flagman got off. The engineer ran back to the caboose, must've talked to the conductor—"

"He's in the caboose?"

Despite his sore shoulder, he straightens, preening at having knowledge she doesn't. "Yeah. Conductor is in the caboose, with the rear brakeman. Front brakeman, engineer, are up front. Flagmen, fireman, we're wherever we're needed for the run—or can fit."

Lily turns on her flashlight, gets her notebook and pencil from her bag. "Can you give me the names and titles of your crew?"

In the ambient light from her flashlight, she sees him purse his lips, reconsider how unconstrained he'd become with her. "May oughta talk to the engineer about that—"

Lily makes herself sound aghast. "I'd hate to delay the train for any longer than necessary. I reckon he'd appreciate you're cooperating with me, speeding this along."

He gives her the names and titles of the crew. When she finishes jotting them down, she shows him; he glances at the page, nods too quickly to have really proofed her work. *Ah.* Her earlier observation was right; he can't read. She puts her notebook away, turns off her flashlight, and tucks it away, too.

"Did you see the body after the train stopped, or talk to other crew members?"

"No. I got off, waited with everyone else to find out what had happened."

"So you stood alongside the train? And you didn't do or observe *anything*?"

He frowns. *Good. Let him be insulted enough to want to prove himself.* "Well, yeah. Mr. Greene—"

"The conductor?" Lily hasn't forgotten already—Greene is the engineer—but she's willing to play the dumb "little lady" from time to time to get more information from men than they intend to share.

Sure enough, he says, "I heard Mr. Greene—the engineer—say he thought the person was female. The body clipped the side of a freight car, and the impact tossed it into the thicket, between the track and the telegraph line." He clears his throat. "I'm sorry if this is too much."

"No, go on."

"Well, that's about all I can tell you, anyway. The conductor sent me to run down the line to the village to fetch the stationmaster. He wasn't on duty, but the deputy was, so he sent the telegram to you from the station. After that, I was sent to wait for you."

They ride on in silence for a few minutes more until the mule stops shy of an embankment. A harsh crop on the mule's flank and the beast pulls them up out of the branch and thicket tunnel, alongside the track.

It takes a moment for Lily's vision to adjust to the brightness of the train headlight, to see westward down a steep grade of track to the tiny village, all shadows and torchlight. Lily cannot make out any buildings or people, but she imagines the torchlights are held by villagers, curious about the hullabaloo at the depot, about why someone's mule and cart have been requisitioned.

Since her husband's death, Lily has found that the absences of ordinary, predictable sounds—Daniel shaving in the washroom, Daniel humming, Daniel sitting on the edge of their bed to pull on his boots and then clunking his feet on the floor—are more noticeable than the sounds themselves ever were.

Lily wraps her arms around her midriff, a sudden hollowness roiling her gut.

Perhaps it was like that for the villagers tonight. They were alarmed by the absence of the regular train whistle, the aural ghost of the expected discordant wail, and gathered outside to ask one another what must have happened.

"Ma'am—you all right?"

Lily hoists herself off the cart and looks eastward at the train, the engine's bright headlight flooding the single track, the tunnel a distance behind the caboose. Above the tunnel to the full moon and the tree-covered top of the Moonvale Hollow Tunnel, from whence the body allegedly had fallen.

CHAPTER 2

※

HILDY

Tuesday, September 21—11:10 p.m.

On this clear night, the full moon rides high and bright, spilling milky light through the dirty bedroom window, onto the thin pillow between Hildy Cooper and Tom Whitcomb. Both now lay on their sides in his bed, eyes locked.

Heat rushes Hildy's face. Suddenly shy, she tries to look away. Can't. Moonlight brightens Tom's blue eyes and there's nothing in the world she can imagine wanting to see more.

The thought only deepens her blush, which makes Tom grin, and she sees in his eyes and smile that he's both amused and touched by her sudden onset of modesty, moments after there'd been not a whit of shyness—or space—between them.

Tom reaches to stroke Hildy's cheek, and in the pale light she notes the coal-stained rims of his fingernails, the rough callouses on his thick fingers and large hands. That such hands could also be tender restirs yearning, though she is still breathless from their lovemaking. Suddenly the spare space between his hand and her cheek seems an impossible distance, the mere moment it will take for him to reach her an unbearable eternity. She grasps his hand, brings it to her cheek.

And there it is again—from his slightest touch, fire dancing over and through her whole body.

Hildy presses her eyes shut, Tom's gaze too much.

But behind her tightened lids, there he is, unwavering, still regarding her, this time from a months-old memory.

One moment, Tom was just another adult student she helped Olive Harding—Rossville's schoolmarm—tutor in letters and reading, a few hours twice a week after the regular school day.

Then one of the other students—a miner like Tom—cursed and banged his fists against his desk, crying out, *Ain't no good, I can't.* While everyone else stared at the man's outburst, Tom gave him a wry smile, saying, *You mean to tell me you can pickaxe your way through a mountain, but you're gonna let a little pile of gray letters get the best of you? If'n I can do this, anyone can.*

As the other man laughed and the tension eased in the one-room schoolhouse, Hildy stared as Tom nearly toppled the child-sized school desk, leaning over to help his friend sort out the source of his trouble. Tom was the quickest study among the adults, speeding along with his lessons, but never braggartly. It struck Hildy that Tom was likely the same way in the mines.

A year before, Hildy had helped her good friend and county sheriff, Lily Ross, with troubles that had arisen in Rossville and then came to know Tom as the widower brother of Lily's other good friend, the union organizer Marvena Whitcomb.

In that moment in the schoolhouse, as he helped the other man sound out the *gr* consonant combination, it was as if Hildy saw Tom for the first time, noting his quiet confidence. His humility and humor. His kindness. Tom must have sensed her looking at him, for he turned his gaze to her, and she'd nearly gasped as she finally saw past his care-worn scruffiness as his sharp blue-eyed gaze took her in. His eyebrows lifting in surprise—seeing her, too, as if for the first time.

She'd also blushed then, redness rising up her chest and creeping over the top of her high-necked dress collar, as she realized for the first time in years—since she'd been engaged to be married to Lily's brother, who had died in the Great War and left her a widow-of-the-heart—she was regarding a man and feeling surprisingly delicious tingles dance over her skin. Tom grinned.

He'd been all seriousness when Hildy came to check on his progress. There was no way out of it, for breaking the usual routine would draw the attention of the others. As she sat next to him, listened to him sound out sentences from the children's primer, she felt herself come alive. And she hadn't even known, until that moment, that since losing her first fiancé she'd been merely going through the motions of life, half-dead even though she still breathed.

That night, back at home in Kinship, after a quiet dinner with Mother, Hildy had gone to bed early, claiming a headache, though really her head pounded with fantasies of Tom peeling back her blouse, of his touch tracing a gentle line down her throat, to her collarbones, clavicle, bosom. She'd tried to banish such sinful thoughts—for she'd been engaged for the past three months to be married to another man.

A suitable man—as Mother would say. Proper. The owner of the grocery in Kinship.

A man everyone—including her best friend, Lily—told her was a great catch for her. Safe. Comfortable. Respectable.

A few days later, Hildy had almost not driven over to Rossville to help the schoolmarm with tutoring. That would have pleased Mother, who found Hildy's volunteerism in a scruffy coal-mining town unsuitable for a properly engaged woman from the Bronwyn County seat of Kinship. But Hildy had been haunted by thoughts of Tom, no matter how cruelly she cajoled herself for such silliness.

She told herself she'd go as usual, see Tom, and he'd have retreated back to being another miner she was teaching to read. Out of Christian charity. Nothing more. And her desires would surely fizzle out as foolish fancies, and her decision to marry the grocer would return to its proper, sensible priority.

Instead, her heart fell when Tom did not arrive at the start of the tutoring session. Blinking back disappointed tears, she'd gone about her tasks alongside Olive. Then when the door swung open and Tom entered—apologizing for his lateness, explaining that his boy had a cough that needed tending to by Nana Sacovech, Rossville's unofficial midwife and healing woman—Hildy had nearly cried out in relief at the sight of him.

He'd lingered after the lesson—to catch up, he said. And Hildy found herself saying she'd be glad to stay to help him. Olive had shot Hildy a knowing, amused look but then looked away when Hildy frowned. After all, Olive was keeping her own scandalous secret—far more serious and potentially dangerous—and Hildy, sympathetic to Olive's plight, was helping her keep it. She'd even told Olive about her father's old hunting shack on a small piece of land between Rossville and Moonvale Hollow, and roughly how to get there. She'd only been hunting a few times with Daddy—an unladylike hobby, according to Mother. They had yet to sell the land and shack.

Olive had left, leaving Hildy and Tom alone together—scandalous enough in its own way. It would be two more lessons before Hildy would find herself letting her fingertips brush his wrist, curious to see if the pull she sensed pulsing between them would simply disappear if they actually touched.

The pull got stronger.

A week later, when they were again alone and he reached for her, she leaned into him, bringing her lips to his.

Now here they are. It's the third time they've made love in Tom's modest company-owned house, his son sent to stay with Nana so she could tend to his tricky, persistent cough.

Hildy opens her eyes. Tom still contemplates her, but he no longer grins. His lined face is taut, his gaze flashing with judgment, though not over her enjoyment of the lovemaking they'd just shared. Even when she'd told him—as she'd never confessed to anyone else—that she and first fiancé Roger had made love before he'd shipped out for the Great War, even when she'd confessed that some small part of her still missed Roger and always would, Tom had shown no judgment, only empathy. In turn, he admitted he still thought with sorrow about his wife, who'd died thirteen years before, not long after their son was born.

No, Hildy realizes, Tom judges her harshly because he reads in her expression her shame at their unlikely, yet miraculous, pairing.

"Folks see your automobile, still parked at the schoolhouse," Tom says. "No one here's falling for the tale that you stay to sweep up and straighten books for hours after school's out."

"You're telling me I should go?"

"No." Tom sweeps a loose strand of her hair back from her forehead. "I'm tellin' you we gotta make this honest. Make it right."

"We will. It's just that Merle—" Hildy stops. Here, in Rossville, in Tom's bed, her fiancé's name said aloud sounds like a foul oath. Yet in Kinship, it sounds a source of pride, as she overhears her mother's friends talk when they come into the grocery, where she works for Merle Douglas several days a week. Once they're wed, he wants her to continue to help in the store.

There's Hildy Cooper—did you know she's engaged to Mr. Douglas?

Why, he's near on old enough to be her father!

Still, a lucky catch for her!

Have they set a date yet?

No—but you know her mother will want the wedding to be fancy!

Well, she'd better get to the altar soon! She's such a quiet, mousy little thing—

Hildy shakes away the voices, refocuses on Tom. "I need time to break it to Merle—"

Tom frowns. "This ain't no good, sugar. You got to choose—and I want it to be me, even though it'd be better for you if it was Merle."

"Easier, you mean."

"In the long run, yeah."

Hildy stares at Tom, considers his lank figure, barely covered under the bedsheet, his thinning hair, the fine wrinkles around his eyes and mouth etched with coal dust ground into his skin. She wishes for his gap-toothed smile to open the stern set of his lips. He is not a handsome man. Weariness and wear show in his overworked, thin lines. But there is that kindness, and humor, and humility in his eyes, even as he gazes at her sorrowfully. She might be hungry at night every now and again in a future with Tom—and by choosing him, she'd horrify

Mother and many people she knows in Kinship, maybe even Lily. She's not sure his sister, Marvena, who seems wary of her, would accept her.

Tom sits up straight, leans his head back against the wall. He pulls away from her touch.

"I can't do this no more." Tom's voice twists on the words, as if he is trying to resist their pain.

"I need to find the right time." Hildy's reply is snappish.

The summer before, Merle's interest in her had been intriguing, flattering, but soon became overwhelming. Still, Merle had also seemed an escape from her otherwise fraught life with Mother.

Yet when Mother and Merle began pressing her over a month ago to commit to a wedding date, she found herself resisting. Hedging, as she is now with Tom.

Oh, Tom. With him, she would find love and, yes, physical pleasure. Over the past weeks, she's come to realize the truth she'd tried to tamp down to the bottom of her heart ever since saying yes to Merle's proposal: life with Merle would be bearable, but she'd never really have any type of passion with him.

That realization was also overwhelming.

Now Tom is pressing her, too, and she needs time to think, time to find the best way—

"You want the impossible."

"What is that supposed to mean?"

"You want to get what you want, upsetting nobody."

Hildy pulls herself over to Tom, leans her head on his chest. He doesn't embrace her as he usually does. She begins to cry. "I'll break it off with him, Tom; I will. I need time—"

Tom finally touches her, but only to ease her off of him, and he stands up from the bed as she tries to grab hold of him, and steps out of reach. "No, you won't. You'd hafta be crazy to do that. What can I offer you but a life of hard work and scarcity?"

"Love. You can offer me love, and I the same to you—"

Tom's laugh, though soft, is abrupt, rueful. "Love? That ain't gonna put food in your belly, nor a fine, fancy hat on your head, and if'n love were enough"—he gives the word "love" a harsh twist, as if it is some rank, foul thing he wants to strangle—"if'n it were—" And here his voice breaks, and he steps out of the moonlight, and she can no longer see his face, and her heart pangs immediately at losing sight of him. But he doesn't want her to stare frankly at the tears she knows are now running down his lined cheeks. He wishes to hide the humiliation she's brought upon him, making him think she could be his when in truth she doesn't have the courage for the only life he could offer her—that of a miner's wife. Tougher still, a union organizer's wife.

"If'n love were enough, you'd have shown that by now."

She hears him step farther away. He picks up her dress from the floor, tosses it to her on the bed. Hildy stares down at it, the modest blue fabric swimming before her eyes, as if she's staring into an endless pond of water, and she wishes that she were, that she could dive in and swim away from all this trouble.

"Don't cry, sugar." Tom's voice hitches. "You'd be crazy to throw over a man like Merle for me, for the life I could give you. I know that. You do, too. Just go, and sooner or later, it'll be like you never spent any time here at all. You'll get your right mind back and settle down to be his wife."

CHAPTER 3

⚛

LILY

Tuesday, September 21—11:30 p.m.

Two men stand by a coal-oil lamp hung on a hook staked in the ground beside the caboose. Lily catches their strident voices but not their words, and they fall silent as she approaches.

One steps forward. In the dim lamplight, Lily sees his hands tremoring, senses the lingering tension of the conversation she's interrupted.

"Ma'am? You should get back to your home—"

Again, she points to her badge. "I'm Sheriff Ross."

He goes stock-still. Then he extends his hand. "I'm the conductor. Mr. Lawrence."

Their handshake is abrupt. *Down to business, then.* Lily says, "I understand the deceased is likely female, fell from the tunnel as the train came through, and was clipped by one of the freight cars? That's what your flagman in training told me."

Mr. Lawrence nods. "The head brakeman was preparing to stop the train down at the depot. He saw the body as it hit, near the middle of the train."

"He was outside?"

Now Mr. Lawrence points, directing her attention to a narrow ladder that scales the engine. "His job is to get up top and set the hand brake."

Lily calculates: frightening enough to scramble up as the train is rumbling through a dark forest, what's more to see a body falling from the top of the tunnel—at least forty feet high. Anyone jumping would know they were risking injury or death.

Voices down the embankment catch her attention. "I hope they haven't disturbed the body. I want to see exactly where it landed."

Mr. Lawrence clears his throat. "They're still looking."

The tunnel is a quarter mile, maybe more, behind the caboose. She's taken a train only twice, both times to Cincinnati with Daniel. But she knows how it feels to stop an automobile going twenty miles per hour; it would take a minute or so. Lily calculates: a train would take longer, but this one had only the engine, the six cars she'd counted walking over here, and the caboose. If the flagman in training was right and the train was going its customary twenty miles per hour, she reckons that the brakeman should have been able to stop the train sooner, closer to the tunnel.

Lily asks, "Does the train come through at the same times every day?"

"Yes."

"So you were scheduled to arrive at the depot at what time?"

"Nine thirty p.m."

"Mighty late. Latest train out of Kinship is on Wednesday nights, eight p.m."

"That's a passenger train. This is freight. Wessex Corporation—over in Rossville . . ." Mr. Lawrence pauses, realization flickering. "You any kin—"

"I was married to Daniel Ross, whose father established the town and the original mining operation." Heat rises in Lily's face, and she's glad for the disguise of shadowy light. The sooty, dank smell of coal, coming from the open train cars, is suffocating.

"Ah, read something about that. Wasn't he killed by an escaped prisoner—"

"I was asking about the scheduled arrival time. Nine thirty, you said?" Behind each sharply snapped word is the hurt that still punches up, a hard fist slamming into her heart, whenever someone asks about Daniel. "Were you on time?"

"Early."

"How early?"

"Not much. We came through the tunnel at nine twenty."

"At your usual speed?"

He frowns. "A bit faster. We left Rossville late, and we were making up time. Wouldn't have mattered if we were going slower. Body hitting a train or the ground from that height—"

"Not blaming the train's speed. Just wondering. Would the train have been able to stop in time to keep from hitting a person, or a body, on the track?"

"Not at that spot. Can't see anything on the other side of the tunnel, even with lights on, until we're nearly out. Most dangerous run for miles, but given these hills, I can see there wasn't no other choice for how to lay the track. What are you thinking?"

"Well, simplest explanation is that a local person would know your train's usual schedule, and decided to jump just before the train would come through. If the impact of the fall didn't bring death, then being run over surely would."

The conductor stares at her, as if this grim, though obvious, explanation is more shocking coming from a woman.

Lily goes on. "If the train came through earlier, wouldn't the person be surprised? Maybe lose resolve? Unless the person wasn't trying to commit suicide, was instead trying for a fast, though dangerous, way out of this area. Ever have something like that happen?"

"Time to time," Mr. Lawrence admits. "Elsewhere, when we're going slower."

"I'm trying to think of all the likely reasons someone would jump from the tunnel onto the top of your train—when it was both going faster and coming through earlier than usual," Lily says. "Smacks of desperation. If you'll pardon the expression."

The conductor frowns, but the other man, until now sitting quietly on the caboose steps, chuckles. "We gotta tell her!" He leaps up, totters toward them, introduces himself to Lily as the head brakeman.

"A highly responsible job." Lily opts to ignore the illicit scent of moonshine roiling off of him. Mama always says you draw more flies with honey than vinegar—and though as a child Lily had argued against the value of more flies, she'd come as an adult to understand Mama's point with the old adage.

"I'm not sure he is feeling well enough to reasonably state—" Mr. Lawrence starts.

"I'd be remiss not to take his statement." Lily looks at the head brakeman, who grins as if pleased that Lily values his witness enough to override his boss. "Please go on."

"Well, ma'am, after the body fell, I saw another figure at the top of the tunnel. One arm hooked around the trunk of one of them there skinny trees."

Lily glances back. Indeed, trees grow to the edge of the top of the tunnel that had been dynamite-blasted right through the hill.

"Were you able to note anything else about the figure? Male or female?" Another person up there with the victim—that complicates things. And raises a new question: if the victim was alone, the fall could be accident, suicide, or a foolhardy attempt to jump to the train top to hitch out of the area. The latter suggested a younger person—in her own youth, Lily liked going with her brother Roger to the Kinship Tree that grows by a still spot alongside Coal Creek. They'd climb out onto their "jumping-off" limb, leap into the water for a swim on a hot day—a choice that has long since seemed reckless. Yet it's one of her fondest memories. . . .

She shakes her head to clear it. Refocuses on the moment. Maybe, as in her youth, the jump had been a foolish dare. In any case, now there is another witness to search for.

"Couldn't rightly say. The figure was all in white, head to toe. A ghost!"

Lily glances at the conductor, who gives her a rueful look: *I warned you.*

"A ghost," Lily says flatly. "You saw a ghost at the top of the tunnel."

"Yep. And you ask me, that ghost pushed th'other person off!"

Ridiculous. And yet . . . she thought she'd seen a phantom boy chasing after something in the woods. Maybe the spookiness of Moonvale Hollow Village and the surrounding woods simply stirred tired—or inebriated—imaginations.

The head brakeman pokes his face close to hers. She holds her breath to keep from gagging at his odors of moonshine and tobacco and sweat. "Dammit, I know what you and Lawrence here are thinking, but I know better still what I saw—a figure up there. All in white. Mayhap a ghost. Or mayhap a person, dressed in white, I dunno. I saw *someone*."

Lily stares into the man's watery, dark eyes. Sees his fear, his adamance. He's not trying to play her as a fool or make a joke. "I believe you saw something, and I will investigate the top of the tunnel—"

"Lawrence!" another man's voice—shaky yet ringing with excitement—hollers up from below the embankment. "We found her!"

Lily angles so that she can sidestep down the slope. There is no path, other than the one made by the train's regular flagman and fireman, their girth snapping tree branches and undergrowth, making it a little easier for her to maneuver while holding a flashlight in one hand, her skirt bunched in the other to keep from getting tangled in the brush.

At the bottom of the ravine, a coal-oil lamp lights the area, so Lily turns off her flashlight and tucks it between her waist and belt. A telegraph pole had stopped the woman's body from tumbling the rest of the way down the embankment into a thin stream. The woman is so small that most of her body is hidden behind the man's stance.

The man eyes Lily's sheriff's badge, lifts his eyebrows, but introduces himself as the B&R fireman. Another glance at her badge—yet he can't help but explain, "It ain't a pretty sight, not fit for a woman t'see."

"I'm not called out for pretty sights."

A retching sound stifles the natural sounds of the autumn night.

Lily lifts an eyebrow. "One of your *men*?" She puts a slight emphasis on the last word.

He frowns. "Flagman."

"Let me see her," Lily says.

The fireman shrugs—*have it your way, lady*—but he steps away from the body.

Lily sets her folded sheet on top of a bush, then kneels before the woman. She swallows hard, understanding why the flagman is so affected. The moonlight and the coal-oil lamp bring a spotlight on the body. Lily breathes slowly, partly to calm herself—her own heart beats hard at the sight of the woman, at once gruesome and piteous—and also to keep the smells, the flagman's sick, the woman's release of bodily fluids upon death, from filling her nose too fast.

The woman is petite. Probably shorter than Lily's own five feet, three inches, by a good two inches. Elderly—gray-white hair, deeply wrinkled skin. So, not likely jumping from tunnel tops on a dare. She is on her side, legs tucked up, left arm across her body—the repose of a nap. Her right arm juts out at an unnatural angle behind her head.

The woman wears a thin, pale blue nightgown. Her feet are bare, except for loose wrappings of cleaning rags. Makeshift shoes.

Why isn't she wearing suitable shoes, or at least house slippers? Mama says shoes tell a lot about a person—something Lily catches herself repeating as she shows her children how to polish their shoes. The elderly woman's lack of proper attire suggests the possibility of wandering out of a nearby home. On a whim? Out of fear? In any case, not likely planned.

Lily gently unwraps the woman's left foot and shines her flashlight on it. No warts or callouses, only a slight bunion, cuts and scratches on the sole, and a still-bloody spot on the instep where it's been pierced by a thorny branch. The well-tended condition of her feet suggest that this woman has lived for a long time with privilege and wealth. Not likely, then, a woman from the hills, or from the rough village of Moonvale Hollow. An outsider. So, also not likely she knew the train schedule, as locals would. If what the brakeman said was true—another person was at the tunnel top with her—maybe that person was from here. Knew the usual schedule.

Next Lily notes chafed raw skin on both wrists—markings that do not suggest injuries from falling into an oncoming train or from landing in this spot but, rather, binding. For the first time since getting called here, shock churns Lily's gut. Who would bind the wrists of an old woman, and why? Outrage on the woman's behalf quickens Lily's pulse.

Moment by moment, the woman's death seems less likely to be the result of unfortunate accident, or self-inflicted by a wish for death or an attempt to escape the area.

Gently, Lily lifts the woman's left foot; the leg moves smoothly enough. Rigor mortis, Lily knows from her days serving as a nurse during the prior decade's influenza outbreak, would start to set in somewhere from two to six hours after death, depending on the condition of the body and the environment—faster if it's cooler and if the deceased had been exerting physical effort before death. Lily touches the woman's neck and jaw, where stiffness would first start. The flesh is slightly taut but depresses easily enough at Lily's touch. So the woman was alive when she fell two hours ago—or was pushed, if the drunken brakeman was right about a figure on top of the tunnel—onto the train. Or had only died very shortly before. It is possible someone killed the woman and hoped to destroy the corpse and evidence by pushing the body into the path of the 9:30 p.m. train. But the train had come through ten minutes early.

Lily goes back to the simplest explanation: the old woman, wherever she was from, seeking to kill herself and mistiming her jump. Or perhaps she had dementia. Maybe the rope marks were from a family member's attempt to protect her? Yet the woman escapes, wanders to the top of the tunnel, falls or jumps.

Then what of the condition of her feet suggesting she is not from there? Of the brakeman's insistence he'd seen someone up there with her?

Both of those questions suggest a not-so-simple explanation.

What if the woman had died while bound and in desperation a family member had pulled the body up, then pushed her off? Had she been bound when she fell from the top of the Moonvale Hollow Tunnel? Did the ropes come free upon impact? Or had she broken free of those bonds before she fell?

The difference strikes Lily as vital.

Lily stares away from the body. Just a dozen yards on, Lily can see nothing but eternal darkness that could lead anywhere. It seems a living thing, the darkness, waiting for her. For anyone who would dare go to it.

Bronwyn is one of eighty-eight counties in Ohio—a tiny scrap of land. And yet, in this darkness, it seems overwhelming and vast. So many places to hide truth or bodies. Most of her work is in Kinship, the county seat, and the coal towns. But death had come here, the most remote part of the county.

There would be much easier ways to dispose of a body in these deep, dark woods. Why do so in a way that would draw this much attention? This purposeful mutilation seems as hostile as murder itself.

Unless Lily is reading too much into those markings on the woman's wrists. Unless the drunken brakeman was hallucinating. And this is a simple suicide, or an unfortunate accident of an old, confused woman. The easiest explanation.

Someone squats next to her. Lily looks over, expecting to see the fireman, but it's the flagman, who'd been retching from the discovery of the woman—God knows what he'll do at whatever sight awaits them once they turn her over.

Lily regards the flagman. He is middle-aged, tough looking, leathery skin, lines well carved in his brow. Even as his arms rest on his thighs, his hands shake.

His voice quivers, too. "She brings to mind my own mamaw."

Carefully, Lily rolls the woman over. The flagman gasps. Lily looks away for a moment, but the image of the right side of her face—a pulverized mash of blood and skin and bone, the unnatural angle of her head—manifests before her. The woman's neck had snapped on impact with either the train or the ground or the telegraph pole. Lily swallows hard. Counts to three. Forces herself to look again.

Lily smooths back the woman's hair, gray-white, yet fine and soft as a child's. In the undamaged part of the woman's face, Lily notes the fine high cheekbones, delicate brow and nose and mouth, the remaining eye, still open, a vivid blue. *Intelligent.* The word drifts into Lily's assessment. Gently, Lily lowers the eyelid. She figures the woman to be in her seventies, a lovely, dignified seventy, and certainly once a beauty, and a woman from wealth.

Lily looks back at the flagman. She feels a rush of gratitude that, despite how upset he is, he hasn't abandoned her. "I'm going to need your help moving her up the slope."

He stares at Lily. His trembling increases, but he nods.

Gently, Lily lifts the woman's feet onto the sheet, then the woman's shoulders and head, trying not to look at the damaged face, the rended arm. She folds the sheet back over top of the woman's body. She looks up. The flagman still stares at her, frozen, and Lily realizes he can't bring himself to touch the body. Lily swallows back a sigh of frustration. "Go ahead of me; light the way. Can you do that?"

He doesn't move.

"I reckon your mamaw would want us to do right by this woman's remains?"

Finally, he grabs the torchlight, steps a few feet up the path. Lily kneels beside the woman, slides her arms under the thin torso. She stands, slowly. The woman might weigh a little over eighty pounds, if that. Not much heavier than a big sack of flour at Douglas Grocers. Lily turns, faces the rise, then launches herself up, steady forward momentum.

At the top, she stops, panting. Men who'd been chatting and smoking go quiet, stare at her, at the sheet-wrapped body in her arms.

Lily hears a low huffing sound and a hoof clomp. She glances toward the noise and sees that the flagman in training has brought the mule cart alongside the train. Gently, with his help, Lily lowers the woman onto the cart floor.

When she turns back around, she sees that another man has arrived—Perry Dyer, a direct descendant of the Dyer who'd established the area, and Lily's opponent in the sheriff's race.

Why is he here? And since he no longer lives here, why hadn't she seen his automobile parked near the turnoff where she'd left her own automobile?

But those questions can wait; she needs to focus on learning all she can about the deceased woman. She walks over to the group of men. "I have a few more questions—"

The conductor shakes his head. "We've lost enough time."

Lily gives the man a stone-cold look—*how inconvenient, the death of this woman.* "It's possible she didn't simply fall, and if that's the case—"

"Good God, woman, you're not taking seriously my brakeman's claim that he saw someone on the top of the tunnel?"

"Enough!" Perry snaps. "I'm hopeful that when I'm sheriff, people will respect my requests. In the meantime, we should respect our *current* sheriff's requests." He accents *current* with a smirk.

Lily sighs. She's dealt with this conundrum before. Snap back—she looks defensive. Don't snap—she looks meek. She turns away from Perry and toward the conductor. "It's up to you," she says as pleasantly as the late hour and her own irritation will allow. "You can delay long enough for me to finish up my questions—or I can report to your supervisor that you've impeded a legal investigation."

One of the men snickers—the head brakeman, still tipsy. Lily walks over to him, stares directly into his watery eyes until his expression goes serious, and the other men quiet. It would be easy to write off those wrist marks as coming from some relative trying to keep the old woman safe, to dismiss the brakeman's sighting as born of inebriation. Run a death notice; if kin claim her, fine. If not, too bad, but she can be buried with county funds for paupers' graves. Then Lily can get on with her campaign.

But the notion turns Lily's stomach.

Just as the flagman thought of his mamaw, Lily would think of her own mama, or dear Nana over in Rossville, or Widow Gottschalk, who lives on the farm with the Kinship Tree Lily'd once enjoyed jumping off of with her brother.

If she's not willing to dig as deeply as she can for the truth about this death—to affirm whether it's an accident or something else—why bother with all the exhausting sacrifices of running for reelection as sheriff? Her job is to uphold the rule of law for all of the people in her county—not a select few. This woman, this death, has to matter. Or winning the sheriff's role would be only a hollow victory.

"I need the truth. As far as I am concerned, no consequences either way, but I must know," Lily says. "Were you drinking before you climbed up the side of the engine, saw the woman fall, saw another figure on the tunnel top? Or after the accident?"

The brakeman gives Lily a long, scrutinizing look. He moves around a wad of tobacco inside his cheek, spits. "I take my job seriously. An' anyhow, I'd be a fool to have a nip afore climbing up—and I'm a lot of things, but I ain't a fool. I was stone-cold sober when I saw that woman fall, saw someone—or some specter—up on the tunnel. An' I'll swear an oath on a courtroom Bible and say it again if need be."

Lily nods. All right then. It's quite possible the woman wasn't from here—no one claims her, and her feet indicate a softer life than this region would offer. And the brakeman was sober when he saw the fall and a possible witness.

Lily turns to Perry. "I need someone from the village to see if they can identify her."

Perry nods. "I reckon I should take a look. If she's from here, or near here, I'll know her."

"You know everyone in the village?" Lily asks.

"There are about a hundred souls that live in or near the village and I've lived here all of my life until I moved to Kinship—so yes, by sight if not by name."

Lily turns and walks toward the cart. She hears Perry following her. When he catches up at the back of the wagon, she carefully pulls aside the cloth. Perry stares as Lily shines her flashlight on the woman.

"I don't recognize her," he says. Then he starts to hurry away.

"Mr. Dyer, what are you doing here?"

He looks at her. When she's seen him in Kinship, he's always given her a hard look and a dubious smile, but tonight his expression is nervous, and his hand trembles as he pushes his hair, hanging in oily strands from too much pomade, back from his forehead. Weariness cloaks his shoulders, and his uneasiness tells her it's not just from the lateness of the hour, or the shocking sight of the woman's damaged head.

"I have friends here." His grin is forced. "Thought I'd campaign a little."

All right—but it seems odd. He'd moved with his family into Kinship, seemingly as eager as his wife to settle in the county seat after his father passed away.

"I didn't see your automobile at the turnoff," Lily says. "Seems a long hike in from Kinship, for a handful of votes."

"You would have left your automobile by the main turnoff," Perry says. "There are other accesses that are more remote, but less of a hike or wagon ride. Besides, my comings and goings are none of your business."

Twenty minutes later, the train has pulled away again. Lily has taken and rechecked statements from all of the train crew, and the owner of the mule and wagon has agreed to take her back to her automobile. He's waiting, impatiently, and yet Lily stands at the top of the Moonvale Hollow Tunnel, grasping a thick tree limb to steady herself. She hasn't found anything to add to her investigation. Her inspection, in the moonlight and with her flashlight, has yielded nothing more than a few broken twigs, which could as easily be from critters as from people. There are no cleared paths to the top of the tunnel, so no footprints in the thick grass and brush. Though low, thorny limbs snag at Lily's skirt, there is nothing so convenient as a scrap of cloth caught in a bush to prove the brakeman's claim.

The sooner the better to drive the body to the undertaker and fetch the town doctor—who doubles as the county medical examiner—to see what they might learn from careful examination.

Still, Lily lingers, edging forward, into the strange pull that open space always exerts on her—that high limb of the Kinship Tree over Coal Creek when she was a kid, the top of a ridge when out walking in the hills, here now on the top of a tunnel. Not an uncommon impulse; she'd heard others speak of it, the pull against all rationality toward open space beyond a rim. Lily toes the earth covering the tunnel's edge. *So easy to fall. So easy to be drawn forward.*

Perhaps, as Perry suggested, the woman had simply wandered from a far-tucked-away cabin, remote to even Moonvale Hollow Village. Found herself here. Felt the pull. Forgot the surety of the plunge to earth that would follow giving into it. Or just stumbled.

No—this isn't a spot anyone would simply wander to. Clambering up the steep side of the tunnel had tested Lily, even though she is fit, and relatively young at twenty-eight. Assuming the woman was alive when she came up here, how would she, more than likely fifty years Lily's senior, have managed it on her own? Coming here must have been purposeful—whether or not on her own volition.

Lily steps back, yet still gazes down to the cart, to the white sheet wrapped around the woman's body that gleams in the full moon. Without anyone willing to claim the woman, it would be nigh on impossible to find out what happened to her in those final moments.

In the distance, a hound dog howls—some scent has caught its attention. In spite of the night's horrors, Lily grins. A good hound could track where the woman had come from. And she knows who to ask for such help. Marvena Whitcomb . . .

Something glimmers, off to the left, catches Lily's gaze. It's the shimmering boy again, still merrily chasing his ball. Or dog. He stops, turns, looks at her, and grins. Lily presses her eyes shut. Weary. Just weary. Seeing nonsense born of her own weariness.

Yet when she opens her eyes and sees only moonlit foliage, disappointment snatches her breath away.

CHAPTER 4

※

HILDY

Wednesday, September 22—2:30 a.m.

In the first moment after startling awake, Hildy looks around wildly, disoriented to find herself on the front porch swing at Lily's house. As she shivers, it all comes back to her—the lonely drive home from Rossville, leaving her father's old automobile at her house, starting to creep in through the back door. Then she'd stopped—the house, even before entering, felt strangely quiet. On nights Hildy got back late from tutoring, Mother was usually dozing in the parlor and would herself startle awake, fuming and fussing. Tonight, Hildy knew, she wouldn't be able to easily deflect Mother's suspicious queries and comments: *Tutoring? So late? A woman should not be out driving at all, what's more at night!*

So Hildy opted for a walk around Kinship, hoping to compose herself before going home, but then she'd seen the parlor light burning in the front window at Lily's house, saw Lily's mother moving past.

Hildy had hurried to Lily's front door—Mama's presence meant that Lily would have been called away. How late? She usually asked Hildy to come stay with the children, Jolene and Micah. That would have awoken Mother. Before Hildy could worry about the implications of that, Mama answered Hildy's light knock and affirmed that Lily had been called out—a body hit by a train just outside Moonvale Hollow Village.

Mama had given Hildy a worried look—without any pestering questions about the lateness of the hour—and tried to send her home. Hildy, noting the basket of laundry in Mama's arms, the weariness etched around Mama's mouth and eyes, had shooed her on up to bed, insisting she'd stay and finish the children's laundry.

After Mama went up to bed, Hildy washed the clothes on the wringer washer in the mudroom, then pinned them up on the clothesline, working by moonlight and coal-oil lamp. Even with her heart hollowed out by Tom's rejection, she smiled as she worked, imagining Lily's grumpy-yet-grateful reaction to Mama and Hildy doing household tasks, unasked. As far as Hildy's concerned, Lily's constant struggle is recognizing that it's all right to take a little help, time to time.

Laundry complete, Hildy went to the front porch swing to sit a spell, hoping the chill night air would keep her awake. She stared at the full moon, contemplated the long silences between cricket chirps so early this fall, portending a tough winter to come. The chirps became sufficient lullaby, and soon in fretful sleep she found Tom. Images she'd hoped to avoid by staying awake.

Now, as she stands to stretch, the porch swing creaks on the hinges. Then she jumps, spotting someone in the street, standing out of the pool of the flickering streetlight. Yet sufficient moonlight silhouettes a woman in a hat and long skirt, and Hildy senses the woman staring at her.

Missy Ranklin? The bedraggled young woman, who lives on a small farm with her husband, seven-year-old son and two older stepchildren, has come into town, either on foot or by mule, several nights of late to complain of her husband's rough treatment. Hildy pities Missy— just seventeen when she wed, and from far back in the hills. She no doubt thought she was finding freedom from poverty by marrying Ralf, even though he is twice her age.

Hildy shudders, thinking maybe she's not so different from Missy. In Merle, Hildy sought refuge from her dreary life with Mother, from the prospect of being an old maid, pitied in Kinship for never quite getting past mourning the loss of Roger. Until she fell in love with Tom. *Yes. Fell in love with Tom.*

What would Lily think of that? Admonish her to speak up, tell Tom she was strong enough to be his? Once, Lily herself, after a fight with Daniel before they were married, had snuck out of her parents' home to go to his boxing match at the Kinship Opera House. Hildy knows that Lily sees her as . . . not weak, necessarily. Tender. Too tender. So more than likely, she'd tell Hildy to count her blessings with practical Merle.

After all, Lily barely contains her frustration with Missy—if she won't file a formal complaint, there is nothing Lily can do, shy of giving her husband a talking-to. Still, Hildy wishes Lily had more sympathy. It is not as easy as Lily thinks for most women to speak up for themselves. At least, it is not easy for women like Missy. Or Hildy.

Now Hildy starts to call after the woman in the street, but an automobile turns the corner, and in the headlights Hildy catches the woman's profile. An old-fashioned full-skirted formal dress. A brimmed hat. Tall, wide shouldered. Definitely not Missy or Mother.

Yet there is something familiar about the stiff stance, the shoulders pressed too far back. As if the woman is preparing for a fight.

Hildy blinks as the headlights flash in her eyes, and when she blinks again the woman is gone. The night momentarily shifts to stillness, and a breeze stirs, as if the night is sighing at Hildy's silliness. For Hildy wonders if she'd seen the woman at all.

The automobile door squeaks shut in the lane beside the house. Hildy hurries inside, reaching the kitchen, dimly lit by a coal-oil lamp burning on a small table, as Lily comes in through the mudroom.

Lily's blouse is smeared with dirt and . . . blood? Yes, blood. Lily does not appear harmed. And yet Hildy's heart thuds as her gaze meets Lily's, gleaming with anger. Whatever she's been investigating has stirred something deep and dark, and Hildy tenses with sudden worry, knowing that her friend will not let go until she sees it through.

Surprise at Hildy's presence flickers across Lily's face before her expression quickly reassembles itself into its standard composure ever since Daniel died. Resolute. Quiet.

Lily washes her face and hands in the pump sink. "It smells good in here."

Earlier, Hildy had made sorghum cookies and left them to cool on a white platter. Hildy looks at the treats, and whereas earlier she'd been pleased with how they'd turned out, had anticipated how the family would enjoy them, now they seem frivolous. Lily has blood on her blouse, for God's sake.

Lily turns from the sink. "Saw that the wash is done."

Hildy nods, eager for her best friend's approval. "Yes. I brought the mail in, too. Left it on the parlor desk and dusted a little. Not that it needed it overly much."

Hildy doesn't want to say where she'd actually been tonight, so she stares down at the sorghum cookies as she offers up an explanation that is at least true, if not complete: "I—I've been having trouble sleeping of late. I was taking a walk, when I saw Mama"—though Hildy never became her daughter-in-law, she's always called Lily and Roger's mother by the affectionate term they used for her—"through the front window and—"

"Must have been a long walk. Sent for you after eleven. No answer at your house."

Hildy looks up, startled. Lily doesn't seem overly concerned. She is eating one of the sorghum cookies, famished. Still, Hildy's heart pounds. Mother is such a light sleeper. Why hadn't she answered the door? Maybe she'd taken an extra dose of Vogel's Tonic for her aches and pains—the tonic is alcohol watered down to barely within the limits of the Volstead Act to make it Prohibition legal, but to hear Mother tell it, it's an elixir from the Good Lord himself.

Lily finishes the cookie and smiles—kind, but patronizing. How must she look to Lily? *Soft. Biddable. No depths to plumb. That's what Tom would say, too. Maybe they're right.*

Unexpected sorrow rises, but she quells it, admonishes herself for being so emotional. Tom had pushed her away. Told her to go ahead, marry pragmatic, safer Merle. Maybe she *is* foolish, wishing at her age that Merle would make her heart flutter like Roger had, like Tom does—

"Hildy? Are you all right?"

She looks up, sees again in her friend's expression how Lily views her: soft.

Hildy's jaw tightens. "I am fine." She gestures at Lily's blouse. "What happened? Mama said you were called out because of an accident on the track at Moonvale Hollow?"

"No one in the area can identify the woman. I'm going to have to go back out."

Hildy moves to the stove, picks up the coffee kettle. "I'll make you boiled coffee, then, and sandwiches."

"No, don't bother."

Hildy's shoulders drop—Lily always seems to wave away her offers of help.

"All right—the coffee."

Lily is patronizing her, yet Hildy is grateful. At the sink, Hildy pumps water into the kettle. "So what were you able to suss out?" Knowing Lily, she'd examined every detail at the site. Sometimes she wishes she could go with Lily on her investigations, but Lily insists she's best suited to her work as jail mistress—though that will end once she marries Merle.

"A woman—elderly, unidentified—was hit by the train. She fell, or maybe was pushed, from the top of the tunnel. At some point recently, her wrists were bound. I don't know if that's coincidence or connected to her death."

Bound wrists? Shocking. Hildy steadies her breath, then busies herself with spooning coffee into the kettle. She turns so that Lily can't see how her hands shake.

"A brakeman swears he saw someone—a person or a ghost at the top of the tunnel. The latter is nonsense, but he's convinced someone in white was up there with her. Anyway, the first thing I have to do is track where the victim came from."

Hildy sets the coffee to heating. "How are you going to do that?"

"I took the woman to Arlington Funeral Home. I kept the rags the woman had wound around her feet as makeshift shoes, as well as her nightgown, wrapped up in waxed paper. Mrs. Arlington gave me the paper—begrudgingly." Lily gives a short laugh. Hildy, despite the grimness of the situation, smiles. Mrs. Arlington is known for being melodramatic about the least thing. "Anyway, I reckon Marvena will know of a hound dog that can track—"

Hildy's next words escape of their own volition. "Oh! I can go with you!"

"You're eager to see Marvena." Lily sounds amused.

Hildy's not, but going along might mean a chance to see Tom, just one more time. Maybe he'd take back his words. Maybe she'd convince him to give her more time, to find the right time to tell Merle and Mother the truth.

Shame at the secret she's kept—not to mention her jealousy of Marvena, who slowly seems to have taken her place as Lily's best friend—makes Hildy's face burn anew. Then she thinks of the letter from Benjamin Russo she'd seen in the mail. For a second, Hildy had been tempted to read the letter, but that would violate privacy, even between best friends. All she knew of Benjamin was that he had been Daniel's friend in the Great War and now works for the Bureau of Mines. Last spring, Lily told her that Mr. Russo had helped settle a disagreement between miners and management, convincing Wessex Corporation, the new owner of Ross Mining, to allow for talk of unionization.

Finally, the coffee bubbles; the aroma is heavenly. Hildy carefully pours the coffee, so few grounds escape into the cup, as she says, "I've been working with Olive Harding. The schoolmarm, over in Rossville. You've met her—"

"Oh yes. You brought her as a guest to a Woman's Club meeting. And to church. She seems bright," Lily says approvingly.

Hildy nods, her hand shaking a little as she gives the cup to Lily. This is a tiny step toward sharing the full truth. "Two evenings a week, Olive tutors miners and their wives in reading and writing. I've been volunteering for a while now."

Lily looks surprised. "Well now. That's good."

A positive response—and yet Hildy's heart falls, as she realizes that as close as they're supposed to be, Lily should already know. Then, too, it strikes her that Marvena must have never brought up Hildy's presence over the past few months in Rossville.

Hildy blinks hard. *Just go, and sooner or later, it'll be like you never spent any time here at all. . . .* Tom's last words come back, stinging as hard as when they'd spurred her to put on her dress, walk out of his house without saying a word or giving him a look, and drive home.

It hits her: Tom is too much of a gentleman to ever tell anyone of their affair, and so long as she keeps her own mouth shut on the topic, she can marry Merle, settle into the proper life everyone seems to think she wants—that she herself had yearned for until a few months ago. And the good people of Rossville would look the other way. They had too much to worry about to care all that much about a brief fling between a miner and a town girl. It would be as if their love affair had never happened.

Lily sips coffee. "It's good. You should have some."

"I'm fine." Hildy smiles, feeling their distance close a little.

Lily shakes her head. "You should take care of yourself, too."

And there it is—the hollow gap between them, borne of the feeling that Lily sees her, may have always seen her, as too fragile. In need of being taken care of. Is that why Lily had been glad about the prospect of Roger marrying her all those years ago, of Merle marrying her now?

Lily doesn't seem to notice Hildy's distress as she takes another sip. "Are there many?"

Hildy startles. "What?"

"Miners who need tutoring?"

"Oh . . . oh yes. Only a few take advantage."

"It's fine that you're doing this, Hildy. You could have told me."

"Well, Mother and Merle don't think so. They say I need to stop."

"Marriage demands compromise," Lily says brusquely. "Trust Merle."

Hildy fights tears welling in her eyes. The Lily from before Daniel's death, from before she became sheriff—and friends with Marvena Whitcomb—the Lily who Hildy had loved as her best friend, even as a sister, for her whole life, would not have been so harsh with her.

She swallows back a lump, manages to say, "Lily, I want to go with you to Rossville, to help you, and maybe while I'm there let Olive know that my availability to tutor may change—"

"This isn't a social call. I'll be out for hours with Marvena, and I need to go while the trail is fresh as possible, before it rains." Lily pushes her cup away. "I also need to talk to someone at the newspaper." Lily rubs her eyes, and Hildy feels a pull of sympathy for her friend's weariness, her frustration at needing to do too many things at once. "I need an announcement to run today about the woman—where she was found, what she looks like, a request for anyone who knows anything to come forward. I need the doctor's assessment, too. I also need to start tracking as soon as possible—"

"I can fetch the doctor. Write the piece up. And make a sketch of the woman. Get them in the *Kinship Daily Courier*."

"Hildy, her body—she's in no condition for you to see—"

"If you won't let me go with you to Marvena's, least let me do this!" Hildy snaps. She slams the coffee kettle against the stove top. "Let me do my job while I can, before I'm married and have to *trust* Merle!"

The women stare at each other, both shocked at Hildy's uncharacteristic outburst. Their silence is cracked by the creaking of the floor above—Jolene turning restlessly in her bed. The poor child had had a nightmare earlier, so fraught she couldn't describe it. Hildy had soothed her back to sleep. Lily hasn't said anything about Jolene being troubled, and Hildy wonders if she should mention it.

Lily looks weary. So instead, Hildy says, "I'm sorry. I don't mean to snap. In a few hours, Mama will be up and can get Jolene off to school. She can take care of Micah and Caleb Junior. And I can sketch the poor woman, make a good guess as to how to . . ." Hildy pauses, then stumbles on—"to fill in her face. You know I'm good with sketches."

Yet for a moment, Lily looks blank, and Hildy is hurt to realize that Lily has forgotten how Hildy had loved to sketch when they were younger—animals, plants, flowers, people.

Then Lily nods, apparently remembering. "This is different." Lily puts her hand on Hildy's arm. "This woman—her face and body— well, it was enough to make at least one of the railroad men retch."

Hildy pulls her arm away. "I was with Daddy when he died earlier this year. I was there with you, last year, when you lost the baby. There after the mine collapsed. When the bodies were pulled out. And I stayed, Lily. I stayed."

Lily stares at her for a moment, then nods. "If you can get it in first thing this morning, there will still be time for the announcement to run in this afternoon's paper."

"Well. To fit it in, I may have to get the paper to drop the society news piece for the Woman's Club. We'll never live down *that* scandal!"

For a moment, Lily smiles softly. For a moment, the distance between them closes, and their friendship is as strong as it's always been.

CHAPTER 5

≫

LILY

Wednesday, September 22—4:00 a.m.

Here, the full moon does not penetrate the canopy of trees covering Devil's Backbone, up which a scant half mile nests the log-and-mortar cabin of Marvena Whitcomb.

Still, Lily doesn't bother turning on her flashlight as she steps out of her automobile, for she well knows the path ahead. May as well save the flashlight's power. She tucks it and the automobile key in her rucksack, alongside the dead woman's nightgown and rag shoes.

Yet, at first, the dark clutches Lily. She forces her breath to steady and slow until her gaze softens and coaxes shadows from shade, then shapes from shadow. The night's soft coolness hints of both past summer warmth and the icy winter to come. A smell of loaminess lingers, coaxed forth by yesterday's rainstorm. Lily had seen the storm clouds roiling eastward, rued that they skirted her part of Bronwyn County, prayed for a good rain to urge on the last of her garden's tomatoes and squash and pole beans for one more round of home canning, before the first hard frost took its futile harvest.

Now Lily prays for the weather—ever changing in Ohio—to stay dry for at least another day, until, she hopes, she can track from whence the dead woman had come.

With her next step up the rutted lane, she considers how her left foot feels. She'd lost her little toe when she was sixteen, rending when caught between rocks the last time she ever jumped with her brother from the Kinship Tree into Coal Creek. Since, her foot aches when a storm approaches.

Now her foot feels fine, portending a dry spell. *Good.*

Lily treks confidently up the incline to Marvena's settlement. She's come up here many a time since last fall, enough that she's lost count, for Marvena is a reliable source for the goings-on in this part of the county.

Lily smells the cabin before she sees it. A whiff of woodsmoke stirs mouthwatering thoughts of Marvena's customary offerings—soup beans and corn pone and dried-apple stack cake. She should have taken Hildy's offer of sandwiches, saving herself from both hunger and Hildy's disappointment. Her friend seems so ill at ease of late. She needs to get over her wedding jitters, settle down with Merle. Then she'll be fine. Safe.

Safe. That's what Lily wants for Hildy. For Mama and the children. For everyone. Surely someone, somewhere, must have wanted that for the dead woman, too. Surely someone is worrying about her, will want to know what happened to her. Another reason not to dismiss her death so easily as mishap.

Lily steps into the clearing at the center of which is the cabin, leaning slightly forward as if eager to hear or smell what might be lurking in the woods. A coal-oil lantern glows inside the one window. For a moment, Lily is pleased that Marvena might already be awake—it doesn't do to startle her, for she is swift to clutch knife and shotgun. Then her thoughts leap to Frankie—Marvena's daughter, who is seven years old, same as Jolene. But while Jolene seems to Lily to be remarkably healthy and even happy-go-lucky in spite of losing her father, Frankie is often sickly, fragility casting a pale glow from within the child.

A snort and snore snags Lily's attention. Guibo, the gray mule asleep in the pen by a shed. The mule, fencing, and shed are all new since Marvena had become an official organizer for the United Mine Workers of America this past spring. With increased hiring in Rossville and other coal towns, the weekly paper becoming a daily, and the growth of Kinship—just over five thousand residents now—prosperity has seemingly reached every nook of Bronwyn County. Even Marvena's. Lily is glad for her, for all the folks in the community, but she is wary of the giddiness that comes with this newfound prosperity, as if it is permanent, as if it can never disappear.

A shadow emerges from under the porch, stretches its forepaws, shakes his head side to side. Shep, Marvena's hound dog. He holds his nose aloft, snuffling, but also looking around confused, unsure of the source of the new smell, the smell of Lily. She smiles, the sight of Shep a surprisingly welcome bit of lighthearted relief in this long, morose night.

Another shadow, much bigger, loosens and stirs on the porch and Lily pulls short, as the shadow lunges forward, holding a shotgun.

Lily puts her hand lightly on her holster. Shep seems unconcerned, but then a scratch between his ears and a food scrap would be enough for him to befriend anyone. Lily's heart races. Someone here fixing to attack Marvena and Frankie? Or maybe has already attacked? Lily grips her revolver.

The man's shotgun lifts. "Can't see you. Can hear you. 'Nuff to aim at."

Ah. Jurgis Sacovech, the miner who had helped Marvena's common-law husband as a union organizer and now, after her husband's death, aids Marvena. Friend, not foe, but still Lily is alarmed. If Jurgis—who lives with his mother, Nana, down in Rossville—is here, it must mean Marvena needs protecting.

"It's Lily Ross!" she calls out.

Jurgis lowers his shotgun, and Lily hurries up the steps.

By the time she's on the porch, Jurgis has lit a lantern. Lily notes Jurgis's sleepy-eyed look, his off-by-one misbuttoned shirt, his hair tousled out of its normally neatly oiled style, his missing belt, his sock feet.

Oh. Jurgis is not at Marvena's cabin for any purpose other than pleasurable. He lights a cigarette, lifts his eyebrows as he inhales, as if daring Lily to question his presence. Except then—why the shotgun?

"Everything all right here?"

Jurgis nods. "There was a bit of trouble today at the mines, is all."

Lily keeps her expression placid, lets silence unspool. It's often the best way to get people to tell more than they mean to.

Sure enough, after a moment he clears his throat. "Marvena is working with a fellow named Clarence Broward to integrate the mines—and the local union. New company has brought in some Negro miners from their operations down south—new seams have been opened up and we can use all the help we can get. This Broward fellow, from the United Mine Workers, well, he took that as an opportunity, came down about a month ago. Good man—but some of the fellows don't like him just because of his race. Which is stupid, if you ask me. We're all risking our lives."

"I see," Lily says flatly. Why hadn't Marvena forewarned her? She doesn't think there should be a fuss over integrating, either, but she also reckons that her, Marvena's, and Jurgis's opinions are likely in the minority. And forewarned is forearmed. "Well, I haven't heard of any trouble over this in Kinship or other parts of the county."

"What're you in need of, this hour?" Jurgis's voice is low, careful. Doesn't want to stir Marvena or Frankie.

"Tracking hound."

Jurgis chuckles. "Well, if'n you need to track a possum a few yards, Shep might do."

Lily scratches between the dog's ears. "Wasn't thinking of Shep."

She means the hounds of the men Marvena employs in her side business—moonshining. Men of distant and uncertain kin to Marvena, a varietal of cousin—second or third removed—and distrustful, working for her only because she toils harder than any of them and knows the secrets for shine made safely. "An elderly woman died, hit by a train. Maybe accident. Maybe murder. Nothing to identify the woman, so I need to track her to her kin."

At that, Jurgis takes a slow drag on his cigarette. "Well. I reckon it's up to Marvena." He gazes with sympathy at Lily. "You look wore out. Sit a spell."

Lily smiles as Jurgis goes back inside—he sounds like his mother, Nana. But she remains standing. No time for resting. She needs to focus on this case, wrap it up quickly, return her concentration to the election, but instead she thinks, *So. Marvena and Jurgis. Jurgis and Marvena.*

She should be glad, for she's harbored, since Daniel's death, even as she became friends with Marvena while they solved his murder, the fear that Marvena had deep down never let go of Daniel. That because Marvena and Daniel had been friends—and, for a time, lovers, long before Lily knew either of them—in some way Marvena too was Daniel's widow.

But here is Jurgis. It makes sense. They are a good fit for each other. Yes, she should be glad.

And yet Lily's heart slumps. No one understands her quite the way Marvena does, and the understanding binds them. Marvena is moving on from her losses. Suddenly Lily is weary from still carrying the weight of hers.

Lily sits after all, bones settling like a sigh into the porch swing. She sways forward, back, forward, and soon it feels as if she's not moving of her own volition, as if the soft, dark night itself is rocking her, as if the squeak of chain on rivet is tenor harmony to a lullaby of sounds— Shep at her feet snuffling and sighing, a nearby critter scurrying, a far-off owl crying.

She stares into the darkness of the forest. The path she'd hiked up is no longer distinguishable in the shadows—shifting, twitching, but giving no clear shape. Lily adds a sharp gasp to the night chorus as she realizes that she's looking for the shimmery, silvery ghost boy.

As the night remains closed and dark, a knot within her eases, and at last she closes her eyes. Just for a moment, what could that hurt? A notion long idling at the back of her mind edges forward—what might it be like, to have her own stretch of land, her own farmhouse, her own porch to sit on at night, so she can stare into enveloping darkness?

A door screech startles Lily, and she opens her eyes to Marvena staring down at her, amused. Lily frowns as if irritated at being caught catnapping, but truth be told, she's glad to see even a glimmer of a smile on her friend's mouth. In the past year, sorrows carved an extra ten years into Marvena's face, and, as Lily roughly rubs her palms to her cheeks, she reckons the same could be said of her.

"You got something to track her with?" Marvena's already dressed for the task—boots, a hand-me-down oversized brown coat, a drab once-white blouse and long blue skirt, cinched up with a man's belt into which Marvena's poked extra holes, a rucksack slung over her shoulder. An old canvas hat, the over-wide brim slouching ridiculously over her eyes. Somewhere in the midst of all that, Lily knows, is a revolver and a knife.

Lily pats her own rucksack, irritated after all. She might be a town girl, but she's no fool. "The woman's nightgown. Rags that wrapped her feet." She stands. "We'd best get a move on. She fell, or was pushed, from Moonvale Hollow Tunnel, so it'll take a while to get there—"

Marvena recoils. "Moonvale? Sorry. If I'da known we were heading there, I'da turned over and gone back to sleep."

She starts to go back inside, but Lily grabs her arm. "What? Why?"

Marvena gives her an incredulous look. "Everyone knows that tunnel—and the holler it cuts through—has been haunted from the get-go. Railmen killed, falling from the train. Girl killed, running through the tunnel, trying to get back home before her daddy can find out she's been consorting with a boy from a feuding family."

Marvena shakes her arm free, sings a mournful refrain: "Down in Moonvale Hollow, where th'sun refuses to shine, her gentle spirit wanders, and her forbidden lover pines. . . ."

Ah. Just an old ballad, conjured from superstition and ghost stories. Marvena's worse than the brakeman earlier tonight. Lily swallows back an impatient sigh, knowing better than to disparage Marvena's sometimes-confounding beliefs—and not just because Lily needs her help. Truth be told, ever since last year, after losing Daniel but also Marvena's older daughter, Lily's friend has turned toward religion, with a generous side helping of superstition.

At least it's brought her some comfort, which still eludes Lily.

A silvery flash. Lily looks toward the dark woods, rubs her eyes. Her imagination conjuring the boy after all, playing tricks on her.

Now Marvena puts her hand on Lily's arm. "You all right? I can get some sassafras tea right quick, if you're feeling puny—"

Lily pulls away. "I'm fine." Marvena looks worried—and a little hurt at Lily ignoring her concern. "The victim is an old woman. Not likely from Moonvale. Probably Nana's age—"

"Now Lily, that's not fair, bringing in Nana, and you know it," Marvena says. "And 'sides, the best tracking hound I know happens to belong to a moonshiner, and if the union gets wind of this, they won't look kindly on—"

"You're saying moonshining's behind you?" A little teasing might ease the tension that's risen, though they both know that Lily looks the other way from Marvena's side business.

"I'm *saying* that if this is an *official* investigation with records and all—"

"Fine. I'll deputize you. That way, if the union gets wind of you helping me requisition a tracking hound from a moonshiner, then I can attest it was all on official business."

Jurgis steps out. He's holding two waxed-paper-wrapped packets— sandwiches, Lily guesses. She smiles to herself. He'd known all along that Marvena would go with her, wouldn't deny her help.

Marvena notes the sandwiches, too, and smiles at Jurgis. "Reckon I'm going to be a deputy now. Who'da ever thought I'd rise to something so official." A prideful note belies her attempt to joke. She switches her gaze to Lily. "Is there a swearin' in, or anything?"

Lily shrugs, impatient again. "I'll file the proper paperwork documenting your deputization later, and if my need of you continues, I can get a badge."

As hurt flashes across Marvena's expression, Lily regrets her snappish tone. *Dammit.* Of late, she's maiming the feelings of everyone around her. It must be the campaign. So much to do—that damned meeting to prepare for her debate, the Woman's Club meeting, the county fair baking contest, the debate with Perry Dyer. She's weary thinking about those obligations. She starts to apologize, but already Marvena has turned to Jurgis, taking the sandwiches and putting them in her rucksack.

Jurgis and Marvena do not touch. Yet the pull between them is palpable, sets to shimmering the thin sliver of darkness between their bodies.

"Frankie'll not want the elderberry tea—" Marvena starts.

"I'll make sure she takes it." Jurgis keeps his voice low, soothing, a balm to Marvena's maternal worries. "And breathes in the steam, too. It's good for her church singing."

"Well, that's all fine and well," Marvena says, "but no future in it. Make sure she studies her multiplication table."

"I will. And I'll pack her a good lunch, too."

Marvena nods, fully entrusting Jurgis with her daughter's well-being.

This moment—this trust—is more intimate than if they touched, than anything Lily might have observed, had she walked into Marvena's cabin a few hours earlier. Lily looks away, across the shadowed yard, back into the dark woods.

The front door opens, closes again gently. Jurgis has gone inside, leaving Lily and Marvena on the porch.

"You may want to visit the privy," Marvena says. "Guibo is a bumpy ride."

Lily looks back at Marvena. "My automobile's down the lane—"

"If'n you want a good tracking hound, and in a hurry, we need to forego your tin lizzie. And do this my way."

CHAPTER 6

❧

HILDY

Wednesday, September 22—5:35 a.m.

Mr. Arlington starts to pull back the top of the sheet but glances at Hildy, concerned. "Are you sure you wouldn't like to wait upstairs? My wife would enjoy sharing coffee with you."

Mrs. Arlington—a stalwart of the Kinship Woman's Club who did not approve of Lily or Hildy's work in law enforcement—would enjoy nothing of the kind. Her harsh gaze had tracked Hildy from the moment she arrived at the funeral parlor.

"I am fine." Suddenly the basement's eggshell white walls close in. Gray spots dance before her eyes. She gasps for air, but the sudden need for breath pulls in an astringent smell, making her gag.

Mr. Arlington smiles sympathetically. "It's the formaldehyde. Perhaps—"

"Can we get on with this?" Dr. Goshen, the town doctor who doubles as county coroner, glares at Hildy. "Go upstairs if you think you're going to have a sinking spell."

Hildy stiffens her spine. "Proceed." She pulls sketch pad and pencils from her bag. She'd been able to slip into her house to get the items without, thankfully, disturbing Mother, though it meant rummaging under her bed to retrieve them.

Mr. Arlington folds back the sheet. For a moment, Hildy and the men stare at the woman.

Hildy wills her breathing to slow, herself to stay present, as she takes in the mangled face, the nearly rended arm. And yet Hildy calms. Her nausea recedes. There is an emptiness to the woman, as if without her spirit her body knows to start slowly melting back to its basic elements. There is nothing to fear from her remains, however grotesquely damaged.

"I guess her to be in her seventies. Or eighties. Hard to tell when women get to a certain age." Dr. Goshen shrugs. "Injuries in keeping with traumatic blow or impact—a fall. Basement stairs are usually the culprit." He gives Mr. Arlington's arm a playful poke. "Tell your old lady to be careful. Hate to see her on one of these slabs." He gestures at the other metal table, empty. The undertaker's attempt at a smile turns into a grimace. The doctor looks back at Hildy. "Looks like more damage than from a tumble down steps. Like she fell from a cliff. She from around here?"

Hildy had not told him the circumstances of the woman's death. "We're still determining identification. That's why I'm here."

He glances at the sketchbook and pencil in Hildy's hands. "Good luck. Nothing to distinguish this old woman from any other." He shrugs again. "Tell Sheriff Ross my official assessment is accidental death due to a fall."

So that's that. Dr. Goshen leaves, clomping up the basement stairs.

"Are you sure—" Mr. Arlington starts.

In response, Hildy pulls a stool alongside the table, by the relatively undamaged side of the woman's body. After the undertaker leaves, Hildy sits. The sketch pad and pencil feel awkward in her hands; it's been so long since she's held them—too long, Hildy thinks, and the realization feels rebellious.

She forces herself to focus on the woman's damaged head, to imagine the woman's face, whole. Gently, she pulls back the lid of the undamaged eye. Pale blue. Mayhap bright blue in her youth. Hildy closes the lid again. Imagines the woman, slightly smiling. Imagines how she might have worn her fine, gray-white hair—up in a tight bun, like Mother's? Hildy studies the woman's intact and elegant cheekbone, her unstooped shoulders—no, though petite, she would have stood tall, unbowed, her hair swooped up in a soft chignon.

Those markings around the woman's wrists—Lily had warned her, yet Hildy shudders. Dr. Goshen, in his dismissive examination, had not noticed them. Shaken out of her imagination, Hildy realizes she's been sketching all along. Before her is a portrait of an elegant elderly woman who looks alive. Regal, yet warm. In the lines of her face, both kindness and toughness.

Now that she is so close to the woman, Hildy notes, below more unpleasant odors, the scent of talcum powder and sweet, floral notes, striking something familiar in the back of Hildy's mind, something she can't quite recall.

She hops off her stool, puts aside sketch pad and pencil, regards more closely the woman's wrists and hands.

They look waxen; even the garish lacerations on the wrists look unreal. Sorrow pulses through Hildy; there is so much life in hands: bread made, clothing and linens washed and stitched, letters written, weeds pulled, berries picked, faces touched. Hildy trembles as she sees again her palms cup Roger's face for the last time, sees her hands taking from Lily the telegram stating Roger's warfront death, sees her fingertips touch Tom's lips, finding love she thought she'd lost forever.

Hildy shakes her head to clear it and returns to her study of the woman's hands. Fine hands that would not have scrubbed pans or pulled weeds, at least not of late. Soft, not overly muscled fingers. Liver spots. An indentation and slight paleness on the ring finger of the left hand—the woman had been married at some point. Most surprising: the carefully pushed-back cuticles on the woman's fingernails, and the remnants of rose-pink nail varnish.

Women from Bronwyn County do not wear nail varnish. Oh—there are ads for it in the big-city newspapers from Cincinnati and Columbus. Not in the *Kinship Daily Courier*. Not carried in Kinship's general store or Merle's grocery or the dress shop. Nail coloring is a new style, for city women. For rich women. Mother would say for "fancy" women, and there's nothing good about fancy.

Yet, in spite of Mother's judgment, in spite of the horror of the woman's damaged head and arm, Hildy smiles at the chips of nail varnish. *Good for you,* she thinks to the woman, *for having adventures, doing what you wanted. Even at the end. Maybe especially at the end.*

Hildy has never been out of Bronwyn County, and her heart pangs at realizing that in marrying Merle she likely never will be. He'd even proclaimed a honeymoon in Cincinnati or Columbus as foolish; the money could more practically be put toward renovations at the grocery. It's not being denied a fancy honeymoon that makes Hildy chafe, or even the notion of no adventures beyond innovating new ways to display canned peas in the grocery window or trying a new tomato aspic recipe for a Woman's Club meeting.

It is the notion of never being someone who anyone would consider bold or strong enough for adventure. Never being someone who others—even people who supposedly love her the most, like Lily and Tom—would take seriously.

Hildy admonishes herself—*such self-pitying thoughts, and right beside a woman who'd died so horrendously!*

But this woman with her chipped rose pink nail varnish—*she* would understand. Yes, far more than any of the women in the Kinship Woman's Club—the Mrs. Arlingtons of the town.

Or . . . *would* some of them understand?

Hildy assumes she knows the women of her community, just as they likely assume they know her. But beyond the surface of names and addresses and preferred tomato aspic recipes, do they really know one another any more than she knows this nameless woman?

She looks back at her sketch, the woman's face made whole. The gaze she'd rendered on paper grips her, offers sympathy. And yet admonishes her to make her own choices. Be her own woman.

A need rushes through Hildy to know everything about this woman. Not just her name, or how she came to her final, strange moment. Nor even the why of her death. Those are Lily's questions, and Hildy has no doubt Lily will find the answers.

Rather, Hildy's heart clenches with the need to know who this woman really *was.* She has lived seven-plus decades—far longer than most people Hildy knows. Who had she loved? Had her heart been broken? Had she broken someone's heart? Did she have children? Work?

Something or someone had compelled her to the top of that tunnel in the last minutes of her life, and surely that means that whatever else she might have been—foolish or smart, kind or cruel, spoiled or giving—she was someone to be reckoned with. Who'd had adventures. Who'd been strong and bold. Who others would have taken seriously.

Hildy realizes that her face is wet, that she's been crying, but not only for this woman.

For herself.

CHAPTER 7

⁕

LILY

Wednesday, September 22—6:15 a.m.

"This's where she fell?" Marvena holds Sadie's leash taut, so the bloodhound heels beside her.

Lily squats at the edge of the tunnel, where she had stood hours before, stares down at the track. The coolness of night still clings to the earth. Lily shudders. "Or was pushed."

Lily pulls out the nightgown and foot rags, then unwraps the pieces, careful to hold the cloth with the waxed paper, so as not to mingle her scent with the woman's. She glances up, sees pity cross Marvena's face as she stares at the nightgown and rags, smudged with blood. The notion of an old woman dressed so wandering alone in these thorny, dark woods evokes shock in even a woman as tough as Marvena.

Lily holds the cloth toward Sadie, as Marvena eases up on the leash. The hound snuffles the cloth. Sadie whines as Lily pulls the piece away, but then puts her nose to the ground, finding the scent again.

The hound eagerly starts down the slope of the tunnel, yanking Marvena along. Lily hurries after them but pulls up short as a snake winds across her path. Lily holds her breath, thinking at first that it's a timber rattler. She notes the upturned nose—it's a hognose snake, a non-venomous variety that likes to make itself seem threatening by rearing up, flattening its neck, in a striking pose. Hard to tell, sometimes, true threats from false ones.

The snake ignores her, slithers on, in search of a toad or two for breakfast.

By the time Lily catches up with Marvena and Sadie, the hound is howling, trying to pull Marvena up onto the track and head away from the tunnel. Then she turns back, nose to ground, straining into the woods.

Lily looks at Marvena. "Is she confused?"

Marvena shakes her head. "Your lady walked from somewhere up to this spot on the track, veered off into the woods before her final stop at the top of the tunnel. So do you want Sadie to take us down the track, or into the woods?"

Lily stares back up the track. "We can double back later?"

Marvena nods. Lily points to the thick dark of the woods.

The farmhouse and grounds are only recently abandoned, a sigh falling into silence. The rails of the generous wraparound porch have recently been repainted a wholesome sky blue, while the shutters are chipped and faded to a dull gray-blue. A large garden patch is weeded over, yet chrysanthemums bloom sprightly yellow along the front porch—the only bright spot in the clearing. Though the sun has now burned off the morning mist, the dimness of Moonvale Hollow feels like a permanently pressing presence.

Lily carefully folds the dead woman's clothing, rewraps it in the waxed paper, and tucks it back in her rucksack.

Sadie strains toward the house but shows no interest in a dirt lane that snakes up to the house. Why would the woman have come to this unoccupied house through thick briars and brush, ignoring the easier path? Why come here at all?

Lily frowns. She'd wanted the identification of the dead woman to be a simple matter, the explanation for her death straightforward. Both are becoming increasingly complex.

Marvena walks over to a scorched area in the front yard, circled by stones. Lily joins her, kneels, studies charred wood and dark ash. The scent of wood fire is strong. Recent. She picks up a stick, pokes at the wood pieces, which readily crumble. No embers. The fire must have been last night, after the afternoon storm that Lily had seen yesterday passed through here. Had the fire been built before the storm, rain would have disintegrated the charred wood, smudged it into the ground. Next Lily pokes the earth. Still soft from that earlier rain. Then she startles, noting boot prints all around the fire circle. Prints with smaller soles, pointier heels. Women had gathered here.

"Wait here," Lily says.

Marvena mutters an oath, which Lily ignores as she hurries over to the porch, trots up the steps. She rests one hand on her revolver, the other on the door. Gives a little push. The door opens easily. Someone hadn't bothered to lock up—or had forgotten to.

"Hello?" Lily hollers. "It's Sheriff Ross. I'm doing a routine . . . property check."

Marvena, right behind her, gives a derisive snort. She glances back— she should have known Marvena wouldn't stay out of the action. Lily shrugs: *You come up with a better excuse.* Then she steps inside, slowly.

The main floor is one open space, with no furniture. The only remnants of occupancy are white curtains, a worn rug in front of the stone fireplace, and on the far wall a coal-fired cookstove. The house feels stiff, empty. Yet more women's boot prints dot the wood floor and the narrow stairs.

Something whimpers upstairs, the thin cry of a baby. Lily's heart clenches.

She hurries up, sees doors open to two empty bedrooms. She follows the sound into the bedroom farthest from the stairs.

She exhales, relieved. It's a white-breasted nuthatch, sitting on top of a curtain rod. Lily goes to the window, which slides up easily enough, as if the track had recently been greased. Another sign that this house— sturdy and decent and strong—had only recently been left behind.

From the window, Lily sees a thin path out back that leads up another hill to a small cemetery—a family plot. At last—a small break in this difficult case and morning. The headstones will bear names, reveal who the house had once belonged to.

She steps back, stares at the small bird. In her presence it's quieted.

Go on, go on, she thinks. *Back to your nest*—probably in a tree outside. Nuthatches can mate for life. Another bird might be longing for its return.

It must have flown in last night as women came and went in the house—but why had they done so? The women's gatherings she knows of are in proper parlors or church fellowship halls, such as the Kinship Woman's Club, discussing how to get a public library for the town.

She goes to the open window. "Go on, shoo, shoo!"

"Lily!" From the next bedroom, alarm pitches Marvena's voice high. The woman doesn't scare easily, so Lily pulls out her revolver as she hurries to Marvena.

Marvena's hand shakes as she points to something on the floor.

A hooded cape, sewn from rough white cotton. The pointed hood has buttonholes to attach a face covering, with slits cut for eyes.

Lily recoils, more startled by this than by the snake from moments ago. As realization strikes, Lily's stomach turns, and bile runs up to her throat. She swallows back rising bitterness, draws a deep breath, forcing herself to think carefully, logically.

The Ku Klux Klan had had a small following in Bronwyn County years ago, before the turn of the century, after the Civil War ended and some former slaves ventured north to find work in coal mines or as farmhands. An ignorant reaction to the end of slavery—that's what Lily's father had been sure to teach both her and her brother.

Her heart pangs—as she thinks of how her father, a kind man who stood firm against injustice, had made sure that his children understood their nation's history, both glorious and inglorious. So she also knows that the federal Enforcement Act of 1871—one of three anti–Ku Klux Klan acts—had helped to nearly dismantle the KKK.

The second rising of the KKK came when Lily was in her teens, around 1915, the excuse for it this time being support of Prohibition, when temperance was a county-by-county, state-by-state choice, well before it became a national mandate. The year 1915 was also when the film *The Birth of a Nation* was released. The film made it to the Kinship Opera House a year and a half after its release, and Lily's father had taken the family.

An image of her dear father's face flashes before her—at home, after the film, both Mama and Daddy had gone quiet, their faces pinched as if in great pain. The next day, they sat Lily and Roger down in the parlor. Lily can hear them again now, explaining why they found the movie offensive. Yet also explaining that there were many in their community who would feel differently—and the challenge was, and always had been and always would be, to live and lead by example, guided by the principle that all are created equal.

Lily tries to focus on the hood and cape. She is not aware of a KKK group in this part of Ohio. Had a chapter opened here, right under her watch?

Yet something seems different about this hood, apparently left accidentally behind.

Like the boot and shoe prints, it's small.

The *women's* boot and shoe prints.

Oh God. This isn't from the KKK.

It's from the WKKK—the Women of the Ku Klux Klan, not just wives and daughters and mothers of men in the KKK, but an auxiliary women's group, born of the KKK but also out of a branch of the suffrage movement that aligned itself with the principles of prohibition and strong sentiments that though women had their specified places in home and society, they were equal to men—as long as they were of European descent, not an immigrant, and Protestant.

The WKKK movement had been making the newspapers of late, with articles and opinion pieces both supporting and castigating the movement, which had begun three years before, combining numerous smaller women's groups that espoused the same beliefs, while drawing strength from a portion of suffragettes who wished to put their political power to work to ensure what they called the American way of life. The WKKK already had chapters in every state, with the biggest and strongest in Indiana, Pennsylvania, Arkansas. And Ohio.

God, they'd hate the sight of her, a female sheriff, fitting their criteria in every way, except in her own beliefs, and in doing man's work, not work sanctioned for women—homemaking or teaching or nursing.

Lily kneels, pokes the hateful hood with the tip of her revolver, as if testing a snake to see if it is still alive.

She swallows hard, another line of bile rising in her throat. Sure, the hood is just cloth, can't hurt her, but what it represents—ah, that is a snake, very much alive, and not a falsely frightening one like the hognose earlier, but a truly venomous one, coming up out of the earth where good people, people like her father, would have hoped it would remain buried. A snake nonetheless reemerged, coiled down tight in its hatefulness, emboldened by the fear it stirred in others, its readiness to strike undoubtable. For snakes always strike.

And evil has a way of slithering forth again and again, its old form disguising itself in new masks, its ancient pretexts of hatred rewritten with new justifications.

This particular evil has its own charter and organization.

In her county.

Her jurisdiction.

And at one of the last places the still-unidentified woman had been alive.

CHAPTER 8

※

HILDY

Wednesday, September 22—6:55 a.m.

Hildy tries to type quietly, so as not to stir Mama and the children, still sleeping upstairs.

Still, to Hildy's ears, each strike sounds like echoes in an empty room—impossible, since she is working at the rolltop desk in Lily's well-appointed parlor. The same furniture and rugs and draperies are positioned as they were when Lily and Daniel had moved in eight years before—nothing new, nothing taken away. Touches of Lily's efforts to make the county-owned sheriff's house a true family home grace the neat, tidy room—a bouquet of purple garden phlox in a red glass vase on a side table, the soft ticks of the nightly wound mantel clock, and, on the settee, pillows embroidered with a lady in a matching pink dress and parasol. Hildy has a similar set, though hers don't display such neat, perfect stitches; they'd made the pillows in home economics class in high school years ago, giggling over something long forgotten, but that at the time had made Hildy's stitches go wobbly, while as Lily kept hers even.

Yet this parlor, this house, no longer feels like Lily's.

Hildy can't quite place when the house became so oddly unfamiliar.

After Daniel's death, but not right away. And not because Daniel is no longer here, though his was a big presence and his absence is just as huge.

Slowly, even with Lily and the children still here, and often Mama and Caleb Jr., too, the house has developed a stiff, empty air. As if the family has moved out, leaving the furniture and decorations as stage setting for a life that was supposed to have been.

Hildy sighs. Mother says she is overly sentimental, that she should learn to be pragmatic.

Pragmatic. That's what Tom had told her to be last night. What Mother wanted her to be by marrying Merle.

Hildy snorts a half laugh at the notion of Mother and Tom agreeing on anything—Mother would scorn Tom as beneath them, and Tom would be amused by Mother's haughty airs.

Focus. For Lily's sake. She must get a clean copy of the sheriff's notice to the *Kinship Daily Courier* in time for it to run in today's afternoon edition.

Hildy taps out the last few words and rolls out the paper. She studies the sheet, rattling between her trembling hands. On the desk and on the floor around her feet are wadded up attempts to document what she and Lily know so far about the deceased woman. It's startling, how hard this task is. Shouldn't there be more on the page? Given all that she had thought and felt about the woman in the basement of the funeral home? There it is. Just a few small facts. A longing rushes over her, a longing to write a thorough description of the woman's life, of who she is. Was.

Overly sentimental.

The mantel clock strikes 7:00. Hildy jumps.

As Hildy reads over her copy one more time, the door to the kitchen opens. Hildy startles and looks up as Mama steps into the parlor.

Mama is carrying two cups of coffee. Only now does Hildy smell bacon, and buttermilk biscuits. She's been so caught up in trying to get this copy right, she hadn't heard Mama crossing behind her in the parlor, or any noise from the kitchen, just her own typing.

She stands, goes to Mama, takes one of the cups, and nods at the settee. "Please, I can tell you've been working hard this morning."

Mama sits. "You too," she says, a lilt of amusement to her voice as she eyes the wadded drafts on the floor by the desk.

"Oh! I'll clean that all up," Hildy says. "It's just that Lily asked me to put together a sketch, and a sheriff's announcement, and—"

Mama pats the spot next to her. "Relax, Hildy. It's hard to get something like that just right." She sips her coffee. "Mmmm."

Gratefully, Hildy sits down and follows Mama's example. She takes a sip of coffee, savors the strong taste and scent.

"Where'd Lily get off to now?"

Hildy smiles at Mama's question, and at the same peeved look Mama had worn when Lily was getting into mischief when they were children—running off to jump into the river from the Kinship Tree or to wander the hills. *Where'd Lily get off to now?* was a question often asked in Lily's youth—usually of Hildy, who everyone saw as the staid one. *Pragmatic.*

"She's off tracking the woman that fell. With Marvena."

Mama relaxes. "Well, I reckon that makes sense. If there's anyone who'd know how to get a good tracking hound and use it, it'd be Marvena."

Hildy stares at her cup. Her stomach is queasy, and her face flames at how jealous she is of Lily and Marvena's friendship. She puts her cup aside, goes to gather the wadded papers.

"Hildy, let me see your sketch."

She suddenly doesn't want to share it with Mama—with anyone. Why would Lily think she could draw a useful likeness? She hasn't drawn in years. The only reason she even had the charcoal pencils is because she'd hung on to them and other childhood mementos in a box she keeps tucked under her bed—overly sentimental, as always. The sketch deserves to be wadded up, tossed aside with the other papers. Lily probably meant this to be a keep-busy task, while she did the real work with Marvena.

Mama has issued a directive, not a question, so Hildy brings her the sketch and sinks back down onto the settee. As Mama stares at the sketch, Hildy feels protective. It's all she can do to keep from snatching it back.

Something passes over Mama's expression. Not judgment but

something like recognition, and for a moment Hildy's heart leaps. Maybe the woman can be identified quickly, the case solved—but then she realizes that Mama isn't recognizing the woman in particular, but that she sees something of herself in the woman: getting older, less relevant, drifting.

"You brought her back to life," Mama says quietly. "You always were a right good drawer." She hands the sketch back to Hildy. "Nearly forgot about that."

"Thank you." Hildy's heart swells at Mama's compliment. The mantel clock chimes the quarter hour. "I—I should get it and the announcement over to the newspaper office. And I should get to Merle's—he's been wanting to show me how he runs the grocery—but the prisoners need to be fed, too, and the children, and Jolene off to school—"

Mama laughs. "You young ladies, stretched so thin these days! Well, I already took breakfast to the prisoners—I couldn't sleep, anyway, I get overheated at night of late, no matter the weather, it seems, and I can handle the children."

"Oh, that was good of you. I'll collect up the plates later—"

"They're a surly lot this morning." Mama sounds amused by her own warning. "Two to a cell, three in one of them!"

Hildy nods. "The commissioners finally had to bring in a security guard for overnight. It'll be a relief when the new jail is done." The facility, started in the past spring, is nearly complete. "It'll be good to have it out of the backyard!"

Mama gives Hildy a long look. "Lily didn't tell you? The county commissioners are also moving the sheriff's office to the courthouse, and working with the mayor to establish a police department for Kinship. Eventually this house will be converted to police headquarters."

"Lily . . . and the children . . . will have to move?"

"In time," Mama says. "Whether she wins the election or not. I've told her that they could move in with me and I could watch the children and . . . Oh, Hildy. I'm sorry. I assumed Lily told you. She should have."

Yes. She should have. That's what best friends do.

"Now, now," Mama says. "She knows that you're set to marry Merle soon, and I'm sure she doesn't want to trouble you as you make your plans. Do you have a date set?"

Hildy shakes her head, blinking back tears.

A faint smile wavers on Mama's lips as she pats Hildy's hand. "Roger would want you to be happy. I don't want you to mourn him forever. I want you to be happy, too."

Oh God. Mama thinks she's delaying a wedding date with Merle because of Roger.

Happy.

She'd been so happy with Roger. His face—young, unmarred, handsome—rises before her. Something in his expression now seems to suggest that he'd never been meant long for the rough-and-tumble and furor and fury of this world.

As his face fades, the one replacing it is not stolid, older, steady Merle, but craggy, thin-faced, hard-etched Tom Whitcomb.

Hildy's heart races, her palms sweating. She looks down, away from Mama, only to meet the eyes of the woman in her sketch and sees an approving glint in the eyes she's imagined, the eyes she's drawn, eyes that say, *Yes, Tom.*

"I can take care of the jailhouse and the children," Mama is saying. "You get on over to the newspaper, then to the grocery."

Hildy looks from the sketch back to Mama. Usually, Mama carries herself with resoluteness, but this morning, a thin gray strand of hair pulled loose from her dark bun makes her seem fragile. What would Mama think—if she knew about Tom? Suddenly her opinion matters to Hildy more than Merle's or Mother's. Or Lily's.

Yet she must choose. She can't remain with both Merle and Tom.

Roger would want you to be happy.

Hildy smiles softly as Mama's words echo in her thoughts.

Well then. She'll choose to deliver the announcement and sketch to the newspaper.

And then go see Tom.

Find a way to make up from their fight the night before, tell him she needs a bit more time to break off from Merle, to break the news to Mother and Mama and Lily.

CHAPTER 9

LILY

Wednesday, September 22—8:30 a.m.

In the family cemetery behind the farmhouse, Lily regards a headstone:

> Murphy Dyer, September 20, 1856–August 15, 1925. Beloved
> father and husband. At Rest in the Lord.

Murphy—father of Perry Dyer. Other headstones, with their cold carved names and dates, testify to the Dyer lineage. Charles Dyer was the first patriarch buried here. He'd have settled Moonvale Hollow around 1796 on land that he'd have gotten in the then United States Military District, payment for service in the Revolutionary War—the way many other farms in this region were originally established. He'd died in 1826, after, as Perry explained in an interview published in the *Kinship Daily Courier,* long years of scrabbling a living off the land, as did his son, Adam, until he had the brilliant idea to lease land to the train lines and Moonvale Hollow grew into a village.

After Adam's passing, his son, Murphy, had overseen the operations, before passing them on to Perry, no doubt assuming Perry and his wife, Margaret, would remain as the generations had before them.

Shortly after Murphy's death, Perry and Margaret had sold the leased land to B&R and used the money to move to Kinship. And the couple had been trying to climb to the top of Kinship society ever since.

Though perhaps there is an additional explanation. Three small headstones—with dates in recent years, two labeled "Infant" and lifespans of a few days, and another for eighteen months, one named Charles after the patriarch who had originally settled this hollow, are tucked in a row near the fence line. From the dates, children born and lost in the early years of Perry and Margaret's marriage.

Perhaps Margaret, knowing that she is old enough that her childbearing years are likely behind her, had wanted to get away from the reminder of such unspeakable loss, readily viewable from the bedroom window. Perhaps both Margaret and Perry had. Sympathy twangs Lily's heart, a note discordant to the usual antipathy she feels toward the couple.

Yet there is also this jarring note: it seems someone is using the old, reclusive Dyer farm for WKKK meetings. The hateful hood is now in Lily's rucksack, alongside the dead woman's gown and foot rags.

Is Margaret the instigator behind the group? Or merely a member providing space? Does Perry know, or care, what his wife is doing?

A bird settles on an old redbud tree shadowing the headstone. The tree is half-dead, its trunk hollowed out, only a few small living branches staggering toward the sky. Yet the ancient tree still provides asylum for the bird—another nuthatch. It trills, then disappears into the hollow trunk. Surely this is not the same nuthatch as the one in the house, or its mate. Still. Wouldn't it be lovely if it were?

As Lily rejoins Marvena at the cemetery gate, Marvena asks, "Learn anything?"

"Let's backtrack. I'll explain along the way."

A few yards from the Moonvale Hollow Tunnel, Sadie stops abruptly. Lily grabs the lead from Marvena, steps onto the track, tugs impatiently. Daylight is at last upon them, revealing dark clouds roiling in from the west. The air is plump with the scent of coming rain, rain that Lily had coveted for her garden yesterday, but that soon would scourge the scent of the dead woman's trail.

Sadie whines, plops down on her hindquarters, immovable.

Marvena wrests back the lead. "Dammit, Lily, wait. She's stopped for a purpose. You can't force things along to suit yourself—"

Lily's feet prickle at a faint tremor in the earth, her ears at a far-off pitch strained high like the whine of a trapped animal. Tremor grows to rumbling, whine to whistle. Lily, Marvena, and Sadie retreat into the underbrush.

The train rumbles into the tunnel, its thunderous progression mounting until at last the engine shoots out, the squeal of iron wheels blighting the murmurs and moans of forest critters, the sooty smell of the coal heaped in the cars smothering woodland scents.

After the train passes, the very air falls into silence, as if the forest had held its breath to endure the piercing of the train and must hold it a moment longer before trusting enough to exhale. Slowly, woodland sounds resume.

"God." Marvena shudders. "Nothin' much would have been left of the woman, nothing recognizable at least, if'n she'd been hit head on."

Lily eyes the sky. Those dark clouds, schooners clipping along, eager to unload their bounty of rain. "We need to hurry."

She reaches in her rucksack, grazing the hooded cape, and jerks back as if she'd reached into a hole and brushed a snake. She extracts the dead woman's foot rags, lets Sadie get another good sniff. Danger passed, Sadie strains again to get on the track—into the tunnel.

"You right sure?" Marvena says. "Don't wanna get squashed like an opossum."

Lily recollects the schedule she'd memorized the night before. "The next train will come the other way, three hours' time."

They walk up onto the track. Even through the thick, good soles of Lily's boots, the track bites her feet. How had the woman walked here in bare feet? As they enter the tunnel, Lily switches on her flashlight. The dot of light barely penetrates the darkness. Something skitters— rats, mice, maybe raccoons. She'd thought the tunnel would be devoid of life.

Focus. Perry had seemed genuinely shocked at the sight of the woman, sworn he didn't know her. But shock and ignorance can be feigned.

A theory sends up tendrils, grasps Lily's mind: What if the woman had been part of the WKKK gathering? Had changed her mind? Or had stumbled upon it? What if Perry had been at the gathering—either sanctioning it or trying to stop it?

What if Perry saw something that could cost him the election? And so *he* had killed her?

Lily places the notion aside for now. She doesn't have enough facts.

At last, Lily and Marvena emerge from the other side of the tunnel. Lily takes a deep breath of fresh air, smiles as Marvena does the same. Lily glances back, stares into the deep darkness. She estimates the tunnel to be a hundred yards or so, short enough that she can see straight through it. Yet the tunnel had somehow felt endless.

There he is again. Shimmering. The boy she had seen earlier—no. Imagined. Now he's running out of the tunnel, still chasing something. He grins at Lily, waves.

Lily presses her eyes shut. Sways.

"Lily? You all right?" Marvena's voice, alarmed.

Lily opens her eyes. The boy is gone.

It's good, good that he's gone. No, not *gone,* for that implies that he was actually *there.* Good, then, that she's not seeing him.

Lily says, "I'm fine."

On they trek, Sadie confident and snuffling. After about a mile, Marvena hums an old hymn—"Washed in the Blood of the Lamb," a grim choice as far as Lily's concerned, but then she's distanced herself from religion, dropping in at the Kinship Presbyterian Church only often enough to keep up appearances, sending her children with Mama most Sundays. Marvena, though, has immersed herself in both unionizing and worshiping at a non-denominational Holy Gospel church with Jurgis, Nana, and Frankie, where the child sings solos.

Wherever Frankie got her gift of voice, it isn't from Marvena, the warbling embodiment of the saying "not able to carry a tune in a bucket." After another half mile, Marvena's humming conspires with the sweat running down Lily's neck to push her into itchy irritation.

Though autumn pokes its nose, like Sadie's snuffling snout, under the veil of summer's last heat, summer is not yet willing to loosen its grip, and already the heat of the morning has burned off dew and mist, even in these deepest crevices of Moonvale Hollow's hills and hollers.

Suddenly Sadie farts.

Lily coughs. What has Marvena's cousin been feeding the hound? Something fouler than skunk, by the odor.

Marvena laughs.

Lily glares at her.

"You wanna talk about it?" Marvena asks. "You've been itchy and irritable since we set out. Why'n't you speak plain 'bout what you're all puffed up over, like a broody hen?"

"You really want me to interrogate you right now, about why in the hell you didn't tell me you're working to integrate the union?"

"So Jurgis told you about that, huh. Well, I reckoned you'd be on the side of integration."

"Dammit, of course I am! Plenty of folks won't be. And that's gonna lead to tension." That hood in her rucksack. Lily realizes that her temples have been throbbing ever since they'd found the grotesque thing. "Looks like it already has."

"I ain't told you because there's been no trouble."

Lily lifts an eyebrow. "You mean to tell me everyone's just fine, working side by side."

"Didn't say that. Said there's been no trouble."

"I'd say this hood indicates trouble." Lily gives her rucksack a vicious poke. She's not foolish enough to think the WKKK is going to stop at rituals around a fire. All those boot and shoe prints signified momentum.

Marvena opens her own rucksack, pulls out a pipe, lights it as they walk. "You don't know that it's related, Lily."

The smell of pipe tobacco—comforting, savory—wafts over to Lily. Her eyes prickle. Daniel's tobacco had smelled like that. "You don't know that it's *not* related. Word that the mines, union, are integrating, I can't believe there's been no trouble in Rossville—"

"None so far!" Marvena snaps. "Folks know that there is plenty of work. That if Wessex can keep up, compete, it's better for everyone. And they also know that the Immigration Act has limited folks from bringing over kin that might take up picks in the mines."

Lily nods. The 1924 act was, at its heart, a national origins quota—limiting the number of each nationality allowed to enter to equal 2 percent of that documented in the 1890 census—in effect cutting out many people from Eastern Europe. She's read heated debates in newspaper editorials and falls on the side against the act. Even in remote Bronwyn County, life constantly changes and rearranges.

"All right," Lily says. "Why not leave well enough alone in the union?"

"You really think the rightful protections of unionization belong only to some?"

"No! Sometimes it's better to be pragmatic." Lily thinks of steady, even Hildy. *She* understands being practical. "How are you going to get folks to accept—"

"This ain't a new idea. You've never heard tell of Richard Davis?"

Lily shakes her head, as she carefully steps over a thick tree root.

"Well, he was a Negro born in Virginia—the very night before old Lincoln's Emancipation Proclamation. He grew up near here—Rendville, over on Sunday Creek. I been reading some of Richard's old letters to the *United Mine Workers Journal*." Marvena's tone turns a little prideful. When Lily had first met her, Marvena couldn't read. Lily had helped her start to learn. "He started writing those letters after the Great Hocking Valley Coal Strike back in '84, and they're about the need for all working brothers, as he put it, to unite against a different kind of slavery—being beholden to low wages and unsafe working conditions with few or no other choices. What does it matter what we look like on the outside if'n the people with power are happy to work any of us like we're Guibo, a mule who's more'n likely treated better than people in the non-union mines—"

"I'm on your side on the question of the right of workers to unionize—remember?"

"Well, anyhow, Richard was one of two Negro men at the meeting to establish the United Mine Workers of America—back in '90. And after that, he was on the Executive Board for two years, in '96 and '97. So the union has a history back to its founding of letting—"

"So Richard was accepted without any backlash? No repercussions later?"

"Well now, I ain't saying that." Marvena eases around a thorny bush. "Just that the fella I'm working with—Clarence Broward, who was sent here from the union—is following in Richard's footsteps. And so far, there's been no trouble—"

Lily sighs. "You can get so fervent, Marvena, that sometimes you don't see the practicalities of a situation."

"How do you know that what we found is a backlash? Mayhap it ain't related. There was the one hood, so maybe that has nothing to do with anything. Jurgis says—"

"Jurgis!" Lily practically spits the name. "*Jurgis* says!" As Marvena recoils, a part of Lily screams at herself to stop. "I thought *he* took direction from *you*. When did you start taking his views as gospel? Since going to his church? Since he's practically moved in with you?"

"I know you miss Daniel." Marvena's voice is wobbly—a rare trait. She clears her throat. "Lily, I know it's been hard—"

The hurting part of Lily lashes out, a whip snapping fast. "What do you know of how hard it's been?"

Marvena's face blanches, tightens, into white-hot fury.

Lily stops, both her words and her stride. Horrified at herself for what she's said. She reaches for Marvena. "Oh God, Marvena, I—I'm . . . sorry—I—"

But Marvena has turned back toward Sadie, now pulled taut as an overly tight string on a dulcimer, plucking forward, no longer humming.

By Lily's estimate, they go on nearly two miles before Sadie follows her nose off the railroad track. Sadie pulls them through brush and brambles that snag their skirts, branches that snap back into their faces. Lily pauses to catch her breath and stares back at the winding way they've followed—but there is no discernible path. Brush and bramble and limb have already closed back over their steps, indifferent, as if they'd never passed through.

When Lily turns back around, Marvena and Sadie are out of view.

"Come this way!" Marvena calls. "Toward the big sycamore!"

The sycamore means they're near some creek or another water source, perhaps an underground stream. Lily hopes it's not a creek—if the woman had crossed a creek, that would make Sadie's work harder.

Lily makes her way over. There is no aboveground stream. Lily smiles at that, and at Sadie happily accepting bites of sandwich from Marvena, who's settled onto a rock like it's an easy chair. Hunger wrings Lily's stomach like a washrag, and a wave of light-headedness sends her staggering into the tiny, dark clearing.

Marvena rolls her eyes. "Come have a sandwich. Your gut's growling so loudly, poor Sadie prob'ly thinks a cougar's coming for us. Grab a pawpaw for me, won't you?" She jabs her forefinger in the air and Lily glances behind her at a pawpaw tree, so laden with abundant green fruit that the boughs nearly sweep the ground. The fruits are camouflaged by the large green leaves. Without Marvena, she would have missed this gift from the indifferent forest.

Lily grabs two ripe fruits, her mouth watering just from the feel of them. She brings a pawpaw to Marvena, who keeps her eyes on Sadie even as she hands Lily a sandwich.

Lily sits on a stump, tucks into her sandwich—ham, butter, greens, between sliced corn pone, so good that Lily finds herself offering up a spontaneous silent prayer of gratitude. Mama would be pleased at her prayerful attitude. Well, while she's being godly, she might as well apologize. Lily looks up at her friend. "Marvena, I'm—"

"Do you reckon the woman stopped here for a meal?"

No outright apologies, then. "I hope so." Lily bites into the pawpaw, carefully sucking fruit off the seeds, which she spits out, then relishes the custard-like creamy fruit, sweet and a bit peppery.

"So, how's Hildy seemed to you lately?" Marvena asks.

Marvena's question catches Lily by surprise. "Fine," Lily says. "Why?"

"I reckon you know Hildy is tutoring, with Miss Olive at the Rossville schoolhouse?" Marvena keeps her expression in check.

What is she getting at—or is she making conversation? But that's not like Marvena. Slowly, Lily says, "She mentioned it to me this morning. She won't be able to continue after she marries Merle Douglas. For the best, really."

A flash of guilt strikes Lily—she'd been so brusque with Hildy this morning, as she'd been with Marvena earlier.

"Is it? Hildy seems right happy when she's tutoring, and I don't reckon a fella who would want her to be happy would want her to stop."

"It wouldn't be proper."

"Proper? You of all women, worrying about what's proper—"

"Hildy isn't like us."

"What d'you mean by that?"

"She needs protecting. She's always been a little shy, not too confident—"

"I don't know; I've seen her hold her own—" Marvena grins. "Even when tutoring a tough nut like me—or my brother."

Lily should be pleased for all of them. Last year, she'd seen first-hand how shamed Marvena felt that she wasn't able to read letters from Daniel—letters that eventually led them to Benjamin Russo, who works in the Bureau of Mines and who was able to help them.

Instead, Lily is miffed. Sure, she's been busy. But Hildy hadn't mentioned her volunteering until this morning, and Marvena hadn't told her about it, either. What else had they not bothered to share?

She's being petulant. Rather than say anything else she'll regret, Lily folds up the waxed paper—Marvena will want to reuse it—and silently hands it to her.

They set back out, and minutes later Sadie whines and strains to go up a footpath that's opened steps away from the pawpaw tree. They follow Sadie to a narrow gravel road.

"Well, I'll be damned!" Marvena exclaims.

"I don't think that's the idea," Lily says.

CHAPTER 10

※

HILDY

Wednesday, September 22—9:00 a.m.

Hildy hurries on a back way from Lily's house to the newspaper office. The direct path would take her past Merle's grocery on Main Street, and today Merle is expecting her to come into the grocery to learn how he wants to stock the shelves and track inventory. She's been working a few days a week as his helper at the register, a task that is simple enough, but that she finds herself resisting. Every time she goes in, she has to push aside the thought of how the grocery had once belonged to Lily's father, had been meant to pass on to Roger.

Now she carefully carries in one hand the notebook, in which she's slipped her sketch and sheriff's notice, and covers her mouth and nose with the other. This alley, which cuts behind the Kinship Inn, reeks of alcohol and trash and even human waste. She steps carefully around a puddle, though it hasn't rained here.

Disgusting, and yet behind her hand she's smiling. She feels, suddenly, important, powerful. Like she's on a secret mission for Lily— and for the dead woman. Merle and Mother would not approve, but recklessly, Hildy thinks, *So what?* For after her mission is complete at the newspaper, she will drive back to Rossville, find Tom, make up with him, make him give her more time to talk to Merle and Mother. They have done nothing wrong, after all, and she wants to let them down as kindly as possible.

She stops short at the sight of George Vogel emerging from the hotel's back entrance—George, the powerful attorney and purveyor of Vogel's Tonic, which barely followed the rule of the Volstead Act for alcoholic content for medicinal purposes. What is he doing here? He lives in Cincinnati, but reports of his mob ties have reached even the local newspaper. Surely he didn't come here for some illicit poker game. . . .

Emerging behind him, a brazen tilt to her chin that nonetheless belies defensiveness, is Fiona Weaver, the widow of Deputy Martin Weaver, who'd died in the line of duty in the conflict in Rossville the year before.

With them are several other men—bodyguards—and George's right-hand man and enforcer, Abe Miller.

Hildy recognizes Vogel from newspaper articles and Miller because he had come to Daniel's funeral, then lingered in the months that followed as Lily settled into her role as sheriff.

She must tell Lily that they're here—and that Fiona is involved with George. Hildy lowers her gaze, hurries past them, heart pounding—then realizes, they haven't even noticed her. She might as well have been one of the alley mice.

By the time she's back out on Main Street, Hildy's resolve is already faltering—and not from being able to scurry past the great George Vogel and Fiona Weaver unnoticed. Her giddiness wilts as she thinks about telling Lily about this, imagines Lily brushing aside this news as gossip. Why hadn't Lily told her that the sheriff's office and jail will move to the courthouse?

There's no use in wondering. She knows why. Lily thinks Hildy will marry Merle soon—and their friendship, already waning, will wither as Lily follows her unconventional path and Hildy takes the conventional way—not side streets and alleys.

Around another corner and there's the *Kinship Daily Courier*, in a narrow building near the end of the street. Inside the office, she finds Seth Robertson, reporter for the newspaper. He's leaning back in his chair, feet on desk, hat on face, with a burning cigarette dangling between his lips. If she were a bettor—like the men at the illicit poker games in the Kinship Inn's basement speakeasy, which Lily, like Daniel before her, prefers to ignore—she'd bet he'd come directly to work from a long night at the speakeasy, and give fifty-fifty odds he's going to either set his hat brim on fire or let the cigarette drop to the pile of paper on his desk.

Hildy raps her knuckles on the desk, and Seth startles, sits up. His hat lands on top of the typewriter, and he stubs out his cigarette in an already-full ashtray. "Dammit, Hildy, are you trying to give me a heart attack?"

"Trying to save you from catching the place on fire," Hildy says.

Seth stands, stretches. He smells as funky as he looks. "I've had a long night because although we're now a daily," Seth says defensively, "Mr. Lindermann is taking his own sweet time adding to the staff—I'm working more hours than ever. Same pay, though." He scratches the top of his head. He grins. "I was composing the editorial for the evening edition, but the sight of you has plumb near driven it from my mind!"

Seth had gone to high school with her, Roger, and Lily. Roger used to tease her that Seth was sweet on her, and Hildy always replied that Seth acted sweet on all of the girls.

Normally, Hildy would stutter out an apology and—of late—worry that someone might overhear and word would get back to overprotective Merle that Seth was flirting. Merle wouldn't confidently laugh it off as Roger would have.

"Good. Then you will have plenty of space for this announcement." Hildy carefully places the article and her sketch to the side of the typewriter.

Seth stares first at the article, then at the sketch, then up at her.

"Normally I only take notices of this sort from the sheriff herself," he says.

"Well, she's indisposed at the moment."

"Indisposed?" Seth lifts his eyebrows and manages to make the word sound scandalous.

"Tracking the woman's recent path with a bloodhound," Hildy says. *And with Marvena.*

Her heart pangs with jealousy—and with nervousness. Hildy is fairly sure Marvena knows about her hidden relationship with Tom. Will Marvena tell Lily?

Seth sighs, picks up the papers at last, reads the copy, glances over the drawing.

He looks up at Hildy. "Where did you get this picture?"

"I drew it from the corpse. Filled in the blanks, with logic and imagination."

He stares at her a long minute, wonder lighting his expression. "You always were a good artist. And full of deep and hidden surprises and secrets, Hildy Cooper." This time his intonation and words are not teasing but serious. "If I run your piece, I'll have to drop a letter to the editor, which the editor is insisting we run in the name of free speech, and my opinion piece responding to it. I was writing it as you came in—"

"Oh, were you? Pro or con for allowing chickens to still be kept in town?"

Seth does not respond with a grin, as she expected. His serious look deepens. "This anonymous woman you care so much about—if she was important to anyone, she wouldn't be anonymous, now would she?"

Hildy's fist rises swiftly, of its own volition, as if it is an entity separate from her, but she has no desire to stop it, cheers it on, as it falls with a thud on the desk, next to her article and picture. It is a gavel coming down with swift judgment, propelled by frustration.

With the thud, Seth jumps.

"This is serious."

"So is this." Seth's hand shakes a bit as he gives her a letter.

> Women of Kinship and Bronwyn County,
>
> Do you want to ensure the Safety and Sanctity of your Family and Home? Fight the forces of heathen change that would threaten the Purity of Hearth and Country, invading our schools with prurient notions?
>
> Even our own Sheriff Ross turns her eyes against the laws of the land, allowing violations of Prohibition law and related ills to go unchecked!

If you wish to put your newfound, hard-won political power to use, to ensure Pure American Values at home, in our schools, and in our streets—be alert for one of our sisters to approach you and listen with a Prayerful Heart to her plea.

Our cause is Just, and we are eager for the Right women—pure of heart and aware of Their Proper place in Society—to join us.

As one of our Great Leaders, the Quaker Evangelist Daisy Douglas Barr, penned in her moving poem:

"I am the Spirit of Righteousness.

They call me the Ku Klux Klan.

I am more than the uncouth robe and hood with which I am clothed.

Yea I am the Soul of America."

Standing for all that is Good and Holy and American,

Bronwyn County Chapter

The Women of the Ku Klux Klan

Hildy drops the letter, as if it's a snake. She stares at him, mouth gaping.

Seth's voice is taut. "We've had the letter for a week. I've thought of every reason to put off running it—though our editor insists we must. I'm trying to find the right words to compose an opposing editorial."

Hildy grins—not joyfully, but grimly. "Well, I'm here officially as sheriff's deputy." Lily had never gotten around to un-deputizing Hildy after the spring of 1925. "And as such, I'm telling you that you'll have to put off running that—that letter—and your opinion piece, in order to run my notice and sketch. For a few days, at least."

Besides hopefully turning up someone to identify the woman, this will allow Hildy to forewarn Lily about this shocking development— which, she is certain, Lily will not write off as mere gossip. Hildy had read articles about the WKKK rising in Indiana, Pennsylvania, other states. But here? Where it's been quiet and sleepy, at least since the year before?

After a long moment, Seth nods, a fresh grin—this one appreciative—lifting his face.

As she reaches the door, his voice stops her. "Hildy? It's good to see *you* again."

She turns, looks at him, confusion rippling her brow. She'd seen him a few days before, in Merle's grocery, but now he's saying this with longing, as if he hadn't seen her in a long time.

Her gaze catches his, and she realizes, with a soft gasp, that he'd put a slight emphasis on "you," that he meant the Hildy he'd known so many years ago.

Announcement submitted by Hildy Cooper at 9:00 a.m. to be published in the KINSHIP DAILY COURIER, September 22, 1926, delivered to Kinship subscribers at 6:00 p.m.

Woman Hit by Train—Sheriff Requests Anyone with Information to Come Forward

An unidentified woman, approximated age late seventies to early eighties, apparently fell from the top of the Moonvale Hollow Tunnel and onto the westbound B&R Railroad freight train on September 21 at approximately 10:30 p.m.

It is not known how the woman came to be on top of the tunnel.

She is Caucasian, 5′ 1″, approximately 88 pounds, of petite bone structure and build. She does not have identifying scars or marks, though her wrists appear to have been recently bound.

Eye color is blue. Hair color is now mainly a snowy gray-white; a few non-gray hairs are sandy brown. She is fair complected, with high cheekbones.

Based on condition of hands at time of death, she is from a well-appointed station in life. No jewelry remained on her body, though from her ring finger, left hand, she wore a wedding ring somewhat recently. Remnants of nail varnish are on her nails. Her only clothing was a nightgown; she was not wearing any shoes but appears to have walked some distance in the woods with her feet wrapped in cloth rags.

Any persons who have any information or who recognize the facial features (a composite sketch given the condition of the victim in death) are requested to come forward with haste and urgency, by order of the Bronwyn County Sheriff, Lily Ross.

CHAPTER 11

⋙

LILY

Wednesday, September 22—10:45 a.m.

A sign identifies the simple rectangular stone building on the other side of the road: Stanehart Hollow Friends Meeting House, est. 1819. Something about its simplicity—bereft of even a porch or window shutters, the yard cropped short save for a mass of goldenrods blooming by a corner of the building—relaxes Lily, makes her think: here, then, one might find ease and rest.

"I bet this is Stanehart Hollow Road," Marvena says. "Shoots off of Kinship Road, right near Rossville, connects up to an old settlement— Stanehart Hollow. We're 'bout five miles from my place. The woman coulda stuck to this road, then the shortcut from my cousin's place to the top of Moonvale Hollow Tunnel. Why'n the world would she take the hard way we just came?"

"Good question."

The door opens. A woman dressed in sturdy boots and a plain, full-skirted brown dress and bonnet—the style of conservative Quaker women—steps out. She holds a broom. The woman gives the top step a brisk swipe, then stops as she spots them, clutching her broom as if it might double as protection.

Even so, the woman calls gently, "Hello, friends!" How must they look to her—two tired, filthy women, one with a tracking dog and another with a sheriff's star and revolver. At least the sky has cleared and they aren't drenched by rain. Lily moves the folds of her skirt so that it partially hides the holster.

She steps forward. "I'm Sheriff Lily Ross. Bronwyn County."

The woman's expression pinches with shock. "You're in Athens County here." She points down the narrow road. "This is Stanehart Hollow Road. County line sign is a mile or so back." She looks at Lily and Marvena, her expression now sedate, even as her grip remains firm on her broom handle. "May I get you water? Bread? My husband and I live up the hill."

Ah, wrapped up in the offer, the mention of a husband—protection from strangers.

"That's right kind of you, but we're tracking a woman," Lily says. "Found last night over in Moonvale Hollow. She was hit by a freight train."

"Oh!" The Quaker woman puts her hand to her heart.

"If our tracker's nose is right, she came by here," Marvena says.

"She was elderly," Lily adds. "When she was found, she was wearing only a nightgown. Barefoot, other than a few rags she'd tied around her feet. No identification."

"If we had seen her, we would have helped her, not let her wander on in such a state."

Lily lifts an eyebrow. "Really?"

The Quaker woman gives a slight, enigmatic smile. "Sheriff, I understand your reservations. Many do not understand our ways. If it's justice you're seeking, I can only wish you well. God's ways are mysterious and—"

"Right now we're looking for facts. Not a sermon," Lily says.

Marvena gives her a hard look, and shame instantly burns Lily's face—it's the same look Mama would give her to reprimand her for unnecessary harshness. Since the events of the year before, Marvena has turned to faith, while Lily has sought to reclaim a belief in justice.

"What I mean," Lily adds, "is that I respect your views. We are very interested in learning all we can about her. To find her family, for one thing. And if it wasn't an accident to find what justice we can for her, to let her rest in peace."

For a long moment, the Quaker woman studies Lily's expression. Finally, her searching look relaxes, and she smiles. "My friend, the woman is at peace regardless. Perhaps this will help you in your quest." She reaches into her pocket and pulls out a gold chain. Dangling on the end, a disc. She holds it out to Lily.

Lily takes it. The item—a pocket watch?—is from the previous century, the case etched in an ornate fleur-de-lis design. Lily presses the side clasp and the cover pops open. *Oh—a compass.* As Lily turns it in her hand, the needle moves to point to the ornate *N.* True north. Inside the cover are the engraved initials *R.E.K.*

The compass is in good shape, not scratched or dinged. Surely if it had been outdoors long, it would not be in such condition.

Lily looks up. "When did you find this?"

"Just this morning. Sweeping the back steps, at the other entrance."

"How often do you sweep?"

"Every morning. We had a meeting last evening. None of us would have such an ornate item. And if it was there last night, someone would have spotted it."

"When did your meeting end?"

"About eight. It was there this morning, looking as if it was meant to be found. It was in the center of the top step, back entrance, the chain carefully coiled around the disc."

"Why would someone leave something so precious on purpose?" Marvena asks.

"And if it belonged to the woman we're tracking, why would she leave it here? Wouldn't she need it?" Lily muses aloud.

"I don't know, except—" The woman's voice hitches, stops.

Lily looks up at her, sharply. "Except?"

"This road, Stanehart Hollow Road? *We* call it Freedom Pass."

The woman's gaze intensifies, as if inviting Lily to reach inside her brain and find the meaning. Lily calculates: In Kinship, dominated by mainstream Protestant churches, Quakers are seen as religious oddities, even more so than the members of the one small Catholic church and the Seventh-Day Adventist church. Daddy, in making sure she and Roger understood the important parts of history that had been left out of instruction in Kinship High School in her class of 1916, had told them that Quakers had been instrumental in helping slaves escape to freedom and avoid bounty hunters who took advantage of the federal Fugitive Slave Law of 1850—selling escaped slaves back to their owners. Under that law, those who helped escaping slaves were themselves criminals, subject to punishment.

Lily glances at Sadie, splayed out and panting from her efforts. Abolitionists had called it the Bloodhound Law, for the hounds that bounty hunters often used to track escaped slaves. Sadie has a talented nose, and they're using her to noble purpose—but what if you were running for your life and baying hounds came after you?

A shiver makes Lily tremble, but she keeps her voice low and steady as she asks, "Was this house—or someplace near here—a stop once on the Underground Railroad?"

The woman looks down. "We are careful about who we share our history with. There have been rumblings of rising hatred, and those among us who oppose speaking out as we once did—" She stumbles to a stop.

Now this woman's face burns with shame. Lily recollects a recent article about the preachings of Daisy Douglas Barr, a Quaker evangelist—and a WKKK leader—who operated out of Indiana but went on speaking tours. At the time, Lily'd shaken her head at the article, dismissing Barr's incongruous message as nonsense.

But it had taken hold for some, in Lily's county. Here too? Was there a reason the old woman had come here first—a Quaker meeting house—before going to what appears to have been a gathering of the WKKK at the Dyers' old house?

Carefully, Lily wraps the compass in a handkerchief and tucks it in her rucksack. What a collection she has now: bloody gown and foot rags, a WKKK hood, an old compass. "I'll need to keep this for now, as possible evidence, Mrs.—"

The Quaker woman smiles. "My name is Anna Faye."

Lily nods, making a mental note. "A moment ago, Anna Faye, you said it doesn't make sense to leave the compass on your meeting house steps, except that—perhaps—the house, or somewhere near here, was a stop on the Underground Railroad. How are the two connected?"

Anna looks down. "I confess I was taken with the beauty of the piece and I opened it up. The initials inside—*R.E.K.* It could be coincidence, but Rupert Edward Kincaide"—Anna looks up again—"well, he was a member of our meeting house years ago. If it's his, he must have kept the compass as a token from his previous life before joining, then found it useful. Rupert was an operator on the Underground Railroad—until he was found slain. Supposedly, by an escaped slave he was helping to freedom. At least, that was the official ruling."

"Did the escaped slave get away?" Marvena asks.

Anna shakes her head. "No. He was hanged to death as punishment for the crime. In the town square. In Kinship."

This part of the journey should be easy. After all, Sadie's sticking to Stanehart Hollow Road. But Lily's feet have puffed up like overly leavened biscuits, filling her boots.

"God!" Lily exclaims. "How could the woman go on, barefoot?" It's unfathomable. What could have driven her so?

Marvena gives Lily a hard look. Then her expression breaks. And Lily knows she's been forgiven for her harsh question earlier—*What do you know of how hard it's been?* "One step at a time, Lily."

After another quarter mile or so, the road turns south, but Sadie insists that they plunge on back into the woods. A few hundred yards later, the intermittent hums of the woods and its creatures are interrupted by a steady rushing sound.

Sadie strains forward and whines, suddenly eager, and breaks into a fast trot. Lily forgets about her aching feet and runs after Marvena and the hound.

Abruptly, all three come to a stop at the edge of a steep gorge, and an old swinging bridge—a shortcut across the Kinship River, to the town of Athens.

Lily looks past the bridge to turrets rising from a grand building, in the holler to the south, on the other side.

The Hollows Asylum for the Insane.

Lily returns her gaze to the bridge. Some slats are missing. A brisk wind sways the bridge, but Sadie sniffs at the first step, anxious to follow the scent across.

"So that's where the woman came from," Lily says, the realization making her stomach queasy, her blood cold. "Give me the lead line."

Marvena shakes her head. "Let's go back to the main road. There must be a proper bridge farther along."

"I only *think* that's where she came from. I have to follow the trail to the end."

"No, you don't."

Lily gives her friend a long look. Sees the fear pooling in Marvena's eyes—fear for Lily.

Marvena's right—Lily could say that the trail ran cold. No one would care. No one would blame her—not even Marvena, at least not at first. This would become another secret decision they made that they could not share with others.

Lily stares across the bridge. Calculates. It's perhaps twenty yards across. Then she looks down to the rocky river. Another twenty feet down. Looks back up. The old woman had made it across, seventeen hours before or thereabouts. It had held for her. Had held for decades. Surely it would hold for one more crossing.

Why?

The question—this time not about the old woman's motives but about her own—ricochets in Lily's mind as surely as if it echoed from someone on the other side of the river.

Because if she doesn't cross this bridge, it will ever rankle her own heart. If she can't do this, for the least of her community, she has no business running for sheriff.

Lily looks back at Marvena, holds out her hand for the lead line. "Get Guibo. Tell your cousin I'll bring back Sadie and payment of fifty dollars for his trouble. Then come to the front of the asylum. I'll meet you there, whether that's where the rest of this trail leads or not."

Lily takes the lead line from Marvena before either of them can change her mind. She pulls the line tight, so Sadie is right by her.

Then Lily smiles at her friend. "One step at a time, Marvena."

She turns, faces the swinging bridge. Puts her foot on the first slat.

CHAPTER 12

HILDY

Back at the jailhouse, the stench is overwhelming—one of the prisoners not only had had diarrhea but also had vomited into his chamber pot. Mama had looked so frazzled that Hildy—who only intended to leave a note for Lily that they needed to talk—had sent her back to her house and insisted on taking over.

Now tears sting her eyes and her throat constricts. Not just from the stench. Somewhere in the brief walk to the pump, the truth has come over her like its own sickness: she's avoiding going back to see Tom.

Seth's comment had boomeranged in her mind. Seth was right—she'd been meant to be with Roger. She'd been happy then, and not just because of loving Roger, but because she did want a conventional life, a pragmatic life, with him.

Now she feels torn. She wants love like she had with Roger—that's Tom. And a conventional, pragmatic life—that's Merle.

And if she feels torn after less than twenty-four hours after leaving Tom's side, maybe he's right. Maybe she's not strong enough for what a life with him would entail, beyond lovemaking and a fluttery heart.

Now, finally, the water runs clear, and there is no mess left to clean.

She's wasting water. She gives the handle another pump, though, and another.

"He-hello? Miss Cooper?"

Hildy jumps, nearly drops the ceramic pot. When she turns, she sees at the gate Missy Ranklin and her boy, Junior. Missy and her boy hang back, as if at any moment they might turn tail and run back through the open gate and up the road. The boy stares down at the ground, so Hildy can only see the top of his cap, as he stubs his toe into the ground, as if trying to dig a hole. His hands are shoved into his overall pockets, and one strap hangs loose over his shoulder, revealing a grubby white shirt. All of his clothes are too big—hand-me-downs, Hildy reckons, from his father or his older half brother. And the boy needs a good washing up. Even from here, having just washed out a foul chamber pot, Hildy catches a whiff on the fall breeze of his sour odor. The boy shivers. Where is his coat?

Missy isn't wearing one, either, nor a hat, and Hildy notes the dark half-moon under her left eye and a red mark along her neck, running down under the collar of her high-neck blouse.

Hildy's heart goes out to them, as relief rushes over her. At last, Missy will press charges against her husband, Ralf.

"Oh, Mrs. Ranklin. I can help you; please come on through the gate; we'll go to the parlor—" Hildy's tone betrays her pity, for Missy stiffens, tilts her chin up defiantly.

"We are here to see Sheriff Ross."

Hildy clears her throat, tries to compose her voice to be as poised as Lily's. "She is not here. I am one of her deputies, so—"

"We need to see the real sheriff!" Missy's voice rises to a near shriek.

"She's away on a—on a case," Hildy says. Seth had accepted her assertion of being deputy sheriff because she is his friend. How many times had Missy come, wanted to complain without making it official, and Hildy had shown pity—a shaming reaction compared to true empathy? No one wishes to be pitied. "As I was saying, I can help—"

Junior peers up at Hildy from under his cap brim. No bruises or marks. Yet his eyes are hollow. The sight freezes Hildy, as the boy keeps stumping his boot toe into the ground.

Without even looking at him, Missy snaps, "You're gonna wear a hole in your boot, and your toes'll freeze off this winter!" She thumps his back, so hard he stumbles forward. Hildy instinctively reaches for him, and the chamber pot she's just cleaned slips from her hand and shatters against the top of the iron water pump. He falls to his knees.

She reaches down for his elbow to help him up, but he shakes her off, angrily. When he looks at her, though, his eyes brim with tears.

"Yoo-hoo!" another voice trills into the backyard. "Oh, there you are, Missy! I wondered where you'd gotten off to!"

Margaret Dyer stands by the gate. For a moment, the old-fashioned lady Hildy had thought she'd seen in the middle of the street the night before flashes before her eyes. Had that been Margaret? No— Margaret is wearing the latest fashion, a drop-waist dress and cloche hat, items Hildy had recently seen and coveted for herself in Kinship's dress shop. She must have imagined the lady last night, in her tired state.

It hits Hildy—other than scattered catnaps, she's been up for more than twenty-four hours. Exhaustion grips her bones, and it's all she can do to stand. Though Margaret is panting, as if she's run a long stretch, Margaret's lips curl, as if she is pleased to catch Hildy so.

"Please, the sheriff! I need to see Sheriff Ross, right away—" Missy clutches her boy. Whatever frustrations she'd taken out on him have dissipated, and now she's protective, a mama bear with arms encircling her cub.

A faint shadow of something—the old-fashioned lady—hovers out of the corner of Hildy's vision. She's not really there, and Hildy knows if she turns to look, the lady will disappear. And yet there's a whisper, too—*Stiffen your spine, Hildy!*

Hildy focuses on Missy. "Sheriff Ross is away on a case, but I can help you—"

She halts as a wail comes from the jailhouse. As stricken looks come over Missy's and Junior's faces, Hildy wishes she'd not left the front door open so the building could air out, but she'd felt sorry for the other prisoners, gagging at the sick man's odors.

"One of the men is having stomach troubles, is all; he'll be fine—" Hildy starts, but fades to a stop as a strangely satisfied smile curls Margaret's mouth.

"Oh my," Margaret says. "Troubling. Say—do you ever have women in the jailhouse?"

"Rarely." Hildy frowns. What an oddly timed question. "They get their own cell—"

"And what of their poor children—"

"They stay with their fathers or family or—"

"And if there is no one for them?"

Hildy glances over at Missy, clutching Junior so tightly that the boy is squirming. What is Margaret getting at? If Missy's here to file a complaint against Ralf, then Ralf would be in the jail, at least for a while, and Missy would need to tend to Junior as well as her stepchildren. Hildy's temples throb from a headache born of exhaustion.

The answer to Margaret's question is *the orphanage in Columbus,* but Hildy refocuses on Missy. "You won't get into any trouble for filing a complaint against your husband—"

"Oh, I doubt that's why she's here," Margaret interjects. "Missy is staying with us for a while. I need a housekeeper while we get settled in as I'm so busy helping dear Mr. Dyer with his campaign."

Hildy gives Margaret a long look—both for the formality of how she refers to her husband, Perry, and at the notion of hiring another man's wife as a live-in housekeeper.

Margaret smiles at Hildy as if she's dim. "The campaign, dear? For sheriff?"

"I'm well aware!" Hildy snaps. Another moan drifts from the jailhouse.

Margaret laughs. "Oh, that's right. You work for the current sheriff. Who is away. Leaving you with all the glamorous tasks." She gives Missy a little poke, and she stumbles. Junior frowns, glares at Margaret, and instead of squirming hugs his mother tighter, as if to hold her stable. "Well, go ahead. I know you were eager to make your report, though I told you there isn't enough evidence."

Missy blanches, turns her wide-eyed gaze to Hildy. "I-I-I . . ."

Another moan rises from the jailhouse. Margaret purses her lips so hard that her chin sinks back into her neck.

"No, no," Missy says. "Never mind. I—I've changed my mind."

Because of Margaret's presence? Or because Lily isn't here—and Missy doesn't trust Hildy to help?

Hildy tries to find the right words to shoo away Margaret, to get a few minutes alone with Missy. Maybe then—

Margaret speaks quickly. "Come along, Missy. I've told you—I can take care of you and your boy."

What an odd statement. Does she really think that Missy leaving her husband to temporarily work for Margaret is a real solution?

Missy finally releases her boy, to follow Margaret. Junior's hand goes slowly, ever so gently, to his mother's back. A light touch, yet a deep plea.

"I could clean up your boy's knee!" Hildy calls. "Since he stumbled at the pump—"

Margaret looks over her shoulder at Hildy. "He'll be fine. I'm taking good care of them."

Moments after Margaret, Missy, and Junior have exited through the gate, Hildy stares after them. Then the shadow of the old-fashioned lady passes by again, in her peripheral vision.

She shakes her head to clear it, tells herself she's weary, shaken by the odd conversation, and as another wail calls her back to her jailhouse duties she turns from the gate.

CHAPTER 13

LILY

Wednesday, September 22—Noon

The scent trail stops. Sadie plops onto the dirt road alongside the asylum cemetery, summoning a last dollop of energy to scratch behind an ear, making it flop so ridiculously that Lily almost laughs. A gnat buzzes by her ear and lands on her sweaty neck. She slaps the pest away and is tempted to plop down next to Sadie, for her legs still tremble, both from exhaustion and from the lingering terror of crossing the shimmying swing bridge. If she gives into temptation, she might not get back up.

So she gives Sadie a moment and gazes across the field of identical headstones laid out in the precise style of a military cemetery, each marker and row an equidistance apart, the design offering illusory comfort of death as tidy and orderly. The stones have only numbers—patient numbers, Lily thinks with a jolt.

Two hawks, circling above, break the brazen blue perfection of the sky. Lily gazes up, then realizes from their wing shape that the birds are actually turkey vultures.

Lily gives Sadie's lead line a gentle tug and, as the hound staggers up, an apologetic scratch between the ears. "Sorry, girl," Lily says. "I can't leave you here."

They continue down the steep, curved road. Past a field with a dairy barn and cows, an orchard, an expansive garden. Men and women work quietly—some dressed in their own clothes, others in pants and shirts or dresses the same shade of blue as the old woman's gown.

If one didn't know they were in a state-run asylum, the scenes would be idyllic.

On a few Sundays in Lily's childhood, Mama and Daddy had packed up a picnic and made the long drive over from Kinship, bringing Lily and Roger to the grounds to enjoy the fountains and formal gardens. Other families, other children, had been there.

Curious, young Lily had asked about the place, and eventually learned that the Hollows had been constructed in 1868, with towns such as Pomeroy and Athens and Kinship all competing to get the asylum, because that meant jobs—nursing, carpentry, groundskeeping— and a beautiful estate with expansive grounds for the community to enjoy. The institution—and others like it dotted throughout the country—took in men traumatized from the Civil War and others deemed insane for various reasons: schizophrenia, dementia, and, particularly for women, hysteria.

Had residents and workers roamed the grounds, mingling with the families? Probably. Lily doesn't recollect anyone scary or odd. Her memories center on the beautiful rose garden and its crowning feature: a tiered fountain, out of the center of which arose a beautiful enrobed woman, water cascading from the pitcher she held.

Asylum, after all, means a refuge. Haven. Sanctuary. Of late, the *Kinship Daily Courier* and other regional newspapers carried reports of overcrowding and understaffing. Would such conditions make it easier for someone like the old woman to slip away, unnoticed?

Lily limps past the entrance to a new hospital wing on the west side of the main building.

From the bowers of remembrance Daniel arises: there he is, coming in their back door from a trip to the Hollows. As sheriff, by court order, he'd been required to deliver a fifty-seven-year-old Bronwyn County woman to the asylum, purported to have hysteria brought on by the change of life. Daniel's normally affable face pinched with sorrow, and he'd pulled Lily to him in a tender hug that lasted longer than usual.

Lily stops mid-stride, a side cramp. She closes her eyes, willing away the pain.

A gentle touch on her arm makes her jump, open her eyes. A man—a resident—stares at her. His eyes are wild, and yet sympathetic. He opens his mouth to speak but gapes, mute. Then he turns and rejoins a group doing calisthenics under the guidance of an orderly. The man goes back to his own movement: swirling around and around, as if in his own perpetual game of "ashes to ashes," never falling down.

Finally, Lily and Sadie continue around the corner of the hospital building and stand before the only entrance to the main redbrick three-story building.

Stone steps rise to the grand porch; towers arise on either side—the turrets she'd seen rising above the tree line on the other side of the Kinship River. Receding back from the central building are two wings, three sections per wing, each farther back than the other—the batwing design championed by Dr. Thomas Kirkbride, the physician who was the father of the asylum movement in the United States. Lily recollects that higher-functioning residents were housed closest to the center section, the more troubled and dangerous in sections farther back, with men in the west wing and women in the east. Numerous windows, as evenly placed as the cemetery headstones, are trimmed with ornate wrought-iron designs—and covered with iron bars. Cottages, like the ones she sees on the east lawn of the campus, had been added twenty or so years before for the higher-functioning residents—and to ease crowded conditions.

Where, Lily wonders as she and Sadie ascend the steps, had the old woman lodged? And why had her scent abruptly stopped—or started—alongside the cemetery?

Lily pushes open the double door to the asylum. Sadie's nails click against the black-and-white tile floor, the sound drawing the alarmed attention of a nurse stepping out of a side office. Lily is distracted for a moment—her mouth waters at the unexpected smell of freshly brewed coffee, strong and rich and savory. She forces a reassuring smile, but exhaustion clings to her as if she's walked through a spiderweb.

The nurse hurries toward them, so urgently that her crisp nurse's cap wobbles on top of her head. She comes to an abrupt stop, out of reach of Lily, and crosses her arms over her thin waist. One hand fidgets toward a pocket on the front of her starched white bibbed apron.

"Miss, where is your escort?" The nurse's voice is sugarcoated with patience, but too thinly to mask a strain of nervousness.

Amused, Lily smiles. She must surely be a sight—haggard and filthy. She pulls off her hat, runs a hand over her hair to try to smooth it, discovers that a few twigs have lodged in her braid, as if something had been trying to build a nest. Her fingers, still sticky from the pawpaw, gum on to a leaf—and too late, she realizes that the nurse is gaping at the holster on Lily's waist.

Lily hastily taps her shield—leaf and all. "I'm here on official business. I'm the Sheriff of Bronwyn—"

The nurse already has her whistle out of her pocket and is blowing it repeatedly, setting poor Sadie to howling. Lily kneels to comfort the hound, and by the time she looks up, two male orderlies have already come from somewhere—for *her.* She staggers to her feet, crying out, "I am here on official business!"—but they're already upon her.

In the small, windowless holding cell, Lily sits on the only furnishing, a bench built into the white plaster wall. She clutches her skirt in her fists, keeping the hem hoisted off the brick floor.

New paint hasn't filled in all of the scratches on the walls, and etched in the plaster across from her is the message: *I never was crazy.*

How long had the man—or woman—been in here, to carve those letters so deeply, and what had they used? Lily forces her fingers between her boot shaft and swollen ankle, to pull up a little higher the leather-sheathed knife she always carries.

At least they hadn't found that, though they had her gun, her rucksack, and Sadie. Poor hound, howling like a crazy creature. Anger rises, and she draws a deep breath. Bad idea. The cell smells of urine. Lily exhales slowly. They'd better not hurt that hound.

As the orderlies had grabbed her, Lily had started to put up a fight, but she heard the nurse, already back in the office, saying into the telephone, "Get me Chief Warren!"

And so Lily had gone quietly with the two burly, brusque men, so that they would not search her and find the knife, figuring that sooner or later Chief Warren—who she knew briefly from a case earlier this past year—would show up to sign paperwork saying that she needed to be "held" and then, upon seeing her, vouch that she really is sheriff of Bronwyn County.

Lily sighs ruefully. If they go through her rucksack—see the bloody rags, the hooded cape, the compass—they'll truly think she is insane. It's a crazy collection, after all. And what do all these pieces mean? If they are connected—how so?

Now Lily closes her eyes, tries to think of something pleasant. Hildy's sorghum cookies. The goldenrods by the corner of the Stanehart Hollow Friends Meeting House.

Instead, images rush in from the asylum corridors, where she'd been hurried along by the orderlies, stumbling on her swollen, protesting feet. Through the main corridor, on either side, were dining halls—one for the male residents and another for the female. They turned down another corridor, to the right, into the women's wing. Here, the doors opened to residents' rooms, many with two twin beds. In some rooms, residents sat quietly, either reading or gazing out the window. In the hall, a few of the women sat on hard wooden benches or curled up on the floor. One sat with her hands bound with twine behind her back; maybe the scratches on her face and arms had been self-inflicted and the staff was trying to help her. Some of the women were dressed in regular clothes; others wore the thin nightgown and robe that the old woman had worn. Lily noted that all had on slippers or shoes.

Lily wonders: Where had the woman's shoes gone? Had she kicked them off, for some reason, on the road beside the cemetery? Is that why her scent trail had started there?

Lily is too weary to consider possible answers, and another image arises from her walk down that corridor: a naked woman, skinny arms wrapped around too-thin legs pulled up to her body, a blanket wrapped around her shoulders. A young, harried nurse, trying to get the woman to put on a robe, gently telling her she should eat something, that she could bring her some applesauce at least.

One of the orderlies pulling Lily along had chuckled at the sight. The resident looked up, her hair a greasy rat's nest, her face gaunt and skeletal, her eyes hollow and lost. *Anorexia nervosa,* Lily'd thought. Their eyes met, but Lily knew that the woman didn't really see her. Lily might as well have been a ghost.

Now Lily feels her heart lurch—she's jealous, she realizes with a jolt, of that woman. What would it be to forget all pain? All loss?

Her eyes prickle as she recollects how harsh she'd been earlier with Hildy, then with Marvena. *What do you know of how hard it's been?* She'd even been unnecessarily brusque with the Quaker woman. This morning, she realizes, isn't the exception. Despair had gripped her heart since Daniel's death, never letting go, at times speaking for her, infusing every moment.

An image of her children comes to her. She does not want to lose them to amnesia—or to despair. She shudders at the very notion of doing so—

Lily startles awake, finds herself curled up on the bench. How long has she been in here? It feels like five minutes. It feels like an hour. It feels like days.

The door squeaks as it opens. The turning of the door key must have stirred her. Lily sits up quickly, stiffens her spine. In the doorway stand Chief Warren and another man in a well-appointed suit.

With an amused grin, the chief says, "Yes, sir, this woman is indeed the sheriff of Bronwyn County. Lily Ross."

"Sheriff Ross, I must apologize. My nurse assumed—"

"I don't require an apology." Lily looks across the wide oak desk at Dr. Harkins—the director of the asylum, who had accompanied Chief Warren to the holding cell.

The wing chair in which she sits is, she admits to herself, a relief after the long day. But she won't let herself entirely relax. She has her revolver back in her holster, her rucksack (and all the contents—she'd checked) in her lap, and Sadie beside her on the floor, napping and snoring, her breath heavy, blubbery sighs. At first, the nurse had looked askance at Lily's insistence that the hound be brought to her in the doctor's well-appointed office—large enough to be a library, with a fireplace, settees, bookcases. But horrified by Lily's rough treatment, Dr. Harkins readily agreed.

Chief Warren, sitting next to Lily, chuckles. She resists giving him a hard look. *Wonder how well he'd be holding up, after a long trek and a stint in a smelly cell?*

The nurse who had earlier whistled for the orderlies at Lily's crazy proclamation of sheriffhood comes in, carrying a tray filled with cups of coffee. The nurse's hands shake so hard that the cups rattle. She is, Lily thinks, probably fearful for her job, knows that if Lily wanted she could get the nurse in trouble.

Lily knows how hard it is to be a working woman, so Lily smiles as she takes a cup. One small sip sets her empty stomach to churning, but she nods in approval.

As the nurse leaves, the chief says, "I'd like to make this meeting brief, if possible, as I have other duties to attend to."

Meeting. As if this were all pre-planned. But the word jolts the realization that she's actually supposed to be meeting at this moment with several shopkeepers in Kinship—all men—who want to give her advice on her campaign and her talking points in the upcoming debate. Lily sighs. She'll have to reschedule. And then she thinks—no. If that elderly, frail woman had trekked all the way from here to Moonvale, surely she can figure out her own talking points without a group of men explaining to her what to say.

Now Lily says, "I am here to inquire about a patient I tracked here."

Chief Warren clears his throat. "This is out of your jurisdiction, Sheriff."

"Not when the patient was *found* in my jurisdiction."

Harkins frowns. "What are you talking about? There must be a mistake."

"The woman was found, barefoot, other than rags around her feet. Wearing a gown like the other patients. My tracking hound traced her scent to the road by the cemetery. Perhaps she was a cottage resident. She is older, in her late seventies. Maybe eighties. Gray-white hair. Thin." The slight weight of the woman, as Lily lifted her from the ground, carried her up the slope, rushes back to her. "Too thin."

The doctor sighs. "That describes too many of our female patients. Unfortunately, they tend toward senile dementia, and when that happens they stop eating enough, and sometimes wander off, trying to get home. Usually someone in town finds them, returns them. Sometimes families take them back in." His voice takes a woeful turn. "We have more than a thousand acres of land, and we serve fifteen counties, and—"

"I'm not here to get an education on your management and facility problems," Lily says.

"Very well," Harkins says. "If you'll bring her back, we'll look at getting her moved from the cottage to a more secure room in the main building."

"I'll send someone to collect her from your little jailhouse," Warren says.

Lily puts her cup down on the desk, too hard, letting coffee slosh. Looks from one arrogant man to the other. "The woman was found dead in my county. Her remains are currently in the funeral home in Kinship. She apparently fell from the Moonvale Hollow Tunnel onto an oncoming freight train. There is cause to think she may have been pushed. Murdered."

The doctor goes pale. "There must be some mistake. You say she's an old woman . . . your hound must be wrong, or if she's from here, how did she get that far—"

"One step at a time." Lily allows herself a small smile at using Marvena's phrase. "She wasn't wearing shoes, it hasn't rained for a few days along the path we traced, and I've been assured that Sadie here"—Lily gives the hound a gentle scratch between the ears—"is one of the best tracking hounds in my county. The woman was wearing one of the same blue gowns I saw on your female residents as I was *walked*"— she hopes the pointed emphasis makes clear that she really means "dragged"—"to your holding cell. So either my hound's nose tracked the path that your resident took from here, or the hound is wrong— which would mean that she got to where she died by another means."

Lily lets the silence carry the implication—that a staff member might have helped the old woman escape for some reason.

The doctor shakes his head. "No, no, this can't be right; we are very secure here—"

"You were saying occasionally residents do wander away, and how overworked you are. How many patients are here?" Lily asks.

"About thirteen hundred."

"About? You don't know, exactly?"

"Now, now, Sheriff Ross, no need to get testy," Warren says.

Lily gives him a hard glare. "Testy" is a euphemism for "hysterical."

"If I had a family member or loved one here, I'd want to know that you know exactly how many people there are—after all, you've numbered them."

Dr. Harkins sighs. "If you're referring to the cemetery, yes, the stones are numbered. The asylum bought a slew of headstones years ago, pre-engraved with the numbers, and yes, our residents do each get a number. We've had thousands of patients come through over the years. We track as efficiently as possible. There are only a few residents, dating back to a few years after the Civil War, whose names are lost to memory."

Lily nods. "Fair enough. Do you allow your residents to keep personal items?"

"The higher-functioning ones, yes," the doctor says, "and often they wear their own clothes as well. If they cannot harm themselves or others with their personal possessions, they can keep them." His voice takes on an eager tone. He wants, Lily realizes, to do the best for the patients, but with overcrowding he's up against an impossible task. "We find familiarity—"

"I assume you saw the compass in my rucksack when you looked through it."

Dr. Harkins frowns. "Well, yes."

"I have a few questions about the contents, Sheriff Ross," Warren says.

"I took the rags with which her feet were wrapped and the gown from the woman—used those clothes for tracking her here. The hood was found along the path—and believe me, I have plenty of questions about that, too, which I will pursue in my jurisdiction. The person where we found the compass says the initials might be for 'Rupert Edward Kincaide.' Does that name have any connection to a female patient here?"

"I wish I could remember all the names," the doctor says. "But I must rely on staff and records—"

"Wait," Chief Warren says. "I brought in a Thea Kincaide two, maybe three, weeks ago."

Lily turns to him. "What do you know of her?"

"Just that her landlady filed a complaint that the woman was creating a disturbance in the boardinghouse—crying out, walking the halls at night, scaring other residents, and making threats that she would hurt the landlady. So the landlady—"

"What's her name?"

"I don't remember," Warren says.

"But you remember the older woman's name?"

Warren chuckles. "She was . . . memorable. Kept demanding notebooks and pens so she could keep writing her story, as she put it. Claimed her journals and story had been stolen from her. Rattled off a bunch of other last names on the way over here—over and over. Names she'd had all the times she'd been married. Said Kincaide was her maiden name and she'd reclaimed it. Crazy, right?"

He looks at Dr. Harkins, but the doctor frowns at the use of the term.

"Nothing about being married numerous times makes a person crazy," Lily says.

The chief turns red. "Well, not if—"

"Even if the person getting married numerous times is a female." Lily looks back at the doctor. "I will need to see the records for Thea Kincaide."

"Finding them may take a while."

"How many new residents do you get each month?"

"As I said, we are facing overcrowding issues, as are asylums all across the country—"

"Just on average, Doctor."

"Perhaps ten."

"And your patients are numbered sequentially, yes?"

Dr. Harkins nods. "True. So if Thea Kincaide came in two or three weeks ago, then we should only have to look through the most recent thirty or so records to find her. And we do take a photograph of each resident as they are processed in. Let me ring for the nurse."

"Please do. I'd like to interview as many of your staff as possible about the missing woman—"

"I wouldn't let her do that without a search warrant," Chief Warren says.

Dr. Harkins looks startled. "But if it helps find out what happened to our patient—"

"Without a search warrant limiting her inquiry, she can poke around anywhere."

"We have nothing to hide here, but—very well. I'll see if we can find the patient record, but beyond that—" Dr. Harkins sighs. The man seems so overwhelmed by his position. "That's the best I can do."

Fifteen minutes later, Dr. Harkins returns with a file folder, hands it to Lily. She opens it.

There, in the folder, labeled "5341," is a single sheet.

A photograph, black and white, of the resident is stapled to the intake form.

This is the woman. Petite, striking face. Hair swept up in an elegant twist. Eyes filled with sorrow—and the realization of betrayal. Perhaps that's too fanciful? No, no, Lily's not imagining the expression. It's there.

On the first line of the intake form, the name: Thea Kincaide.

Lily scans down the page.

Comes to the last line: next of kin.

And stares in shock at the name.

Mabel Cooper.

Hildy Cooper's mother.

THE HOLLOWS ASYLUM FOR THE INSANE
OFFICIAL USE ONLY

DATE: August 30, 1926

IDENTIFICATION:

NAME: Thea Kincaide **AGE:** Approx. 75 **SEX:** Female **RACE:** Caucasian

PLACE OF BIRTH: Unknown **HAIR:** Gray-white **EYES:** Blue

HEIGHT: 5′ 2″ **WEIGHT:** 103 lbs. **INMATE NUMBER:** 5341

CONTACT: Mrs. Maryann Pothoulis (boardinghouse)
59 Elmwood Avenue, Athens

NEXT OF KIN: Mrs. Mabel Cooper (cousin)
61 Plum Street, Kinship

CASE INFORMATION:

Mrs. Pothoulis contacted the Athens County Sheriff after repeat-edly asking Miss Kincaide to refrain from entering other boarders' rooms. Miss Kincaide would come down to the common room only partially clothed, muttering to herself, and several times screaming at "a large man" or other times "a scary woman" to "get away" and "leave me alone," but other boarders say these were imagined people, as she was staring into space. On two occasions, once with scissors and another with a paring knife, she tried to stab Mrs. Pothoulis, ap-parently mistaking her for the "scary woman." Mrs. Pothoulis reports that Miss Kincaide came to the boardinghouse with two satchels but could not describe her background, other than mentioning her cousin Mrs. Cooper. Mrs. Pothoulis says that Miss Kincaide paid her room rent of $2 a week in a timely fashion, and at first was quiet and kept her room neat, but then seemed to think she was on a luxury oceangoing liner and complained others were not attending to her needs, and asking about ball dances and such.

Upon admission, Miss Kincaide was generally calm, exhibited a well-educated demeanor and vocabulary, but was disoriented. She is assigned for the time being to Women's Cabin 3.

CHAPTER 14

꙳

HILDY

Wednesday, September 22—6:40 p.m.

Dinner should have been on the table more than a half hour ago.

After Missy, her boy, and Margaret Dyer left, Hildy had taken a spare chamber pot into the jailhouse for the sick prisoner. Then Mama had come back, Micah and Caleb Jr. in tow, to get lunch for the prisoners, but Mama still looked so weary that Hildy didn't have the heart to leave her alone with the task. By the time she'd helped Mama clean up after lunch, it was 2:00. Hildy had returned to her home, planning to clean up herself and drive back over to Rossville.

She'd leaned back against her headboard for a moment, meaning to only close her eyes to the count of ten . . . then she'd startled awake to Mother banging on her bedroom door, to the Big Ben clock on her nightstand ticking away at 5:30. For a moment, Hildy came close to telling her mother about Tom—or to simply leaving after all—but then Mother had one of her coughing fits, looking so pitiful, gasping for air, begging Hildy to fetch some Vogel's Tonic, and reminding her that tonight Merle will be over for dinner.

Now, in the kitchen, Hildy wipes her brow as she scrambles eggs. It is too late to make chicken and dumplings and biscuits, which was supposed to be dinner tonight, to show Merle how well she could cook his favorite dish. A plan concocted by Mother—who must sense that Hildy's interest is wavering, that Merle is getting nervous as well. A plan Hildy had forgotten about, until she'd opened her bedroom door to Mother.

Hildy instead fries green tomatoes and scrambles eggs. The kitchen is warm and suffocating, and she cranks open the kitchen window.

The crickets' long, lonesome chorus sifts in from the dark, stirring an impulse to run out into the yard, even at this late hour. Run to her daddy's old automobile, start it up, drive away from Kinship, to the dark, cool hills and hollers in the eastern part of the county. To Tom.

Is he thinking of her tonight? Wishing he'd come after her as she walked away after his hurtful proclamation?

As the suffocating hot kitchen rebuffs the evening air, Hildy imagines herself making supper instead for Tom, him coming home after a long day in the mine, her greeting him at the door, not caring that he is sweaty and dirty and smells of dank, dark earth, taking his face in her hands, grateful that he is all right, kissing him fully, satisfying another sort of hunger—

A charred scent snatches her attention back to the moment. The eggs are burning in the cast-iron skillet.

Distractedly, Hildy reaches for the skillet handle, scorches her hand, yelps.

She grabs a crocheted potholder, moves the skillet off the heat. As she scrapes burned scrambled eggs into a bowl—her hand already throbbing—she hears Mother's and Merle's voices from the dining room, murmuring and low, sodden with propriety, converse to cricket song. Maybe neither had heard her cry out. Or maybe hearing her hadn't given them pause.

Hildy takes a platter of tomatoes and a bowl of eggs into the dining room. Merle sits at the head of the table in Daddy's old seat, Mother at the other end, her accustomed spot.

Hildy's hands begin to shake, the platter quivering so that the fried green tomatoes jiggle. Two drop to the floor.

"Such a messy girl," Mother says. "I'm sorry, Mr. Douglas, I thought

I had Hildy trained up better than that. I'm sure she'll be daintier by the time of your nuptials—"

Hildy freezes. Merle takes the platter and bowl and puts them on the table. "It is fine, Mrs. Cooper!" Firmness grips Merle's voice, and he gives Mother a harsh look. Hildy knows she should be grateful for Merle coming to her defense, but the hard tone—he'd used it a few times with her at the grocery—sets her skin to prickling.

Hildy drops to her knees before the spilled green tomatoes, as if in supplication, and stares at the blue rose and vine pattern on the red Victorian rug—a point of pride for Mother, who would not want grease spots, even though the rug is thin and worn. She stares at the tomatoes, about to pick them up bare-handed, but then Merle kneels next to her, scoops up the tomatoes with his handkerchief—a kind gesture.

Dammit, how can he go so readily from harsh to kind? It was the kindness, the easiness, that drew her to him a year before, a kindness that reminded her of Roger. But Roger was also spirited and funny and smart. Like Tom.

"Well, don't worry now, Mr. Douglas," Mother is saying. "I'm sure Hildy will wash and press your handkerchief."

Hildy reaches for the handkerchief—relieved at an excuse to go back to the kitchen—but Merle snaps, "It can wait!"

Hildy sighs. That hair-trigger anger—neither Roger nor Tom was like that. As she takes her seat between Merle and Mother, Merle also sits and puts the handkerchief-wrapped green tomatoes on the table.

Hildy clears her throat, starts, "It's a light supper tonight—"

"You wore yourself out at that wretched jailhouse! Where was the sheriff all day?" Mother pokes at the eggs, inspecting them. "I myself will be voting for Perry Dyer for sheriff, such an unsavory job for a woman, and—"

"Shouldn't we have a blessing?" Hildy's voice, shrill and thin, cracks the room. Merle and Mother stare at her, and she looks down at her plate. "Daddy always prayed before meals."

"Course he did." Affront tinges Mother's voice, as if Hildy were suggesting otherwise.

Her father's sweet voice comes back to her, his simple unrehearsed prayers, thanking the Lord for food and work and health and family, going on too long, Mother always said, so the food got cold, but the coldness of the food isn't what's going to ruin this meal. Hildy opens her mouth to pray, hoping something simple but wise like her father's words will issue forth, but then there's Merle's voice, booming in her ear, as if loudness is what draws God's attention.

"Amen," they murmur, and Hildy puts egg, the burned part, on her plate.

For a moment, they eat without conversation, just the sounds of chewing, fork tines on plates, Mother snuffling, the parlor clock ticking. Merle talks of a shipment of Campbell's soup brought in by truck, all the way from Columbus, and Mother comments it's such a shame that modern women—so spoiled!—don't cook from scratch like they did in her day, and Merle says this is a sign of the economy growing, deregulation helping business, and thank God there will never be a recession again like 1893, and Mother says she remembers that, how awful it was.

Merle goes back to his food, shoveling in the fried green tomatoes and eggs, making smacking noises as he eats. Hildy pokes at her eggs. She forces herself to swallow a bite, spears another bit, but the fork feels too burdensome to lift.

"I had to be at the jailhouse today because Lily was called away," Hildy blurts. "She got notice of an elderly woman who had fallen from the tunnel in Moonvale Hollow. There was no identification—"

"This is not appropriate dinnertime conversation!" Mother says.

"She had no identification on her, this woman. Lily had me write up a description of the woman. And draw a sketch." Hildy realizes with a start that she hasn't checked for the newspaper on the porch. "They should both be in the paper tonight, if you want to see."

Mother looks at Merle. "Hildy always was good with drawing and crafts. I'm sure she'll bring a bright spot of decoration to your home. Tatted pillow covers can really—"

"Did you hear what I said?" Hildy drops her fork to her plate, letting it clatter. "The woman fell to her death, onto the train! You wanted to know where Lily was all day so that I had to be at the jailhouse. That's where she was—investigating—"

"The woman should have stayed where people take care of her. Just as I know that I'm going to be taken care of by you." Mother looks at Merle, smiles.

Merle pushes back from the table. His plate is clean, other than some greasy smears from the eggs and fried green tomatoes.

"I'm hopeful there's apple cake. You should know how much I like apple cake, Hildy—"

Hildy ignores Merle, stares at Mother, her thick face wadded into frowning twists and folds, crevices etched out of frustration with Hildy. And yet she cannot resist pressing. "I'd hoped you'd be more sympathetic, Mother—"

"Enough, Hildy!" Merle snaps. "Hildy, you will not be going to work for Lily anymore. Starting immediately."

Hildy stares at him, wide-eyed. He is not her husband. He has no right over her. They have not even set a specific date for the wedding. And yet he is already presuming control. She wishes to argue back, but she is so weary, even after her fitful nap, and there is something fiery in his eyes, and his hands are now clenched on either side of his plate, and she shrinks back. She clenches her hands, too—then releases them. Her burned palm is throbbing.

Oh God. She is just like Missy Ranklin.

Tom's words haunt her. *You want to get what you want, upsetting nobody.*

Merle regards Mother. "If I may say so, Mrs. Cooper"—his tone is more modulated for her—"you might gain more compliance from your willful daughter with a bit of sweetness."

A bubble of hysterical laughter rises, an impulse tickling the back of Hildy's throat. If she laughs, they will think she is crazy. But the idea that she is willful is itself crazy.

"Of course, Mr. Douglas." A gentle smile settles Mother's quivering features, but Hildy knows that the minute Merle leaves, Mother will harangue her for not being sweet and compliant enough, for risking losing Merle—the best prospect Hildy has, since she's dithered away her time after Roger's death and now she's an old maid and who else would have her?

Tom. Would he? If she told Mother and Merle about him and went straight over to Rossville and told him she'd thrown over Merle— would it be enough? Or would he dismiss her, so she would indeed be an old maid, destined to live for the rest of her life with Mother?

Then she sees another face—the elderly woman. Even after the woman's gruesome death, Hildy was able to find in that face more compassion and passion than she ever sees in her mother's face. She looks down at her hands, sees instead the woman's rose-pink nail varnish.

Merle and Mother stare at her.

"I—I burned my hand," Hildy says, by way of explanation for her vacuous expression, her unusual outspokenness.

A sharp rap comes at the front door. Relieved by the distraction, Hildy rises and hurries to answer the knock. There, on the front porch, is Lily.

Hildy leans forward, propelled by a rush of relief at seeing her friend, about to collapse into her in a hug—though Lily isn't much of a hugger—and confess, as she did when they were young, her confused, scared, swirling emotions.

She notes Lily's stiff expression. The dirt on her face. Lily must have just now gotten back from wherever she'd been, wherever she'd traced the woman to. . . .

"I need to talk to your mother," Lily says.

After Lily finishes speaking, silence gathers in the parlor. Holds them all stunned and mute.

Hildy looks first to Mother, but she stares at her hands, neatly folded in her lap. Merle is focused on the clock, as if entranced by each *tick, tick, tick.* Lily gazes at Hildy, and finally Lily's face softens with concern for Hildy.

Hildy covers her burned palm with her other hand. She wishes for a cold compress, to ease the aching throb, but she can't bring herself to move. She's pinned in place by Lily's news.

The dead woman—the woman she'd sketched. Thea Kincaide. The paperwork listing Mabel Kincaide Cooper as the next of kin.

Mother.

Hildy looks at Mother, searching for any resemblance between the two, beyond both being older females. She doesn't see it.

Finally, Mother looks up at Lily with distaste, regarding her smudged face and dirty boots. "Yes. I have a cousin named Thea Kincaide. She was the only child of my father's brother, Rupert Kincaide. We weren't close. We had our differences. I have no idea why she would have listed me as her next of kin."

"She didn't," Lily says. "The landlady where she was staying, a boardinghouse in Athens, did. The landlady's name is Maryann Pothoulis. Did you ever hear anything from her?"

Mother shakes her head. "No. I had no idea Thea was back in the area. I haven't seen her since I was a child."

As Lily makes a note, something about Mother's assertion that she hasn't seen Thea since childhood niggles at Hildy. A shadow . . . a face emerging. Thea Kincaide . . . her first cousin once removed. A younger Thea entering this very room, about twenty years ago . . .

Hildy presses her left thumb into the burn on her right palm, pushing in the pain, as if that will stave off the image, as the conversation swirls around her.

"You visited often?"

Mother laughs, a sharp bark. "Hardly. Our fathers weren't close."

"She told her landlady about you. Surely there's more to your relationship?"

"She wrote now and then."

"From where?"

Mother sighs heavily. "I believe she moved to New York City. Later to Europe."

"Europe is a big continent. Do you recollect any specific postmarks?"

"Paris. Rome. Maybe London."

Paris. Rome. London. New York. These sound like dream cities, floating high above in gilded clouds.

"Would you happen to have those letters?" Lily is asking Mother.

"Of course not. I threw them away." Mother says this as if it is a point of pride.

Oh. Hildy's heart pangs—a bit of life, captured, tossed away. Dismay flickers across Lily's placid features. Mother's cavalier comment tickles a memory. Something about postcards. Lily's father giving them to her quietly. Telling her to enjoy them—hide them away—and not let Mother know.

Lily lifts an eyebrow. "Do you remember anything she wrote?"

"Certainly not. Probably bragging about her exploits—unfitting for a lady." She looks at Merle. "And certainly not a predilection that's reached our branch of the family."

Hasn't it? Hildy feels heat rising in her face. She'd had exploits. Just to Rossville. Unfitting for a lady, certainly for a betrothed lady, a lady of her status in Kinship . . . A different heat rises in her as she recollects Tom's hands running over her.

"Why does any of this possibly matter?" Mother asks.

"Thea Kincaide is dead. And possibly not by accident," Lily says. "Everything matters at this point. So I must ask again—do you remember anything she wrote?"

Mother shakes her head. But Hildy remembers now.

Merle bounds to his feet. "Mrs. Ross, you are upsetting Mrs. Cooper—"

Lily squares her shoulders, stiffens her spine. "Mr. Douglas, I am here in an official capacity. You can sit quietly, if you insist on bearing witness, or you may leave. If you disrupt again, I'll bring you in for interfering in an investigation."

Merle sinks back down in the chair. He glances at Hildy, as if she might—given her position with Lily—speak up on his behalf, but she is gazing at Lily with admiration. Her coolness has hurt Hildy over the past months, and yet she wishes for some of that demeanor for herself.

Lily looks back at Mother. "The landlady of the boardinghouse where Thea Kincaide had lived said a man, about forty, claiming to be her son, brought Miss Kincaide there four months ago. Prepaid three months of Thea's rent. The landlady didn't take down his name. My guess is, he didn't want to give it and she wanted the money. A month ago, Mrs. Pothoulis—the landlady—complained to the Athens police that Miss Kincaide was behaving crazily, and soon after a judge signed paperwork committing her to the Hollows Asylum."

What a horrifying fate! Hildy puts her hands to her mouth, holding back a cry of sorrow.

But Mother laughs sharply. Lily's carefully neutral face contorts with anger. Even Merle looks aghast. Hildy feels some part of herself disembodying, as if untethering at last. Everyone in the room looks and sounds so distant.

"Finally!" Mother says. "She was crazy, delusions of being a dancer in New York—of all things! An actress! And her claim that she was going to go to Europe!"

Lily's voice is tight and hard. "I thought you barely remember her, Mrs. Cooper? And she was not committed for delusions of grandeur. Apparently, she sometimes thought she saw people who weren't there, but in the main, confusion and memory loss were the sins that, officially, consigned her to the asylum."

Lily's unspoken point—Mother had claimed to be confused and forgetful of Thea—echoes in the parlor. Mother presses her lips together so tightly that her mouth seems sewn shut. She cracks it enough to speak, finally. "Well. She was quite a bit older than me. Fifteen years. She came to visit when I was five. I only have a vague recollection. That was when she said she was going to New York to be a dancer and maybe an actress."

"A surprising thing for a five-year-old to understand."

"I didn't. My father"—at this, Mother looks down at her hands and, to Hildy's surprise, a vulnerable look flashes over her face—"my father always brought her up as an example of what not to be. Referred to her as . . . well. As a vulgar woman."

Hildy shudders, recalling her grandfather. He'd been a hard man, prone to outbursts and preachy rages. Once, upon visiting him, after Grandmother died, Hildy had, without asking, taken a piece of the cake that Mother had brought him. Grandfather had yelled at her, mocked her for crying, and Mother hadn't stopped him, though she had looked horrified, even comforted her daughter later. Daddy hadn't been along on that trip. Hildy was five.

A shadow moves in the corner of the room—the elegant lady. Hildy stares. It's not a shadow she's glimpsed—instead, a memory. A woman, entering the room, sifting back up to life from the dust motes. Gliding, graceful, like a dancer. In her long dress, with the cinched waist, and a wide-brimmed fancy hat. Doing a twirl. Here. After Grandfather's funeral.

"She came here." Hildy's voice sounds so distant, as if coming from behind her, rather than from within her. "After Grandfather's funeral. She was there—" Hildy's hand rises, her finger pointing, but not in the room. To the back of a small gathering at the Kinship Cemetery. "At the back of the crowd. Not with the rest of us. I wondered . . ."

Hildy falters. She'd wondered who the beautiful lady was. Perhaps an angel come to reap Grandfather's soul, but she had thought no—an angel would not have come for such a mean man's soul—and she'd felt immediately guilty at thinking this. The lady had seen her stare, had stared back, smiled warmly, and Hildy had smiled, too. A connection made.

"I was six—maybe seven. Yes. My seventh birthday was a few days before. Same day Grandfather died." Her birthday had been marred for years by her mother's wailing that it was the anniversary of her father's death, until finally Hildy's own father told Mother to stop—the only time Hildy had overheard her father be cross with Mother.

"She was alone." Hildy smiles, as if in a trance, seeing the beautiful lady, floating before her, a vision of the woman she'd sketched, but so much younger, plumper, filled out. Oh—as old as Mother is now, and yet she'd looked so much younger. Vibrant. Happy. An energy peeling off of her, filling the room. "Except for her driver. She had for some reason a driver for her carriage. She came to the funeral, then here, later that evening—"

"Nonsense!" Mother snaps.

Hildy looks at Mother. What an odd, shrunken little woman. So terrified and small. She smiles at Mother, benevolently. At the angry, tense quiver in the corners of the woman's mouth. At the fear in Mother's eyes. Why had she never seen Mother as she really is, before? A peaceful warmth spreads over Hildy. She feels like she is floating, floating.

"It's not nonsense. She was at Grandfather's funeral, then here—"

Mother stands up, fists clenched by her sides. "No, no—"

"Let her speak!" Lily says.

Hildy looks at her friend, sees Lily's gaze, gentle, searching. Lily believes her.

"She came here." Hildy looks past her mother to the chair where Merle is sitting. She sees Thea sitting there, in a blue silk dress, on the edge of the chair, her ankles primly crossed. And Thea smiles again at her, a little girl, snuck down from the upstairs, and Thea beckons her forward, and in spite of her mother's dismayed cries, she crosses to Thea, enchanted.

"She was beautiful," Hildy says. "And kind. And she seemed to like me. It's like remembering . . . a feeling. A feeling of warmth."

Yes, a feeling of warmth and a scent like cinnamon. Warm, spicy, enveloping. A real scent, right here, in her nose, and yet she knows it's a memory. She hadn't seen the much younger Thea in the maimed face of Thea's corpse, yet she'd sensed a connection. The scent she thought she'd detected, lingering below all the sad, awful odors in the mortuary.

"She said she came because she wanted to see her uncle— Grandfather—buried. To be sure he was gone at last. She told me something else, something encouraging—"

"Hildy! Enough!" Mother screams. Her expression is taut with . . . jealousy. *Yes,* Hildy thinks—Mother doesn't like her only child remembering Thea so warmly. And yet her only few warm memories of Mother come from before Thea's visit.

Merle says, "You've upset your mother, dear, and the sheriff doesn't need to hear—"

Cousin Thea fades, and whatever she was going to hear Thea again whisper to her withers to silence. The smell of burned eggs obliterates the warm, cinnamon scent. Hildy wilts back into her chair, the confidence she'd found remembering Cousin Thea hollowed out of her.

All she can feel is her hand throbbing.

Mother glares at her, and not only out of annoyance. Fear has turned Mother's pupils to pinpoints. "I remember now," Mother says. "She came to gloat over my dear father's death!"

"Why would she do that?" Lily asks.

"Our fathers—though they were brothers—disliked one another greatly."

"Mrs. Cooper, why did your father and uncle dislike each other?"

"I can't imagine why it matters!"

"As I said, at this point everything matters."

"They had different points of view on abolition. My father was against getting involved. He supported states' rights. My uncle—Thea's father—was adamantly supportive of abolition." Red rises in Mother's face, and she adds in a half whisper, "To the point that he was involved in . . . illegal activities."

Hildy stares in shock at Mother. She means the Underground Railroad. Hildy'd heard mutterings about it, here and there, that some folks in the area worked to sneak runaway slaves, who made it across the Ohio River at Portsmouth, northward. But this is the first that she'd heard any inkling she had kin who was involved.

Mother goes on. "Well, it was an embarrassment to my father that his own brother defied the law of the day. It split them—and the family."

"And yet Thea Kincaide came here when your father died."

"To gloat!"

"That seems odd—holding on to such bitterness when the last time you'd have seen her she would have been much younger."

Mother tilts her chin defiantly. "Clearly, my cousin was given to odd behavior."

"Would she have tried to come see you last night?"

Hildy's mind returns to last night, the old-fashioned woman she thought she'd seen in the street, when she'd come awake on Lily's porch.

"Of course not," Mother says.

Lily makes a note. Then she looks up at Mother. "I have to ask—to be thorough, mind you—where you might have been last night?"

Lily's question siphons the air from the room. For a moment, Hildy can't breathe, recollecting how last night, after she got home late from her heartbreaking visit with Tom in Rossville, the house had felt empty—but she'd dismissed it as Mother not waiting up to harangue her, for once. But what if that—like the notion of being satisfied with Merle, or having the courage to be wooed by Tom—was another delusion? Like the phantom old-fashioned lady?

"Well, of course I was here. As usual." There's not even a hint of nervousness in Mother's voice.

Hildy starts to question that assertion. Mother gives her a hard, warning look.

"Hildy?" Lily's voice is a soft nudge as pity flashes across her expression.

Earlier, when Hildy'd made herself sound insane, going on about remembering Thea, and she'd seen belief on Lily's face—what if she'd imagined that, too? Maybe it was just pity.

Hildy's courage slips away. She stares down. A blister is rising on her burned palm.

"Very well," Lily says. "I will no doubt need to ask more questions— but I'll leave you in peace for tonight."

An hour later, Hildy finally heads upstairs.

Soon after Lily left, Merle had stiffly thanked them for dinner. Under Mother's watchful glare, Hildy had hastily, wearily promised to go to his grocery the next morning. It seemed the easiest way to put an end to the dreadful evening—and surely, after a night's rest, she'd find the courage to break off their engagement and go at last back to Rossville.

As Hildy cleaned up from dinner, Mother scolded her for not being a better hostess to Merle, for her "display of nonsense" during Lily's visit—but Hildy only half-listened, berating herself for not stopping Lily as she left, to tell her about spotting Fiona leaving the Kinship Inn with George. About the odd visit from Missy—and Margaret chasing down the poor woman and her boy. About the editorial from an anonymous WKKK member. She hadn't even reported on submitting the sketch and sheriff's notice—but that wouldn't matter, now that they knew the dead woman's identity.

When Hildy started the dishes, she promised herself she'd leave after Mother went to bed, go down to Lily's house, and explain all. By the time Mother had finally gone up to bed, and Hildy finished the dishes, exhaustion overwhelmed her. She finally applied a cold compress to her hand and headed upstairs.

Now, as she enters her bedroom, all she wants is sleep. To not feel the pain in her hand. Or in her heart. *Dreamless sleep,* she prays.

There on the desk, flickering in the light of the coal-oil lamp she carries in her good hand, she sees the mess of sketching pencils she'd pulled out earlier from under her bed.

Hildy puts the lamp on the bureau and starts putting the pencils back in the old cigar box that had once been her father's. She notes the thin rectangle of wood, once used to divide a bottom layer of cigars from the top layer. And it is wobbly.

Hildy pries up the rectangle and stares at the contents at the bottom of the cigar box.

Postcards.

She picks one up, reads quickly.

Postcards to her, from Thea Kincaide.

> *Carte Postale*
> *April 12, 1906*
> *Bonjour, Mademoiselle Hildy, from Paris! Oh, the fashions, the cafes, the pastries, and the sights. How I trembled on the lift ride to the top of the Eiffel Tower—not fear, but joy at such a monument! At night, the city has a pulse of its own. I hope when you are older you can come visit me! You'll be brave enough, I know.*
>
> > *Love,*
> > *Your cousin Thea*

CHAPTER 15

LILY

Wednesday, September 22—10:00 p.m.

As Lily lets herself in through the mudroom at the back of her house, the parlor's mantel clock chimes a faint 10:00 p.m. Twenty-four hours since the telegraph boy came to the house with the news of a dead woman near Moonvale Hollow Village.

Dear Lord. More than twenty-four hours since she last slept.

Lily rubs the heels of her hands into her eyes. So hard that she sees speckles. She longs to peel off her now smelly, filthy clothes, to release her feet from her boots, to soak in a hot bath upstairs with a heaping dose of Epsom salts. She tears up at the tasks such luxury will require: heating water on the stove, toting it upstairs to the washroom—created last year from the nursery, now outfitted with a cold-water sink and a clawfoot bathtub.

She can't bring herself to go to bed so filthy, either.

She will settle for a cold-water sponge bath at the sink.

Lily carefully locks the door behind her. The house is quiet. A coal-oil lamp flickers on the small kitchen worktable, its flickering light illuminating a plate with a sandwich and one of Hildy's sorghum cookies.

Mama's handiwork. A guilty pang contracts Lily's heart. She'd given little thought to Mama or any of the children on this long, wretched day.

A day that had led, at long last, to the identity of the dead woman: Thea Kincaide.

Hildy's mother's cousin. Hildy's cousin, for that matter—first cousin once removed.

Lily shakes her head, recollecting the haunting, awful scene she'd left at Hildy's house, the shock that the news had brought to both Hildy and her mother. And the sense Mabel Cooper is holding something back.

If it has to do with Thea Kincaide, eventually she will share it. Lily will find a way to pry it from her.

Now, though, she slowly extracts her swollen feet from her boots. *Ah.* A brief rush of relief. Then throbbing pain. Lily limps to the mudroom, leaves her boots to air out, locks the door again. Back inside, she washes her hands and face under the cold-water pump. Next she eats the bologna sandwich and the cookie, taking comfort as well as sustenance in each bite. She's home too late to see her children or tuck them into bed, but at least she's sufficiently revived for the nighttime rituals at hand: Unholster and unload her revolver. Put the bullets, and her sheriff's star, in the red dish on top of her pie safe.

The red dish that had once held her blue ribbons for prizewinning pies—*oh Lord.* The dish reminds Lily, as Mama had twenty-four hours before, that she needs to enter *something* in the county fair baking contest. A quick mental inventory of what she has on hand and how pressed she is for time. She'll have to settle for making vinegar pie. It won't be a blue-ribbon winner, but the tangy-sweet pie will do.

Lily sighs as she picks up the coal-oil lamp and heads to the parlor, where she puts her notebook on the rolltop desk next to the typewriter, and her unloaded revolver on the mantel.

She crosses to the front of the parlor, about to go upstairs, but then sees mail on the desk. Lily quickly sifts through: a Sears Roebuck catalog and—*Oh.* A letter from Benjamin Russo. Daniel's old friend.

The Cincinnati postmark is from more than a week ago. Lily swallows hard, recollecting that in the wee hours of this morning Hildy had mentioned doing chores—including bringing in the mail. She must have seen the letter. Heat rises in Lily's face. Had Mama seen, too?

Lily picks up the envelope. Now, after everything the past twenty-four hours had brought, her hand trembles. *Cincinnati* . . . Suddenly the far-off city seems too close. Had Benjamin moved there, from the Bureau of Mines in Washington, D.C.? Or been on a visit?

She tries to remember—had Benjamin ever written to Daniel? If he had, it doesn't stand out in her memory. She should throw the letter away . . . but she finds the letter opener in her hand, and seconds later she's quickly scanning the letter:

> Dear Mrs. Ross,
>
> I write to let you know that I have been moved to the Cincinnati location of the Bureau of Mines, and will, along with three other engineers, be setting up a field post in southeastern Ohio. I might take up lodging in Athens with my colleagues, though Kinship offers more economical options and better access to many mining communities, as well as other charms. We have yet to work out the details.
>
> I trust that Marvena, your mother, and the children are doing well? Below please find my Cincinnati address in case I can ever be of help in any way.
>
> Respectfully yours,
>
> Benjamin

Lily's face flushes. *Charms?* What is charming about Kinship— unless he means the rare moving picture show at the opera house, or the hotel basement's liquor-fueled poker games she opts to ignore. *Yours?* She's reading too much into that. After all, he'd referred to her as Mrs. Ross, as was proper, and asked after the children. The letter falls from her still-shaking hands. Lily chuckles at herself. *Silly. Becoming undone over a perfectly courteous letter—*

"Mama?"

Lily startles and turns in the chair. There's Jolene, sleepy eyed and dark curls askew, emerging from under the dining table, a teddy bear in hand.

Oh. Lily's heart softens and tumbles, downy feathers shaken from a pillowcase.

Lily scoops up her daughter. She means to quickly embrace her, gently admonish her for being down here rather than in bed, then send her back upstairs. But Jolene's arms and legs latch around Lily in an embrace of deep relief, the sort that can only follow fear. As Lily breathes in the sweet scent of her daughter's hair, her resolve to quickly put the child to bed unravels. Lily's reciprocal embrace tightens at an image flashing of the silvery, shimmering boy.

"Mama." Jolene pulls back a little, and Lily lightens her grasp. Jolene wrinkles her nose. "Mama, you're stinky!"

"Jolene!" The reprimand comes from Lily's mama, who, as she comes downstairs toting a lantern, gives both daughter and granddaughter a stern look.

Lily laughs. "Yes, yes, I am, sweetheart—Oh!" Lily gasps, seeing the mottled purple and blue bruise underneath Jolene's right eye. "Oh, child, what happened?"

Jolene's eyes well up and her chin quivers. "Mama, I already got a whipping at school, and Mamaw gave me a talking-to."

Lily carries her daughter into the parlor, sits down on the settee, holding Jolene in her lap. She looks at Mama. "Turn up the lamps. I want a clear look."

Mama lights the chandelier and turns it to full brightness, then eases herself stiffly into a rocker. Lily cradles Jolene's little face in her hands. No serious gashes; the child should heal quickly enough. Lily exhales, slightly relieved. "Tell me what happened, Jolene."

"It was Junior Ranklin! At recess, he shoved me down, and snatched the ribbon from my hair, and started kicking me, and I got up and ran, but he came after, and shoved me into the fence—" Jolene starts crying and hiccupping all at once.

The county school for grades 1–8 is just outside Kinship proper, up a lane off Kinship Road, and abuts a farm. The farmer has put up a fence to keep his cows from wandering into the school yard and ragamuffins (as he once put it) from spooking his cows.

"It's all right, baby girl. Take your time." Lily looks up at Mama. "Could I trouble you to warm her some milk? And add a dollop of brown sugar."

Mama rises from her rocker and heads to the kitchen.

Lily refocuses on her daughter. "Go on," she gently urges.

"Well, I said give me back my ribbon, and he said I didn't deserve nice things like that, 'cause you couldn't help his mother, like Daddy did, that *his* daddy wouldn't listen to you. Junior said that you shouldn't be sheriff at all because you're a girl." Jolene's face crumples up as she wails out the rest of her tale. "And then he tried to punch me, but I caught his arm, and kicked him right between his legs, and he doubled over howling, like I'd stabbed him, and grabbed himself, and he ran—well, sort of—for Teacher!"

Mama comes into the parlor with three mugs. She puts one on the side table and brings the other two to the table in front of the settee. Lily picks up a mug, helps Jolene take a drink. "Sweetie, I want to make sure—Junior picked on you first, and you ran away?"

"Yes, Mama. But I got pinned at the fence."

"All right, sugar." Lily gives Jolene her warm sweet milk. "You didn't start the fight. You tried to walk away. You couldn't, so you finished the fight. You did what you should have."

Mama stares. "Lily, girls shouldn't—"

Lily stops her mother with a hard look. She'd been about to say "fight." "No one should fight—unless they have to." Lily looks back at Jolene, tilts the little girl's face up so they can look in each other's eyes. All that blue and purple around the child's eye—Lily quivers with anger at the Ranklin boy. And how dare the teacher punish her daughter! "You listen to me, child. You did what was right. You defended yourself. I want no less from you."

"Miss Ellen said girls shouldn't fight, no matter what, and that I'd given Junior a black eye! He told her I'd hit him!"

Lily frowns. "You said you kicked him."

"I did. But I didn't hit him! You have to believe me." Jolene starts crying again.

"I do," Lily says. "Let's do a little detective calculating, you and me. Did you notice if Junior already had a black eye, when you were at the fence?"

Jolene nods. "He did, Mama. I'll never forget how he was looking at me."

Lily's heart drops. *Oh God. Seven years old and already Jolene has a memory of assault seared into her mind.*

"Jolene, how long did it take for your eye to turn black from him hitting you?"

"I don't know."

Mama says softly, "Her eyes were red when she came home. I thought it was from crying and rubbing her eyes. I read the note the teacher sent home, and gave Jolene an early supper, and sent her up to bed. I didn't realize it was purple until now."

Lily ignores her mother for the time being. "Jolene, you did what was right. Never let anyone hurt you like that. You can have a day off of school tomorrow." She looks at Mama, whose expression is so guilt stricken that Lily's anger at her softens a little. Mama nods—yes. Yes, she will take care of the children again tomorrow. "And I will talk to Miss Ellen— and point out to her that Junior's black eye couldn't have been from you. There wasn't enough time between you defending yourself and him telling Teacher. And I'll buy you a new hair ribbon. A whole passel of them!"

Jolene looks up at her mother, relieved. "Really?"

Lily smiles and nods. "Really. But now, young lady, you need to get to bed!"

As Lily carries Jolene upstairs, her own words echo in her mind: *You defended yourself.* And yet she'd spent a good portion of her day at the Hollows Asylum, where her only defense had been, at least at first, to act placid.

After tucking Jolene and her teddy bear back in bed, Lily comes back downstairs to find Mama at the dining table, sipping on her milk. Lily's mug is at the spot catty-cornered from Mama.

A bottle of Vogel's Tonic, lid off, is on the table.

Lily sits down, pours a splash into her mug. "You know this is really alcohol, watered down to be barely legal under the Volstead Act."

Mama nods. Taps her mug. Lily's surprised but pours in a dash. Mama nods—*go on!* Lily smiles, pours more into both mugs. For a few minutes, they sit quietly together, sipping.

"I'm sorry," Mama says quietly. "I read the teacher's note, that she'd given Jolene a light switching, for hitting the boy. Jolene's becoming such a tomboy, like you were—"

Lily arches her left eyebrow.

"Not that you've turned out anything but right nice, it's just that, it's, it's hard for you, and I don't want it to be so hard for Jolene—"

"You've always been proper, Mama! How has that made it easy for you? And how is it going to be easier for Jolene if people around her— her mama, her mamaw, her teacher—show her that her word doesn't matter?" As Mama's expression turns to hurt, Lily puts her hand on Mama's. "I'm sorry, too, Mama."

Mama pats the top of Lily's hand, then lets hers rest there, too. For a moment, they sit like this, and Lily's heart blooms with gratitude for her dear mama.

Oh, Hildy . . . The memory of her friend, so nervous, around her mother and fiancé, quickens that bloom into sorrow.

Mama gives Lily's hand a reassuring pat, then gently pulls away to take a long sip of her sugar milk and tonic. "Go on. Tell me of your day."

Lily shares the facts of the day, from tracking the woman to the Dyers' old house in Moonvale Hollow Village, to finding the compass, to talking with the Quaker woman, to tracking the dead woman to the Hollows Asylum and discovering the identity of the woman as Hildy's first cousin once removed, to breaking this news to Hildy and her mother.

She leaves out the horrid comment she'd made to Marvena about not knowing loss. The swinging bridge. The guards at the asylum.

The visions of a young silvery boy, laughing and chasing his ball through the woods.

Mama looks worried enough. Her expression had pulsed with revulsion at the description of the WKKK caped hood and then settled into concern for the remainder of Lily's recitation.

For a long moment, Mama is quiet. The parlor clock ticks the half-hour mark. The sounds of early autumn—the last of the crickets, an occasional hoot of an owl in the not-so-far-off woods, the sigh of wind—leak into the house.

Then Mama says, "Well, if I were you, I'd get to the newspaper office tomorrow. I don't know anything about Rupert Edward Kincaide, but if this Thea was retracing his steps from long ago, and if he was murdered, the newspaper would have covered it. And you'll need to find all the facts you can. Now you need to get to bed!"

And in spite of her weariness and all that has transpired over the past twenty-four hours, Lily smiles at how much alike she and Mama can sound.

Later, as the parlor clock chimes midnight, Lily quietly comes down the stairs, taking care to step over the squeaky third step from the bottom.

She'd had her cold-water sink bath, donned her flannel gown, and slid under the blanket and quilt in her now too-big bed. Thoughts—not of the eventful, bizarre day, but of all things, of the letter from Benjamin Russo—flood over her. She'd tried to fall asleep by counting back from one hundred—twice. By the third time she hit thirty-seven, more awake than before, she flung off her blanket.

Now, fueled by a second wind of energy, she crosses the parlor, finding her way in the dark by the coal-oil streetlamp shining through the front picture window, glinting off her shotgun hanging over her fireplace. She brushes against Daniel's leather chair. She lets her hand linger on the smooth arm. This is as much as she's allowed herself in the year and a half since his death. She has not sat in it. She'd wondered, a few times, how she'd react if either Jolene or Micah, or even little Caleb Jr., climbed in it. None of them have. It sits silently by the fireplace in the corner. Sometimes Lily thinks she can smell Daniel's cherry-scented pipe tobacco, as strong as if he'd just lit the pipe.

She inhales—but tonight there is no phantom scent to tease her. She makes the rest of her way to the desk, lights the coal-oil lamp, and spots Benjamin's letter, still out. *Yes,* she reassures herself, *it's perfectly proper. Nothing more than checking in on a friend's widow.*

She pushes aside the letter—better to put this sprout of energy toward organizing all she's learned today. Lily rereads her notes and calculations: Thea Kincaide likely leaving the Hollows Asylum between 4:05 and 4:55—given her age, the distance, and the rough terrain—in order to end up at the top of the Moonvale Hollow Tunnel right as the train came through at 9:20 p.m.

She'd have left, then, when there was still daylight, before dinner. Surely someone had to miss Thea, notice her absence. What would drive an elderly, senile woman to leave the asylum, make that trek? Surely not a WKKK meeting. Would she have learned of the meeting at the asylum? Felt she had to get to it? Mrs. Cooper had said that Thea's father was allegedly killed by a runaway slave he was trying to help. Would Thea have remained sympathetic to the Underground Railroad cause?

On a fresh notebook page, Lily lists questions: "What drove Thea to leave the Hollows? Who saw her leave? What happened to Thea's shoes, by the side of the cemetery? What does the Athens landlady know? Who is Thea's son—or did she really have one?" These are questions Lily cannot hope to pry into until she has a search warrant for the asylum.

And she needs to start a list of who might have purposefully or accidentally killed Thea. Someone at the WKKK gathering? A random stranger from Moonvale Hollow Village? Perry Dyer?—he'd been acting strangely enough. Even . . . Mabel Cooper? She'd been so shaken by the notion of her cousin possibly coming to see her. About being listed as next of kin.

Lily shakes her head. She's never particularly liked Mrs. Cooper—but she can't imagine her at a WKKK gathering. If nothing else, she'd find the rituals ridiculous and improper.

Or maybe that was the point of hiding under such bizarre garb. Anonymity offering freedom to embrace the grotesque, the darkest impulses, the anger and fear and hate that couldn't be discussed over coffee and ham salad sandwiches and pie at ordinary, harmless women's clubs.

Now Lily's head throbs. She closes her eyes, rubs her temples.

So many questions. Maybe the sketch and the article Hildy had run in the newspaper will miraculously inspire someone to come forward with all the answers. Wouldn't that be lovely.

In the meantime, tomorrow Lily will request the search warrant. Go to the newspaper and read all she can about Thea's father—Mrs. Cooper's uncle. Go to the school, talk with Jolene's teacher. Talk, again, with the Ranklins.

Oh, and make the damned vinegar pie for the county fair contest.

When Lily opens her eyes, her vision is swimming. She tries to focus on her notebook, blinks hard, ends up staring at the letter again.

Well, here at least is something she can do now—write a reply:

> Dear Mr. Russo,
>
> Thank you for checking on me and the children. We are doing fine.
>
> Congratulations on your new post.

Lily hesitates. She could simply end right there.

Her hands shake again. *Oh, for pity's sake!* She'd been able to write out questions and theories about a murdered woman and the rise of hatred in her community—but a simple reply rattles her. She should just sign the letter—*Cordially, Mrs. Ross*—confident, even after only meeting him once, that Benjamin would know she was signaling him to not come calling.

As her heart pounds, she writes instead:

> I believe you would find Kinship an excellent location for eco-nomical lodging. Should you need guidance or a home-cooked meal while searching, please do let me know. My mother and I would be glad to host you.
>
> > Cordially,
> >
> > Mrs. Ross

Lily's second wind gives way to exhaustion. She pushes the letter aside, too weary to dig out an envelope and postage. She stands, staggers toward the stairs, and stumbles into the side of Daniel's chair. For a moment, she wants to collapse into it, curl into a ball, the chair wide enough to enfold the whole of her.

Her face flaming from the letter she'd just written, she instead trudges up to her bedroom.

CHAPTER 16

※

HILDY

Thursday, September 23—8:00 a.m.

Hildy hurries up Plum Street toward Lily's, determined to quickly dispense with her duties at the jailhouse. And since she hadn't the night before, she will tell Lily about seeing Fiona with George but, more important, Missy coming by, followed quickly by Margaret, and their strange conversation—so odd that Margaret has taken such an interest in Missy. Plus, Lily needs to know about the WKKK editorial that Seth had bumped for the sheriff's notice and sketch of Thea Kincaide.

Oh—and she will show Lily the postcards from Thea.

She'd barely slept the night before, reading and rereading the postcards—just three of them—but they'd emboldened her. They'd been sent when she was young. Daddy had collected their mail every few weeks at the post office. Would he have snuck the postcards to her, so Mother wasn't aware? Yes. That made sense.

After meeting with Lily, Hildy would go, at last, to Tom. Apologize. Surely he'd take her back. Give her time to find the best way to break off with Merle. To break the news to Mother—who had kept to her bed this morning with another coughing fit, so that Hildy had to bring her breakfast in bed.

Thea would approve of Hildy's plan. She can almost see her elegant cousin taking shape before her, nodding encouragement. She smiles at this fanciful notion—obviously she can't see Thea, except in her imagination—but she also doesn't see the man lunging out at her from between the houses. He grabs her by the arm, and she yelps, pulls away, stares up at his face, for a moment not registering that this is Merle. His face is ravaged with anger, his eyes glinting dark and dangerous.

"Oh!" Hildy looks desperately back at Lily's house. He jerks her away, grasping her so tightly in his meaty hand that pain shoots up her thin arm, pulling so hard that she stumbles. People out on the street—other shopkeepers heading to their stores, mothers with strollers, men on the way to the courthouse or train depot—glance away as if they've seen nothing, though the swiftness of their looking away reveals they've seen everything. Hildy's face blazes with humiliation and fear, her earlier resolve crumbling.

Soon they are at Douglas Grocers, and Merle pulls a key from his pocket, clumsily trying to unlock the door one-handed. He has not let go of Hildy's elbow, as if she might run off.

"You were going to Lily's." Merle's voice is deep and gruff, but also weary, and Hildy guesses that he's been up all night, obsessing about last evening's scene. "I knew you would this morning—no matter that I told you that you need to quit."

Guilt washes over her, along with doubt that Tom will take her back. The question that plagued her the night before returns: Which would be worse? Living the rest of her life with Merle, but wanting Tom? Or breaking off from Merle and living the rest of her life as an old maid, much of it with Mother's constant bitterness—and still wanting Tom?

Suddenly she wishes to be alone. But how could a woman in this world function and survive alone, unless, like Lily, a husband had left her well situated?

Finally, she finds her voice, but only to say, "Please let go of me. I'll stay and help you."

Merle gives her a petulant look but releases her. As Hildy rubs her arm, he quickly finishes unlocking the grocery door. Then he pulls her inside. The bell over the door gives a merry, welcoming chime. It is the chime that Lily's father had put over the door years before.

Hildy stops, gazes around the small grocery. Waits for her usual feeling of comfort at being back in the grocery that had been Lily's father's, that was supposed to be Roger's, supposed to be McArthur & Son Grocers—to come back over her. This morning, the usual comforting smells—the briny pickle barrel, the sweet of the penny candy, the cheese and bologna—make her nauseous.

Hildy focuses on the checkout counter and soda fountain, the polished wood and gleaming brass fixtures and NCR cash register. Where she'll work day after day after she weds Merle. The counter suddenly reminds her of an animal pen.

"I told you last night that we have a new shipment of Campbell's tomato soup and other canned goods in the back," Merle is saying. "I'm thinking of taking out the penny candy counter, adding some new shelves for canned goods—"

The rows of shelves rush in at her. She focuses on the first thing she sees on the counter—a jar of licorice.

A memory hits her hard. Just before Roger was to leave with the American Expeditionary Forces Thirty-Seventh Division, they'd had an argument. She was terrified that she'd never see him again, a premonition of death crawling over her like an army of ants. Roger came to her house, stood in the doorway with his hand behind his back, then presented a fistful of licorice whips, like a bouquet of exotic flowers. She couldn't help but laugh.

She stares at her face, a hollow, ghostly reflection in the glass of the candy case.

Roger would want you to be happy.

That's what Mama had said the day before.

What Lily would say—if Hildy had only the nerve to tell her the truth.

And—as fanciful as it is—what she is sure Cousin Thea would say.

She thinks again of Roger's gentle face, eager and pleased at his goofy gift.

Then sees Roger's face fading away like the moon at sunrise, and another face rising before her, like the sun promising a new day. Tom. Not to take Roger's place, for no one could. A new promise.

"Hildy?"

She jumps, looks at Merle, realizes she'd actually forgotten him for a moment. He looks so sad, she feels sorry for him, despite his earlier brusqueness. She isn't being fair to him, either. Marrying him would, eventually, make both of them miserable.

Merle regards her with concern. "I'm sorry. I—I shouldn't have rushed you so fast. How 'bout you sit on the stool back here, take care of any customers, I know you can do that, and I can handle the inventory myself; I should never have asked you. And I know you're nervous about the wedding. Soon, though, we'll have you settled in my house!"

Now. Now is the time to tell him the truth—

The bell gives a merry chime as the door opens, and Margaret Dyer walks in. She is perfectly, primly dressed, as if going to church or a Kinship Woman's Club meeting.

For a moment, she looks from Hildy to Merle, and back again. A slow smile crawls up Margaret's face—she's sensed the tension between Hildy and Merle and finds it amusing. "The store is open, is it not? I'm not interrupting anything?"

"Of course we're open," Merle says quickly. "What can we help you with?"

"Well, I saw in last night's newspaper . . ." Margaret pauses and flicks her eyes toward Hildy, and for a moment she wonders if Margaret might actually know something helpful about Thea, might help resolve what had brought Thea to the village where the Dyers had lived until the previous year. She looks back at Merle. "I saw an advertisement for Campbell's soups. I prefer to cook from scratch, but with the pressures of helping on my husband's campaign—"

"Oh yes, we have them, just not out," Merle says.

"I can go fetch them," Hildy says, desperate to get away.

"Please—let Mr. Douglas get them. I want to talk with you about another matter." Margaret gives Merle a coquettish smile. "About the Woman's Club, and the fundraiser at the county fair this weekend. Women's talk."

Merle nods approvingly. "I'm glad to see Hildy expanding her friend circle. Good influences, like you."

As soon as Merle exits to the storeroom, the smile drops from Margaret's face—not unlike, Hildy realizes with dismay, hers just moments before. Margaret turns a coal-hard gaze to Hildy. "I'm glad to find you here. I was on business at the newspaper to file a complaint that an item I'd expected to see in the paper was not included last night. The reporter—a friend of yours, I believe?—told me you'd used your influence to knock it from the newspaper with the sheriff's announcement."

Hildy swallows hard, keeps her breathing even. Had Margaret been behind the WKKK op-ed piece? She forces her eyes to hold Margaret's gaze. "I used my authority as deputy sheriff to request that the announcement was run."

"Oh—your *authority*. So glad it wasn't your *influence,* given your pending nuptials."

Hildy clears her throat. "May I ask—what was the newspaper item you wanted to run?"

"Of course. I worked on it so hard, after all, with your dear mother." The blood drains from Hildy's face. *Oh God.* Margaret's smile returns. "It was an announcement about wishing for fine women to join us— the Kinship Woman's Club, that is—in raising funds at the county fair for a library. Your mother hasn't mentioned anything like that to you, has she?"

Hildy shakes her head.

"Oh, that's too bad. As Mr. Douglas just said, it would be good for you to expand your circle to include a better sort of friend."

Ire clenches Hildy's heart. "Lily is the best sort of person, and friend, possible—"

"Is she? How lovely. But I wasn't talking about her. I meant Olive Harding. The schoolmarm over in Rossville? I liked her well enough when you brought her as a guest to a Woman's Club meeting a few months ago, but there have been rumors lately of, shall we say, illicit activity between her and Clarence Broward."

Hildy's legs tremble. Even as it seems everything around her falls away and all she can see is Margaret's face scrunched up with hatefulness, she forces her breath to slow. Her legs to not give way.

Oh God. Even as she'd covered for them, she'd warned Olive—not against falling in love with Clarence. She knows all too well that the heart will find its own direction, whatever the mind dictates. But to be careful. Some people wouldn't care. Most would look askance. But some—some would be cruel. Even dangerous. She'd noted the varieties of responses just about the integration of the mines—what's more, the move to integrate the union. It suddenly strikes her—she'd told Olive about her father's old hunting shack between Rossville and Moonvale Hollow. Had they come close to where Thea had wandered by Moonvale?

Then the editorial that Seth had shown her flashes before her. *We are the soul of America!*

"Don't you volunteer over there, with Miss Harding in Rossville, tutoring those ignorant miners? I think your mother has mentioned this. At the Woman's Club. Which she says you're a member of, but you haven't been coming of late."

"I—I've been busy—"

"Volunteering with Olive? So perhaps you've seen—"

Hildy forces her voice to stay calm, but it still wavers a little as she says, "I do volunteer with Olive. All I've noted is that she is an excellent teacher. It's an honor to work with her."

Margaret sighs. "I should have known that the *current* sheriff and you as her little helper would offer no sympathy to concerns about the moral decay—"

"Olive has broken no laws," Hildy says. "And Sheriff Ross upholds the rule of law."

"Oh, does she? She certainly doesn't when it comes to moonshining and bootlegging by the likes of Missy's husband—and others."

Merle comes huffing out of the storeroom, toting a crate of canned soup. He puts the box on the case, knocking over the jar of licorice. Hildy catches it before it can crash to the floor.

"Here's the tomato." Merle smiles encouragingly. "They're only twelve cents a can!"

"Oh, I'll take three cans," Margaret says. "You wouldn't have the vegetable soup, too, would you?"

"I do—let me go get the box," Merle says.

"Wonderful! Hildy and I were having such a lovely time, catching up," Margaret says.

"I'll get some cans for you!" Hildy dashes around the counter, ignoring Merle's protests. She slams the storeroom door shut behind her, picks up another crate of soup, and puts it in front of the door, and then rushes out the back, down the alley.

She must get to her automobile, and over to Rossville.

Not just to find Tom.

To alert Olive and Clarence.

CHAPTER 17

LILY

Thursday, September 23—9:50 a.m.

Lily hurries out her back door toward the jailhouse. She's overslept. Mama had left a note saying she'd watch the boys today and take Jolene to school on a breakfast tray outside Lily's bedroom door— biscuits and jam, and boiled coffee already cold by the time Lily arose.

She'd gulped down the food, both grateful and guilty.

Now men's voices clamor angrily from within the jailhouse, the door to which hangs open. Inside, Lily fights back the urge to gag. The place stinks of human waste.

"Quiet!" Lily yells, and the men in the jail cells settle down to a grumble. She looks at Leroy Gregson, one of the security guards Lily had insisted the county commissioners ante up for as the county's population has grown. They'd been reluctant—until Lily reminded them that their positions were also elected and no one expects their daddy or husband or brother to be tossed in jail for a routine twenty-four-hour hold and come out roughed up worse than he went in.

She frowns at Leroy. "What is going on?"

He rubs his face nervously. "They're upset that the chamber pots aren't cleaned up—"

"And all we got for breakfast was leftover, cold biscuits!" yells a prisoner.

"Where is Hildy?" Lily asks.

Leroy shrugs. "Never showed." He steps outside the jailhouse.

Dammit! Of late, Hildy has been so withdrawn, reserved. She'd been so delighted when Merle first wooed her, and Lily was relieved that Hildy had found someone who would keep her safe.

She can't worry about her friend at this moment. Lily looks around, assesses. One of the men is unperturbed, but he's snoozing by himself in one of the cells. The other two cells each hold two men. In one, a man lies on his cot, moaning. His cellmate sits on the opposite cot, hands clasped over his nose and mouth.

"Has he been sick long?" Lily asks.

"Something hit him wrong sometime yesterday," says the sick man's cellmate.

Lily nods. "All right. I'll send a doctor."

She exits, finds Leroy on her back stoop, spitting tobacco juice into her chrysanthemums by the cellar door.

"What the hell is going on?" Lily demands.

Leroy looks up at her, shocked, as if a lady using an ordinary curse word is the most shameful thing about this situation. Then his eyes narrow with anger—and also fear. Lily has learned that look well over the past year. She gets it as much from women as men. She's learned to pretend it's not there, to not respond, to go on about doing her job, to let the rule of law speak for itself—and for her.

"What the hell do you care about the scum you have in lockup?" Leroy asks.

"The prisoners are people with rights under the law."

Leroy scoffs, "The right to a clean cell? Where's that in the lawbooks, missy?"

"There's the law of man—and the law of a greater power." In spite of her doubts, her withdrawal from church, Jesus's words from the book of Matthew in the Bible rise from deep within her. "'Then shall they also answer him, saying, Lord, when saw we thee an hungred, or athirst, or a stranger, or naked, or sick, or in prison, and did not minister unto thee? Then shall he answer them, saying, Verily, I say unto you, inasmuch as ye did it not to one of the least of these, ye did it not to me.'"

For a moment, Leroy pulls back, rebuffed. Then his grin returns. "Now you think you can be a preacher, too? No woman can be behind a pulpit!"

"No. But they can be in a Sunday school room. Your mother was an excellent teacher. I still remember her lessons."

As Lily walks away, frustration rattles her every step. She wants to give her complete attention to the case of Thea Kincaide—but first she needs to get help for her prisoners.

Three hours later, Lily steps out of the courthouse—her second trip there today.

On her first trip, she'd found one of the county commissioners, informed him that she's firing Leroy and that she would be replacing him with one of the other guards, a retired barber who usually only filled in when needed on weekends.

Then she'd gone to the doctor, and requested his immediate attention for the prisoner, who, it turned out, was suffering from a kidney stone, so she released him from his hold early so he could get back to his home and moan in privacy.

By then the retired barber was at her house, along with his wife, who was willing to take on jail mistress duties.

Lily's next stop was to both Douglas Grocers and the Cooper household—neither Merle Douglas nor Mrs. Cooper knew where Hildy has gotten off to. Merle thought she wasn't feeling well and had gone home; Mrs. Cooper thought Hildy was at the grocery; both Merle and Mabel Cooper were curt.

Lily had wondered where could Hildy have gone? Just for a drive, or maybe over to Rossville to tutor? She'd have to find her soon—she doesn't want Hildy to learn from anyone but her that she's been officially relieved of her jail mistress duties. And yet Lily was irritated at having to track her down. She had more pressing matters to attend to first—namely, returning to the courthouse and filing a request for a search warrant for the Hollows Asylum for any information that might help her with Thea Kincaide's case.

Now Lily stands on the top step of the courthouse, taking a moment to draw in a deep breath, to survey the calm, the normalcy, of the town. She considers the courthouse—the scaffolding on the end of the building, the addition that will have a proper county jail and an office for her, assuming she is reelected. Progress. Change.

And there—at the bottom of the courthouse steps, an older woman bending over the pram that the younger one has been pushing, both women beaming, and Lily can imagine their conversation, yes, their new baby boy, baptized last week at the Presbyterian church, yes he's doing well, waking them up at night, but they're so pleased with his growth....

Lily's smile falls away. What if one, or both, of the women had been at the WKKK gathering the night before on the old Dyer farm? Both of those women—and Lily—are in the Woman's Club, along with Margaret Dyer. Was Margaret responsible for the meeting? Or had the farm been used without any of the Dyers' knowledge?

Lily can't imagine that either woman, chatting so amiably and innocently at the bottom of the steps, could be part of such an ugly gathering. But then they would be shocked at some of the things she's had to do, to keep secret. Can anyone really know their neighbors—what's more, their neighbors' hearts?

The women stop talking, look up at Lily. They wait as Lily comes down the steps, and then chat for a few moments—yes, Lily says, she will bring her pie on Friday to the county fair, yes, yes, she's looking forward to the Woman's Club meeting at Mrs. Perry Dyer's home. She'd actually forgotten about the meeting, or where it was to be held, and looks away from the women to coo at the baby boy. He smiles at her and coos back. Yawns.

A sudden stiff breeze stirs his blanket. He starts to fuss.

It is enough for his mother to say "goodness" and she must get him home, settled for a nap. The women go their separate ways.

Lily heads to the *Kinship Daily Courier*.

"What can I do for you, Sheriff?" Seth asks.

"Well, first, thank you for running Hildy's sketch and article. I have another favor to ask. I need to see some old newspapers—how far back do your archives go?"

"All the way back—the newspaper started shortly after Kinship became a village in 1842. They are in cabinets in the basement."

"Good. I need to see editions from 1857. I've been able to identify the woman from the notice—Thea Kincaide. I need anything about her father, Rupert Edward Kincaide. He died in 1857—allegedly at the hands of an escaped slave he was helping."

Seth lifts an eyebrow. "Sure, I'll find those editions for you. Hey— will you give me the exclusive if this turns out to be really interesting?"

"All right." He'd been like this even in high school, for the newspaper that came out once a year, though there wasn't much to report for a school with at most eighty students.

"Thanks! My editor is out now, doing the interview I wanted. Said I'm not seasoned enough to handle it. I've been here more'n ten years!"

Lily's curiosity is piqued. "What interview is that?"

"George Vogel. He's in town, but no one seems to know for sure why. There were a few theories at the Kinship Inn—Lily? Are you all right?"

As Seth's voice grows more distant, Lily sits down, hard, on a chair. Seth stares at her with concern. "Lily? You're not gonna pass out on me, are you?"

Vogel, Lily had learned after Daniel's death, had exerted far too much control over her husband. The year before, she'd managed to maneuver out from under similar control—or so she thought. But Vogel, a powerful attorney and businessman, managed to not only sidestep bootlegging laws but also cleverly use the Volstead Act to sell his "tonic" with a legal percentage of alcohol and become even more rich and powerful. There was probably no permanent way to get free of such a man's reach.

"I'm fine." Lily forces her voice to be even.

Seth looks doubtful. "All right. I'll find all I can about Rupert Edward Kincaide."

"Thank you." Lily starts to the door but stops. "How did Hildy seem to you yesterday?"

Seth's eyebrows go up at that. It's an odd question—everyone knows that Lily and Hildy have always been best friends. Seth chooses his words carefully. "Hildy has always been more tender than most people. Yesterday, she seemed more determined than I've ever seen her."

A few minutes later, it's spitting rain as Lily hurries past the train depot.

A small crowd under the awning catches her attention. At first she thinks maybe they're hoping to avoid a downpour, and then she hears his voice—loud, bombastic, jocular.

The great George Vogel.

Lily stops, mid-stride.

After Daniel had come back from the war, their plans were up in the air—perhaps Daniel would go into the grocery business with Daddy, since Roger had died in the war; or perhaps they'd move somewhere new, start fresh. Daniel had run for county sheriff instead, his boxing career and war heroism a sure platform. Then, after Daniel died and Lily became acting sheriff, Lily learned Daniel's real motivation— George had held a terrible secret over his head from his boxing days. George—Cincinnati attorney, pharmaceutical mogul, and alleged mobster, whose deeds are fearfully whispered about—is not a man you want to be in debt to.

Yet after Daniel's death and Lily becoming sheriff, George had promised that he would leave Bronwyn County alone.

"How are you doing, Sheriff Ross?"

Lily jumps at the sudden presence of Abe Miller—George's right-hand man and enforcer—looming over her with an umbrella. Lily's gaze hardens as she looks up at Abe, the tallest man she's ever met, and so slender it's hard to imagine he takes any joy in eating. She'd dealt with him in the past. Now Abe doesn't deign to look down at her, so all she can see of him is his well-pressed suit lapels and shirt collar, his exaggerated Adam's apple as still as a stone lodged in his throat, his chin and jawline shaved so smoothly as to suggest that even stubble is too scared to brush his face. No matter. She already knows from past experience the only expression his dark eyes ever hold—sharp expediency.

"I'm quite well," Lily replies. "What is Vogel doing here?"

"Visiting."

"To what purpose? He gave me his word that he'd release my county from any hold—"

Abe cuts her off with a flat bark of a laugh. "As I told you once before, Mr. Vogel is always on the side of his own business."

Oh yes, he'd told her that. Lily looks back at the crowd at the depot as if she's simply a casual observer. There's the newspaper editor, the mayor, one of the commissioners, and—*Is it? Yes. Perry Dyer.* Lily frowns. *What is he doing, cozying up to George Vogel?*

Then some of the men in the crowd shift, and Lily sees her. *Oh God. Surely not—but yes. That's Fiona Weaver, widow of Martin Weaver. Martin, who had been Daniel's top deputy.*

Beside Fiona is a steamer trunk. She is wearing a fancy new dress, a style depicted in illustrations in newspaper serials, but not for sale in the ladies' shops in Kinship—a drop-waist lavender sheath, all the way up to her knees, with sapphire blue embroidery work, and a matching hat that accentuates her pert bob haircut.

In her shock—not at the dress or hat or hair, but what it all likely means—Lily runs down the slope to the depot, breaks through the men, stops in front of George and Fiona.

George looks at Lily, momentary surprise quickly masked by a sneer. "Why, Sheriff Ross, you're not here to arrest me, are you?"

The men who know Lily all laugh a little nervously. There's no doubt it's likely George is guilty of at least a few crimes. There's also no doubt that, even if she had cause, she couldn't make an arrest stick. The men who don't know her—reporters and photographers from other towns' newspapers, and Pinkerton hired guns as his security detail—look a little confused, then surprised as one points out her sheriff's star.

Lily ignores them and turns her attention fully to Fiona. She steps closer to her under the awning of the depot, as Fiona looks imploringly at George.

"Ah, let the little women talk, shall we, fellas?" George gives Fiona a proprietary pat on her arm, before abruptly turning to enter the depot. The men quickly follow, except Abe, who has come down the slope and stands off to one side, smoking a cigarette, looking away as if he doesn't notice them at all. Lily has no doubt that he is taking note of everything. She's just as sure that George wouldn't have left Fiona alone with Lily if he thought Lily would have any influence over her. Still, she has to try.

"Fiona, what are you doing?"

Fiona's bright red lipsticked mouth pinches into a tight knot. The wind nudges her hat, and as Fiona lifts her hand to adjust it, Lily notes the large sapphire on her left ring finger, the carefully painted pink crescent nails.

Lily's shoulders and heart slump. "Oh, Fiona."

At this, Fiona's eyes brighten with tears, as much of anger as of sorrow. "Don't you dare, Lily Ross. You've barely done more in the past year and a half than say hello to me at Woman's Club meetings—and only out of cordiality. If you had, you might have learned that George invited me and Leon to visit Cincinnati a few times, staying at the hotel of course, because he thought it might be good for Leon."

Lily has to think for a moment before it strikes her—Leon is Fiona and Martin's now fourteen-year-old son.

Fiona correctly reads Lily's expression—confusion, then recognition—and her mouth twists into a small, bitter smile. "Do you even know your own children's names anymore?"

At that, even Abe Miller shifts uncomfortably from foot to foot. Lily swallows back her rising anger. "Fiona, I understand. Missing your husband. But you deserve a good man. Martin was a good man. George has done terrible things—"

Fiona grabs Lily by the shoulders, gives her a hard shake. "I *had* a good man, Lily. I had Martin. And he . . . he believed in you. Respected you. Trusted you. More than the men he knew. And that got him killed."

Fiona releases Lily with a final, small shove and stares past her. "I'm not like you, Lily. Not every woman can be like you. We live in a man's world. So I'm doing the best I can, and right now that is going to Cincinnati to marry George." Fiona returns her gaze, hard and dark as coal now, to Lily. "If there is a reason, a real reason, why I should not go with George, you tell me now. Tell me now, Sheriff Ross."

Lily glances at Abe Miller, who has not moved a grass blade closer, yet somehow seems to be right beside them. His stare remains steady, his face expressionless.

She looks back at Fiona. Even if Abe weren't standing right there, Lily knows she wouldn't tell Fiona the truth about the barter she and Marvena had made with George the year before to resolve their investigations—and to help their community.

For a second, she feels the earth dropping away below her, her legs weightless, and she feels for the first time the heavy dreadful certainty that the ripples from that barter will be never ceasing in her life—and in the lives of others.

Now she clears her throat. "What of—what of Leon?"

Fiona smirks, turns away, walks into the depot.

"He is away at private school in Boston," says Abe, suddenly beside her. As Lily startles, a smile twitches across his lips. "Has been for a month, thanks to the generosity of Mr. Vogel."

Lily stares at him.

"You are done here." Abe's twitchy smile flutters away. "Unless you'd like to help me with Mrs. Weaver's trunk?"

Lily turns and heads back toward her house.

The two older Ranklin children—a twelve-year-old girl and an eleven-year-old boy—sit quietly beside Lily on the drive from the Bronwyn County Primary School, just west of town on Kinship Road, into the part of the county that flattens out into cash crop farms: buckwheat, some tobacco and sorghum, and in a few cases subsistence farms.

After they'd first left the school, Lily had tried to engage the children in conversation: Favorite subjects? Books? Friends? They'd only answered in single words or grunts, sitting as far away from Lily as possible, their grubby faces pinched with a mix of defiance and defensiveness. The boy's hair is chopped unevenly short, the girl's in greasy strands, nary a ribbon to hold it back from her face. A sour odor wafts off of them and their smudged, stiff clothes. Neither of them has a coat or hat, and late September's turned chilly.

Lily'd thought she'd been doing the children a favor, saving them the three-mile walk back home, but now she realizes she's only terrified them, that they'd likely said yes because they recognized the sheriff's emblem on her automobile.

And so they all remain quiet for the rest of the drive, except for the girl telling Lily to turn at the "big rock" onto Forbidden Creek Run. Up a steep rise and then the narrow dirt road etched between brush and trees opens into a clearing to a small single-story farmhouse, slant roof capping the front porch like a hat brim. In the distance are garden plots, a field with a few cows and goats, a chicken coop, a barn that is small yet twice as big as the house. The barn has been freshly painted red, and the blue tin roof on the house is new. Missy, from her hardscrabble life in a deeper, farther holler, had seemingly married up and well.

And yet, despite the signs of prosperity, the Ranklin property has the air of shrinking in on itself, as if it had been salted down, like a ham. Maybe Missy had sensed it, too—the lack of sweetness about the place—as she took care of another woman's children and ran afoul of her husband's quick temper.

Lily pulls to a stop on the first flat stretch of yard, but not too close to the house. She wants Ralf Ranklin to have to take his time coming toward her automobile.

"Get on out," Lily tells the children, but as softly and kindly as the words will allow. She wants Ralf to see his children first.

They stare back at her. Their wide eyes remind her of several of the asylum residents—gazes fraught with fear and uncertainty.

Lily smiles, even as she glances toward the house—the front door is creaking open. She inches her hand toward her holster. "Go on," she urges. "I'll make sure your father knows you're not in trouble."

At that, the boy opens the passenger door and tumbles out, his sister quickly following, running toward the house, until their father steps out, shotgun at the ready. The children bump into each other as they come to an abrupt halt, staring up at their father.

Lily quickly gets out of the automobile, keeping her hands spread wide but knowing full well she can quickly get to her revolver if she has to. Her heart pounds. She doesn't want to have to. Not in front of these children. Not at all.

"Mr. Ranklin!" she hollers, keeping her voice steady and respectful. "I was at the school, needed to chat with you a bit, thought I'd give your boy and girl a ride home."

He takes a step forward. "Ain't no sheriffs pay a visit to *chat*." But at least he lowers his shotgun a mite.

"First time for everything!" Lily calls. She gives a quick side-eye to the children, frozen in their spots, even as a big hound comes loping from around back of the house and is sniffling at the boy's hands. "Teacher says they're right good students. Well behaved."

"Does she, now?"

Lily nods. The schoolmarm had said that, about these two. She'd been less complimentary about their younger half brother, seven-year-old Junior Ranklin, who'd attacked Jolene. Though she hadn't been particularly flattering about Jolene, either.

Lily's anger over the ridiculous situation reflames, but Mama's voice reminds her: *You catch more flies with honey than vinegar.* And, *Can't go wrong, complimenting people's babies.*

"She does. Says they're good with their chores at school." Lily picks her next words carefully. "Probably have some chores here, too."

Ralf looks at the children. "You heard the *sheriff.*" He works the words around a plug of tobacco in his left cheek, then spits, as if spitting out the very notion of a woman in such power.

As the children run toward the porch, Ralf sets aside his shotgun. They stop before him, and he kneels, scoops them up in a big hug. Lily inhales sharply at the unexpected moment of tenderness and almost looks away to give them privacy. But she catches herself. This is a man who Daniel had repeatedly warned about smacking his second wife, Missy. And the schoolteacher had admitted, after Lily pressed, that Junior, Missy's boy, had shown up to school several times with bruises around his eyes and lips—markings the other children didn't have.

Ralf releases his children and gives them a kindly smile. "Bumper crop of string beans out back. A mess of 'em will make a right tasty supper." The children drop their books on the porch, dash around to the back of the house, the dog at their heels.

Lily exhales slowly, relieved that the children are out of the scenario.

Ralf strides quickly toward Lily, until he is a few feet before her and she is forced to look up to keep her eyes on his. His face is rough and ruddy, his nose thickened and pockmarked, his eyes rheumy.

Lily lowers her hands, puts her left one near the fold of her skirt that only partially covers her holstered gun. Though he'd left his shotgun on the porch, it's more'n likely he carries a gun or knife in his pocket, a sight she'd seen a few times, men who think they are so impervious to misadventure that they don't even bother with holsters.

"Don't think you're going to haul me in on Missy's say-so," he says.

"I don't. I can only bring you in on formal charges. There aren't any at this time."

"Then where's Missy?"

"She's not here?"

"Been gone five days, now. Kids see Junior at school, but he won't tell them where he and his mother are staying."

Well. That's a surprising bit of news. "I do not know where she is. I came out here to talk with you about Junior. And my daughter. Seems Junior hit my daughter."

"Yeah? Way the other two told it last night at supper, she hit him."

"In self-defense. I don't care if you have a problem with me being a lady sheriff. Vote for my opponent. But tell your boy to stay away from my children. The teacher admits that Junior comes to school with bruises, so I'll be keeping an eye on him—and your other children—and if I see signs of abuse, I'll be filing my own charges against you."

Ralf steps forward and it's all Lily can do to keep herself from stepping back. "I don't hit my children." While his breath doesn't smell of shine, Missy had complained that he often drank—and became more violent. For a moment, Lily considers returning with backup, searching and finding his illegal stash or home still, and hauling him in on those charges. Then she thinks of the children, who'd been glad for his embrace. How gently he'd sent them out back, to pick a mess of green beans for supper. And she turns his words over in her mind. She'd assumed Ralf had hit Junior—but what if it was Missy? Taking her own anger and frustration out on her boy? If she hadn't had him, she could more easily leave Ralf. Having the boy complicated her situation. And while Ralf might tolerate her smacking her own son, he wouldn't put up with her hitting his children by his first wife.

"Where's Missy?" Ralf asks.

"I told you, I don't know."

"Don't know? Don't know?" Ralf's voice turns mocking, and he pokes her sheriff's star hard, sending her stumbling back. "Some sheriff you are!"

Lily quickly regains her stance, plants her boots wide. "Touch me again, and I'll bring you in on assault charges."

Ralf laughs. "You think you can take me on?"

"Yes." She puts her fists on her waist, doesn't reach for her revolver. She quickly assesses: a swift kick would knock his feet out from under him, and from there she could quickly flip him to his stomach and cuff him.

Then what? She couldn't leave the children here. She'd have to take them back to town, too, away from their home and their hound dog and their mess of green beans for supper, and find a place for them to stay, and eventually Ralf might be released, or if Missy presses charges after all, emboldened by him being in jail, they'd probably end up in an orphanage. If Missy doesn't even really want her own son, she won't want her stepchildren.

"Look," Lily says. "I don't want to haul you in. But I can't let you attack me. Missy keeps wanting me to give you a talking-to. If I see that she's been hurt, I'll have to haul you in even if she doesn't file a formal complaint. The teacher said your boy defended his attack on my daughter because he thinks I'm too weak to stop you from hitting his mother. So we now have witnesses—your son and the teacher. Consider this a fair warning—and a suggestion that you and Missy work out whatever's eating you, peacefully."

Ralf glares at her but backs up and folds his arms across his chest. "Never had trouble with Arlene." His eyes water up at simply saying the name of his first wife. "Man oughta be able to discipline his woman if she gets outta line."

Lily swallows back the inclination to admonish that Missy is his *wife,* as well as her frustration with the knowledge that many men and women would agree with Ralf's view.

"You tell her to get back home," he goes on. "And I bet I know where you can find her—with that Margaret Dyer. Or at least she'll know where Missy is."

Before she can catch it, shock registers on Lily's face.

"That's right. Missy's joined some women's group that the Dyer woman's leading. Missy's gotten these ideas that she can tell me what I can and can't do."

"This women's group—did Missy tell you the name of it?" Lily holds her breath, expecting Ralf to say, *The WKKK.*

Ralf shakes his head. "She didn't go into that detail, 'cause I didn't want to hear the other crazy ideas she started spouting. Didn't want the kids hearing them, either. Forbade her to keep going to meetings, but Missy won't listen."

A door slams. The children, entering the back of their house with their mess of green beans. Lily looks past Ralf at the simple yet neat farmhouse, trying to settle and sort out this much bigger mess. She doesn't support Ralf's drinking to excess, yet she's found Prohibition frustrating and nearly impossible to enforce, an endless drain on resources.

She definitely doesn't support the stomach-turning principles of the WKKK, yet the group has the right to free assembly and free speech, and she can't stop them from meeting—or recruiting vulnerable women like Missy—until they violate the law. That's assuming the group Missy's joined is the WKKK. Just because the group had gathered at the old Dyer farm doesn't prove Missy's involvement—the farm is abandoned, isolated, and could be used by anyone as a meeting area. For all she knows, Missy has connected up with Margaret and is trying to get in the Woman's Club. There are certainly enough ideas bandied about at those meetings that Ralf most likely would disapprove of.

"You got any kin, nearby?" Lily asks.

"A cousin, on up the road," Ralf says. "You got a beef with her, too?"

"Need to know where your children can stay, if I need to take you in. I'll let your *wife* know you miss her—and your son. If she comes back, mind you keep your disagreements civil."

Ralf gives her a long, hard look, then strides back to his front porch. He stops, turns, looks back at Lily.

"I prob'ly never should have married Missy. She was too young— not just in years. She's simpleminded. But pretty. And I ... well. I reckon you can understand, Sheriff." At last, Ralf uses Lily's title without irony. "I wanted a whole family again."

He stoops to carefully pick up his children's schoolbooks and goes into his house.

CHAPTER 18

※

HILDY

Thursday, September 23—7:00 p.m.

"You don't have to stay, Hildy. I don't think anyone's coming tonight—"

"No, I'm here now. And I, I need to talk with you." Hildy finally stops sweeping the same spot in Rossville's one-room schoolhouse, around the coal-fired stove at the back, that she'd been sweeping for the past hour.

Olive gives Hildy a long, annoyed look. Olive has been irritable with her all day—and no wonder. Hildy had shown up at the schoolhouse, on the far edge of Rossville, at 10:00 this morning.

After running from Merle's grocery, she'd rushed to her automobile—well, her daddy's old automobile—and started it up, and driven as fast as she could to Rossville. On the hairpin turn on Kinship Road, between Widow Gottschalk's house and the house where Daniel Ross had grown up, she'd nearly overturned her automobile.

She'd driven cautiously the rest of the way, until at last she came to the top of the hill and saw Rossville laid out below, a collection of humble buildings, pinned down by a coal tipple, in the holler below. Joy lifted her heart. *Tom.*

Then dismay overcame her as she drove down the hill and into the coal-mining town, past the scant miners' houses lined up like a necklace strung around the base of Devil's Backbone, the mountain that held the coal that had teased the town into being.

Of course the men were at work in the mines. With all the others, Tom would have taken his lunch pail with him and not come back out until after work ended.

Turn; go back; apologize to Merle; don't act so insane; be reasonable, a voice had thrummed in her head. Yet on she'd driven, heart pounding.

Olive and the children had all stared at her as she burst into the schoolroom, out of breath as if she'd run miles, though it was only her thrumming heart that made her gasp so.

When Olive rushed over, asked if anything was wrong, Hildy had said no, she'd come early to help with . . . with—she'd paused, then stuttered awkwardly—anything that might make tonight's tutoring session easier.

Olive's gaze turned from alarm to concern. This was not one of the two evenings per week for tutoring.

Hildy forced a smile to her face, brightly chirped, *It will be a special extra session tonight!* Then she'd turned to the students, focusing on Alistair—Tom's son—and said they should be sure to tell their parents about the extra session.

Even to her own ears, Hildy sounded manic—almost hysterical— and she knew she'd alarmed the children, who nervously looked at one another.

Olive had rapped a ruler against her desk and announced that Miss Hildy would be helping students that day and they should be respectful. To Hildy's surprise, the day went quickly, and she'd enjoyed working with the children on their numbers and letters. At the end of the day, she had caught Alistair gently by his shoulder as he went out, and gave him a long look. *Don't forget to tell your father,* she'd said.

Now Olive says, "Hildy, I don't think anyone's coming to this extra session tonight, and I know it's not me you really want to talk with."

Olive's pitying gaze grasps Hildy from across the room, makes her look down. *Oh. So Olive has figured it out. Does everyone in Rossville know?* Tom had suggested as much two nights before, and now—given

Hildy's announcement of a special tutoring session—Olive must think she's here to throw herself at Tom.

Well, she does want to see Tom, but there's a more pressing matter.

Olive sighs. "I'm closing up the schoolhouse, and going home. You should, too."

"No, wait!" Hildy snaps.

Olive looks at her, startled.

Hildy sets aside the broom and crosses over to Olive. "I've learned that there's a WKKK group in Bronwyn County. I think I know who the leader is—Margaret Dyer, the wife of the man running against Lily for sheriff. I don't know for sure, but some things she said today make me suspicious. And Olive—she was asking about you. And Clarence."

The blood drains from Olive's face. She staggers back, sits down hard in a chair.

"What . . . what did you say?"

"Nothing, really. Just . . . that you're a good teacher, that there are no laws against—"

"Oh God, Hildy, do you really think such people care about the laws—or my goodness as a teacher? Did you confirm that . . . that . . . Clarence and I—"

Hildy shakes her head, hard. "No! Of course not."

"Are you sure there's a WKKK group here? How do you know?"

"There was going to be an editorial in the *Kinship Daily Courier* from an anonymous member of the WKKK. I only learned about it because, well, a woman died over in Moonvale Hollow Village, hit by the train," Hildy says. She swallows hard. "In the same general area of my daddy's old hunting shack."

Alarm grows in Olive's expression as Hildy continues. "I've been helping Lily find out who she is—and we did. It turns out, she's a distant cousin of mine. Her name is Thea Kincaide. She used to send me postcards. . . . Anyway, she's older and she'd been gone a long time, and ended up at the Hollows Asylum, but got out somehow, and wandered all the way over to Moonvale Hollow, and fell, or maybe was pushed—the sheriff isn't rightly sure yet—from the top of the tunnel over the train, and before Lily figured out all of that, I wrote up a notice and made a sketch of her, and took it to the newspaper. To have space to run it, the editorial had to be bumped. Margaret Dyer made references that sounded so much like the editorial, and asked about you. I'm not sure how or if it connects, but the Dyers used to live over in Moonvale, and—Olive?"

Olive's eyes are wide, her mouth agape. "This—this woman—you said she was elderly?"

Hildy nods.

"What did she look like? What was she wearing?"

The odd question spurs images of Thea Kincaide to rush back— first the slender, frail body on the mortuary table. Then the face she'd pieced back together in a sketch. Then the childhood memory of Thea alive and whole, in her elegant blue dress and proper hat—the one time, Hildy thinks, she'd ever seen Thea alive.

But Olive means when she was found. "She was elderly. In her seventies. Soft gray-white hair, a plain blue nightgown, no shoes save rags, rose nail varnish—" Hildy stops. Why would Olive want to know any of this? "Olive, are you—"

The schoolhouse door opens, and in strides Tom, and Hildy is no longer concerned about Olive, who quickly moves out the door, muttering something about taking all the time they need, to lock up after themselves.

Hildy stands stock-still, breathless, quivering, staring at him as he strides toward her. As if she had not seen him just two days ago. As if it has been years.

Tom stops out of reach of her and she steps forward, but he holds up his hands, signaling she should stop.

Hildy's heart cracks. Tom is not going to embrace her, and it takes all her will to keep her feet planted on the slanted wood floor, to keep from rushing toward him.

Tom's face droops with sorrow, his hands trembling as he scrunches his hat together, but his voice is pickaxe hard and certain. "This ain't no good, sugar. Told you, you've got to choose. It'd be better for you if it was Merle."

"Easier, you mean."

"In the long run, yeah."

Hildy takes in Tom's long, lank figure, his thinning hair, the fine wrinkles around his eyes and mouth. Weariness accumulated over years has worn its way into every bit of his overworked, thin lines. But there is an intelligence, good humor, and a love for life in his bright blue eyes, a kindness to his gap-toothed smile.

"What if I don't want easy?"

Tom shakes his head. "I can't do this no more, and you can't come running over here making a fool of yourself."

Hildy stiffens at his cruel words. "I'm not making a fool of myself. I'm here to tutor—"

"This ain't a tutoring night, and I'm going to stop coming for tutoring anyhow—"

"What? No, no, you're doing so well!"

Hildy lunges forward, grabs his arms, pulls herself to his chest, holding on tightly, even as his arms refuse to embrace her. She doesn't care that she is humiliating herself. She starts sobbing. "I'll break it off with him, Tom; I will!"

Tom then finally touches her, but only to gently push her away from him. His eyes harden. "No, you won't. You'd hafta be crazy to do that. What can I offer you but a life of hard work and scarcity?"

"Love," she sobs.

"Love?" Tom gives the word a harsh twist, as if it is some rank, foul thing he must stomp out. "That ain't gonna put food in your belly, nor a fine, fancy hat on your head."

He lets go of her, lifts his hand as if to wipe away her tears, but then drops it to his side.

"Don't cry, Hildy." His voice hitches on her name. "Like I said th'other night—you'd be crazy to throw over a man like Merle for me, for the life I could give you. I know that. You do, too. Sooner or later, you'll get your right mind back and settle down to be Merle's wife."

Tom walks back out the schoolhouse door.

The door shuts behind him.

For a long moment, Hildy cannot breathe or move.

Then a shadowy form—the elegant lady she'd imagined seeing in the street the night before—flickers in the corner of her eye. *Go.*

Hildy runs out the door, lets it bang behind her, calls Tom's name. He ignores her, keeps walking, but she races after him, and is almost to him, when they both hear, from somewhere in the woods, Olive's wailing cry. "No! Clarence—you can't!"

A few moments later, Hildy and Tom have followed Olive's voice down a slanted path into the woods. They stop at the scene that awaits them.

There, standing under the rising moon in a small man-made clearing, stands Clarence Broward. He is well dressed, though his gray-and-tan houndstooth checked cap is askew. Clarence and Olive hold each other.

"What the—" Tom starts.

Clarence jumps back from Olive, but she won't let go.

Hildy puts her hand on Tom's arm. "Please—"

Tom shakes her hand off. "Don't go lecturing me about love. If they find love with one another, it's none of my damned business. It's other folks I'm worried about—"

"That's what I'm trying to tell him—" Olive says.

Clarence gently pulls away from her. He walks over to Tom and Hildy and looks at Hildy imploringly. His jaw flexes nervously, pulsing the long, thin scar across his left cheek. "You work for the sheriff, right?"

Hildy nods.

"Olive and I—we saw the old woman night before last. Wandering, confused, lost. Nearly got hit by the train, but I pulled her back. We wanted to get help, but she was determined to go a path that made sense to her. Now Olive tells me she's dead. We have to talk to the sheriff—"

Olive rushes over, throws her arms around Clarence's waist, but looks at Hildy and Tom. Her eyes are desperate, pleading. "Please. Tell him he can't tell Lily that we saw the old woman. Please. Word will get out and if they know we . . . we've been . . . that we're—they'll lynch him."

CHAPTER 19

⋙

LILY

Thursday, September 23—9:00 p.m.

"'The golden-rod is yellow; The corn is turning brown; The trees in . . .'" Micah falters, trying to remember the rest of the rhyme. He stares up at his mama, eyes widening. His lips quiver, and he pulls his cheery red-and-blue quilt up to his nose.

Lily is bone weary as the mantel clock downstairs chimes nine in the evening. She blinks her bleary, gritty eyes. Rubbing them will show her son she's tired, and she wants him to feel how much she cherishes him. She dismisses the temptation to finish the old-timey rhyme for him, forces an encouraging smile, and says, "Hmmm. Something about applesauce?"

Micah pulls the quilt down, sputters excitedly, "And . . . 'trees in apple orchards; With fruit are bending down'!"

Lily laughs. "That's right! You've got it!" She scoops her son into a big hug, her heart softening at his little head cradling against her chest. She closes her eyes. She could fall asleep like this, right here. But more tasks await—chores, mainly, to make the next day easier. She hopes she'll get that search warrant for the Hollows Asylum tomorrow, which will mean needing her mother's help again. And poor Mama was so worn out from a day with all the children, Lily had sent her and Caleb Jr. home right after dinner.

Micah wiggles loose, but not fully free of Lily's embrace. He stares up at her. Those big brown eyes, like Daniel's. The tiny freckled nose, like hers. "Mamaw taught me that, on our walk to Mrs. Gottschalk's." Micah, who has lost his first baby tooth, lisps from the gap, especially over the difficult name.

Lily lifts her eyebrows. "Really. You all walked all the way out there?"

Micah nods. "Mamaw said we should see the area where she grew up. Across the road from where Daddy grew up." A shadow crosses his little face. "Someone else lives there now."

A lump rises in Lily's throat. She nods.

"I think Mamaw wanted to visit her friend. She said someone said Mrs. Gottschalk's house was for sale."

Lily does a double take. "Was it?"

Micah shrugs. "I dunno. I just know Mrs. Gottschalk is grumpier than Mamaw and her sugar cookies aren't as good, but I liked her goats and running around outside."

"You know we have to move from here in a few months, right, sweetie? Maybe where we live next will be a place we can have animals outside."

They have to move whether she wins or loses the election. Such a big choice looming.

Micah's face lights up again. "We could get Mrs. Gottschalk's place! Couldn't we?"

Moving to the farm on the hairpin curve of Kinship Road? The farm where grows the Kinship Tree, right by the river? The farm so close to the spots where she'd first met Daniel and fell in love with him . . .

Truth be told, Lily had neglected checking in on Widow Gottschalk, too, though Daniel would have been disappointed, as if such neglect could ease her heart. *Oh, Lily,* she recollects him saying a few years back, when she chastised him for working too much, *this job requires hardness—but that ain't the same as hard-heartedness.*

"Mama?" Micah says the word like a soft chirp.

Lily clears her throat. "I'm fine, baby boy. Now, prayers."

Obediently, he bows his head and prays as she'd taught him—her own variation of a traditional prayer. "Now I lay me down to sleep, I pray thee, Lord, my soul to keep, and when I with the sun arise, I pray to know thy love so wise." A few minutes later, satisfied both children are settled, Lily treads carefully down the stairs, intending to finally make the damned pie for entering in the county fair contest. As Mama keeps reminding her, she might be running for sheriff in her own right, but townsfolk will want to know that she hasn't wandered too far astray from feminine interests. Especially those unsure about whether to vote for her.

So as Lily crosses the parlor, she considers the important question of the moment: Does she have enough lard in the icebox for the crust?

She stops mid-way, her gaze caught by new mail on her desk.

Oh God. The reply she'd written to Benjamin Russo the night before—when she'd been tired and weary. She rushes to the desk, thinking she should toss it in the fireplace, on the remaining embers from the fire earlier tonight.

Her envelope is right beside the new mail. Had Mama seen it? Face burning, Lily picks up the letter, turns toward the fireplace—then jumps at a knock at the front door. Quickly, she stuffs the letter into the rolltop, shoves it closed, and hurries to the door.

Seth Goodwin, the reporter from the *Kinship Daily Courier,* steps in without being asked, rushing into the parlor. Even in the dim parlor light, she sees he shakes so hard that the old sheaf of newspapers he holds jitters loudly.

"Oh God, Lily. This isn't the sort of town history they taught us in school. I found the old articles. About Hildy's grandfather and great-uncle. That is, about Thea Kincaide's father. And uncle."

Seth holds the rattling stack out to her.

Kinship Weekly Courier

LOCAL QUAKER MAN DISCOVERED DEAD, BY HIS OWN DAUGHTER—QUESTIONS ABOUND

September 28, 1857
By: Edwin Clarke

A week has passed since Thea Kincaide's horrific discovery of her father, Rupert Edward Kincaide, hanging from a noose affixed to a tree atop the Moonvale Hollow Tunnel, built three years ago by the B&R Railroad upon land owned in Moonvale Hollow Village by Adam Dyer.

It is unknown why Thea, seven years old, was out on her own at 10:00 p.m., the time that Mr. Dyer and his wife, Joyce, reported to Bronwyn County Sheriff Thomas Langmore that Thea arrived at the Dyer farm atop a hill near the rather peculiar and certainly remote village.

The couple averred that the child either was unable or refused to speak, but they followed the distraught lass down the hill from their home on a shortcut to the tunnel, and quickly understood her being struck mute, as Thea pointed to a figure hanging from the tree. Several men from the village retrieved the body of Mr. Kincaide, known in the area for his outspoken views on abolition. He was a faithful member of the Stanehart Hollow Friends Assembly, in the tiny farming settlement of Stanehart Hollow, north of the Kinship River and of Athens.

Sheriff Langmore and a posse of his deputies found an escaped slave, who would only say his name was John, hiding in the woods near the Stanehart Hollow Friends Meeting House. Members of the Friends Assembly have refuted any familiarity with John or with Mr. Rupert Kincaide's alleged activities in defying the Fugitive Slave Law of 1850, which criminalizes assisting runaway slaves rather than returning them to their owners.

However, Mr. Rupert Kincaide's brother, Claude Kincaide, who many know as the proprietor of the Kinship blacksmith shop, was beside himself with anguish upon learning of his brother's death, in spite of their disagreements over Rupert's alleged activities.

"I always knew that Rupert would get hisself hurt or killed by one of them," Claude declared when this reporter called upon him. "Let this be a warning to anyone who is as foolish and naive as he was."

Shortly following Thea Kincaide's reportage of her father's death, slave bounty hunters discovered the escaped slave in the hills near Moonvale Hollow Village hiding under a makeshift shelter of tree limbs in a creek bed that runs alongside the B&R Railroad line.

Sheriff Langmore has avowed that from wounds, including injuries to the head as if from rocks or another heavy object, he can assuredly infer that Mr. Rupert Kincaide had been beaten before his hanging. Though John vehemently denies any role in Mr. Kincaide's death, he refuses further testimony as to events that led to his hiding in the creek bed. Furthermore, on the escaped slave's person has been found a compass, bearing the initials *R.E.K.*, which Mr. Kincaide's widow and daughter affirm belonged to the deceased. The sheriff is thus currently holding the escaped slave John in the Bronwyn County jail in Kinship, but has hired able-bodied guards on duty around the clock, as many men of the region have called for the immediate death of John.

"Rule of law shall prevail," avers Sheriff Langmore, "and we are still in the business of interrogating possible witnesses as to events leading up to Mr. Kincaide's death. Our prisoner will either be returned to his owner, or face swift justice here, depending on what we find."

At this time, services for Rupert Kincaide will be held at the Stanehart Hollow Friends Meeting House in a private funeral and burial. Thea Kincaide is now reunited with her mother, Mrs. Cleo Kincaide, on their farm near Stanehart Hollow.

Kinship Weekly Courier

COURTROOM PACKED FOR DRAMATIC TESTIMONY IN BRUTAL MURDER

October 8, 1857

By: Edwin Clarke

The Bronwyn County Courthouse was suffocatingly packed with those wishing to bear grim witness to the proceedings of October 6, forcing Judge Winchester to repeatedly thunder his gavel upon his bench to bring the disorderly crowd to order in the trial of an escaped slave accused of murdering outspoken abolitionist Rupert Edward Kincaide, who was allegedly easing him north via the so-called Underground Railroad.

Many were outraged that the slave escaped to Ohio from South Carolina should be given a trial at all, what's more one equal to that of a Caucasian man; however, Judge Winchester issued a stern reminder of Ohio's Personal Liberty Laws, designed to protect slaves escaped from states south of the Ohio River, and to in some cases counteract the Fugitive Slave Laws set forth by the federal government, providing Afro-Americans some of the same protections under the Constitution, including the right to a fair trial.

Also packing the courtroom were many members of the Stanehart Hollow Friends Assembly, of which Rupert Kincaide was an active member until his death by hanging from the Moonvale Hollow Tunnel, on the B&R Railroad line, just outside of Moonvale Hollow Village.

Nevertheless, silence fell like a shroud over the room as Thea Kincaide, age 7, gave her testimony, her voice a quivering chirp, yet heard clearly throughout the room.

"Pa and me were taking hams and Mama's canned green beans to a family in need," the child stated. "Then we were beset by him."

Though quivering, Thea pointed distinctly at John. The courtroom erupted—as did John, who cried out his innocence, wailing, "No, no, no!" After John was taken away, Thea sobbed out the rest of her testimony, that she ran for help up Stanehart Hollow Road, and then became disoriented, wandering the region for hours, before finally finding her way to Moonvale Hollow Village, and the horrific sight of her father's corpse hanging from the tunnel.

The child was returned to the bosom of her mother, who then passed her to the care of one of the women from the Friends Assembly.

Upon taking the stand, Mrs. Rupert (Cleo) Kincaide affirmed that the child knew the way to Moonvale Hollow Village, for she had taken the child with her on regular visits to the farm of Mr. and Mrs. Adam Dyer in order to do light housework, laundry, and mending for the family, as well as other villagers, for extra money, since her husband had fallen upon hard times on his own farm, distracted, she said, "by his well-meaning but ill-conceived beliefs as an abolitionist." Upon making this statement, she too fell into a fit of sobs, but recovered sufficiently to testify that she had been bedridden on the evening of her husband's murder, due to women's troubles, and did not know that the child Thea had hidden away on her father's wagon.

After this emotional afternoon of testimony, Judge Winchester adjourned for the day. It is not known if the jury will hear additional testimony.

Kinship Weekly Courier

MURDERER HANGED TO DEATH IN KINSHIP TOWN SQUARE

October 20, 1857
By: Edwin Clarke

Though a chill wind swept through Kinship on the afternoon of October the 19th, stripping the trees along Main Street and on sleepy side streets alike of their golden autumnal splendor, the sky was a bright sapphire blue, reflecting none of the mostly somber—though in a few pockets celebratory—crowd that jam-packed the town square.

The makeshift gallows, constructed over the past three days, was situated in front of the Kinship Inn. Armed guards, in the county sheriff's employ, kept the crowd a distance of several yards from the gallows platform.

Sheriff Langmore, wearing a suit fit for a funeral, came out first onto the gallows and asked if anyone would care to speak for the escaped slave John, found guilty of aggravated murder. Several men hooted at the notion, until the sheriff warned that there should be only silence, lest any merrymakers wished to spend a week in the county jail on charges of public disturbance.

A silence then fell over the crowd of mostly males, though some women were in attendance, and even children. From the silent crowd then emerged a Quaker woman, who refused help up the steep steps, relying on only her cane to aid her assent onto the gallows platform. Though her visage was frail, her voice was firm and resolute.

She introduced herself as Charity Claymore, and said the following, which your reporter faithfully transcribed: "In our assembly we sit in silence, awaiting the voice of God to move within us, and it is with rarity that we share His words. Today"—and here her voice broke, trembling, so that even the hardest men lost some of their bloodthirsty expressions—"I am so moved to aver that John, though deemed a lesser man on earth for the hue of his skin and decried as a killer despite his protestations, is a child of God, and as such, the spirit of God is within him, and the spirit of God"—and here her voice rose as strong as a sword thrust heavenward—"has no color, but burns brightly and purely, and it is to this spirit I commend the spirit of John!"

Murmurings of protest against what many in the crowd would decree as religious heresy began to arise until a walloping shout from Sheriff Langmore silenced the crowd.

Then John, arms cuffed behind him, was brought up onto the gallows, and the sheriff, as executioner for his county by the law of the great state of Ohio, fitted first a burlap bag and then a noose over John's head, and with another rope bound his ankles. John himself said nothing, nor showed any expression, so quiet and still that one might think his spirit had already left his body.

Though the sheriff, who has the right to choose the means of execution, elected death by hanging as it is considered the most humane and quickest means, he nevertheless was pale and trembling, only steadying once he had the lever in his grasp. Then he closed his own eyes, and without further warning to the crowd, pulled.

Some in the crowd gasped, and a few—who had undoubtedly wasted no tears over John's fate prior to execution day— wailed, though most remained quiet at the specter of death overtaking John's body, within minutes of the fateful pull of the lever.

Though my reporting has been as humanly impartial as possible, I add on a personal note that I hope to never again bear witness to any execution—and I daresay that many in the crowd, even those who started out the most enthusiastic, would share the same opinion.

CHAPTER 20

※

LILY

Sunday, September 26—10:00 a.m.

Sunday morning, Lily parks her automobile down the hill and walks up to the Stanehart Hollow Friends Meeting House. She's dressed in her Sunday-go-to-meeting best, a crisply ironed navy blue dress, and her brown jacket. First frost has nipped the morning air, a brisk forewarning of fall that's singed the roadside clover and bowed the black-eyed Susans. Some trees have turned from green to crimson and golden and orange, bold against a pensively pale blue sky. All these changes in just four days since Lily and Marvena had emerged at the behest of Sadie's nose from the woods across from the meeting house.

Now Lily can't help but smile. What a sight they must have been to Anna Faye, the Quaker woman who'd seen them as she came around the corner.

Lily looks for her among the people walking to the Friends meeting house. As she moves toward the worshipers, Lily realizes that she's overdressed. The men and women are in plain clothes—some traditional Quaker garb, others not—that they would wear to work in their fields or kitchens. No one speaks as they go up the stone steps and enter the meeting house, though some folks give her a silent, welcoming nod.

Inside, Lily sits in the last row of pews. Everyone else moves up to the front, sitting as close together as possible. To her surprise, the men and women do not separate, as is still the custom at the Presbyterian church she occasionally attends. Here, family groups stay together.

Lily searches for a placard listing hymn numbers, for hymnals and Bibles tucked in the pew racks, for a pulpit from which a pastor will speak—but none of these items are to be found here. Where are the instructions, the order of worship, about what she is supposed to do?

A woman several rows up turns and looks back at Lily. It's Anna Faye. She dips her head, a gesture inviting Lily to come up and sit with her family, but Lily stays put, waiting for the meeting to begin.

No one stands or speaks. Entering in silence was the start of service, Lily realizes. The only sounds are the rustle of clothes on wooden pews, of children fussing, but as mothers reprimand only by pulling them close even the children soon quiet.

This is it, then. The congregants are simply going to sit in silence. As people bow their heads, or lean forward, or tilt their heads back—howsoever they're moved—the silence strengthens with a somber yet beguiling quality, binding the congregants.

To Lily, the silence is unsettling. Itchiness overtakes her skin, making her all too aware of the cloth of her dress, of the tight lacings of her boots. Itchiness claws her, nearly spurring her to spring to her feet, run out the door just behind her.

Her mind jumps to the tasks awaiting her at home, even on a Sunday. The past two days had been exhausting. The overnight guard had quit. One of the commissioners strongly suggested she hire his nineteen-year-old nephew, and in desperation she'd agreed—though she hoped the scrawny lad wouldn't shoot his foot off if one of the prisoners whispered, *Boo.* She had gone to the judge's house to ask him if he thought she might get the Hollows Asylum search warrant Monday morning—and backed off when he told her she'd be lucky to get it at all if she didn't leave him alone over the weekend.

Now here she sits, pinned in place by the great demanding silence suffusing every breath she takes. What is she to do? Listen, as her own pastor admonishes from the pulpit, for the still small voice of God?

All right, then. Listen. Inhale. Exhale.

"Oh!" someone cries out. It is a young woman from the front pew, standing up. "Oh, oh, oh!" Tears prick Lily's eyes—the moans of loss could be her own. A man leaps to the side of the young woman and puts his arms around her. Probably her husband.

Silence rides the rhythm of the woman's sorrowful "ohs!" until an old man, sitting next to Anna Faye rises gingerly. His words are strong: "Find the wisdom in your grief."

A surge of anger writhes forth in Lily. *What nonsense! How can grief provide any wisdom—other than the knowledge that life is more often cruel than not. This life, this world where a child like Thea discovers her own father hanging from the Moonvale Hollow Tunnel.*

Where an escaped slave—identified only by the young Thea—would be condemned for her father's death.

Where the sheriff—back then both lawman and executioner—must pull the lever to execute the man.

Where years later elderly Thea would wander from the asylum, past where once she and her family worshiped, searching for God only knows what or who, only to die brutally, falling onto the train from the top of the same tunnel from which her father was hung from a tree.

Where is the wisdom in any of this grief?

From the silence, this knowledge strikes Lily: her grief over Daniel, which she has tried to sublimate by working each day until exhaustion slays her each night, has shaped her every thought, like a hand rising from a grave to squeeze her heart, barely allowing it to keep beating.

Suddenly service is over. Worshipers stir from silence to shake one another's hands. Some folks come back to Lily, and though she contemplates leaving, waiting for Anna Faye outside the meeting house, soon she's caught up in the simple, warm welcome of hand grasping hand, a shake, a smile, a nod.

Next people take turns speaking—announcements about the fall picnic immediately following the meeting, about a family in need of food and prayers, an elderly person passing on, a baby born. The individual details of life and death, and the demands they make for community succor and support.

The announcements blend into one another until another silence falls.

"Are there any other announcements?" asks the elderly man.

Lily feels herself rising from her pew, as if she's being lifted. She clears her throat. The congregants all look at her, their gazes asking why has she stood? Lily herself isn't sure. She'd come here intending to speak to just Anna Faye, but something compels her to speak to the congregation as a whole. "I am Lily Ross, the sheriff from Bronwyn County. I came by here with a deputy and a hound four days ago, tracking a woman who died, likely at another person's hand, over in Moonvale Hollow."

Murmurs and worried glances stir the small gathering as Lily continues. "I have since learned the identity of the woman—Thea Kincaide. This name might be familiar to some of you. Her father, Rupert Kincaide, was a founding member of this Friends group. He was found—" Lily notes a young girl, about Jolene's age, staring at her wide-eyed over the back of a pew. Lily chooses her words thoughtfully. "Thea found him in the same place. Of late, Thea was a resident at the Hollows Asylum."

A murmur rises in the crowd at that, and nervous glances exchange.

Lily clears her throat. "Something compelled her to escape from the asylum. I believe she was retracing her steps from that night, probably along a trail he used as part of the Underground Railroad years ago. She was also at a site where I believe a local group had gathered—the Women's Ku Klux Klan."

Murmurs crescendo into alarmed gasps.

"Surely you of all people must know how dangerous such a group could become, especially as not far from here good people are working to integrate the mines in Rossville. I beg of you, if any of you know anything about Thea Kincaide—or her father—that might help me find out what happened to her, please, come speak to me."

As if all the energy had been gut-punched out of her, Lily sinks back down to the pew. People file past her, some pausing to give her a worried look or a handshake, but many looking away as if she is not there.

She's failed. By making such a dramatic announcement, instead of stealthily speaking with Anna Faye and others one on one, she's done nothing more than scare these good people. Or rile them up. After all, Daisy Douglas Barr is an Indiana Quaker who speaks on behalf of the WKKK around the country.

A hand alights gently on her shoulder, and she looks up. It is the elderly man who had spoken during the meeting. *Find the wisdom in your grief.*

"My name is Harold Claymore. Anna Faye is my granddaughter. She told me about your visit a few days ago. May I sit with you?"

Lily smiles, the tension and anger in her heart slowly easing. "Of course."

He sits down next to her, and he's short enough that his feet dangle over the edge of the pew like he's a small child. Harold smiles up at her, the lines in his grizzled jaws deepening. "Born up the hill, grew up here, and never left—except to fight in the War Between the States."

Lily's eyebrows rise and he laughs. "Yes, I'm that old. Eighty-five, next month." Harold coughs deeply, his chest rattling. "If'n I make it, that is."

"I was reacting more to your fighting. You being a Quaker and all."

"I rebelled. Turned my back on the faith. After I came back, my parents took me back in. So did the meeting house."

"Claymore—I just read in an old news article about a Charity Claymore, who spoke out against the execution of the man accused of killing Rupert Kincaide."

"My dear grandmother." He tears up. "Our community was nearly destroyed by those awful events. That's one reason I left—disgusted by some in our community refusing to help on the Underground Railroad. When I returned, my grandmother in her final years helped me back to a semblance of peace. She taught me that forgiveness is a cornerstone of peace, and peace is the cornerstone of faith. I visited a good friend of mine, over at that asylum. He'd lost his leg, but more than that, he lost his mind. There's a special plot there, for Union soldiers who lived out their time there. And one Confederate—captured during Morgan's Raid."

Lily nods. In high school, she'd learned about the 1863 panic when it seemed that Confederates, led by a Rebel general named Morgan, would overrun Ohio. The campaign faltered.

"Met that Confederate fella—would have shot him dead, gladly, in the war, but seeing him all hollowed out with terror like he was? Well. I couldn't hold anything but pity for him."

Is that what this old man meant by *find the wisdom in your grief*? In sorrow for his friend's inner torment—and in, Lily reckons, trying to overcome his own—had he found empathy for his enemy?

Lily's heart shellacs over at the notion. She is not ready to let go of her distrust and dislike for some people, such as George Vogel.

Harold smiles gently. "You're not here to listen to an old man's war stories, are you?"

"Papaw?" Anna Faye approaches them. She looks with concern at her grandfather. "We're having our fall picnic. Perhaps you and Sheriff Ross could join us."

"I'm fine, baby girl. Could use some lemonade to wet my whistle, though."

Anna Faye looks skeptical but wanders outside. Two men—one of them her husband—remain standing near the pew, well within earshot. What are they afraid of Harold revealing?

Lily looks back at Harold. "I'd love to listen to all your stories. But I'm interested particularly in anything you—or anyone else—can tell me about Thea Kincaide? Or her father?"

"We lived on the farm next to the Kincaides. Helped Mr. Kincaide out from time to time. He had the one daughter—Thea. I didn't take much interest in Thea. She was a little girl, and I was sixteen. I do recollect this—after her father died, my whole family went to call on her and her mother. They needed all the help they could get. Rupert's own brother wouldn't do anything for them, and the mother, Cleo, refused any of our help."

"Why?"

"I think she was out of her mind with grief. Let it make her hard." Harold stares at Lily with such intensity, even with his fading pale blue eyes, that she looks away. Is her own hardness all that obvious? "Said she didn't want anything more to do with the Friends. Ran the farm on her own as best she could for a bit, then went to work over in Moonvale Hollow."

Lily looks at Harold, stunned. "Where her own husband had died so brutally?"

Harold nods. "She'd been doing laundry and mending for the Dyers for several years before that, to bring in extra money. It seems Rupert wasn't a particularly successful farmer. He was too keen on his books and studies, and didn't stick well to a farm schedule. My own father was always trying to help him, but he'd come home shaking his head, saying Rupert would have been better off sticking to his books and being a teacher. Pa would say—"

One of the men standing nearby clears his throat, and Harold stops. Lily gives him a sympathetic smile. No disrespectful talk of past members.

"Well, anyhow," Harold says, "Mrs. Dyer was always sickly. Must'a been a blessing to the Dyers when Cleo and Thea went to work full-time for them—cooking, housekeeping. 'Specially after Mrs. Dyer was blessed with a baby, late in life, their only child. Murphy Dyer."

Lily turns this over—*Murphy. Perry Dyer's father.* Something pings at the back of her mind, about the dates she'd read but not fully noted when she and Marvena had been at the Dyer cemetery. Something feels off to her.

"The girl, Thea, and her mother lived there. Mrs. Dyer was still sickly after she had Murphy. Not long after Mrs. Dyer died, Thea's mother, Cleo, married Mr. Dyer. Reared Murphy as her own."

Lily shudders. *Poor Thea—she'd grown up on that farm, then. And Murphy—Perry Dyer's father—would have been a young stepbrother to Thea.* It's believable that Perry never met his stepaunt, Thea, but wouldn't Murphy have mentioned having an older stepsister? Is that why she was returning there, after she escaped from the asylum? Had she gone to the top of that tunnel, hoping to save her poor father from his terrible fate? Perhaps she'd grown up shuttering away the memories of finding him like that, of the courtroom scene, of seeing the tunnel from time to time as she grew up in that hollow, and then, in old age, the barriers she'd put up broke down, and it all came back in a terrible flood.

Anna Faye comes back into the meeting hall with a glass of lemonade and gives it to her grandpa. He takes a long drink, smacks his lips. "That's good." He regards Lily. "You look a mite peckish, young lady. Come have supper with us."

Lily smiles. "That's right kind of you. But I have plenty to attend to—"

"On the Lord's day? It's meant for rest and reflection," Anna Faye says.

Lily looks at her, sees that she means no harm with the admonition, and yet, before she can catch them back, the words fly from her mouth: "The law knows no rest."

Shame rises in Lily as redness dots Anna Faye's cheeks. Lily looks back at Harold. "I think Thea was retracing a path she learned from her father. Do you know—or are there any records—of the paths he'd have taken? Anything I can learn about her last moments might help."

Harold starts to speak, but Anna Faye's husband steps toward them. "There were no records of routes on the Underground Tunnel. No proof except hearsay that this assembly was involved. If you'd like to join us for supper—fried chicken and potato salad—"

Lily shakes her head. "Thank you, though."

Harold hands his glass back to Anna Faye and rises wobbly to his feet, leans on his cane. He shoots a harsh look at the two men hovering nearby, then looks back at Lily. "No hushing up an old man," he says. "I don't know what paths Rupert may have taken. More'n likely, that knowledge is lost for all time. But it sounds to me like the beasts of hatred and oppression are trying to rise again—so if you or anyone needs sanctuary here, rest assured it is yours."

Two hours later, Lily stands in the cemetery outside the old Dyer house, wishing she'd picnicked after all at the Stanehart Hollow Friends Meeting House. She's hungry and tired from her hike, retracing the mule path from the same spot where she'd left her automobile on the night of Thea's death, into the village, and then up this hill to the Dyer family plot.

Yet the hike, though making her tired and sweaty, had finally brought her the peaceful stillness that had so eluded her at the Friends' gathering. Now, even as she stares at the headstones, she savors the soft wind blowing over her, the damp smell of autumn, the rustle of the crimson and golden foliage. It's always been in nature that she could find a moment's respite from the ravages of sorrow and anger. A bird trills and Lily looks up at the hollowed-out tree on the cemetery's edge. *The nuthatch?*

She makes herself focus on the headstones, the mathematics of them summarizing birth, life, death of generations of Dyers.

Charles Dyer, d. 1826, age seventy.

Adam Dyer, "Beloved Founder of Moonvale Hollow Village," 1802–1888. Dead at eighty-six.

Joyce Dyer, "Beloved wife and mother," 1806–1858. Dead at fifty-two.

Murphy Dyer, "In Faith We Rise Again," 1857–1925. Dead at sixty-eight.

No headstone for Cleo Kincaide Dyer, Lily notes. Had she left Adam? Been buried elsewhere?

Lily refocuses on the existing headstones. Though the men had lived unusually long lives—and produced few children, and then at older ages—what bothers Lily about her calculations is that Joyce would have given birth to Murphy when she was fifty-one.

That hardly seems possible. Why, Mama had had Caleb Jr. when she was forty-one and she was considered old to have a child. A change-of-life baby, he'd been called.

Adam was old to father a child—fifty-five—but certainly siring a child could go on much longer than birthing a child. Lily supposes it would be possible that Joyce was really Murphy's mother—but she'd be more likely to believe it if Joyce had had other children, had been described as healthy. Harold Claymore had remembered her as often "sickly."

But what other explanation is there? More than likely, the oddities of the Dyer family's dates of births and deaths mean nothing. Still, Lily is glad she took the time to confirm the dates of the Dyer family's births and deaths, even if it means Mama will scold her for returning home sweaty and unkempt just before the Woman's Club meeting.

She turns, starts her trek back to her automobile.

For a moment, she thinks she sees him again—the silvery, silently laughing boy, merrily chasing his ball. Then she sees only trees and brush and shakes her head at her imagination that seems to go wild in Moonvale Hollow, even as she sorrowfully longs for just one more glimpse.

CHAPTER 21

⁂

HILDY

Sunday, September 26—10:00 a.m.

Hildy's legs tremble as she climbs the steep slope. *Soft town girl,* she chastises herself. She's determined not to fall too far behind. Even Olive—with her bowed shoulders and drooping head—is keeping up with Marvena, who is leading the trek.

A thorny limb snags at Hildy's sleeve, and she pulls free, tearing her blouse. She ducks under a low limb. She'd rushed out of Kinship, over to Rossville, with no coat or hat, and having no notion that she'd end up spending several nights in Marvena's scant cabin, or that this morning she'd serve as rear guard to Olive up the thorny spine of Devil's Backbone.

And yet, though she aches and shivers, peacefulness settles over like a cloak woven of bird chatter and skittering leaves, of deep scents of lichen and moss and earth, of sunlight teasing through the forest canopy. Her gaze is drawn to dollops of goldenrod in sunnier spots, and tiny white blooms of snakeroot. Each sighting stirs an unspoken delight, eases Hildy more and more, as if she is finally unspooling—and she hadn't even known, until now, how tightly wound she'd become. Maybe she's not such a soft town girl, after all.

Thursday night, after their shocking discovery, Tom had told Clarence to go back to Rossville, his lodgings where he'd be safer, away from white miners who oppose Clarence's cause to integrate the union—housing is segregated in the town, as it is in most mining towns. Olive had protested, begged Clarence to run away with her, but Clarence had refused. Tom had then told Hildy to take Olive up to Marvena's cabin. *Marvena will know what to do,* he said. Then he'd looked away from Hildy.

At Marvena's cabin, the only indication of surprise Marvena showed—both at Hildy driving Olive up to her cabin and at her hurried explanation of Olive and Clarence as a couple—was a slight lift of her left eyebrow. She showed more surprise—both eyebrows lifting, her lips tightening—when Hildy announced she would not be going back to Kinship.

Marvena had given her a long look, and in that gaze Hildy saw that Marvena had known all along about her and Tom. That Tom had confided in his sister. And that Marvena, though she might like Hildy all right, did not approve of Hildy as Tom's lover. *Weak tea,* she might say.

Hildy had squared her shoulders, kept her gaze steadily locked with Marvena's, until finally Marvena simply nodded. They'd had a supper of soup beans and corn pone—Olive barely eating, but Hildy surprising herself by finding the simple meal delicious. Olive poked at the beans, asking what was going to happen next, until Marvena snapped at her, *Stop sniveling!*

Then Hildy had played checkers with little Frankie, getting whipped at least half of the games. Goodness, that child was smart. After Frankie was to bed, Hildy had helped Marvena get out quilts for Hildy and Olive to sleep on the floor. Olive fell asleep quickly, occasionally moaning and muttering in her sleep in her part of the room, but Hildy remained wide awake.

When the cabin door creaked open, she'd gone stock-still, except for her heart thudding wildly. Hope surged at the notion that Tom had come to her? No—it was Jurgis. He'd tiptoed quietly through the cabin, back to Marvena. Floorboards creaked as he eased onto the straw mattress next to her. Their voices, soft and low, mingled and drifted across the room, but Hildy couldn't make out anything they said, and soon they fell silent.

On Friday morning, Jurgis was gone. To Olive's dismay, Marvena insisted that Hildy would need to substitute for Olive at the schoolhouse. Hildy and Frankie walked back down to Rossville, and though exhausted by the end of the day, Hildy found the time sped past and the work was thrilling. On Saturday, Hildy and Olive helped tight-lipped Marvena and Frankie—who merrily sang the day away, seemingly unaware of any tension—in the garden and with other chores. Hildy heard Jurgis come back again last night, and this morning Hildy awoke to Marvena putting out a breakfast of leftover corn pone and buttermilk and boiled coffee. Both Jurgis and Frankie were gone. As they ate, only Marvena spoke, saying, *Take care of your needs at the outhouse. We won't be stopping. I'll lead, and Hildy*—and here she gave Hildy a look that said, *Here's your chance to prove yourself worthy— Hildy, you'll be right behind Olive. Make sure she doesn't do some fool thing, like try to run off.*

A half hour later, here they are climbing, endlessly it seems.

Abruptly, Marvena turns westward, and they're on a ledge, earth falling away into an open holler. Below them, in the hollowed-out earth, over the patchwork of orange and red and yellow treetops, a hawk glides, then swoops down. For a long moment, Hildy stares, mesmerized, but Olive whimpers. Olive had come here from Boston to take the Rossville schoolteacher position. Was she thinking she'd find freedom from whatever strictures held her there? Hildy doesn't know; for all their time working together, they'd never had personal chats.

Now Hildy feels sorry for Olive, so fearful of heights—and no doubt of what the future holds. "You're fine," Hildy says. "Keep your eyes on Marvena's back. One step after another."

Around the slick, rocky rise, the earth flattens out again, giving them wide berth from the ledge, and they come upon a cave. Flat, flinty rock juts out over the opening, like a porch roof carved by God's hand.

Marvena turns, regards Hildy and Olive. "Not my usual meeting spot. This calls for something even more remote."

Then she enters the cave. Olive looks at Hildy, a pleading gaze. She's trembling. Hildy takes her arm, gently nudges her on in. "It will be fine." Hildy keeps her tone even, as if she knows what Marvena is up to, though she does not.

As they enter, the scant light of coal-oil lanterns shimmies against the cave walls. Tom, Jurgis, and Clarence are gathered around a small, crackling fire.

"Oh!" Olive breaks free from Hildy, runs to Clarence, and they embrace. Hildy thinks she should look away, give them a moment of privacy, but she's both enchanted by and jealous of their tenderness with each other. She looks at Tom, who pointedly stares away from her.

Jurgis kneels and stirs up the fire with a long stick, looks up at Marvena. "Frankie is settled in with Nana. They'll go to church this morning."

Finally, Tom looks up at Hildy, as if not looking at her has become unbearable. Tears spring to Hildy's eyes. He comes to her, takes his coat off and drapes it over Hildy's shoulders, and gently pulls her toward the fire. "No use catching your death of cold." As soon as he gets her there, he lets go, steps away.

Only then does Clarence finally relax into his embrace, close his eyes in relief.

Hildy knows she should look away, but she can't. She so longs for Tom to embrace her.

Marvena clears her throat. "Well. Here's how we all see it. If someone finds real love, they should cherish it." She gives Hildy a pointed look. *God,* Hildy thinks. She's been such a fool. Such a coward. Olive and Clarence—especially Clarence—are willing to risk their lives to be together, but Hildy has been afraid of a few raised eyebrows. Marvena turns that same look on Tom. He stares down into the fire. Marvena takes Jurgis's hand. "We've learned the hard way how quickly such love can be ripped asunder—how rare it is to find it again."

Jurgis nods. "Plenty don't see it that way, though."

"Who all knows?" Tom asks.

"We've kept it well hidden," Olive says.

Tom lifts his eyebrows. "You sure? Me and Hildy found you feet from the schoolhouse."

Olive looks at Hildy. "She told me about the old woman who died at the Moonvale Tunnel. I panicked, ran to find Clarence; I wasn't thinking—"

"Luckily," Clarence says, "I was already near the schoolhouse, at our meeting spot. Usually we're quiet, then head further away. To an old hunting shack Hildy told Olive about."

Hildy reddens as everyone looks at her. "It was my daddy's. Same general area as Moonvale."

"You knew about them, kept your tongue?" Marvena asks. To Hildy's relief, respect, rather than irritation, fills Marvena's question.

Hildy nods.

"All right." Jurgis's voice is taut as he looks at Olive. "Why did you panic over Hildy telling you about the woman?"

Olive looks at Clarence. Both seem reluctant to answer.

"She is my cousin," Hildy blurts into the growing silence. She shifts awkwardly from foot to foot. "I found out four days ago. Lily tracked her to the Hollows."

"Huh," Marvena says. "After I picked her up at the Hollows, Lily said nothin' about the woman's identity."

A frisson of pleasure—Lily didn't tell Marvena everything! But this is not the time for petty childishness. "The woman's name is Thea Kincaide. She and my mother are first cousins. My mother was listed as next of kin on the asylum's paperwork, but Mother swears she has had no contact with Thea for years. The last time they'd have seen each other was at my grandfather's funeral. I was just a child. It's possible she was coming to see my mother—"

"Is your mother's name Garnet?" Olive asks.

Hildy shakes her head.

"She kept calling me that. And called Clarence 'John.'"

"She was old, and confused. We wanted to get her to help." Clarence's voice, mournful, breaks on the words. "Tried to nudge her toward the village. I was going to wait in the woods, and Olive was going to take her to a house."

"Leave her there, like an abandoned baby?" Marvena snaps.

Clarence turns to her, his look pleading for understanding. "We couldn't . . . be seen."

"Well, course not! And now you've put integration in the union in jeopardy. It's one thing, men of all sorts working together, but quite another—"

"Marvena!" Tom uses his sister's name as admonishment. "Love is no respecter of boundaries." He casts a glance at Hildy, and for a moment her heart jumps. She sees the sorrowful look to his eyes. He does not believe in her. Does not believe she is strong enough. He looks back at Marvena. "Anyway, it's no use going on at them now. We have to figure out what to do."

"You didn't get the old woman—Thea—to a house in Moonvale," Jurgis says.

"No. She was determined to go her own way, so we followed her. Hoped maybe she knew where she was going. Then we came upon—" Clarence stops, shakes his head.

"It was awful. A group in hoods and capes, taking an oath," Olive says. "Maybe fifteen or twenty women, but in that garb—it felt like a mob of a hundred. Anyway, we couldn't be seen by the Klan. The woman ran to them. So we ran the other way. We didn't have a choice!" She starts crying, puts her head to Clarence's chest.

"We did." Clarence looks shot through with guilt. "We should have gotten someone."

Hildy looks to the others. Tom and Jurgis look bewildered, too.

Not Marvena. Her face has hardened, as unyielding as the cold stone around and over them. "Olive is right. You did the right thing." She takes a deep breath, exhales slowly. Hunkers down to the fire and holds her hands over the flames, as if beset by a deep coldness. "Lily and me, we traced Thea to the old Dyer farm. We found boot prints, from women's boots. Inside the house, a hood, like Olive described. The WKKK. That's Lily's supposition, anyhow."

"That's why I panicked—Hildy told me that Margaret Dyer had come by asking about me and Clarence. And said that she thinks Margaret might be the leader of the WKKK."

"Could be—given what Lily and Marvena found at the Dyer farm," Tom says. "Hildy—when did Margaret ask you about Olive and Clarence?"

"Three mornings ago. I think she was fishing for information—and any interest I might have in the group, which she probably sees as important for proper women," Hildy says. "See, there was an anonymous editorial for the WKKK that was going to run in the newspaper—but my sketch and piece on Thea, when we didn't know who she was, took its place."

"You learned all this on a social call?" Marvena asks.

"I was working in the grocery store, you see, when she came by. . . ." Hildy's voice trails and her hand goes to her mouth as Tom stares at her, hurt flickering across his face. *Oh God*. He'll think she's toying with him, that she never really meant to break off with Merle.

Marvena flicks her gaze back to Clarence and Olive. "You were right, to skedaddle out of there when she went to them. But what if she told them about you?"

Clarence shakes his head. "I don't think it was like that. She didn't seem shocked or upset to see us. We reminded her of people, probably from her past. And Hildy here just said the poor old woman was at the Hollows Asylum."

"For dementia," Hildy says quietly. "So yes, she probably thought you were someone else. And her father—my grandfather's brother—was an abolitionist. My grandfather . . ."—she pauses, giving Clarence an apologetic look—"was not." Clarence looks nonplussed. *Oh. That's what he would expect.* Hildy looks back at the fire. "Surely she wasn't going there because of wanting to attend such a meeting. And how would she have known of it anyway?"

"Overheard nurses talking about it at the asylum?" Olive suggests. "And people change. Not always for the better."

Hildy looks at Olive, irritated with her insinuation about Thea possibly wishing to join in such a hateful meeting—and a sense of defensiveness rises swiftly. "After Thea went to the house, where did the two of you go?"

Everyone goes silent. Hildy's face flames as she realizes what she's implied—the possibility that they might be lying, might have harmed Thea. No, surely not—but they'd have motive, wouldn't they? To keep Thea from telling the WKKK about them? They only have Clarence's and Olive's word that Thea broke from them and ran into the WKKK meeting at the old Dyer farm.

Jurgis clears his throat. "The both of you need to get out of town."

"No one else saw us," Olive says.

"Are you sure 'bout that?" Marvena asks. "That Margaret Dyer was asking Hildy about you two, after all."

"I'm not leaving. My work isn't done—" Clarence says.

"And my students. I can't abandon them—" Olive says.

"You have to go. For your own safety." Tom looks worried. "Olive back to Boston, Clarence to New York, maybe not at the same time, 'cause that'll look suspicious, but—"

"No!" Hildy's voice ratchets and ricochets around the cave. She squares her shoulders as everyone looks at her. "As deputy sheriff, I have to speak up on the side of the law. Lily will want to question you, about what you saw that night—"

"A bunch of people who'd like nothing more than to string us both up!" Olive cries.

"Well, as deputy sheriff also—" Marvena stops as everyone looks at her. She shrugs. "What? Lily needed to make tracking that poor old woman official." She gives Hildy a pointed look. "Nothing worth fussing over."

Hildy shrinks back. It is important, serving the law. Working for Lily. She can see in Marvena's face that she knows it, too.

"Anyway, I agree with Hildy," Marvena says. "Clarence can stay another few days. Jurgis and Tom—you can keep an eye on him, ears to the ground if there's trouble?"

Both of them nod.

"Olive, you're still sick with a fever, just like on Friday," Marvena says. "Staying at my place."

"My students—"

"I can keep teaching them." Again, Hildy surprises herself by speaking up. "I'm good at it—"

"She is," Tom says quietly.

Hildy looks at him, heart leaping. But he stares down at the fire, away from her.

"And I can listen, too. Let Marvena or Nana know if I hear of danger. I could stay with Marvena, too." Surely, as Tom comes to visit, he'll see how she can fit in. How serious she is.

Jurgis shakes his head. "Better you stay with me and Nana."

Hildy's heart falls as Tom and Marvena nod agreement.

"When will I get back to my schoolhouse?" Olive asks.

Clarence looks at her gently. "As soon as we know we're safe. You have to be prepared to leave if need be—"

"What about you?" Olive's voice is a strangled cry.

Clarence squares his shoulders. "I'll leave when I know whether or not Negro miners are welcome into the union. I will not let down the United Mine Workers."

"Enough yammering here. Someone has to go tell Lily about this." Marvena sighs. "An' I reckon that someone is me."

The men start from the cave. Hildy reaches for Tom, but he avoids her touch, refuses to look at her. "Your coat—" she starts.

"Keep it."

He strides out of the cave, and Hildy feels the pitying gazes of everyone else upon her. She wants to run after him, but pride stops her. No—more than that. Self-respect. She holds her head up, chin forward. Looks at Olive. "Well go on. I'll help you around the ledge again."

CHAPTER 22

LILY

Sunday, September 26—2:00 p.m.

Lily takes another sip of tea and keeps smiling, even as her eyelids droop, and a mousy woman, usually quiet at these gatherings, says hopefully, "What about a taffy pull? An appeal to nostalgia might be what we need. . . ."

Lily nearly laughs at the prim tone, and wishes Hildy were here to share a glance of amusement with—but neither Hildy nor her mother are here. No doubt Mrs. Cooper's chronic coughing fit—and her desire for Hildy to attend to her—kept them away.

"Oh, heavens, why don't we pretend we're our grandmothers and have a cakewalk, then!"

The rebuke comes from Margaret, who is hosting, for the first time, the Kinship Woman's Club meeting at her new house.

Lily gives Margaret a hard look. "Or instead, let's hear everyone's ideas and then discuss them."

The mousy woman who Margaret had chided gasps—probably both grateful, Lily reckons, for her defense and nervous about the repercussions with Margaret. This is the first time this afternoon that Lily has really looked at Margaret. Until now, she's avoided eye contact, not trusting herself to keep from lashing out—does Margaret know there's been a gathering of the WKKK at her husband's old family farm? That Thea Kincaide had trekked all the dark, difficult miles from the Hollows Asylum to the farm and been murdered not long after?

It seems a ridiculous question, seeing Margaret now, sitting properly on the edge of a Queen Anne wing chair, a seat that is too small for her statuesque frame and surely uncomfortable, chin in an imperious tilt, as if she herself is a queen. Since moving to Kinship, Margaret has gone to great effort to appear prim and proper, campaigning to become the newest member of this club, which normally takes years, and straining to live up to the gabled, overwrought beauty of this Victorian house—one of the finest in all of Kinship, built on top of the town's highest hill by an owner of one of the many iron excavating and furnace sites that once dotted the southwestern part of the county, before the businesses began dying out two decades ago, leaving only cold, crumbling stacks in the hillside. This house sat empty and neglected after the previous owner left the area, and the Dyers have returned it to its former glory. Now Kinship's reigning ladies—and those who aspire to such stature—are all too eager to cater to Margaret's whims. And Margaret is all too eager—even anxious—to deserve their regard.

"Very well," Margaret says primly. "Let's hear all of the ideas—however trivial."

A silence ensues, until a brave soul mentions the possibility of a raffle, which sets the more conservative members of the group to wondering if this is akin to gambling, and soon the rest of the conversation dissolves as exhaustion shuts Lily's eyes and ushers her thoughts into welcome downy fuzz.

A moment later, a loud clatter and warm tea spilling on her legs startle Lily awake. And standing before her, a young boy. He stares up at her from underneath shaggy, dark hair. He looks to be about seven, Jolene's age, holding up a toy wooden popgun, squinting his left eye as he focuses his aim on her, and Lily's mouth drops open in surprise—not at his gruesome pantomime, but because she recognizes in him the narrow forehead, the forward tilt to the ears, that his half siblings and father, Ralf Ranklin, share.

Ka-pow, pow, pow! he mouths silently, jerking the top of his wooden gun with each mute *pow,* as if his hand is jumping at the recoil.

Lily grabs his arm, causing him to drop his toy, and fixes a hard gaze on him.

And immediately regrets it as his eyes widen and tear up and she notes the bruising around his right eye. He might be the boy who'd attacked her daughter, who'd said awful things, but he was still just seven. And he'd learned such behavior somewhere.

"Lily! He didn't mean to run into you."

Lily looks up, startled that it's Margaret who's come to his defense. The Sunday afternoon gathering of the Kinship Woman's Club take in the confrontation between Lily and Margaret, twenty faces of Kinship society's top tier frozen into various expressions ranging from shock to bemusement to dismay, with one exception. Mama looks concerned.

"Come here, Junior," Margaret says.

Lily releases the boy's arm. He scoops up the toy, runs to Margaret, who puts a soothing arm around him. "Now, son, I told you to stay in the kitchen, help your mother." Her voice is gentle, kind. *Son?* It's a commonly enough used term, but the image of the three babies' grave markers flickers across Lily's thoughts, along with Ralf supposing that Margaret might be housing Missy and their son.

It seems Margaret is playing a dangerous game with the Ranklin family, and yet, seeing the tenderness on Margaret's expression as she regards the boy, Lily momentarily feels pity for Margaret.

As Junior runs out of the room, Lily notes her china cup and saucer upended at her feet. At least the dishes are not broken. She pulls her wet skirt away from her lap.

"Was our fundraising discussion boring you, Mrs. Ross?" asks Margaret, her voice coiling back to its customary haughtiness. "Or should I say *Sheriff* Ross? Perhaps a shooting contest would be more amenable."

Lily starts to remind Margaret of the protocol of politeness of Woman's Club meetings—even when already-exhausted guests are lulled to sleep by cookies and tea after a tedious presentation comparing Mary Robert Rinehart's *The Circular Staircase* to her newest thriller, *The Red Lamp,* and somehow making both sound dull, followed by a tiresome discussion of efforts to raise monies for a public library.

Mama, across the room, clears her throat—and Lily knows that sound is an admonishment to behave.

"I'm so sorry I made a mess." Lily looks at the women who had been talking before her embarrassing mishap, and adds, "And that I drifted off while you spoke. I've been exhausted of late—I'm sure all of you, denizens of our town, busy with many important works—can understand. And certainly fundraising for the library is important. A truly public library"—the ladies of the club maintain a private, members-only one but have been debating for years since the disappointment of not receiving Carnegie funding for a public one about how, or if, to get a public library—"would be a boon to our fine county. And perhaps even, in a few years—"

Mama coughs and gives a subtle shake of her head. Lily sighs. *Mama's right. Pushing for a mule-drawn or even automotive bookmobile so the whole county could be served would alienate the more conservative members of the club.*

"Who knows how the library might grow," Lily falters. "To address Margaret's suggestion—a shooting contest might not be the best idea, especially for a sleepyhead like me."

A few titters of laughter. She's regaining the women's sympathy. "Why don't you all come to the debate between myself and Mr. Dyer, and pass the bucket for funds?"

"Beg for money?" Margaret frowns. "At a political event?"

A few of the older women nod, pinch lipped, at the impropriety of the very notion.

"Oh, of course not," Mama says. "Lily and I were talking this morning about an idea—we're all baking to enter the county fair contest, and I'm sure we're making practice batches, so why not bring those items to offer, but without a set price?"

Lily forces her face to be still and not hint at the truth—they'd had no such discussion. In fact, they'd argued. Lily hadn't wanted to come here today at all. She'd rather be catching up on assorted domestic chores—not to mention the pie for the county fair baking contest.

When she'd returned home after the Quaker meeting this morning, Mama had been waiting for her, envelope in hand—another delivery from Seth Robertson. *Gossip column items you might find interest-*

ing was all he'd say, Mama had explained, showing her the envelope. Then she'd put it on the desk—Lily watching anxiously, fearful Mama might mention the letters between her and Benjamin. But Mama was on a tear, insisting, after Lily expressed weariness and a desire to skip the Woman's Club meeting, that she must attend, that she'd need the votes of the members. Now Lily forces herself to smile.

"It will be a great opportunity to raise awareness for a library, and why it's good for the whole community—and maybe get some of the men to provide funding." Mama turns her stern look to Margaret. "I'm sure, as the newest business owner here in Kinship, your dear Mr. Dyer would love to donate? Whether he becomes sheriff, or not?"

Attention turns back to Margaret, who flushes brightly and looks perplexed—how had this conversation turned on her? Lily presses back a smile—because Mama is not only one of the revered founding members of the Kinship Woman's Club. She is also a more adept politician than Lily or most elected officials.

As the conversation turns to the details of how to best execute Mama's plan, Lily murmurs to excuse herself from the parlor to go and blot some of the tea from her skirt.

In the kitchen, Lily spots Junior, now playing under the worktable in the center of the room, and Missy, standing at a pump sink, back to Lily, humming to herself while washing dishes from the luncheon the members of the Woman's Club had just enjoyed in the dining room.

"Kapow, pow, pow!" Junior yells.

"Junior, I told you to hush up! You're already in trouble for going out there!" Missy spins around, hissing her words, but stopping as she spots Lily.

Lily bites back a gasp. There is a fading yellow mark on her left cheek, but a shiny new bruise mars her right. Lily calculates: The marks on Junior are probably from Missy, and the older bruise on Missy from Ralf. But the new injury? That is too recent to be from Ralf. It must be from Margaret or Perry. Why is Missy staying here, if she's abused just as badly here as with Ralf? Or is there another explanation?

Missy is shocked at the sight of Lily. "Sheriff?" Terror shadows her expression. She looks like she wants to say more, but then her expression closes. The moment for sharing whatever Lily's appearance brought to mind has passed.

Lily smiles gently. Maybe she can coax it out of her. "I'm here for the Woman's Club. Spilled some tea." She picks up a dishrag and presses it against the damp spot on her skirt. Then she puts the rag aside and starts drying a just-washed plate with a clean towel.

"I don't need help." Missy's tone is prideful. "That's what Mrs. Dyer is paying me for."

"Truth be told," Lily says, "I'd rather be back here anyway than with that stuffy group."

A smile flits across Missy's lips, and a knowing look—she'll never be good enough for the ladies of the club, but if they're dull, who'd want to join them anyway. Then Missy frowns, not so easily taken in, and says, "Just go."

"I'd rather not," Lily says.

Missy shrugs, turns back to the dishes. "Suit yourself. I'm paid same either way."

"How's that? Room and board here? I'm guessing no real pay?"

The young woman scrubs at another plate so hard that Lily fears it might crack in Missy's hands. "Beats where I was."

Lily dries another dish. "Went to your place the other day, talked to Ralf."

Missy is quiet for a minute, but Lily can see the sudden tension in her shoulders, can almost feel her wanting to ask if Ralf had inquired about her.

"About your boy, there," Lily says. "Seems he got into it with my daughter. Said some awful things."

Missy glowers at the boy, now scooted way under the table, and Lily regrets her words. Though she's purposefully steering the conversation, she hopes she's not set the boy up for another backhanding.

"Didn't know that. Reckon he must have heard some of the points Mr. Dyer is planning on making 'bout you."

Lily's hands stop, mid-swipe on a plate.

"So—that son of a bitch have anything to say?" Missy asks.

"What?" *Oh—Missy means her husband, not Perry.* Lily takes a deep breath, resumes drying. *Fine.* Let Perry resort to such cruelty—throw

Daniel's death at her in the debate. It'll more'n likely backfire with as many women voters as it will resonate with some of the men.

Lily considers the boy hunkering under the table, swallows her wrath. "It's a nice enough day for late September. Maybe your young 'un could go work some steam off, outside?"

Missy gives Lily a long look. When Lily purses her lips to indicate their conversation is not going to proceed in the boy's presence, she sighs and says, "Go on outside, then, Junior. Mind you don't get too dirty, or wander far!"

The boy pops out from under the table and glares at Lily. She grins back at him. She reckons the boy has had a hard-enough time of late without being too fearful of the sheriff. Plus, Jolene had already bested him.

After the boy runs out and the back door slams shut, Lily says, "If you mean does Mr. Ranklin want you back, then yes. He did ask after you."

Missy looks pleased. "Well, tell him I ain't coming back. I have it good here. Helping Mrs. Dyer around the house, and with . . . other things."

"Like the gathering this past Tuesday night, up at the Dyer farm in Moonvale Hollow?"

Missy opens her mouth, about to respond, then stops. Catching herself.

Dammit. She'd pressed too soon. "Look, Missy, I know you're in a tough spot, but—"

Missy lets a handful of cutlery clatter loudly to the bottom of the sink. "What do you know of it? I come to you for help, an' all you can say is same as your husband said. Can't do nothing if I don't file formal complaints. Well, I do that, then what? Ralf goes off to prison and I'm stuck with my kid *and* his'n. Or he don't, and he comes back and it gets worse. Truth be told, he only married me 'cause he thought I was pretty, looked like his first wife when she was younger, and I only took up with him 'cause it seemed better'n, well, everything at home."

Lily's heart starts to go out to the young woman, but then Missy goes on. "An' now I'm saddled with a young 'un I can't shake off on Ralf. Might as well be a noose around my neck!"

At that, Lily's sympathy shuts off, like a spigot twisted tight. She clears her throat. *Focus.* "You're in a hard way, I know, but is working for Mrs. Dyer the best choice? I mean—" Lily leans toward Missy, as if they're conspirators. "I know about that gathering last Tuesday night. Now I have reason to believe a crime might have been committed there." Missy's eyes widen a mite, and her pallor blanches—indicators, by Lily's reckoning, that indeed she'd been at the gathering. With a bit more careful pressure—

A sharp rap comes at the back door, and they both jump.

Missy stomps to the door, making more of a racket than the knock had, muttering, "Dammit, Junior, I told you to stay hushed up—"

It's not Junior, coming back.

It's Marvena.

"Neighbor lady said I'd find you here." Marvena's face is taut. Sweaty too. God, she'd walked the whole way here from her place on Devil's Backbone. Marvena wouldn't have made the trek to Kinship for less than urgent purpose. The last time she'd done so was to seek Daniel—not yet knowing he was murdered—and ask for his help in tracking her older daughter. Immediately, Lily's heart races, as her thoughts go to Marvena's brother, Tom, to Jurgis and his mother, Nana, to Tom's son, Alistair, and Marvena's daughter Frankie. They've all woven themselves into the fabric of her life. Her family.

Missy's eyes cut to Marvena, as she listens with intense curiosity.

"Very well," Lily says as primly as possible. "How may I help you?"

"Need to talk," Marvena says.

Lily turns to Missy. "Please give my apologies. I need to return to my home."

With that, Lily folds her dish towel neatly and hands it to Missy, then steps out with Marvena. They start walking, neither one speaking, each knowing by instinct that whatever has to be said and heard best unfold in the privacy of Lily's house.

Fifteen minutes later, Lily and Marvena sit in Lily's kitchen at the worktable. Lily has taken a moment to pour them each a glass of lemonade. Lily says, "Have you heard something about the women's Klan gathering, among your people?"

Marvena lifts her eyebrows. "Among my people? *My* people are working with Clarence to integrate the union in Rossville. I found you at the home of one of *your* people, a well-to-do woman whose old house was the stomping ground for that gathering. You reckon just 'cause *my* people are ill-paid coal miners—"

"Dammit, stop, Marvena! Hate takes up lodging wherever it's welcomed—and don't give a rat's ass whether the door that opens to it is plain or fancy." Lily takes a sip of the lemonade, grimaces at the taste. A mite bitter. The lemons had been old, and she's running low on sugar. "Now, I reckon you didn't track me down for less than urgent purpose, and right at the moment I can't think of anything more urgent than the fact we have a Klan presence in our county, and a dead woman who spent at least some of her final moments on earth at their gathering. Can you?"

Marvena looks at her steadily. "Yes. You seen Hildy of late?"

Lily shakes her head slowly, her blood running cold, a frisson of fear for her friend.

"That's 'cause she's with me. Came yesterday, partly to confront Tom. Well, to ask him to have her back, more like it. They've had a dalliance, for a time now. Hildy's been wanting to break it off with Merle, but keeps losing heart. Seems to think you and your mama—not to mention her own—will think less of her, taking up with the likes of my brother. Tom finally came to think maybe Hildy herself feels that way, so he broke off with her several nights ago."

Lily sets her glass down, hard. Lemonade sloshes to the table. The tiny kitchen feels burdensome, suffocating. All at once, she's shaky, yet feels as thuddingly heavy as stone.

Marvena clears her throat. "Way you're acting, I reckon Hildy was right about how you'd feel. Guess we hill folks is good if'n you need tracking, or help of some kind, but other'n that—"

"Dammit, stop!"

Shock widens Marvena's eyes.

"Hildy—Hildy is my . . ." Lily pauses, realizing as she looks at Marvena how much the woman has come to mean to her. So she amends her statement: "Hildy is *one* of my best friends. She could have told me. Told Mama. Believe me, we'd have both supported her against her own mother's protests—and Merle's." Their rough treatment of Hildy the other night washes over her in a wave of shame. She hadn't stood up for Hildy then. She'd been so weary from the long day. "We . . . we've always told each other ev-er-y-th-in-g." Lily's voice breaks on *everything*, cracking the word into six pieces. "Did you know she was engaged to my brother Roger?"

Marvena bites her lower lip, slightly shakes her head.

"Roger died in the Great War. Daniel was with him. Held him as he died."

Tears spring to Marvena's eyes, and Lily blinks her own back, dashing her hand to her eyes. "Roger would have approved of Tom and Hildy. I know they had their differences, but by now, I think Daniel would have, too."

Lily drops her head to her hands. "Life is short. And cruel enough without borrowing trouble. If someone finds love, real love, they should take it. If Tom and Hildy love each other, they should be together. Why wouldn't she trust me? Why?"

A year and a half before, with the loss of Daniel, and all that came after, Lily had been impaled with grief. The wound set deep, rending her spirit, and all the tender emotions she'd used to pack the lesion now break forth, and Lily weeps in great gulping sobs that burst from her of their own volition. She wants to pack them back down again, into the gaping pain, but she cannot, and she's swept away by the force of them gushing free.

Marvena pulls her chair alongside Lily's, puts her arms around her.

Lily accepts her friend's embrace for a long moment. Then she pulls away and rubs her eyes. When she brings her hands away, she sees him, there, behind Marvena. The silvery boy. She'd thought she had glimpsed him on the walk back here, even commented to Marvena, then when she looked back again, she laughed it off. She was so tired. But here he is again. He has followed her here, from Moonvale Hollow—but no. As he stands still and stares at her—not laughing, not chasing a ball—Lily understands. He'd never been a part of Moonvale Hollow. He'd been a part of her, all along.

A haunt from another life—in which Daniel lived, and Lily was never sheriff, and a third child was born—a life she would never live, yet haunting the one she is trying to live.

Lily frowns at him—*why, why, are you haunting me?* She blinks, rubs her eyes again, and in the next instant he is gone. As always, it is just as shocking when he melts away as when he appears, and Lily saddens at the mundane sights left in his absence, of mere checkered floor tile and icebox and pie safe.

"Lily? You look like you seen a ghost." Marvena hands her a handkerchief from her pocket. Lily takes it, blows her nose hard, and the great honking sound, bouncing around her tiny kitchen, strikes her as absurd. She laughs, and then Marvena does, too. When at last they're spent of both tears and laughter, Marvena scoots back around to the other side of the table.

"Lily," she says gently, "if'n I'da known it'd hit you so hard, Hildy not telling you, I'da eased into it. Truth be told—there's a reason you've been tired and some people, specially sensitive ones like Hildy, might be pulling back from you. You're sad, Lily. It's been more'n a year, the length of time people give for mourning, but there's no clock running on sorrow."

Lily studies her friend's face. "But you . . . your loss—"

"Everyone's different. Still, I can tell you that with Jurgis, I've found comfort"—Marvena's voice creaks—"that lets me set aside the pain, now and again. You, though, you just keep hunkering down, waiting for the sorrow to stop, and I understand that. I do. But it'll never stop, not entirely. You know that. All hunkering down does is give sorrow a way to burrow in, carve a hollow in your heart. Go too deep, and sorrow is all that will ever fill it."

Lily's glass shakes as she picks it up, and she has to hold it in both hands to keep it steady, to take a sip. "All right. Hildy is in Rossville. Staying with you. In love with Tom. That is her business, though—and I'm guessing you didn't come all this way to carry tales."

"You gotta know how she and Tom came to spark on one another. Hildy's been tutoring some of the miners—and, and, folks like me—on their letters and numbers. In the schoolhouse, after regular hours, along with Olive Harding. Well, in tutoring Tom, she grew sweet on him." Marvena gives a rueful smile. "Don't see why—my brother's nothing pretty to look at, and more stubborn than Guibo."

Lily offers a small smile. "Kin of yours? Stubborn?"

Marvena snorts. "Anyway, what I'm getting at is that it turns out Hildy's been keeping a secret for Olive and a man that Olive's more than a little sweet on." Marvena clears her throat. "The man is Clarence Broward."

Even as Lily stares at her in shock, Marvena's gaze is unflinching.

Lily feels flattened, as though all the air in the room has been pressed out. She draws in a great breath, as if coming up from underwater. Lily forces her mind to start again, calculating. This time, not the details of crime. The desires of the human heart.

There had been talk that Mama had tried to keep from her, but that Lily had been aware of, about Lily marrying Daniel years ago—he was, after all, half Indian from his mother's side; some would whisper *savage*—and had been a fierce boxer, a sport that was cheered and honored and yet used as a mark against him whenever it was convenient.

Many would sneer at Jurgis and Marvena consorting without benefit of marriage.

Certainly, the women of the club would be appalled at Hildy choosing a common miner like Tom over a business owner like Merle.

But this? Olive and Clarence . . .

Lily considers: the state of Ohio repealed its anti-miscegenation laws all the way back in 1887—the most recent state to do so. Mixed-race marriages have been legal here for nearly forty years but remain illegal in most states, and in recent years there have been two attempts to make a constitutional amendment to ban interracial marriages nationwide.

So though Olive and Clarence *could* sanctify their relationship under law, that doesn't mean that it will be treated with respect by everyone in the community. Simply by courting, they're putting themselves in danger.

Lily clears her throat. "Well. Like I said. If someone finds real love, they should cherish it." She's learned the hard way how quickly such love can be ripped asunder.

Marvena's stiff expression relaxes, and she gives a small nod. Yet her expression becomes more grim. "Plenty don't see it that way."

"Who all knows?"

"I want to think just you, me, Hildy, and Tom. They've kept it well hidden—it was a surprise to me. Hildy says that Margaret Dyer came by the grocery and asked if she'd heard anything about Clarence and Olive—that's what sent her back to Rossville a few days ago, to warn them. And Clarence and Olive have had a shock of their own." Marvena sighs, as if the world and all its tangled troubles and rules and expectations have ensnared her very soul. "Seems they were out, meeting up, the same night as Thea Kincaide left the asylum and trekked to the Dyers' old farmhouse in Moonvale. They spotted Thea, near the tunnel, so entranced by something that she stayed stock-still on the track, about to let herself get ran over. Clarence pulled her off. She snapped out of it, called him 'John.'" Marvena pauses. "Lily? You all right?"

Lily rubs her eyes. John—the escaped slave who Thea's father had been hiding from bounty hunters, who had been accused of hanging Rupert from a tree on the Moonvale Hollow Tunnel, who Thea, as a little girl, testified against. Her testimony had been enough, at the time, for John to be found guilty—and to be hanged to death himself.

Something had thrown Thea back into that time and place, sent her on the search for who knew what—and had been sufficient for Thea to think she'd found John alive again. But what?

Maybe there would be a clue in the new set of clippings that Seth had dropped off?

"Is that it?" Lily asks. "That Olive and Clarence spotted Thea, saved her from the train?"

Marvena shakes her head, her mouth pulled taut in a grim line. "They followed her—worried about her. She was talking nonsense, and they kept asking her where her people were. And she led them up to the Dyers' old property. When Clarence and Olive seen all them robed and hooded people—they took off, right quick. Not that anyone could blame them."

"So . . . so they're witnesses? To the WKKK gathering on the Dyer property? To the fact that Thea was definitely there the night she died? I need to talk with them."

"Separately," Marvena says. "And somewhere no one will see you talking with them. We have cover for them now—Hildy is taking over for Olive, and the story is she has taken ill. Hildy's at Nana's, and Olive's with me, so she won't take a fool notion to run after Clarence. He's more level-headed, going on with work as usual, with Tom and Jurgis watching out for him. I'll take back word." Marvena stands.

"I'll drive you back," Lily says.

Marvena shakes her head. "Walked in rather than getting a ride so as not to stir wonderings about why I'm seeking out the sheriff again."

"Well, at least let me get you down the road a bit."

"To the turn on Kinship Road? Got a backwoods shortcut from there."

Marvena means the hairpin turn that's right by Widow Gottschalk's house as well as the house where Daniel had grown up.

Lily swallows hard but nods. "Give me a second. I . . . I have something to drop off at the box outside the post office. Likely to forget to mail it tomorrow, with all I have going on."

Then she goes into the parlor, to her desk, pushes aside the new packet of clippings from Seth, and opens the rolltop. Her hands tremble a little as she regards the letter she'd written to Benjamin. Silly. She's being silly. She starts to shut the letter away, but Marvena's words come back: *All hunkering down does is give sorrow a way to burrow in, carve a hollow in your heart. Go too deep, and sorrow is all that will ever fill it.*

Quickly, Lily picks up the letter and tucks it in her pocket.

May 26, 1905
Submitted by Mrs. Mabel Cooper

Claude Kincaide, age 77, of Kinship, passed to be with the Lord on Saturday, May 27. He was preceded in death by his beloved wife, Bertha (Gregson) Kincaide, and two infant children.

Mr. Kincaide is survived by his daughter, Mabel (Kincaide) Cooper, his son-in-law, Chester Cooper, and his grand-daughter, Hildy Lee Cooper. He is also survived by many good friends at the Kinship Presbyterian Church.

Born July 17, 1827, to James and Lee (Marshall) Kincaide, he grew up on a modest farm outside Athens, Ohio. He served in the Mexican-American War, and upon his return established his profitable business. A devout Christian and staunch sup-porter of the laws of our land, he served as deputy to Sheriff Thomas Langmore each year during the sheriff's tenure, 1850–1858, and briefly considered his own run but decided to devote his life to his business, a blacksmith shop, to teaching Sunday School, and to hunting and fishing.

Family will receive friends on Friday, June 2, 5:00–8:00 p.m., with funeral services on Saturday at 10:00 a.m. at the Kinship Presbyterian Church. Burial will immediately follow services on Saturday, at the Kinship Cemetery. A supper will be held in the community room of the Kinship Presbyterian Church.

June 4, 1905
Callie's Corner
Tidbits from Around Kinship

—Mrs. Hugh Laney reports that she has more strawberries than she knows what to do with, and is willing to barter for eggs, as a fox got several of her hens earlier this year and her remaining hens haven't been quite right since.

—The Methodist Church Quilting Circle, which meets each Tuesday afternoon, is collecting clothing and household linens which are beyond repair but still good enough for quilting squares, as they begin work on baby quilts for new mothers this coming Christmas.

—We grieved the passing of Mr. Claude Kincaide a few weeks ago, but would be derelict to the duties of this column if we did not note that his funeral drew several mourners from out of town, including former sheriff Thomas Langmore, who served Bronwyn County from 1850 to 1858. Mr. Langmore, who now lives with his son and daughter-in-law in Columbus, is now, we are sorry to report, mostly infirm and relegated to a wheelchair. He spoke to no one while here, and when asked why the sheriff—who moved to Columbus as soon as his tenure was complete in 1858, according to Mrs. Arnold Greystone (my next-door neighbor)—would care to make the surely arduous journey for this particular funeral when he has not visited Kinship since leaving, Mr. Langmore's son's only reply was to say he did not know, but it was an ardent wish of his father and he felt it was his obligation to fulfill any wishes of his failing father that he could.

A more surprising and colorful attendee at the service was a woman, bedecked in a resplendent burgundy dress with black lace trimmings, and the most ostentatious matching hat ever witnessed atop a head anywhere in Bronwyn County—complete with ostrich feathers!

The woman was none other than Thea Kincaide Dyer, daughter of Rupert Kincaide, Claude's brother, though neither was mentioned in Mr. Claude Kincaide's obituary. I learned her identity by questioning her after the funeral service. She stated that she had learned of the passing only because, after coming into "some wealth," she had contacted an "anonymous friend" and pre-paid said friend a "handsome sum" to send a telegram should any of her Kincaide kin pass away. She was resolute in not divulging who the friend is, and no one I've talked to has owned up to being the friend or having a clue who the friend might be. In any case, upon learning of his passing, she immediately made the long train trip from New York City to Cincinnati to Kinship. I asked her about her marital status and children and what she's done with her life since leaving Bronwyn County. She demurred, and asked if I could guess her age. I declined to take on such a gauche game, though she must surely be in the matronly range, and commented that she looks youthful and has retained a younger woman's figure. She then boasted that it is to her advantage to have a youthful visage and form that suggests a younger age so she is able to continue the works she loves, dancing in a burlesque show, which she said is like a variety show, but is soon to marry the show's producer and move to Paris, France.

What a bold life for Miss Thea Kincaide Dyer—who, I've since learned, was last seen in Kinship in a trial of an escaped slave accused of murdering her father, Rupert Edward Kincaide, who, it was alleged, was an abolitionist. As a seven-year-old, Miss Thea—as she asked me to refer to her upon learning of my columnist duties—identified an escaped slave as her father's attacker, and then lived with her mother as in-home caretakers of the Dyer family in Moonvale Hollow Village; after Mrs. Dyer passed away due to complications bearing a late-in-life baby, the Widow Kincaide married Mr. Dyer, with both Miss Thea and her mother taking the Dyer last name. Miss Thea ran away when she was seventeen years old. She was quite vague as to the details following this shocking choice.

When asked why she would return now for her uncle's funeral, Miss Thea only gave an enigmatic smile, but she was observed later calling upon the grieving daughter, Mrs. Mabel (Kincaide) Cooper, who is a first cousin to Miss Thea, so we can only assume that Miss Thea never lost her love for the region of her birth, and perhaps regrets living so far away, and upon learning of the death of her uncle wished to be welcomed back to the bosom of her remaining family.

June 11, 1905
Callie's Corner
Tidbits from Around Kinship

—I must begin by first apologizing to any that I may have offended by referencing the brazen lifestyle of Miss Thea Kincaide Dyer in last week's column. My dear husband explained to me just what "burlesque" might entail in a big city like New York, and my editor promises to more carefully review all items from his correspondents. (Note: The newspaper is short staffed, due to Mr. Baer moving to Cincinnati for a position at the *Post*.) What's more, Mrs. Mabel Cooper corrected my assumption that Miss Thea was warmly welcomed. Why, given her improper choices as a young lady (she ran away with a traveling pots-and-pans salesman at the start of her journey to New York!) and her scandalous lifestyle even now as a fifty-five-year-old woman, not a drop of tea or a single biscuit was served, Mrs. Cooper assures me. As to the motivation for the return, Mrs. Cooper theorizes that Miss Thea was hoping to inherit in order to help fund her follies, and states that not only is this not the case, but that Miss Thea serves as an example—which Mrs. Cooper uses if needed with her daughter, though Hildy is so biddable it's rarely required—of what happens if a child is not brought up properly, and goes astray.

—Meanwhile, Mrs. Hugh Laney reports that she is out of fresh strawberries for bartering. . . .

CHAPTER 23

❧

LILY

Monday, September 27—10:00 a.m.

"Coffee or tea, Sheriff Ross?" Mabel Cooper gestures toward the parlor—as if Lily doesn't already know her way around the house.

Lily enters the parlor, where the draperies are drawn even though it is a bright sunny day. Draperies are always drawn at the Cooper house. *To keep the sun from fading the upholstery.* The stern admonishment echoes forward from Lily's childhood, on the rare times she came to visit Hildy here, instead of Hildy coming to Lily's parents' house. As it had then, and a few nights before, the overbearing smell of too much furniture polish stuffs her nose.

The memory of last Wednesday evening comes back to her—poor Hildy. So suffocated by both her mother and Merle. No wonder she'd wanted to roam free—even take up with Tom, so different from Merle. So different from Hildy. Maybe that is part of the attraction?

"Please, have a seat, Lily!" Mrs. Cooper hurries over to the love seat, as quickly as her girth and arthritic hip will allow, and pats a stiff embroidered pillow.

Lily lifts an eyebrow. This particular love seat, a Victorian era piece with carved and curved mahogany, is Mrs. Cooper's pride and joy—a seat that Lily remembers sitting in, giggling, despite Hildy's horri-fied protestations about what her mother would do if she came in and found a child in the seat. Sure enough, her attention pricking at the sound of Lily's giggles, Mrs. Cooper came in and saw Lily and yelled so abruptly that eight-year-old Lily, who almost never cried, started wailing with terror. She'd run from the house, but not before catching a glimpse of Mrs. Cooper's satisfied grin—as if she'd finally ridden her house of vermin.

A few days later, at school, Hildy had been red-eyed and puffy faced, and Lily had run over to her, worried that she'd gotten her friend whipped. At that, Hildy had started sobbing in relief. She hadn't been whipped, but she'd been distraught all weekend, certain that Lily would no longer be her friend after her mother had acted so harshly. Lily had hugged Hildy and reassured her—no, no, she would always be her friend, no matter what.

Now Lily's eyes prick, as she wonders if she'd kept that promise. Why hadn't Hildy trusted her with the secret of her love for Tom? She hadn't even hinted at it. Had Lily gotten so lost in her own grief that she was unable to see how sad and lost Hildy was as well? Yes. Just the other day, she'd dismissively told Hildy to listen to Merle.

Mrs. Cooper is still patting the embroidered pillow, as if the gesture will refluff the pillow and the room and the home with sweetness and softness. And she looks at Lily with her usual disdain, but something else. Anxiousness. That's new.

Lily sits on the edge of the nearest chair. Mrs. Cooper's eyes narrow at Lily's unspoken denial of the offer of the prime spot and stops pat-ting the pillow.

"I'm not here on a social call today—any more than I was the other night," Lily says. "I'm here as sheriff—"

"Oh! Have you come with news about . . . about Hildy?" For a moment, Mrs. Cooper's face softens—and another early childhood memory comes back to Lily. She and Hildy must have been only five or so. They were here, playing with a doll Hildy had gotten for her birthday. Mrs. Cooper made them tea and cookies and didn't fuss over crumbs or spills but laughed with them. Now Lily can't remember what—but it's startling, this memory of Mrs. Cooper as happy. Almost carefree.

That would have been before Thea's visit. Lily realizes with a start that Mrs. Cooper has been sour ever since Thea's visit all those years ago. Why? What had that visit triggered?

Lily reassures Mrs. Cooper. "Hildy is fine." The second Lily says it, though, she wonders. Hildy may well be besotted with Tom, but Lily knows her friend well enough that she is sure Hildy is feeling deeply guilty about duping both Merle and her mother. Physically Hildy may be fine, but emotionally and spiritually? Mayhap not.

In the next instant, instead of relief coursing Mrs. Cooper's brow, her mouth tightens as if she has just bitten into something bitter. "Well, where is she then?"

Lily sighs. *Well, that flicker of tenderness in Mrs. Cooper died out quickly.* "She is staying for the time being in Rossville. Substituting for the schoolmarm, who is recovering from a severe bout of flu."

"Well, Hildy should be home, not messing around with the likes of those grubby people," Mrs. Cooper says. "She has a fiancé to think of, her reputation; what would he say if—"

"I believe that is between Hildy and Merle!" Lily snaps.

As Mrs. Cooper's face tightens, Lily hears her own mama's voice, reminding her again, *You catch more flies with honey than vinegar.* So she forces a smile. "Do you remember the column 'Callie's Corner'? I believe you were featured many times. For your county fair wins—"

Pride flushes Mrs. Cooper's face. "Oh yes. I kept all of those columns in my scrapbook. I believe she referred to the cross-stitch work on those pillows as exquisite"—she gestures at a pillow with peacocks, turquoise and orange feathers on full display—and Lily has to smile at the choice of cross-stitch pattern. Mrs. Cooper hasn't changed over the years.

It's time to puncture that pride, catch Mrs. Cooper off guard. "Did you keep the column that mentioned Thea Kincaide's visit to this house after your father died?"

The air in the already-stuffy room thickens. "I . . . Surely you are mistaken. I told you all I know of Thea the other night." Mrs. Cooper pulls a handkerchief from her pocket but doesn't use it to dab at her nose. She wads it. "I was only vaguely aware of her as a child—"

"Yes, you said that the other day, that Hildy was wrong about Thea visiting here when your father died. That you only saw her a few times as a child. I've done some background research. According to a set of 'Callie's Corner' columns, Thea came to your father's funeral back in June of 1905. And she visited you, and your husband, and Hildy here. The other day you claimed that Hildy was mistaken about Thea's visit—"

"Callie was known for embellishing, bless her heart—"

"Was she embellishing when she wrote about your exquisite cross-stitched pillows?" Lily gestures at them. "I think she was right about that."

Mrs. Cooper presses her handkerchief to her nose, after all. "Perhaps *Thea*"—she snaps the name as if trying to break it in half, like a stick—"did visit. Can anyone blame me for forgetting? I was awash in grief, I am sure, and, and"—she straightens up, tilts up her chin imperiously—"well, dear, you are too young to realize, but grief puts details in a blur, and most likely if she attended or visited, she was not a detail worth noticing—"

"I am all too well acquainted with grief, Mrs. Cooper," Lily says, "and in my experience the details after time begin to stand out in stark contrast, emboldened by the emotion that surrounds them. Plus Thea's presence was quite notable and shocking to the community, according to the 'Callie's Corner' columns. She stood out, well, rather like your peacocks there." Lily gestures toward the pillows, as Mrs. Cooper stares as if seeing them for the first time, with a look of distaste. Lily realizes that she has now ruined the pillows for Mrs. Cooper by comparing them to Thea. Why such strong, bitter hatred toward a cousin, one she so rarely saw?

"What I'm wondering is," Lily says, "why you denied the other day that Thea came here twenty-one years ago?"

"As I said, I must have forgotten—and what does it matter anyway?"

"Because I do not believe that you have forgotten. I think that visit has rankled all these years, like a thorn digging deeper and deeper in your foot. The memory itself won't let you forget it. And yet, you wish to deny it. It matters because now Thea is dead and she was on her way somewhere—and I have to wonder if she might have been trying to come here? If she never quite made it here, because she was sidetracked or stopped for some reason."

"I can't imagine why she would visit me. She knew quite well that she wasn't welcome here—" Mrs. Cooper stops short, her face pinching at the realization of her admission.

"Hildy said a few nights ago that she recollects Thea saying she came to your father's funeral to make sure he really was dead. As if she found satisfaction, or peace, from that. Why?"

"Our fathers had very different views on . . . many things. Another reason why she would have had no reason to return here."

"Your name is listed on the asylum form as her next of kin."

Mrs. Cooper shrugs. "I must be the only kin that she has."

"She has a son. What is his name?"

"I don't know. I've never met him, and wasn't aware until now she had a child. Poor thing—having a mother like her!"

Lily pinches her lips, holding back a snap about the irony of Mrs. Cooper's opinion. "You weren't aware of her presence in this area, of her being at the asylum?"

"I've already said no."

"The asylum didn't contact you about her?"

"No."

"You didn't see her at the WKKK gathering at the old Dyer farm?"

"No, I didn't see her there—" Mrs. Cooper stops, her face reddening at being caught in Lily's battery of questions.

"You were at the gathering?"

Mrs. Cooper straightens up primly. "I don't believe my comings and goings are of your concern. And how do you know that such a group met there—or anywhere?"

"In tracking your *cousin*,"—Lily emphasizes the word—"our path took us to the old Dyer farm in Moonvale. I found evidence of a large gathering of women, and that it was likely for a chapter of the WKKK."

Mrs. Cooper sniffs. "The right to free assembly extends to all groups—whether you like them or not."

Lily suppresses a smile. Mrs. Cooper knows Lily well enough to correctly intuit her opinions. "So long as they gather peaceably. Were you at the gathering, Mrs. Cooper?"

She stares at Lily but says nothing.

Lily sighs. "I can always interrogate Mrs. Dyer about whether she was there. As if she knows your cousin was there, and that she later died, likely by foul play—"

"I didn't see her there!" The admission bursts out of Mrs. Cooper.

Another question arises—did Hildy know of her mother's involvement with the WKKK? Could she have even been pulled into it, too?

The fear of such must flash on Lily's face, for Mrs. Cooper smiles at last. "I'd like to formally report my daughter as missing. When you find her, you can ask her what she knows of the group. I insist you bring her home—or I may have to share among my new friends in the WKKK that you are unfit as sheriff and derelict in your proper duties. You might be surprised how much influence we have in voting in the upcoming election."

Two hours later, Lily peers out the window, scanning the tree line, until she finds the opening to the narrow path she'd just walked, an unsanctioned shortcut from the Hollows' formal gardens, up to the women's cottages. Even outside, the path was easy to miss, but surely most longtime employees would know of it. Maybe even take a resident to it, for the right bribe. From the formal gardens, it would be a quick jaunt to the road that goes to the cemetery. The spot where Sadie, the tracking hound, had lost Thea's scent.

After leaving Mrs. Cooper, Lily had gone back to her house and a few minutes later received a delivery of the search warrant for Thea Kincaide's lodgings at the Hollows—this room and this room only. A blown tire and the tedious process of swapping it for the spare had added to the long drive to Athens. But she made it to the asylum in time to catch Dr. Harkins as he was leaving for the day. He'd reviewed the search warrant, then told her he'd send a nurse to escort her to the women's cottages and Thea's room.

Lily waited nearly an hour for the nurse.

When she finally got to it, searching the room hadn't taken any time at all. She could have been on her way a half hour ago. Something told her—*stay.*

Now Lily turns from the window and again scans what had been Thea's room, shared with one other woman. It's surprisingly large, ornate—delicate plasterwork in the high ceiling, polished oak wainscoting—outfitted with two each of beds, wardrobes, and end tables. Both beds are so neatly made under crème chenille bedspreads that Lily wouldn't be able to tell which had been Thea's, except the end table by one bed

is clear of everything, and the other holds a small framed daguerreotype—a woman in a bonnet. Lily hasn't looked too closely at this portrait of the woman's loved one—daughter? Mother? Sister? It feels too
invasive.

On the other bed is a box—Thea's items, said the nurse who had
walked her over here. Boxed up, put in storage, gotten out for Lily a
few minutes after arriving at the cottage. *Take all the time you need.*
So cooperative. And yet an hour to find a nurse to escort her over—
not to mention the five days since tracking Thea here—was more than
all the time the director would need to curate the items in the box,
if there was something among Thea's belongings that might point to
something suspicious.

And how can she be sure that the few items in the box—a dressing
gown, a few blouses, underclothes, a skirt, a robe—were even Thea's?
There was nothing distinctive about them, other than they were old-
fashioned and high quality. And they held a faint but distinctly cinnamon scent.

The only thing interesting about the box is what is not in it. No coat.
No shoes, or even house slippers. No jewelry, brooches, or other personal items.

Why hadn't Thea at least put on the robe?

Lily stares back out at the barely discernible path. While waiting,
Lily had ample, restless time to study the few items on the waiting area
wall, including a framed and signed copy of the architect's original
plans. The cottages, added later, hadn't been on those plans. The formal gardens had, and between the plans and Lily's memory of childhood visits she realizes that down that path would be the gardens.

Lily calculates. This room is at the back of the main floor, near the
shared bathing room, which includes a pump sink and flush toilets—
nicer bathroom facilities than she has at the sheriff's house. The bathroom is by the rear exit to the cellar. So easy to slip out. No creaking
steps to descend from the second floor. No other rooms to walk past.
Just a quick walk down the hallway, as if to the bathroom—and who
would question the toiletry needs of an elderly woman in the middle
of the night?—then slip out the back.

The back door has a lock on it. Maybe bribe someone to meet her there? Unlock it, then guide her through the shortcut to the garden and, from there, to the back road by the cemetery? Where, for some reason, she started walking in rag-wrapped feet?

A thud startles Lily. She turns, sees a petite young woman in the doorway, who kneels, picks up the dust mop she'd dropped.

"Sorry!" the girl yelps, so nervous that Lily might think she is a resident, except she wears a pink-striped nurse's aide uniform.

"Wait!" Lily says as the girl turns away. The poor thing jumps—this is not the place for the timid or easily spooked—and Lily gives her a gentle smile, even as she taps her sheriff's badge. "I have a few questions."

The girl's eyes go wide. "I—I don't know nothing!"

"Of course you do." Lily keeps her voice soft and gentle. "I'm Lily." Pointing out the badge had been enough to keep the girl from scampering away. Better to take the honey-over-vinegar approach sanctioned by Mama. "What's your name?"

"Helen."

Lily smiles. "Well, Helen, how long have you worked here?"

"Half a year."

"Have you always been assigned to this cottage?"

"Oh no, ma'am. This is a plum assignment. I'm filling in for the cottage's resident aide, who left to take care of a family member who is ill." For a moment, Helen looks honored—even though temporary, this is an assignment to be proud of. "When she's back, I'll be back up at the big house."

"Resident—so you live here?"

"Yes—for now." Helen points to the room across the way. "It's right nice, nicer than where I'm lodging. . . ." Her voice trails off. She shrugs, as if relinquishing the relative luxury of the room later will not really matter to her.

"You were here when Thea Kincaide arrived? Knew her?"

Helen looks down. "I knew who she was, yes." A tremulousness to her voice belies the statement. She knew Thea better than she is letting on.

"I can tell you're a quick study." Lily flashes another smile as Helen glances up. "So, did Mrs.—" Lily hesitates. What is the proper way to refer to a woman who took an adopted name, then a married name, then divorced—but was listed on her asylum record under her maiden name?

"Miss Thea. That's what she said to call her."

Lily considers—the same mode of address Thea had asked Callie of Callie's corner to use. "Did Miss Thea wear shoes?"

"All the residents must wear shoes. If they don't have any, then they're issued a pair. Thea—Miss Thea—had a very nice, comfortable pair."

"When she was found, she didn't have on her shoes."

"Perhaps . . . perhaps she lost them along the way?"

"Poor woman walked miles in no shoes, in the woods and brush, on the rocky ground," Lily says. "I'm sure you can imagine what that did to her feet."

Helen whimpers, and Lily sees in the sorrow on Helen's face that not only is she empathetic, but also she liked Thea. Lily glances at the box, and then back to Helen. "No shoes in there. I doubt that she lost them," Lily said.

Helen looks down. "Sometimes residents trade items of value for things they want that they're not supposed to have." Her voice is a half whisper.

"Like . . . tobacco? Or alcohol?"

Helen nods.

"Or getting help to leave?"

Helen looks back up at Lily. "It's . . . it's possible."

Lily turns this over—that would explain why Thea's scent abruptly started along the path by the cemetery. She must have convinced someone—Helen?—to help her leave the cottage without raising an alarm, and then given them her shoes. And maybe other valuable objects.

Or, in the hour or so that passed before Lily was brought to this room, the shoes and any valuables had been removed? That doesn't make sense. The absence of shoes, of at least one precious item—Lily glances at the roommate's daguerreotype—raises more questions than it answers.

Lily gives Helen a questioning look.

Helen looks taken aback. "Oh no, ma'am, it wasn't me, I swear! I wouldn't help her escape in any case. It is too dangerous, especially for someone like her."

"What do you mean?"

"She was so forgetful. And too trusting."

"I see. Did she have any possessions besides her shoes that might be missing from this box? Any jewelry for example?"

"She had a brooch that she liked to wear on her lapel. And a fine silk scarf—she said it was from Paris!—that she would wind over her head sometimes, like a turban."

Neither of these items is in the box. Perhaps they'd been thieved since her death. Or perhaps Thea had bartered dearly to get her escape.

"The items aren't in here. Is there anything else of value that should be in here?"

Helen looks away, gives her head a shake, and Lily reckons from the blush rising up Helen's neck that she's lying. Yet this girl doesn't seem like the sort who would take items of value from patients. So perhaps she's covering for someone else who would take them?

"She was well thought of by her next of kin," Lily says lightly. Not an entire lie—Hildy seems to have an admiring memory of her, or of how she made her feel at least. "I'm sure if there are things that have been put aside for her, her family would love to have them."

"Oh! I'm so glad her son loved her. Miss Kincaide talked of him often, though he never visited. A shame." An apologetic look crosses Helen's face at what must seem, to her, a harsh judgment. She rushes on. "Sometimes family have a hard time with visiting their loved ones here, at least at first, even if it is the best place for them."

"Ah, her son," Lily says. "I'm having trouble remembering his name?" A bit of a white lie—Hildy's mother swore she didn't know Thea's son, and the landlady where Thea had lived stated he never gave it to her, or an address where he could be found.

"Neil Leitel," Helen says. "Dr. Neil Leitel. Miss Kincaide was right proud—always said 'Dr.' when referring to him! Said he was very important, very busy, but he'd come soon to visit."

"He was a physician?" Lily keeps her voice light, though she is fuming at the son—this Dr. Neil Leitel—caring so little for his mother.

"No—a professor. Of philosophy, Miss Kincaide said. At Ohio University."

CHAPTER 24

❀

HILDY

Monday, September 27—4:00 p.m.

Hildy is sorrowful to see the school day near its end. Little Becky had a breakthrough with her multiplication tables and is bouncing with delight. Jameson is practicing his cursive letters, the tip of his tongue poking out of the corner of his mouth as he concentrates. As Hildy flitted from desk to desk, her energy has only increased since the beginning of the day.

As much as she'd enjoyed working with adults, with the children she'd found a joy like she'd never known. To be sure, there had been challenging moments—Alistair had gotten into a fight with another boy at lunch break, and one of the girls is distraught at Frankie's absence. Even so, solutions came naturally to Hildy—giving the boys the task of washing out lunch pails for the other students, explaining that Frankie had a touch of flu but should be back soon. Something sparked within Hildy, as if it had long lay dormant and needed a chance to break free. But now it is time for the children to leave for home.

Alone in the schoolhouse, Hildy sits for the first time since lunch break at her—no, Olive's—desk. Last Thursday, Olive had hurriedly left behind gloves and lesson plans. On Friday, Hildy had followed the lesson plans, but over the weekend, she'd found herself considering new approaches. This morning, Hildy had put the plans in the desk drawer alongside the gloves and, with a surprising, wild impulse, decided to follow her own instinct for teaching—one-on-one attention as much as possible; showing, rather than lecturing.

Effective, but exhausting, yet only now does tiredness overcome her, as if seeping out from every pore. This exhaustion, though—it's a satisfying bone weariness born of good labor. Different from being plain tired after a long day working as jail mistress for Lily—not that she minded. She likes being useful, working hard. Bur this work calls to her. Is that how it is for Lily? For despite her deep sorrow over Daniel, Lily's face often lights up as she conducts her duties as sheriff. Does Lily know how her satisfaction with her work shows in her expression?

Hildy is already eager to come back the next day, her mind racing ahead to how she can help each child. She already has their names, and many of their quirks, memorized.

Tomorrow, sure. Maybe the next day. Soon enough, Olive will have to come back. Definitely after the vote to integrate the union, whichever way it goes. For after that, Clarence has promised to leave. Olive will stay until a new, proper teacher can be found. Then she'll likely go to Clarence. They'll be together, and Olive will teach elsewhere.

Hildy's joy collapses, and she slumps forward. What is the point of allowing herself such elation? Stolen moments. That's all today's teaching had been. Just like her time with Tom.

The door squeaks open, and Tom—as if beckoned by her thought—enters.

His face is drawn up with fear, and her heart drops. He is not here for her.

"We were hoping Olive was here," Tom says.

"She's up with Marvena and Frankie." Frankie had taken ill that morning, unable to keep down her breakfast. Flu, Marvena had said, but more likely, the child had a nervous stomach, from all the comings and goings at Marvena's cramped cabin, the tension exuding from Olive, and Marvena's barely contained annoyance. In Frankie, Hildy sees something of the child she had been—too tender for this harsh world.

Tom shakes his head. "Frankie took a bad turn—"

Hildy stands quickly, exclaiming, "Oh!" For a moment, Tom's face softens, gratitude at Hildy caring so for his niece, but then he swallows hard.

"It's a fever Marvena couldn't get to break, so she brought Frankie down to Nana's. After a while, Marvena went back up to her cabin to check on Olive." Tom swallows again. "Olive's gone. Marvena came back down, sent Jurgis to check with—" He stops, afraid to say Clarence's name, in case someone passes by, overhears. "I offered to go, but she sent me here."

The air in the small schoolhouse stiffens, draws the walls closer. *Ah.* Marvena had thought she was doing a kindness, giving them a chance to come to some reckoning—or if not that, given Olive's disappearance, at least a shared moment to soften the hurt between them.

Tom won't meet Hildy's eyes, stares down at his hat clutched between his hands. *Damn his pride!* Why couldn't he have given her time to ease the news to Mother, to Merle?

It hits her. Tom didn't want to give her time, because he doesn't believe she would ever choose him.

Hildy's heart sags.

He might be right.

It's easy to be brave here—away from Mother's pressure, from the expectations of a lifetime to marry well and become a fine town woman. A lady of the Woman's Club.

Hildy clears her throat, and yet her voice still sounds ragged, harsh. "Olive isn't here. She hasn't come here at all today."

Tom wearily rubs his hands over his dusty face. He hasn't had time to go home, wash up. A flash of earlier fantasies sparks Hildy's thoughts—her awaiting him with supper, relief that another day in the coal mines, though hard, has been uneventful.

Tom steps toward Hildy, and of its own accord, her heart quickens. She forces herself to remain still, rigid. *It's over, it's over. We're not brave—not like Olive and Clarence.*

Yet . . . perhaps he'll reach for her? Touch her, a graze of fingertips on her cheek?

He stops short of coming close enough and says, barely above a mumble, "Marvena says we're gonna need to track Olive. Need something of hers."

Hildy stares at him for a long second. *Track.* Marvena and Lily had tracked poor Thea, using the rags from her feet.

She opens the desk drawer and points at Olive's gloves.

"And this is a picture of Buckingham Palace," Hildy says.

Frankie, sitting in Hildy's lap at the Sacovech house, points at the palace on the front of the postcard. "And that's where the princess lives?"

Hildy smiles, kisses the top of Frankie's head. "Yes, that's where the princess lives!"

They've gone through the postcards at least five times. Hildy had left Kinship without coat or hat, but she'd brought the postcards with her, overcome by a sense of protectiveness, imagining Mother searching her room for clues to her departure, finding the postcards, and ripping them up with satisfied glee. During her duties at the school, simple awareness of the postcards in her pocketbook had brought Hildy strength and comfort.

Hildy had wanted to go with Tom, Marvena, and Jurgis to track Olive, but Tom had been firm. She was to go to Nana's. Help with Frankie and Alistair.

At first, Hildy had sulked over Nana's supper of potato pierogies and a poke salad. Again, she had been judged and found lacking. Too soft, too weak to go with the other adults, just as Lily hadn't wanted her along to track Thea.

Nana's good cooking had improved her spirits, though she saw how tired Nana was from taking care of Frankie, who only sipped bone broth for her supper, and how Alistair too, who'd been so rambunctious at school, was sulking at being left behind.

Near the end of supper, Alistair caught Hildy studying him, and he scowled. Hildy half-grinned at him, crossed her eyes, and stuck out her tongue. Alistair had giggled, and then Frankie too, while Nana sighed as if in dismay at such shenanigans, though a smile twitched at the corners of her mouth. After supper, while Frankie napped in the front room, Alistair and Hildy helped Nana can a batch of late-harvest tomatoes.

Then Nana made peppermint tea for all of them. "Life is hard," Nana had said. "Have tea."

Now, a few hours later, Nana sits in her rocking chair, crocheting a length of lace. The tiny house is humid and stuffy with the arch smell of tomatoes. Nana gives Hildy a long look. *Why are you filling the child's head with such fancifulness?*

Yet looking at the faded pictures on the front of the postcards awed Frankie. The child couldn't read cursive yet, and even if she could, Thea's taut, slanted handwriting would prove a challenge. So Hildy had made up stories to go with the pictures.

Alistair looks up from a well-worn old copy of *All-Weekly Story*— Hildy's father used to get the magazine, and Hildy had taken several to Tom to inspire his reading. Mother certainly wouldn't miss them. Alistair says, "No such thing as princesses and castles!"

Hildy holds back a smile. This, from the boy raptly rereading the exploits of John Carter in *A Princess of Mars,* a soldier who'd somehow ended up on Mars and become immortal.

"Yes there are!" Frankie says. "Here!" She points to the picture of Buckingham Palace again. She looks up at Hildy. "Aren't there?"

Hildy nods. "There are."

Frankie stares up at her. "Do you think I could sing there someday? For a princess?"

Such a wild dream. As wild as going to another planet.

Hildy turns over the postcard, stares at Thea's script, rubs her thumb lightly over the stamp. Then she ruffles the top of Frankie's head. It doesn't feel as hot as earlier. With Nana's tender care, the little girl's fever has broken. "Of course."

Nana stops crocheting for a moment, gives Hildy a long look. "Sometimes, what we want is right here, in front of us. Just takes a little courage, is all. Mayhap, a little forgiveness."

Hildy frowns. *Forgiveness?* Tom, the stubborn ass, has yet to tell her he is sorry!

Nana smiles, shakes her head, returns to her crocheting.

"Tell me the story again, about the princess!" Frankie says.

Alistair groans.

"Well, once there was a princess who lived in a palace, but she didn't want to wait for a prince to take her on adventures. So she decided to go find her own adventures! One day—"

The door swings open. Tom. Only Tom. Alistair jumps up, runs to his dad. Tom looks past Alistair, even as the boy throws his arms around his father's waist. Hildy's eyes lock on Tom's—and she reads his gaze, immediately and without doubt. *Come. Please.*

Hildy gently lowers Frankie from her lap. She wants to tell her that everything is going to be fine, but she can't bring herself to say this. Such a hard and bruising world. Things rarely are fine—or stay that way for long. As Frankie's eyes well up, Hildy hands her the precious postcard, all the way from London. "Can you take care of this for me?"

Frankie nods, eyes widening.

"Good. When I see you again, tell me a story you made up from the picture. All right?"

They don't have to drive far, but the mule towpath is so narrow and rutted that Hildy's automobile bounces on its frame as branches lash the sides. Hildy drives as swiftly as she dares. Not too hard. Breaking down on this route meant for mule carts heaped with coal wouldn't do any good.

"You're doing fine, Hildy, fine."

Tom's voice, tender and admiring, sifts through the darkness of the automobile over to her. A caress. Here, in this dire situation, hurtling through the night, anxiety making her heart thud, she finally hears the Tom she's so missed.

And yet a hardness encases her. Tom—the others—need her. But when she'd needed him to give her time, help her through, all she'd gotten was brusque pride.

Hildy presses her automobile to go a smidge faster.

Well, damn if she is going to let her emotions give her pause now. Olive needs help. Tom had explained at the start of the drive: Marvena bartered to borrow Sadie; with the glove, they'd tracked Olive. Found her—bloody, beaten, broken. *Beyond what Nana can tend to,* Tom had said, *if'n it were safe to bring her back to Rossville. But it ain't.*

"There!" Tom points.

Hildy sees only darkness and branches before her, but she slows her automobile. Before she can fully stop, Tom opens the door, jumps out, takes off running. Hildy sets the parking brake, follows after him, and then she sees the coal-oil lantern.

Marvena and Jurgis hunched over another form.

Hildy rushes over and drops to her knees next to Olive.

Oh God. Her face—one cheek knife slashed, eyes beaten to swelling and cracking. Locks of hair, snatched from her scalp. Her arm, twisted and broken behind her. Her lips, puffy and split.

Hildy's stomach turns; hot tears overflow her eyes. *Oh God. What animal, what monster—for surely no human could do this—had beset poor Olive?*

Then Hildy spots the note, pinned to Olive's dirty, ripped dress, like a child's name tag for school: *A warning for all—Bronwyn County Chapter WKKK.*

Not an animal, then. Human. No, monsters. In human form.

Hildy blinks back her tears, sees with a rush of relief that Olive is breathing. Still alive.

"She was able to talk when we found her." Marvena's voice, strumming low and tight, and Hildy knows that if the monster who'd done this were before them Marvena would not be like Lily, asking questions, trying to suss out the *why, why*? She'd simply shoot the monster dead. And Hildy, in this moment, would cheer her on. "Fool woman, went to wait for Clarence, hanging back in the woods behind the boardinghouse. Then they got her. Three women. In their cowardly hoods and capes—" Marvena stops, strangling on her words, and Hildy realizes that Marvena too is crying.

"Margaret suspected," Hildy says, "but how did they know for sure—"

"It's my fault. Found Lily in Kinship at some fancy women's meeting—"

"The Kinship Woman's Club," Hildy says, remembering that she was supposed to have been at that meeting. "Oh God. The meeting was at Margaret's house."

Olive moans, tries to speak, attempts to lift her broken arm, to sit up, but falls back.

"Easy, easy." Jurgis shivers. His coat is spread over her as a blanket.

Hildy leans over Olive. "Did you get a glimpse? Was Margaret Dyer one of the ones—"

"Hood . . . fell. . . ." Olive nods. Agony pulses her face.

"Dyer—that was the farmhouse where we found the hood," Marvena says.

Hildy looks up at Marvena. "Anyone see you at the Dyers' house, in Kinship?"

"I found Lily in the kitchen. There was a stringy-haired woman, a boy, working back there, but Lily and me, we went to her house before I told her anything." Marvena hesitates. Her face pulses, stricken, and her hand goes to her mouth. "Oh God . . ."

"What?" Tom snaps.

"Lily kept glancing behind us on the walk back," Marvena says, a half whisper. "Said she thought she saw a boy, but then she laughed it off, said her imagination had gotten the best of her when we'd been out tracking—but, mayhap . . ." She stops, unable to finish the terrible thought.

Hildy realizes what Marvena's trying to express: Lily had been working so hard lately, was so tired. Maybe she had imagined a boy. Or maybe she had caught a glimpse of Junior, following them, overhearing through the back door, reporting back to Missy, who would have reported back to Margaret.

Jurgis slides his arm around Marvena, comforting. "Nothin' to do about it now."

Tom's hand closes over Hildy's arm. She looks up at him. "She's beyond Nana's poultices. Rossville doctor's good for nothing. She needs help—a safe place—right quick."

Olive's breaths are now quick gasps from the pain. Hildy knows what she must do for Olive, though it will draw her back to Kinship, to the orb of Mother and Merle.

She gently removes the hateful note from Olive's lapel, wishing to rip it to shreds, but the note might serve as evidence later, so Hildy folds it, puts it in her pocket, to give to Lily. Then Hildy takes Olive's hand. Looks at her directly, as Olive stares up at her through the slits between her swollen eyelids.

"I'm taking you to Mrs. Gottschalk's. She's a good woman, on a farm. It's safe there. And I'll get the doctor from Kinship."

Postcard
May 10, 1907
My dear little Hildy—I am now settled in London. The love that swept me to Paris was not to last. But do not cry for me. My flat, as they call lodgings here, is small and cold, but it is mine, as is a new job in a hat shop. And I've found the most quaint and proper tea shop! I may return to the states though—New Orleans will be a better fit for me, I think. And when I am there, you can come visit me! Do not give your heart easily, my sweet cousin. You must see the world first!

Love,
Your cousin Thea

CHAPTER 25

LILY

Tuesday, September 28—1:00 p.m.

"Is this a stunt?" Perry's voice is low and tight, but his face is ravaged with rage, his brow pulled down so low in a frown that his eyes are glinty slits. "A way to defame my wife, try to make me look bad before our debate tonight?"

Just behind him in the doorway of the Dyer household stands Margaret. Perry holds his arm awkwardly twisted backward, across her midriff, his hand grasping her arm, as if he is holding her back from imminent, dire danger—the danger being Lily.

Oh! The fact that tonight was their debate had clean run out of her head, with all that had transpired last night and this morning. Today, she'd planned to go to Cincinnati, for yesterday she'd learned at Ohio University that Neil Leitel had taken a position at the University of Cincinnati, right after he'd left his mother at the Athens boardinghouse. She wanted to find out how his mother had ended up in his care, why he'd abandoned her, and what—if anything—he knew about why the poor woman had wandered away from the Hollows. Perhaps she'd been motivated to find her father—confusing past with present in her addled condition. What had triggered that? An event at the Hollows?

Something that happened, while with her son, even before he left her in Athens? The motivation of Thea's wandering might be tied to the reason behind her death—whether purely accidental, a heat-of-the-moment attack, or premeditated murder. In any case, understanding her motivation seems key to putting her—and the case—to rest, and now Leitel seems the most likely source for insight into that motivation.

Then late last night, Hildy had appeared at her door with horrific news. If only she had gone to interview Olive and Clarence on Monday after her trip to Athens, rather than returning directly home. But the call of her own hearth, the desire to spend time with her children, and the need to prepare for the upcoming debate had won out.

This afternoon, as Lily left the courthouse with proper paperwork in hand, a sudden downpour had opened up over Kinship. Now she stands on the Dyers' front porch with a warrant for Margaret's arrest, the wind blowing the hard, cold rain onto her back and head. She wishes she'd listened to Mama's warning—the ache in her hips and knees foretelling calamitous weather—and grabbed her hat, rather than giving Mama a dismissive wave.

Now Margaret, peeking out from behind Perry, looks far from terrified and in need of Perry's protection. A smile of wry satisfaction curls her mouth. The sense of triumph Lily had carried along with the warrant dissolves in a rush of foreboding. Has Margaret already thought several moves ahead of Lily, to some outcome that Lily can't foresee?

"It is not a stunt," Lily says. "Olive Harding verified to my deputies, Hildy Cooper and Marvena Whitcomb, that Margaret was one of three women who attacked Miss Harding, unprovoked. Their testimony as to Olive's injuries and complaint was sufficient for me to receive this warrant for Mrs. Dyer's arrest."

Perry laughs. "Ridiculous. Why would my wife—or anyone—want to harm some schoolmarm over in Rossville?"

Lily shivers as rivulets of rain drip down her collar. "Probably because Miss Harding was being courted by Clarence Broward."

Perry looks blank.

"An employee of the United Mine Workers. Working with Marvena

Whitcomb to integrate the Rossville union." Perry's face remains bereft of understanding. Lily sighs. "Clarence is a Negro man."

Perry's eyebrows rise. "Oh. I don't see what this has to do with my wife—"

Lily points to Margaret. "Because she is in the WKKK. In fact, likely leading the group that has been meeting at your old farm."

"I believe you should come in," Margaret says, her voice as cold and pitiless as the driving rain.

Lily sits on the edge of an overly stuffed chair in the parlor, rain dripping from her hair.

Perry snaps, "Margaret, get her some coffee—"

"Oh no, I'm fine—" Lily starts.

"Nonsense. I don't want you to say at our debate that we weren't hospitable—or were the cause of you catching cold." Perry gives Margaret a quick wave of his hand.

Ah. He wants her out of the room. Though clearly Perry is unhappy with her, Margaret gives a little shrug and a simpering laugh as she heads back to the kitchen.

"Margaret cannot be in the WKKK," Perry says, "because I would expressly forbid it."

Does he really believe that Margaret will meekly accept his imperatives without question? There is nothing to be gained by pointing out the delusion of such a belief, so Lily tries another approach. "Would you forbid it because you do not believe in the tenets of the WKKK?"

Perry smiles. "Clearly, I do not believe in women taking leadership roles in any form. Their place is in the home. That's only one reason I'm running against you. As for the other beliefs—I do not agree with violent approaches or secret meetings, but I do agree with the view of separation of races. I can understand how you might see otherwise— having been married to a half-breed yourself."

A pulse of anger zips up the back of Lily's head. How dare he make this reference to Daniel? Lily takes a long breath, says, "Back to the matter at hand. Hildy and Marvena received testimony from Miss Olive Harding—"

Perry pummels his hand against his chair's arm. Lily jumps, but Margaret glides into the parlor, followed by Missy carrying a tray with a coffee urn and cups. The tray quivers in her hand, making the urn and cups jiggle. She looks ashen, drawn.

"They must be lying!" Perry exclaims. "I've forbidden Margaret from joining—"

"So she has expressed to you her desire to join? And you're confident she'd put your wishes as a priority over her own?"

Perry's deepening frown acknowledges his realization that Lily has maneuvered him into admitting that he is not completely unaware that it's possible Margaret has gone against his wishes. Missy puts the tray on a side table, but her hand shakes so badly that when she picks up the carafe she sloshes coffee out on her hand, and she yelps in pain. Margaret frowns, gives her a dismissive wave, and Missy runs from the room. Margaret takes over, gracefully gliding around the room, setting out the cups and pouring the coffee.

Lily reminds herself that she can't worry about Missy now. "I tracked Thea Kincaide—the woman found dead near the track by Moonvale Tunnel—to your old house, Perry. I also found footprints indicating a large gathering of women at the house and a WKKK hood that someone had left behind in the house. Not only that, but Miss Harding and Mr. Broward, who were out that night, happened upon Miss Kincaide and, concerned for her safety, have testified that they followed her, until she came upon your Moonvale property. When she ran to the gathering of women in WKKK garb, they decided to retreat. As you might understand."

Perry's already-ruddy face turns a deeper red. "That doesn't mean that Margaret knew anything about it. The house is remote; that's why we moved here after my father died—"

"Remote, but you were in Moonvale Hollow Village."

Margaret perches on the love seat and sips her coffee. Neither Lily nor Perry touches theirs.

"Visiting friends," Perry says.

"That late at night?"

"There's not a curfew on adults visiting friends."

Margaret clears her throat delicately and puts her cup back on its saucer with a pointed clink. "While this is a charming preview to the upcoming debate, let me save us all some time before it becomes tiresome. Perry was in the village because he was trying to stop me from holding the meeting at our old house. Though it's causing us distress, I'm sure he'll come to see why women need to gather to rally for protections, and against changes that will surely only hurt families. Such as men being able to use physical force against their wives—"

Lily looks at the entry to the parlor, through which Missy had fled. "I've already said that I'd love to stop Ralf Ranklin from hurting his wife. She has to file charges—"

"I know, before you can legally do anything about it. In the meantime, you turn a blind eye to his moonshining—"

"I have no proof of that," Lily says.

"You mean, you're not willing to look for it."

"I've been a bit too busy to track down every home still in the county! I've tracked the path of a woman before she died, and that path happened to lead to your old house, on the night you were holding a WKKK meeting!"

"Ah yes." Margaret's smile curls wider. "Thea Kincaide. That's who you said she was? She did come onto our property—we didn't know her name at the time. I think you're focusing on the wrong issue. You can't seriously claim to be fine with the notion of Miss Harding being courted by someone like—" She stops, shudders.

Lily clenches her jaw. She doesn't give a damn who courts who. Her and Daniel's love had been as worthy as anyone else's—no matter what people like the Dyers think—as is Olive and Clarence's.

Lily abruptly stands. "Perry has a point, Margaret. My only role is to bring you in until you face the charges against you—"

"I'll post bail and she will be out in no time!" Perry exclaims.

"That's up to you," Lily starts, but then Margaret shouts.

"Listen to me, both of you! The old woman did come onto our property, being chased by that—that disgusting couple. It was clear she was afraid of them. I have no idea why, but the way that . . . that . . . man was coming after her—"

It is all Lily can do to keep from rolling her eyes at Margaret's unlikely story. It's much more believable that Olive and Clarence assumed, as they'd told Marvena, that Thea would come to no harm with the women at the gathering—and was perhaps trying to find her way to it—and then quickly departed for their own safety.

"Margaret, stop; you shouldn't say anything more—" Perry starts, but Margaret gives him a dismissive wave, much like the one she'd given Missy. She yells the young woman's name. Quickly, obediently, Missy appears, like a dog answering a whistle.

Margaret gives her a magnanimous smile. "Don't worry, dear. I haven't told them. I've left that for you. Go on, about your boy. You should be proud of the lad!"

Missy steps forward. She clears her throat. "Junior followed you home th'other day. When you left here, so abruptly. He's a smart one, knows you're up to no good, like that smart-mouthed daughter of yours! And he heard that filthy woman—" Lily's ire rises to hear Marvena described in this way. She clenches her jaw, keeps her eyes steady on Missy. "—tell you all about Olive and her . . . her unnatural . . . love for that union man, stirring trouble over in Rossville." Missy squares her shoulders. "He did as any good boy would do. Came back, told me. And I reported it all to Marg—to Mrs. Dyer."

As Missy looks at Margaret, her expression asks, *Was that good?*

Margaret gives a small nod, another wave of the hand, and Missy leaves. Then Margaret looks at Lily, her eyes dark. For a second, Lily imagines those eyes peering through slits, soulless hollow voids.

"After that, I had no choice but to confront Miss Harding," Margaret says. "I didn't beat her because she would not foreswear her unnatural love."

Perry gasps and Lily stares at Margaret, shocked by the admission. Suddenly the room is quiet and suffocating, as if all air had been sucked from the room along with sense and reason.

Into this void, Margaret smiles again. "The old woman—whose name I didn't even know that night—ran away of her own volition, for some reason. And Olive bragged that when the old woman came across them again, Clarence dragged the woman to the top of the tunnel, and pushed her off as the train came through. Threatened that he would do the same to any of us. That is, I admit, when I lost my own temper and beat Olive. And I have two witnesses—upstanding members of Kinship's best and of the WKKK—who will testify to Olive's admission that he murdered the old woman."

Margaret stands, holds her hands forward, wrist to wrist. Gracefully. Coolly.

Lily's jaw tightens. The hood accidentally left behind at the old Dyer farmhouse—that would have been the result of some anxious member's carelessness. Margaret wouldn't have left it; neither would she have let her hood carelessly fall to reveal her face to Olive. She had only let herself be seen because she wished to be seen. Only let Olive live because she wished for Olive to accuse her.

Margaret's smile widens. "Will you still stand on the rule of law, Sheriff Ross?"

A few hours later, Lily startles awake at a creaking sound. As she rouses, she winces at the stiffness from falling asleep on Marvena's porch swing. Shep moans as Lily's hand moves—and she realizes she's been half resting her hand, half petting the hound's head, the whole time she's been waiting here. She gives his silky ears another rub, then looks sheepishly at Marvena, who stands before her, regarding her with an amused grin and a shake of her head.

Lily looks beyond Marvena to twilight softly claiming the woods, her gaze catching on a maple tinged with orange. The rain had stopped but cooled the air and stirred the loamy scents of earth. Soon the whole forest would erupt with the resplendent hues of autumn—and after that, the quiet and cold of another winter. Whenever she would complain that it was so cold her bones ached, Daniel would tell her to think of the snow as a soft blanket letting the earth rest.

Then she sees him—the shimmering, silvery boy perpetually chasing either a ball or a dog, pausing in his pursuit to peekaboo at her from behind the oak. *Dammit.* A real boy—Junior—had followed Marvena and Lily home, overheard Marvena explain to Lily about Olive and Clarence. And she had been so used to dismissing the silvery boy that she must have also dismissed a glimpse of a real one. She could chalk her oversight up to exhaustion if she is looking for an excuse—but she isn't.

Lily shivers and sneezes. In the split second her eyes squeeze shut for the sneeze, the boy has disappeared. *Dammit.* Marvena looks concerned. "Lord a mercy, Lily. You look spooked. I reckon you didn't come on a social call, but let's get you inside before you start yammering—"

"I don't yammer!" Lily sneezes again.

Marvena swiftly unlatches the door. "If'n you say so."

Ten minutes later, Lily sits in front of Marvena's warm stove, a heavy quilt draped over her shoulders, sipping mint and chamomile tea, doused with some of Marvena's shine. The scent and taste of the tea is soothing, and she feels her chest relax. She hadn't realized, until now, how tense she's been since finding Thea, and now she feels even more twisted up after taking Margaret to jail—all the while Margaret never flickering her gaze or dropping her odd smile.

Lily takes another sip of tea, breathes in the steam, savors both taste and scent of Marvena's concoction. "Where is Frankie?" Not school. Without Olive—or Hildy—the children of Rossville will go without school for a time, a thought that saddens Lily.

"She's down at Nana's. Jurgis will bring her home when he comes up—" Marvena stops, clears her throat. "How long you been sitting up here, anyway?"

"Probably since three."

Marvena turns from the one table in the cabin, where she's been stirring up biscuit dough, and shoots a look at Lily. "You coulda found me in town, you know."

Lily lifts an eyebrow. "Well, as sheriff, I came straight here. To be efficient in upholding my duty as law enforcement. Since this would be the most likely place for me to find you."

Marvena whacks her wooden spoon against her bowl, making such a racket that outside Shep howls on the front porch. "You tryin' to tell me that you're takin' me in again for moonshinin'?" Lily had had to arrest her friend once before—though she hadn't held her long. "What's in your cup is left over—should I take it from you?"

"Not on your life." Lily takes another sip. "No, no, I'm here because as a union organizer, you're the most likely to tell me where I might be able to find another union organizer—Clarence Broward."

"Lily, you know—"

Lily holds up her hand to shush Marvena. Then she fills her in on the events at the Dyers' house and the arrest that followed.

As Marvena takes it all in, her expression goes from shock to outrage—and Lily knows that Marvena has sifted the details and sorted out how Margaret has trapped Lily. She can arrest Margaret for assault, sure. But if she neglects to bring in Clarence, too, why then she's taking the side of a potential murderer against the upstanding wife of her political opponent.

Lily finishes, "So I'm here, since I don't know where Clarence is, and since you might be aware of where he lives, you need to tell me that, so I can bring him in for questioning." Surely Marvena is savvy enough to understand what she's really saying.

Marvena finally says softly, "I don't know where he lives, but if'n I see him, I can tell him." Then Lily exhales with relief as she reads in Marvena's expression that she understands: Lily had come here, where she wouldn't see Clarence, but plenty of witnesses in town would have seen her drive up to Marvena's to ask about his whereabouts; and that Clarence needs to clear out of Bronwyn County as fast as he can—and not because of any threat from Lily.

Then Marvena's expression collapses in sorrow and fear. "Lily, he won't—"

Lily shakes her head, interrupts. "Oh, Jurgis won't be home for a bit? Well then, tell him I said howdy." She stands, finishes her tea, puts the cup on the table, and folds up the quilt.

She pauses at the door and says, without looking back at Marvena, "Olive will be fine. I've been to check on her. Course, I can't be everywhere at once. So I've brought on several men as deputies to be at Mrs. Gottschalk's around the clock. Once the charges are resolved against Mrs. Dyer, I can't imagine Olive will want to stay in the area, though. She'll want to figure out where to go next. She'll want to go where she is safe—well, safer at least." Lily cuts a meaningful look at Marvena: *Where Clarence should go to join her.*

With that, she puts on her hat and steps out of Marvena's cabin.

CHAPTER 26

❦

HILDY

Tuesday, September 28—8:00 p.m.

In the thick of the crowd outside the Kinship Opera House, Hildy can barely breathe. She's pressed between several men and can only see a sliver of brick, of the dimming sky. Her head tingles. She had picked over dinner, skipped lunch, had only a biscuit and jam for breakfast.

But Hildy is determined. She will see Lily debate Perry.

And here, in the throng of people who also want to see this debate, it will be impossible for either Mother or Merle to find her, to pull her away—assuming they had come after her.

Mother had forbidden her to come, of course. All day, she had harangued Hildy for being away. Fussed at her, while Hildy polished the furniture and scrubbed the kitchen floor, that she should go to Merle, offer her help at the grocery, apologize to him—for what, Hildy was unsure. Neither Mother nor Merle knew about her affair with Tom. Mother had, she repeatedly told Hildy, informed Merle that Hildy had run home from the grocery due to "female troubles" when Merle had come to find Hildy—both proud at coming up with the ruse and angry at Hildy for "forcing" her to lie. Quietly, Hildy had scrubbed the day away, biting her tongue to keep from pointing out that Mother had lied, all on her own.

At dinner, Hildy asked if Mother would like to go to the debate—a mistake. Of course Mother didn't want to, and she'd told Hildy she must not go, either. It would be improper for her to go support Lily, to be seen there, and Merle would surely think Hildy crazy if she went.

Fine. She'd go anyway. Slide out the kitchen door, quietly, after dinner.

Then a knock had come at their door. Merle—looking worried and sheepish, holding a bag of the penny candy. Supplication. Apology, though he'd never say it outright.

As Merle pressed the bag at Hildy, the flash of memory from a few days ago returned to her—Roger, grinning widely, holding his ridiculous bouquet of licorice whips. Merle had smiled, assuming Hildy's gasp was in pleasure at his offering, but she'd pressed past him and, for the second time, ran from him.

Now someone at the front of the crowd hollers out. The doors to the opera house are opening.

"Well now, it's been a novelty, standing here, debating Sheriff *Lily*," Perry says.

How can she endure it? Hildy wonders. Earlier, she'd managed to work her way to the front of the throng, and now sits a few rows back from the stage. Though her eyes are fastened on Lily, she is sure Lily hasn't seen her. Throughout the past hour—back and forth on topics such as curfews or the increasing number of automobiles speeding on the country roads—Lily has kept her eyes fixed at some spot above the crowd. The topics have been mundane, yet Perry has managed to work in digs about how these issues would be too hard for Lily to take care of, especially as a widow with small children.

Lily has not denied that, not once, sticking instead to her opinions on the issues. The crowd had started divided between the two candidates. Now Hildy senses a shift in its sympathy toward Perry.

It's time for the closing comments. "Ladies first!" Perry says, to the tittering crowd. Lily demurs, asking Perry to go first.

"It's been a novelty having a lady for a sheriff for the past year, but as our county grows and prospers, is that what we want?" Perry says, to the crowd's growing cries of approval. "Novelty? Why, who knows what she might do, especially if she gets nervous. Just today, she pulled my own wife into jail! Accusing her of attacking another woman—Olive Harding, the schoolteacher over in Rossville." The crowd gasps. "Why would my wife do that? Well, seems she learned Olive was consorting with the Negro who's trying to integrate the Rossville union!"

Now the crowd roars. Lily stares at that same damned fixed point. *Why won't she say something? Anything?*

"My wife told her that Miss Harding admits that that same man, Clarence Broward, killed an elderly woman. The same poor old woman—who could be any of our own mothers!—whose image was in the *Kinship Daily Courier*."

Hildy shudders. Her own drawing, twisted and used in this way. Yet, even with angry jeers growing, with wadded papers and apple cores and even a pipe being hurled at her, Lily remains implacable.

"Is he locked up? No! Is this the kind of law enforcement you want for your county?"

The crowd roars. Perry grins.

Lily stands stock-still.

Oh God. He's won. He's whipped up the crowd, and won.

Hildy wonders, *Why won't Lily move, or speak, or at least blink?*

Soon others must be wondering the same thing: *Why is Sheriff Lily Ross standing fixed and solid as a statue? No hint of emotion flickering across her face?* Perry's smile fades. The crowd slowly quiets.

Lily's hand starts to float up from the podium but then comes down again, grasping the edge. *Did anyone else notice?* Hildy wonders. A jeer from the front row seems to startle Lily at last into focusing on the moment.

"I'd like to answer that question," Lily says.

Someone in the crowd chuckles, and someone else shushes him.

"I think my kind of law enforcement is exactly what all of you want for Bronwyn County. Let's start with the matter of Miss Harding and Mr. Broward. It has been legal for couples of mixed races to court and marry in the state of Ohio since 1887."

"Well, that ain't right!" hollers a man. "It oughta be more illegal than moonshining!"

Several in the crowd crow in agreement.

Lily breaks her distant gaze, stares down at the man. "I think we all know that I'm not a fan of the law of Prohibition because it's hard to enforce." An appreciative whoop from the back of the crowd sets several to chuckling. Lily waits until the crowd quiets to go on. "But activities can't be more or less illegal. They either are, or they're not. I defend the rule of law."

Now the crowd fully hushes as Lily scans the packed seats.

"I defend the rule of law," she says again. "And that law says that Miss Harding and Mr. Broward may assemble as they see fit. That law also defends the right to free assembly—including the right of Mrs. Dyer to assemble a group of women in a chapter of the WKKK. I can do nothing to break up either assembly—so long as no other laws are violated.

"Today, Mrs. Dyer freely admitted that she beat Olive Harding nearly to death. There is a law against that. And though Mrs. Dyer says that Miss Harding claims Mr. Broward killed Thea Kincaide, Miss Harding denies saying so. Neither of the two WKKK members that Mrs. Dyer claims also heard Miss Harding say this has come forward. And why, I wonder, would that be?"

Lily scans the crowd, and now it seems as if her eyes alight on each person there. The crowd is rapt. Lily's eyes finally meet Hildy's—but just for a second. A second that is long enough for her to see that Lily wishes Hildy weren't there. That she doesn't believe that Hildy can handle a gathering this intense. That she would agree with Mother and Merle: Hildy should be at home.

Lily's eyes move on. "They have not come forward, because they are cowards. Only cowards hide under masks and cloaks."

Now some in the crowd stir angrily. A chill runs over Hildy. There must be women here who are part of the group. Maybe men who are part of their own KKK group.

"Only cowards," Lily repeats firmly. "As for Thea Kincaide—I will find out how she died. I didn't even know her name a week ago—but now I do. I know so much about her—but not enough. Not yet. If you wonder why I haven't been coming to your businesses, your houses, campaigning, it's because I've been working for justice for her. For this woman who"—Lily looks at Perry for a moment—"could be any of our mothers. Who was, in fact, Mr. Dyer's father's stepsister. Mr. Dyer's stepaunt."

The crowd murmurs, and Perry turns ashen. "Father never mentioned, never . . ." His voice trails off.

Lily waits for the crowd to quiet, and then finishes her statement. "Here is why you should vote for me. Not because I'm a novelty. But because I do not think the rule of law is a novelty. Because I think it should be applied equally, for justice for all."

Someone in the crowd breaks the silence with an approving whoop. Other cries follow, and soon there is applause. But Lily only gives a curt nod, leaving the stage, not staying to hear the crowd's applause rise to its full swell.

For a long time, Hildy stands as the crowd shuffles out around her.

"Miss? Are you all right?"

Hildy startles, then sees an older man, sweeping up the opera house, look at her with concern. The crowd has almost entirely left.

"I'm fine," Hildy says. She gives him a reassuring smile and turns to go home, but the man's next comment stops her.

"I liked what Sheriff Ross said, 'bout rule of law," he says. "She's darned bright. Doesn't stand a chance of winning, but she's got my vote."

Hildy starts to rebuke the notion Lily can't win the election, but that phrase, *rule of law,* stirs an idea. A brilliant idea.

And tomorrow morning, she will convince Lily to believe in her, to trust her.

CHAPTER 27

LILY

Tuesday, September 28—11:00 p.m.

At last, Lily is alone. She turns up the coal-oil lamp on her bedroom nightstand, pulls the quilt up to her chin, and sips her peppermint tea. Marvena had been right—her cough needs tending. She'd managed to choke back coughing at the debate. It would have made her seem weak.

Now Lily picks up a novel she's been unsuccessfully trying to read for the past few nights, *The Red Lamp,* by Mary Roberts Rinehart. She keeps dozing off. It's not Mrs. Rinehart's fault—the story is thrilling.

Tonight, though, she is too wide awake, still buzzing with energy postdebate. She glances at the Big Ben clock on her nightstand. *Oh God. Eleven p.m.* She'll be lucky to fall asleep before midnight—but that will give her time, at least, to finish her book. Tomorrow, she heads to Cincinnati. Mama and Caleb Jr. are spending the night, so Mama can watch all the children. *Dear Mama. Of late, she spends as much time here as at her own house.*

Lily opens to her bookmarked page—sinking into the world of Twin Hollows, of William Porter's "diary" entries, of the question of whether Jane really had caught the ghost of Uncle Horace on her camera or she was only imagining things. . . .

Lily gazes up from the novel. *Only imagining things.* Tonight, she'd seen the silvery, shimmering boy standing at the very back of the debate crowd, smiling at her with amusement. For a sliver of a moment, everyone else dissolved, and it was just him and her, alone, as if in some mist from a dream—and then he was gone, the crowd was back, and she saw her hand floating up to reach for him. Just a momentary lapse, not enough for anyone to notice, and she'd returned quickly, smoothly, back to her comments, and yet she'd caught Hildy at the front of the crowd staring up at her, always so sensitive to her every nuanced shift of mood and mannerism. A jeer from the front row— Leroy, the guard she'd fired a few days ago—had finally jolted her back into the rhythm of the debate.

Jolene's voice filters into the bedroom. "Daddy rounded up all the bank robbers, all by himself! But on the way back here to the jail, one broke away—"

Lily sits bolt upright, *The Red Lamp* tumbling from her hand to the floor. *What in the world is Jolene telling Micah?*

Lily leaps out of bed, tosses on her robe, and flings open her bedroom door. She crosses the hall to Micah's room, enters, and finds Jolene sitting on the edge of Micah's bed.

"What in the world—" Lily starts.

She stops as Jolene's eyes go wide and her lower lip trembles. "Micah wanted to know the story of what happened to Daddy. He's—He's been having nightmares." She whispers, so as not to stir Caleb Jr., sound asleep in his bed.

The chastisement that had immediately sprung to Lily's lips—that Jolene knows better—fades away as the realization hits her that she hasn't even been aware of Micah's nightmares. Surely Hildy or Mama should have told her.

Another thought pushes aside irritation at not being told: It's only human to create a narrative to fill the gaps we don't know, the gaps that terrify us. The visions—like a shimmery, silvery boy appearing and disappearing—that haunt us.

It's what her children are doing, with the vague explanations she'd offered for their father's death.

Lily rushes to her children, needful and scared in this moment, and sits on the edge of Micah's bed and scoops them both to her. "Oh, my little sweet peas. I miss your daddy, too. He wasn't killed stopping a bank robbery, though. He was killed by an escaping prisoner." She swallows hard, giving her children the lie that she had at first been given.

"Is the pris'ner gonna come back for us?" Micah's voice trembles.

"Oh no, no," Lily says. "He . . . he was caught. He's in prison now."

"Behind our house?" Micah sounds truly alarmed now.

"No, that's just the jailhouse. Truly bad people go to prison. He's in the Ohio Penitentiary, all the way in Columbus." Lily clears her throat. Another lie.

"Well, then I wanna go see him! Beat him up! For what he did to Daddy!" Micah wails.

"We can't do that—" Lily starts.

"Why not?" Micah asks.

"We have to let the law govern what happens to people who break the law—"

Micah stares up at her now, eyes wild with confusion and anger. Her answer might have been the right thing to say to tonight's debate crowd, but she hasn't said the right things to soothe her little boy. She's only made things worse. As she strokes his head and tries to think—now her head is pounding—Jolene speaks up. "That Ranklin boy was back at school today."

Lily tucks her hand under Jolene's chin and gently tilts her child's head up so she has to look at her. "He didn't hurt you, did he?" She scans Jolene's face for fresh marks.

"No-o-o." Jolene drags out the syllable so that it's almost a moan. "He said I might see Daddy's ghost. That when people are gone before they're supposed to be gone, they sometimes don't go away completely. Like the ghosts at the Moonvale Tunnel!"

"G-ghosts?" Micah's voice cracks on the word, and he grips his mother tightly, the small tremors of his body ricocheting through Lily.

Lily almost smiles—relief at the subject changing from the circumstances of Daniel's death, albeit to another tricky one. She keeps her expression somber. "Do you know, I heard those same stories when I was your age?"

"You did?" Jolene's eyes widen with wonder. "Those stories are that old?"

Lily chuckles. "Yes, that old. But you know what? I've been investigating out there—"

"Why?"

"Oh, an older lady got hurt, and—"

"How?"

"By the train, sweet pea."

"Is she dead?"

Lily hesitates. She wants to comfort her children, but instead she keeps letting the conversation spin in the wrong direction. She squeezes Micah and Jolene, her arms easily wrapping around them. Soon that won't be the case. They are growing up quickly and asking questions that become trickier by the day. Maybe they would be better served by real answers. So Lily says, "She is. But you know what?"

"What?"

"I haven't seen any ghosts. Not of her. Not of anybody."

"Really?" Micah's tone is a mix of disappointment and relief.

Lily's stomach clinches, as she thinks of the silvery boy. Still, she answers quickly, "Really."

Jolene starts crying. "So, I'm never gonna see a ghost of Daddy?"

"Oh, sweet pea." Lily's heart aches under the weight of seeing the hurt her child bears, a hurt that makes her long to see a ghost. "You don't want to see your daddy's ghost, do you?"

"N-no," Jolene stammers. "But it would be better'n not seeing him again. Wouldn't it?"

Lily smooths her daughter's hair back, gently wipes the tears. "I see him, in you and in Micah. In your beautiful eyes, and how smart you are, and sometimes stubborn. . . ." She pauses and gives Jolene's belly a little tickle, and Jolene hiccups a small laugh. Then she looks at Micah, tousles his hair. "In your mess of black hair, and in your funny and feisty spirit."

Both children brighten for a moment, but then Micah's expression darkens again. Lily's heart flips. *Another way in which he looks like his father.* "I'm already forgetting what Daddy looks like." He hiccups.

"And his smell," Jolene says. "I think he smelled like tobacco?"

Lily pulls her children back to her. She rocks on the edge of Micah's bed, as if they're all in a rocking chair. "Your father did often smell like tobacco. Don't worry. Someday, the both of you, you'll sense him—maybe when you need to do something very brave, or maybe when you need some guidance—and you'll know what to do. That will be him. Letting you know." She presses her eyes shut. She doesn't know if she believes this to be true. She must tell her children something to ease their fears. To ease her own fears, of both her and her children forever being haunted, not by Daniel's presence in the form of a ghost, but by his very absence.

She presses her eyes shut, breathing in the sweet, soft scents of her children. A surge of gratitude for Mama swells her heart. She must have helped them get their baths. Then a surge of longing to protect her children from all the cruelty of the world.

The thought crosses Lily's mind—Jolene lost her father at almost the same age as Thea lost hers.

The stark image of Thea fills Lily's mind's eye, even as she rocks her children: her small, almost childlike body, in just the nightgown, tossed like a doll into the woods alongside the track, her head and body broken by the impact of the train and then the hard, cold earth.

Had a ghost from the past caused her to make the trek from the Hollows Asylum to the Moonvale Hollow Tunnel? Something that had haunted her since her childhood, something that had happened when she'd lived on the old Dyer farm?

Lily sighs, and her children grow heavy against her. The rhythms of their breaths lengthen and even.

Tomorrow in Cincinnati, she will somehow find Thea's son, and hope that he knows something from his mother's past that will lend insight—and that he'll be willing to share it.

Finally, Jolene and Micah have fallen asleep. Lily carefully lets Micah down onto his bed. He sighs as his head rests on his pillow. Lily carries Jolene to her bedroom, careful not to disturb Mama on the other twin bed, tucks her in, then goes back to Micah to make sure he's covered by his blanket. She checks on Caleb Jr., still sound asleep. She smiles. Her little brother could sleep through anything.

Then Lily stares at her bedroom door. All that talk of Daniel . . . she does not want to be in their bedroom—her bedroom—alone. It's late, but she might as well get the damned pie made for the weekend's county fair. She can ask Mama or Hildy to deliver it to the judging tent, while she goes to Cincinnati on the morning train.

She makes the pie with only half her mind on the task, mixing up the lard crust, then while it bakes, cooking the filling on the stove top, comprised of simple ingredients always on hand—eggs, sugar, flour, water, white vinegar. Then Lily pours the filling into the crust and while it bakes a while longer cleans up and nearly laughs out loud as she thinks how Mama calls this (along with its sorghum and sugar cream cousins) a desperation pie, as in, pie is called for, but very few ingredients are handy. Desperation fits her mood—desperate to solve the case of Thea's death, to stem the hatred rising in her county, to take care of her children, to find a way back to being gentler with Hildy and Marvena and Mama. . . .

After Lily puts the vinegar pie to cool on the worktable, she heads back through the parlor. Surely, now, she can sleep. But in the parlor, she pauses by her desk. She'd only just mailed her reply to Benjamin Russo in Cincinnati. Would it be odd to find the Bureau of Mines office in Cincinnati, drop in, wish him luck in his new post in the Kinship region? She closes her eyes, trying to imagine how it would play out. *Hello, Mr. Russo. I happened to be in Cincinnati on a case, and thought I'd drop by to wish you the best.* . . . Implausible. Cincinnati is a huge city, not a town like Kinship where it's commonplace and simple to "drop by." *Hello, Mr. Russo. I'm in Cincinnati on a case and thought it would be efficient for me to discuss how area law enforcement might help with your office's research into safety practices.* . . . Ridiculous. How could it help? Oh God, another possible reason to visit arises unbidden from the deepest part of her: *Ben, I'd love to see you when you're in Kinship, to get to know you better.* . . .

Exhaustion overcomes her, like a sudden fever. She places one hand on the back of Daniel's old chair, swaying from weariness, but she can't bring herself to sit down in it, not yet. After a moment, she opens her eyes and makes her way back upstairs.

Hours later, Lily stirs to confused, fuzzy wakefulness.

She sits up, rubs her eyes, the mist of some strange, troubled dream quickly receding. She sighs, letting it go, not trying to grasp its last slippery tentacles and pull it back to her. It is a relief to be free of whatever it was.

Now a shout from outside, below her window, startles her. More voices rising. It must be this commotion that awakened her.

Lily rushes to her bedroom window, pulls back the drapery, and stares at the sight below.

A cross, erected on her front lawn. Burning. In the light of the flames, hooded and caped figures. One turns its hollow, soulless slits for eyes up to her window.

Oh God. So this is why Margaret was so willing to be taken to jail. To whip up her followers into rash, hateful action.

The children. Mama. She must get them out.

She wakes them, hurries them down the stairs, to the kitchen door. Lily thrusts Micah into Mama's arms, even though Mama is already holding crying, confused Caleb Jr. Poor boy—he couldn't sleep through *this* atrocity.

"Go to Hildy's! Get her to take you to Mrs. Gottschalk's!" Lily orders her mother.

"Mama!" Micah screams, reaching for her, and Jolene grabs on to Lily's nightgown. But Lily shoves her daughter toward Mama. "Make sure Mamaw does as I've said!"

Then Lily rushes back in, grabs her shotgun from the mantel. By the time she is out on her front porch, the Klanswomen have gone, disappeared into the veil of night.

Anger seethes and rises, and Lily lets loose with a fierce scream.

The corrupt cross, its flames a desecration of all a cross *should* stand for, crackles and collapses, falling toward the porch roof. Lily jumps back, into the house, runs back to the kitchen. It seems hopeless, but she puts her rifle on the kitchen worktable, nearly knocking off the vinegar pie, and fills a bucket at the pump sink. The water sloshes out, soaking her gown, as she runs out the back and around to the front of her house, gasping with desperation and shock, and sorrow at the impossibility of her task. She'll never get the flames out, alone.

But as Lily comes around to the front, she sees that she is not alone. Men and women in neighboring houses have heard the commotion, too, seen the burning cross, the flames now spreading across the roof porch. They've come with buckets of their own water, and someone has a ladder up alongside the house, and a bucket brigade gets under way, as more and more people pour out of their homes and join the communal effort.

A process is already unfolding—a few older people in line to pass along the full buckets to the man going up and down the ladder, while sprier folks bring buckets of water to toss on the burning lawn. The air is filled with the smell of woodsmoke and the hiss and crackle of the flames already dying out and the alarmed voices of people calling out to one another.

Someone hands her an empty bucket, but she shakes her head. She can't become part of the brigade, not yet. "The prisoners! I have to get them out of the jailhouse in case the fire spreads." She must get the prisoners to safety. Even Margaret. Lily'd spoken tonight about the rule of law, and she knows she must stand for it, even for those she considered the community's vilest members.

A man holding a bucket of water turns and looks at her. It is Leroy, the guard she'd fired, one of the men who had jeered her at the debate. He pauses for a moment, giving her a look that is a mix of regret and sorrow, and then he hands his bucket to someone else.

"I'll help you," he says. "We can get them to the courthouse."

As Lily runs alongside Leroy, she glances back at the brigade that's quickly formed to douse the hateful burning cross, to save the sheriff's house.

This too is her community.

CHAPTER 28

※

HILDY

Wednesday, September 29—10:00 a.m.

"I wish to take back my statement," Margaret says.

Hildy looks up, startled. As she'd swept the threshold to the jail-house, her thoughts had been on the news that Lily had received from the undertaker that Thea would be buried today in the Kinship Cemetery. Though it should fall to Mother or Thea's mysterious son as Thea's next of kin, Lily had agreed to pay for the burial out of her personal funds, but would not witness the internment, as she was making sure her children, Mama, and her little brother were safely settled in at Widow Gottschalk's—and after that, she was determined to be on the train later this afternoon to Cincinnati.

Now Margaret sits primly on the edge of her straw mattress, as if she is waiting at the train depot, rather than in jail for having beaten a woman.

For once—more'n likely because it is mid-week—the jailhouse is relatively empty. Margaret is in her cell. Another is empty, and in the third a man sleeps off too much moonshine, face to wall, his snores so loud they nearly rattle the cell bars.

"You heard me," Margaret says. "I wish to retract my statement about beating Miss Olive Harding. I would never do such a thing. I only said as much because Sheriff Ross intimidated me. My husband will attest to this fact. He stepped out of the room to bring me a drink of water, and while he was gone, Sheriff Ross threatened to hurt us—to, to burn down our very house if I didn't confess! Missy Ranklin happened to come into the room, and hear the threat."

Hildy stares in shock at the woman. Lily would do no such thing.

But Perry would back up his wife, and Missy would vouch for her benefactress.

Margaret snaps her fingers twice, impatiently. "Well, go!"

Hildy flinches. Margaret's smile crawls farther up her face.

For a moment, the exhaustion, the smell of bleach Hildy had used to disinfect the cell where the ill prisoner had been, the memory of the night before, all spin Hildy around. The earth comes up toward her and she grabs the doorframe.

She thinks of Olive's beaten, broken body. She does not rush to get Lily, as she once would have. Instead, as Lily would, Hildy calculates.

Margaret's willing admission to Olive's brutal beating . . . of course that would get her arrested, put her in the jailhouse, her flock stirred up, but she herself with the perfect alibi for last night's WKKK attack. Maybe she'd even ordered them to act as they had if she was ever arrested.

Hildy leans her broom against the wall, tapping the handle loudly enough to stir the hungover prisoner. As Hildy strides to her jail cell, now Margaret flinches—*how satisfying.* It's Hildy's turn to smile as she says, "You planned this."

"I have no idea what you're talking about. Go fetch the sheriff—and ask your dear mother what she thinks of your liaison with that filthy miner."

Hildy recoils. *How does Margaret know about Tom—unless some of the women of Rossville are in the WKKK? Why reference Mother—Oh God. What if Mother is part of the hateful group? What if she'd been at the Dyer farm that night? What if she recognized Thea?*

Hildy turns, runs from the jailhouse after all. As she goes out the door, she brushes against the broom, knocking it to the ground. The sound of its crack against the earth does not mask Margaret's trill of laughter.

"I don't know, Hildy." Lily sighs, busily folding a few items of clothing for her travel bag. "Yes, your mother implied to me that she is part of the women's Klan—but I don't know."

Hildy stands in the doorway to Lily's bedroom. "What if she was there? Saw Cousin Thea? What if—" Hildy's voice withers. Does she really think her mother would be capable of murder? Mother clearly still hates Thea. What on earth could be between them from all those years ago to keep alive such vile emotion?

Lily turns abruptly, her gaze scorching Hildy with impatience. "Thank you for telling me about Margaret. I will let the judge know before I leave. Hildy—you look weary. Just rest while I am gone. I have the deputies in place that I need—"

"You're angry about me and Tom."

Lily jerks back as if stung. "Oh, Hildy. I—Yes, I wish you'd told me, rather than Marvena. I know I've been preoccupied—" Lily looks down. Maybe, finally, if only for a few moments, they will talk, find their way back to friendship. When Lily looks back up, her expression is again shuttered. "Hildy, go to Thea's burial today, and after that lay low while I'm gone. It will just be for a few days. Tell you what—you want to help? Just type up my notes from this case." Lily picks up a notebook, hands it to Hildy. "I've filled up this one, and hopefully, I'll fill up pages in the new one with information that will put an end to this case." She gestures at her bag, holding the new notebook.

Hildy stares at the notebook she's holding. A typist for Lily. Busywork. Surely not—but as she looks up at Lily, she sees the pity and worry in her friend's eyes.

Lily looks away, as if ashamed at being caught pitying Hildy. She picks up a hairbrush, pushes it into her bag, adding, "If anything, go to Mrs. Gottschalk's to check on . . . everyone, and if Olive decides to press charges, go immediately to the judge, and—"

"I have an idea," Hildy blurts. "I've been thinking about a way I could help us learn more about Thea's motivation to leave the asylum—"

Before Hildy can explain, Lily crosses the room, as quickly as if she'd flown. She grabs Hildy by her shoulders and gives her a shake. "No! Hildy, don't do anything! I will see what I can learn from Thea's son. Just do as I ask."

A few hours later, Hildy alone stands in the Kinship Cemetery, save for the three gravediggers waiting quietly outside the gate. The closed pine box holding Thea's remains is next to a neat rectangle they've already dug.

A stiff wind blows across the top of the hill, making leaves chatter mournfully to one another. Far off, a bird chirps. One of the workers spits a stream of tobacco.

Hildy wishes for Frankie, who would know a song to sing. Or Lily, who in spite of her gruff doubts would have a Bible verse handy. Marvena or Mama or Nana would all know something to say. Tom might put a gentle, comforting hand on her shoulder.

Hildy, by herself, finds her mind a gray blank—and not just from the hour and a half she'd spent typing up and organizing Lily's notes. A blur of impressions, interviews, even dates from the Dyer family cemetery. A jumble of facts and tidbits, like rags in a box saved for a quilt, but none of them yet coming together in a clear pattern.

Still, she'd fulfilled her obligation. Left the notes on Lily's desk. Her hands are stiff from typing so fast, so hard. Now she forces herself to reconstruct at least an outline of what she and Lily had learned about Thea Kincaide.

Thea had lost her father when she was just seven, in 1857. She'd said it was at the hand of John, an escaped slave her father had been helping, and remarkably, her identification of him had been sufficient for the court at the time to convict John and hang him to death in the town square.

In 1857, Thea and her mother, Cleo, had moved to the Dyer farm, working full-time, for room and board, for the family they'd once done laundry for. Tending to sickly Joyce, to one-year-old Murphy Dyer. After Joyce died, Cleo married old man Dyer and Thea stayed—until she was old and brave enough to run away to chase a life of glamour and adventure.

Eventually marrying, having a son, divorcing, remarrying.

Yet—she'd come back once, for her uncle's funeral, her uncle being Hildy's grandfather, Mother's father.

A few postcards sent to little Hildy. Why? Had Cousin Thea seen something of herself in Hildy—a girl trapped by circumstances, yearning for a bigger life?

Then a large blank—except for the postcards Hildy had forgotten about—until Thea at last ended up back in Athens, where her son was a professor. He'd provided minimal room and board for her and then set her up to go to the Hollows Asylum—but didn't leave his name as contact. Instead, Mother's name.

Thea left the asylum, determined to get back to the Dyer farm, on the night of a full moon. The light of the full moon had made it easier for others to be out, too—Clarence and Olive. The WKKK gathering at the recently unoccupied Dyer farm. After coming across Clarence and Olive and persistently going to the Dyer farm, Thea had either fallen or been pushed to her death in the path of an oncoming train.

Why? Now Hildy looks around, wishing for some glimpse of the old-fashioned lady she thought she'd seen several nights ago, as if a specter might hold all the answers—the lady who, she realized, she wanted to believe was Thea.

Just your fool imagination. She can hear Mother saying it.

The cold fall wind stings her eyes, and Hildy dashes her hand across her face. Not tears of emotion. A mere physical response. For ever since her conversation with Lily, she's felt nothing. Been unable to think anything, beyond wanting to follow through on her plan. No matter what Lily said.

No one thinks she is strong enough. But she is.

Yet she doesn't wish to do this just to "show" them.

She wants to do this for Thea. For herself.

Or, she fears, she will never feel anything again. She will be so numb that she herself might as well be in that box.

Now Hildy crosses over to the mound of dirt. She picks up a small scoop, stares at the dark, loamy earth. Inhales its strong, musky scent. Perfect earth for burying.

She goes to Thea's box, lets the earth sift through her fingers onto the lid, the bits of dirt softly tapping.

Maybe that is enough for a funeral song.

"I'll try my best," Hildy whispers.

Maybe that is enough for a funeral prayer.

An hour later, Hildy is back home, in her bedroom, packing her own travel bag. Mother and Merle wait downstairs.

Her plan is in place. She has told them about Tom. About seeing the ghostly figure of an old-fashioned woman. About how confused and lost her mind has been.

It had been too easy to convince them—as if they'd been waiting for this all along—that in the next few hours, after Lily is gone, they should take Hildy to the Hollows Asylum.

I've been acting crazy, she'd said. *Out of my head.*

They'd readily agreed.

If I have time at the Hollows, to clear my head, I think I'll get right. Be . . . worthy of Merle.

He'd, at least, look shocked at the notion.

Mother had agreed quickly—so quickly that Merle looked even more shocked by that.

Just for a week or so, Merle had said quickly. *Then we can marry. Right away.*

In that moment, Hildy knew she would never marry Merle. But she'd smiled. Nodded.

Now something crinkles in Hildy's pocket. *Ah.* The third and last postcard from Thea.

Postcard
May 2, 1908
Dear Hildy,
Oh, how I had hoped to send you cards from Rome, Madrid, even Oslo and more exotic locales! Alas, I hope you are not too disappointed in your old cousin to see that I am back in New York. Economic needs necessitated my return. At times, the hardest thing to do is the right thing. Though I long to return to the stage as a dancer, that is no longer feasible at my age. I've found a position as a typist, and sometimes, I think of my fingers as dancing on

the typewriter, as if the machine is a stage. For it was only on the stage, playing a role—for that is what dance is as much as acting— that I feel truly myself. Is that odd? Or wisdom? When you are old enough, I hope that you will come to New York—which has as many charms in its way as Europe, and certainly more than Kinship!—and help me answer the question!

All my love,
Thea

CHAPTER 29

LILY

Wednesday, September 29—4:00 p.m.

"Sheriff Ross, would you comment on the events of last night?"

"Where is your family staying?"

"Have you identified any of the culprits?"

"Will you be pressing charges when you do?"

"Why are you leaving town now—especially after last night and with an election? Are you going to withdraw? Pay closer attention to your family?"

While swiftly winding her way through the crowd that has gathered on the Kinship depot's platform, Lily has ignored the barrage of questions from newspaper reporters from the *Kinship Daily Courier,* the *Athens Messenger,* and even from Columbus, blinked at the flashing lights of cameras but not paused to pose. That last set of questions catches her attention. She stops short, looks at the faces of the men blocking her way to the station, and steadies her searching gaze when she comes to a man with a self-satisfied smile curling up under his mustache—pleased he was the one who'd managed to get the little lady sheriff to stop.

As Lily keeps her stare locked on his face, his smile dissolves under his mustache and his caterpillar eyebrows creep up. The other reporters glance at one another, then back at their notepads, pencils poised.

Finally, Lily asks—her voice steady and clear—"Which newspaper do you work for?"

The man straightens a bit. "The *Columbus Dispatch*."

"Take careful notes for your readers. I am not withdrawing from the election. I am taking a brief trip out of town because I am doing my job—following up in the case of the death of Thea Kincaide. Unless any of you boys have any leads you'd care to share?"

Most of the men exchange confused glances—all except Seth, who gives her a quick nod of solidarity and an amused look: *Give 'em hell, Lily.*

Lily presses on through the reporters and now townspeople who have stopped to see what new ruckus has beset the usually boring depot. The last time such a crowd had gathered here, George Vogel was leaving town with Fiona. Thank God that Cincinnati is such a big city—she is not likely to cross paths with the man.

"What about your children? Don't you have a mother and little brother to watch after—"

Lily turns on her heel at the question. "They are fine. Leave my family out of this."

She finally enters the door. Thankfully, the train to Cincinnati is in the station and she quickly buys her ticket, then boards. She'd considered driving, but she still hasn't replaced the spare on her automobile with a new tire and driving would take longer than the train—especially if she broke down along the way. Once in her seat, she opens her satchel and pulls out *The Red Lamp*, which she still hasn't finished. After stowing her satchel under her seat, she opens the novel, stares down at the last page she'd read.

The words swim before her. She'd said her family was fine—but they weren't. Micah had wailed, clutching her legs, begging her not to leave, and Jolene had tried to look stoic, but Lily could see she was terrified. Even Caleb Jr., who reminded her often he didn't have to listen to her because she was "just" his sister, had welled up and begged her for a good-bye hug.

Meanwhile, Mama and Mrs. Gottschalk had reassured her they'd be fine, and Lily tried to convince herself this was true—after all, she's only going to be gone for a few days. She had deputies keeping watch at Mrs. Gottschalk's house—as well as at the sheriff's house and jail, where Margaret, despite her protestations, remains.

The train jerks forward, several uneven jolts as it pulls out of the station.

Lily closes *The Red Lamp* and clasps her hands atop the novel. Her mind is too aswirl to concentrate on reading. She stares out the window, taking in the countryside of southern Ohio as the train passes out of the Appalachian foothills and into the flat land near the Ohio River. Dusk is upon the land, brushing and infusing the trees and small villages—even smaller than Kinship or Rossville—with hues of lavender and sage and coral.

It's not her family members' faces she sees in her mind's eye. She can't stop seeing Hildy's devastated visage at catching her gaze of pity. She was trying to protect her friend—but now she fears she's wounded her.

Focus.

Her job now is to get to Cincinnati, talk to Dr. Neil Leitel. Find a way to get him to tell her everything he can remember about his mother, Thea. Surely there must be something he can tell her that will help crack this case.

She opens her satchel, returns the novel, and pulls out her notebook. Her notes had all seemed a jumble; she hadn't had a chance to review them, try to piece them together like a quilt, finding patterns and order. Her jaw slackens as she stares at the blank page. *Oh yes*—she'd shoved her notes at Hildy to type up.

With a sudden sharp aching that feels like a knife to her gut, she wishes for her dearest, oldest friend, Hildy. Lily closes the useless blank notebook, shoves it alongside the novel in her bag, and presses her eyes shut.

I'm sorry. I'm sorry. I'm sorry, she thinks to the rhythm of the train, to Hildy's visage floating, ghostlike, before her.

The train jolts and Lily's eyes open. Darkness fills the train window.

Night has fallen, and now they are pulling into the station in Cincinnati.

Thursday, September 30—9:45 p.m.

"Do you require more coffee, miss?"

Lily pulls her gaze from the restaurant window to the waiter standing next to her table. He stares down at her, unsmiling, no coffeepot in hand, eager for her to leave.

Behind him, most of the tables, covered in red-and-white-checked tablecloths and topped with candlesticks, are empty, except for a few where couples still linger over coffee and dessert. Lily is the only person sitting at a table alone in Sonny's, and she's drawn stares—her singularity a curiosity, but so too her long-sleeved, collared, modest dress. The other women are garbed in sleeveless, glittery dresses, their heads topped with feathered caps. Her clothes—and probably her demeanor—mark her as a rube from outside the city.

Yet she can't be annoyed, so sated is she from a heavy, exotic meal—a soup with meatballs and spinach, salad with black olives, lasagna rich with mozzarella cheese, garlicky breadsticks, and a dessert she's never heard of before: a slice of *zuccotto,* a cream-filled sponge cake topped with chocolate icing. Though she doesn't require, or even desire, more coffee, she lifts an eyebrow and says with exaggerated politeness, "That would be lovely."

As the waiter turns on his heel, Lily's gaze wanders to the cold window, as it has so many times during the meal. She'd tried to focus on the moment, rejoice in the outlandish tastes of the extravagant meal, think how she might describe it to Mama and Jolene, Hildy and Marvena. And yet, every few bites, her attention turned from warm restaurant to rain-streaked pane, from the bustle of pedestrians and automobiles on the main street in Cincinnati's Over-the-Rhine neighborhood, to Boyd's Gymnasium across the street, where a neon-lit marquee advertised the evening's featured event: a boxing match. Eddie Tyler versus Frank Leoni.

She's never heard of either man, never been a fan of boxing. More than a year ago, she'd come to hate the sport when she discovered how it had once brought out the worst in Daniel, and permanently connected him to George, who'd backed Daniel as a boxer long before she'd met him.

Yet here she sits, idly stirring the remaining coffee, staring through the window at the boxing gymnasium across the way, all because George is likely in there.

She's this desperate because so far, her trip to Cincinnati has proven fruitless. She'd slept fitfully in her room at the Sinton Hotel the night before, then this morning gone to the University of Cincinnati in search of Dr. Neil Leitel. But he didn't have office hours today, and the philosophy department secretary—a gaunt man who made the Sonny's waiter seem downright jolly—had declined to share Neil's schedule or classroom location or home address, even when Lily had introduced herself as the sheriff from Bronwyn County and explained why she was looking for him. In fact, the secretary had scoffed, giving her a quick appraisal, followed by a dismissive look. When she'd loitered in the hallways, asking students if they knew Dr. Leitel, she'd gotten similar reactions. A few hours into that, and a member of the Cincinnati police—summoned by the secretary—had arrived to tell her she was causing a disturbance. She'd then challenged the police officer to take her in, and he'd done so. Lily managed to talk her way up to a lieutenant on the force but still couldn't get anyone to help her locate Neil. She had no jurisdiction here, she was reminded, and if Dr. Leitel had broken ties with his mother, well, that was his business.

Finally, Lily had returned to her hotel room, tried to nap, but restlessly tossed and turned, trying to think of any other way to track down Leitel. The only one she could come up with was to ask George for his help.

But if getting someone to tell her where Leitel lived was impossible, she stood no chance prying that information out from anyone about the powerful and secretive George. Then the notion arose from the back of her mind: if there was one thing George cared about besides power and money, it was boxing. And Boyd's Gymnasium was where, she knew, Daniel had boxed when George was his sponsor.

So Lily had taken the streetcar to this part of town, her heart pounding when she saw the marquee was alight. She'd crossed the street, walking up and down the sidewalk, ignoring the occasional stares, telling herself this was a fool's errand. She stopped in mid-stride as an automobile pulled up and Abe Miller stepped out, holding the door for George as he followed. She'd stopped breathing when Fiona emerged. She'd almost not recognized Fiona, in her short, glittery dress, mink stole, and feathered hat.

But as soon as something—perhaps the power of Lily's stare—made Fiona look over her shoulder in Lily's direction, Lily had ducked in the nearest business: Sonny's Italian Diner, in business since 1912.

She'd remained, and asked for a table, and ordered an expensive meal, and lingered over it. Sure—if anyone had the connections to unearth Leitel's address, it would be George. But would getting it be worth becoming, even in a small way, obligated to George? Why not go home, rule Thea's death an accident—the easiest and, most would agree, the prudent thing to do. Then return to her campaign. Take care of her family. Make amends with Hildy.

Why, tomorrow she could even go shopping, get presents for Mama, Hildy, Mrs. Gottschalk, the children. And Marvena—she wouldn't wear it, but she'd get a good laugh out of a sequined cap. And while shopping downtown, if she happened to drop into the Cincinnati office for the Bureau of Mines to wish Benjamin Russo good luck—a warm gesture on behalf of the folks of her county before his move to her area—why, now, sitting in this sophisticated restaurant rather than late at night in her parlor, that didn't seem so ridiculous—

Lily startles at a man clearing his voice at a table near hers, and when she looks up he's glaring at her. She realizes she's been tapping her spoon hard and loud in her cup, sloshing coffee out on the tablecloth. She gives him and the woman with him a quick, apologetic smile, puts aside the spoon, looks from her nearly empty cup to the window, back again.

What if she does enjoy her coffee, return to the hotel tonight, to Kinship tomorrow, and tell everyone who cared—which, really, was Hildy—that she'd done her best on behalf of Thea, and return to focusing on her campaign and the problems back home?

Take the first choice, and she'll know she has given up on an old woman whose death is too easy to discount.

Ask for George 's help in finding Neil—on the thin chance that Neil will have any information that will shed light on Thea's motivation to leave the asylum, and thus on her death—and she'll owe George a favor in return. Favors from people like George are never given freely, without strings. He'll collect. Probably not right away. Sometime when she won't see it coming.

"Madam? Your coffee?"

The waiter is back, and Lily's hand with the spoon is hovering over the cup.

She looks out the rain-glazed window, at the boxing club. As Hildy's face crosses her mind, her heart pinches at remembering Hildy's hurt expression when Lily had rebuffed her friend's idea for helping uncover the truth about Thea. She hadn't even bothered to find out what the idea was. Why, she'd lectured Leroy, the guard she'd fired, for not caring enough about the least among them, even quoting her favorite Bible scripture. And yet he'd helped her secure the prisoners away from the house until the danger was over. If she is not willing to do what she must for the most vulnerable—a frail, elderly woman with dementia who'd suffered a brutal end—she'll always wonder, even if she wins the election, if she really deserved to be sheriff in her own right.

Lily sighs. Maybe her request will be so pathetically small in Vogel's world that he'll forget to come collect. If not, she'll have to trust herself to be clever enough to deal with his demands. Dealing with difficult choices—and making uneasy compromises—is also part of the job. She smiles at the waiter. "I'm sorry. I've changed my mind."

Half an hour later, inside the gymnasium, Lily presses her handkerchief to her nose. The smell of sweat and body odor is overwhelming. As in the restaurant, she is the only unaccompanied woman, but here that meant she'd already slapped away hands grabbing for her rear end.

Determinedly, she forces herself through the crowd, down to the first row where George, Abe, and Fiona all sit. She's almost there when a man grabs her arm this time. Without even glancing toward her, Abe lifts a hand. The man mutters something, but Lily can't hear it as the crowd erupts when one of the boxers lands three fast blows on the other fighter. But he lets go of Lily's arm and she stumbles forward.

She slides past several people, who yelp in annoyance even at her temporarily blocking their view of the fight, and finally gets to George. There is nowhere to sit, so she stands in front of him, blocking his view. He looks up at her, and it is all Lily can do to not turn away from his hollow dark eyes, the pleased grin that lifts his thick jowls, saying without words, *Ah, Lily, at last. I knew you'd come to me someday.*

"Hey, lady, move your ass!" a man a few rows up shouts down at Lily.

"Or get in the ring and put on your own show!" hollers his friend.

Lily's heart pounds, but not at the men's crude catcalls. There is still time to back away—but abruptly, Abe stands, gives a curt nod to Fiona, who pointedly avoids looking at her as she follows Abe out to the aisle.

George pats the seat next to him.

Lily slowly sits next to George. She doesn't want to look at him, but the sight before her—one boxer on top of the other, punching him repeatedly in his face—turns her stomach. She's starting to regret her heavy meal. One referee pulls the top boxer off, and another kneels next to the one on the floor, counting to ten as the man goes still.

"Mr. Vogel, I—"

He holds his hand up.

Lily waits for the count to come to a conclusion. Half the crowd roars with pleasure, while the other half groans at the outcome. George does not react. Surprised by his silence, Lily looks over at him. He looks not quite bored but not intrigued, either.

Without looking at her, he says, "Tell me what you came for, Sheriff Ross. Or walk away now and we'll pretend that you never tracked me down."

CHAPTER 30

⋙

HILDY

Friday, October 1—11:30 a.m.

Hildy stirs the chicken noodle soup in her bowl. To her surprise, it smells delicious. Even more surprising, she is ravenous.

Her hand trembles, though, and she can barely get the spoon to her mouth without dripping its contents back into the bowl. Finally, she slurps down a noodle and some broth.

Tasty. Well seasoned. Not what she'd expected from lunch at the Hollows.

In the next instant, her stomach roils. She gags—not at the taste or the smell, or even sitting packed onto a hard bench with so many others in the women's dining hall. The soup hits her stomach wrong. She's been nauseous, worse than her monthly menstrual cramps, since she woke up this morning. Her head—so woozy. Her skin—tingly, almost numb.

"You'll get used to it."

Hildy looks up at the handsome woman across the table from her. The woman appears to be older, maybe fifty or so. Stout, hair in a tight gray bun. She could be a member of the Woman's Club. Nothing in her demeanor indicates a need to be here—except maybe the lines of sorrow dragging her face. One eyelid, twitching rapidly, out of her control.

Hildy looks past the woman, across the sweeping hall. Light filters in through the long windows in the grand, elegant room—the floor tiled in black and white, the tin ceiling stamped with ornate, interlocking circles, pastoral paintings gracing the walls, and silk draperies pulled back with tassels from the windows. There are perhaps a hundred women in here, quietly eating their tasty soup, served in real china bowls by polite workers.

This—This would be easy to get used to. Asylum. Rest. Respite.

Yet walking here with the group from her wing, Hildy had been horrified to see a half-dressed woman trying to writhe away from the orderlies who held her, while a nurse forced some concoction into the woman's gnashing mouth. Her thin gown hung from her protruding ribs like a cloth over a table edge. And her eyes—so dark and empty. Yet, for a second, they'd snagged at Hildy, who'd looked away and an instant later felt shame at doing so.

"I mean the medicine they got you on," the stout woman says.

Hildy's gaze returns to her. "Aspirin." The word comes out raspy and garbled, though.

A few of the women around her laugh softly, cutting their eyes at the nurses dotted around the hall, keeping a benign gaze over their herd.

That scene in the hall. Hildy shudders. Benign gazes could turn harsh at any moment.

The stout woman leans closer. "That's what they *tell* us. Aspirin."

Hildy drops her spoon with a clatter. It sounds so loud to her, but no one notices. Maybe it isn't loud. Maybe it just seems so. Everything feels disjointed. She picks up her roll, tears off a piece, but even that is hard to do. Her fingers feel too thick.

Now she wonders—the thought floating to her as if from a great distance—why would they give her aspirin? She hadn't complained of aches and pains—had she? Maybe she'd said something about her hands being swollen from all that typing?

Hildy drops the piece of bread back to her plate. She's suddenly not hungry. The image of the skeletal, hollow-eyed woman in the hallway comes back to her. She shakes her head again. The shake. It's becoming, already, a twitch.

She forces herself to look up at the woman across from her. "A friend of mine is here. Was here. Thea Kincaide."

Hildy waits for someone to exclaim, but everyone at the table is nonplussed. They keep eating, occasionally muttering to one another.

She'd thought—assumed—the name would stun everyone. How could someone—one of their own—wandering off not shake them? Her heart thuds, heavily—*ba-boom, ba-boom.*

"I—I've lost track of her. My friend. Thea."

The woman across from her stares hard. Cold. For a moment, her eye stops twitching. "You'll get used to it."

A few hours later, Hildy sits alone in the garden. The sunshine warms her face and hands, which feel almost normal again. She stares at the statue of the woman in the fountain. How would it be to remain forever so still, so placid, like this carved, beautiful woman, with her graceful arms, her curling tendrils of hair? The flat, empty eyes?

Someone brushes against Hildy's back, and she startles from her reverie. That's right. She's not alone. She's part of a small group that had been walked out here for fresh air and sunshine. It's cold, though. She pulls her sweater more tightly around her.

Her mind is clearer now. She recollects the notes she'd typed for Lily—that Thea had lived in a separate cottage here, that there was a path that led from the garden to the back door of the cottage, and a young aide named Helen had taken a liking to Thea.

Hildy stands. No one notices. She edges to the side of the bench, then behind it. The nurse is preoccupied with several other women who are squabbling. She hesitates. Where is the opening to the nearly secret path? Lily hadn't made note of that.

The flat gray eyes of the woman in the fountain seem to snag at Hildy. She stares, as if the statue might speak—but of course it won't.

Then it hits her—if she were a resident and wanted to devise a nearly hidden path, she'd also want some indicator to prick out its opening, no matter if spring growth or winter snows covered it over. She follows the line of sight of the statue, where the sculpted woman would be looking if only she could see.

There—behind her, to her left—the slightest break in the woods.

Hildy looks up. The nurse is still preoccupied, and none of the other residents notice her. She glances at the statue, the dull, flat eyes. Sees them, in her mind's eye, pop open. *Go!*

Hildy scrambles backward, to the path, and disappears into the woods.

Once she is in the building and standing in front of the door to what should be Thea's old room, Hildy is not sure what she should do next. The door is slightly ajar, and she sees one woman curled up on a bed, sleeping. Another is reading from a Bible.

Tears prick her eyes and her whole body starts to tremble. What has she done? She is not going to learn anything about Thea here.

She should run, just run.

But she can't go back to Kinship. She'll look crazy. Merle and Mother will bring her back. A laugh burbles up, and Hildy claps her hand over her mouth. Maybe she *is* crazy, after all. Crazy like Cousin Thea. Laughing and crying at the same time.

Tom. She could run to Tom.

No. He hadn't given her time. She'd just needed time.

She could just run. See where her legs take her. Where fate takes her.

The image of Thea—shattered face, rags on feet—flashes before her. Thea had run, too.

Hildy's legs give way, and she crumples to the floor. There's a wailing sound, lonesome and long and grinding, like the warning cry of a train.

But it's her—just her.

The women in what had been Thea's room are sitting up, alarmed, staring out at her, the one with the Bible clutching it to her chest like it's a life raft. Rough hands pull Hildy up. She struggles, but her arms are pinned behind her and she's pulled away, down the hall.

A young woman pops out of the room across the hallway. She's not dressed like a resident, and she stares at Hildy with alarm. For a moment, Hildy quiets, studies the girl. Just as described in Lily's notes . . .

Helen. Resident Aide.

"I'm Thea's cousin!" Hildy tries to stop her sudden sobs, but the effort only makes her gasp in convulsive bursts. "I'm Hildy, Hildy Cooper, Thea Kincaide is my cousin; she sent me postcards. From London and France and . . ."

Hildy's voice fizzles to a hissing stop. Helen pales, ducks her head, and dashes back into the room she'd been cleaning.

"Thea," Hildy manages to whisper, like a prayer, as if the beautiful woman in the blue dress could be conjured back to life, could turn Hildy seven years old again, could sweep them both far, far away.

CHAPTER 31

※

LILY

Friday, October 1—3:30 p.m.

Lily looks from the white sateen couch to the tiny chairs dotted around the resplendent room, big enough to contain the whole first floor of the Bronwyn County Sheriff's house.

She reckons she ought to be impressed, but she's irritated. Sit on the couch, risk leaving a smudge at the base from her boot heels? Sit on one of the fragile chairs and be uncomfortable?

Not that she's going to be comfortable, in any case. This afternoon, after a long morning waiting to be summoned, hunger had finally driven her down to the hotel's dining room. She'd just started sipping her coffee and was anticipating her lunch when the concierge rushed in and alighted his anxious gaze on her table—the only one taken by a woman, alone. He'd rushed over, said she needed to come to the lobby at once.

Rather than a message conveying a home address for Professor Neil Leitel, as she'd expected after last night's discussion with George, there was Abe Miller.

"You couldn't leave the information in an envelope and have someone bring it to my room or my table—where I've got coffee going cold?" Lily had said to Abe.

"Plenty of coffee available at Mr. Vogel's house," Abe replied.

Now she stares around Vogel's expansive parlor, overwrought with paintings in gilt frames that rendered the enclosed art to diminutive smudges.

"Just pick a seat, Lily."

Fiona enters the room. A green satin dress overwhelms Fiona's slender figure; like the paintings, she seems a smudge of what she's meant to be. Dark circles punctuate her eyes. A chunky ring, set with emeralds and diamonds, anchors her left hand.

Lily strides to the white couch, sits. Might as well be comfortable. Inasmuch as possible.

As Fiona primly deposits herself on the edge of a small chair, a butler enters with a tray of coffee service and pours a cup as he regards Lily. "Do you take cream or sugar, ma'am?"

"I don't need—"

"We were informed you did not appreciate being taken from your coffee," Fiona says.

"Cream, then."

The butler pours her a cup. He leaves the tray on a sideboard and then exits the parlor.

Lily looks at Fiona. "You could come back with me."

Fiona laughs. "To that horrid little town? I have the perfect life here."

Lily sees in Fiona's eyes blame for last year's death of Martin, her husband and Daniel's deputy—and the death, too, of a life she'd been satisfied with. Until Martin was gone. Something else glints in Fiona's gaze: there is no going back, once you've gotten in bed with George Vogel. For a moment, Lily is tempted to drop the coffee to the floor—fragile cup and white couch be damned—and run away. Would George let her escape? Or—having already made a tacit bargain by being here at all—would she be caught and brought back?

Lily takes a sip of the coffee. It is delicious. Better than the hotel coffee. Which was better than the boiled coffee she makes on her cookstove back home.

Damn. Her heart pangs. She's been here, in Cincinnati, for just over a day, and already Kinship and Bronwyn County seem so distant.

As Lily puts her cup down, Fiona picks hers up, sips, smiles over her rim. *See how easy it is to get pulled in? To get comfortable?*

Suddenly there is the grand man himself. Bellicose, stuffed into his suit, his eyes narrow and pale and rheumy. George doesn't look healthy—and yet he has the commanding presence of a man who believes that he just might live forever.

Behind him, Abe has a man by the elbow, steering him into the room. Lily notes the man's slender build, his sharp nose and thin mouth. She hasn't met the man, yet there is something familiar about him.

Neil Leitel. Thea's son.

Such confusion and fear mottle his face that, for a fleeting moment, Lily feels sorry for him. He has no idea why he's been brought here—likely pulled out of his classroom or office by some of George's thugs. Or from his home, as a woman rushes into the room behind him. His wife, Lily surmises.

As George sits on the end of the couch opposite Lily, Abe gives her a long look; one eyebrow arches. *There's still time to back out.* But in Neil's face, Lily sees dashes and hints of Thea. Sees, again, her bashed head, her rag-wrapped feet. So Lily nods, and Abe shrugs, releases Neil's elbow, points to the couch opposite George and Lily. Neil and his wife perch awkwardly on the edge of the couch—as if there is a chance they might yet escape—while Fiona at last settles back in her chair, crosses her legs, sips her coffee, as if awaiting a show. Abe remains in the entryway, stiff and still with hands down at his sides, like a soldier at only half ease.

Introductions made—yes, this is Neil Leitel and his wife, May. Lily introduces herself. Neil and May look stunned, and George chuckles. "Times are changing."

"I'm sorry to inform you that your mother, Thea Kincaide, has passed away," Lily says.

She waits, watches Neil's face for a reaction. Something passes over his face—but it is not sorrow. It is, she realizes with a start, relief. Then his face hardens.

"I will be more than willing to pay for her funeral services and interment—"

"That is not at issue," Lily says flatly. "She has already been buried."

May cries, "Oh, if only we had known—"

"We wouldn't have attended. Send us the bill."

"That is not why I'm here—or why you're here, Professor Leitel," Lily says. "You are a very hard man to track down. The landlady was loath to share your name, and your department secretary did a fine job of keeping me at bay."

"If Mother died in Athens, and you're from Bronwyn County, why—"

"She didn't die in Athens County," Lily says. "She died in Bronwyn County, which is why I'm here. She was at the Hollows Asylum soon after you left."

May gasps.

"Oh, please," Lily says. "Neither of you can really be shocked that the landlady had her transported there, kept the money, and was able to then rent out the room."

"How did she die?" May sounds genuinely concerned.

"She left the asylum one night. Walked for hours through the woods . . ."—Lily hesitates, then decides to include the cruel details—"with only rags for shoes. She made several stops along the way but ended up at the top of a train tunnel, outside of Moonvale Hollow Village. She fell, or was pushed, onto the oncoming train. Died upon impact—or so I hope. I'd hate to think she lingered in the ditch where she landed."

Fiona moans, and even Abe arches an eyebrow. George looks amused, as if pleased by Lily's capacity to box with words.

"I have been in Cincinnati this whole time. I have not left the city. My wife, my colleagues, my students, my dean, can all attest to this."

"I'm not here to accuse you of murdering your mother," Lily says.

"Then what? A simple telegram—"

"I came to see what you might be able to tell me about your mother that might help me sort out her death and why someone would kill her. She lived for a time at the Dyer farm in Moonvale Hollow

Village—her last stop before coming to the top of the tunnel. Did she ever share anything about her time growing up there, about her past—"

Neil gives a sharp, barking laugh. "What did she share? What do I know about her? I barely remember her! Shocking as it is, my parents divorced, and my mother left me with my father when I was seven. I suppose she tired of being a mother. All my father told me, years later, was that she was going to pursue a life as a dancer. That they agreed he would provide a more stable life for me. That she would visit when she could—but she rarely did. And when she did, she'd start the visit by doting over me, but quickly get bored—though she tried to hide it—and take off again."

A chill creeps over Lily. Neil's story is sad, and she can't imagine making Thea's choice. Lily's children mean the world to her. But her reaction is not at what Neil is saying. Perhaps Thea knew she wasn't really cut out to be a mother, and she made the best choice she could for herself and her son. No, Lily's frisson is in response to the slow smile rising on George's face. Has she really traded a piece of her soul, made herself beholden to George, left behind her family and home, to track down Neil on the thin hope that he can tell her something about Thea—only to find he knows nothing useful?

Lily pulls her notebook and pencil from her bag. Her hand trembles—*so annoying!*—as she makes notes.

"Then when she's old and desperate and out of money, she turns up," Neil says, his nostrils flaring as if he's trying to expel a foul odor. He cocks an eyebrow at Lily. "But I take it that you know nothing of mothering."

Lily's hand stills. She looks up at Neil. "I am here as sheriff—"

"She's a mother, with two children she's abandoned to come here!" Fiona blurts. Her face turns crimson by the time she finishes the sentence, and she looks away, avoiding Lily's hard glance. Vengeance, Lily realizes, for her judging Fiona for sending her own son off to boarding school so she can come live with George.

Yet Lily's heart softens toward Fiona. *God, it's hard enough to deal with choices—or lack of them—as women. The right to vote was great but didn't mean women could be independent in every other way as well. Why do women make it harder for themselves by fighting with one another, judging one another?*

She looks at Fiona, at the splotchy redness in her otherwise pale face. "We make the best choices we can—"

"Oh, hardly!" Neil's voice snaps with disparagement. "My mother could have stayed. She ran off to pursue some silly dream. Certainly my wife would stay with our children."

Lily looks back at Neil, who does not seem to notice the flash of disgust in May's eyes. "I'm not here to debate mothering practices. I need to learn what I can about your mother. Anything she might have said after she came into your care that might pertain to why she left the asylum, headed toward Moonvale Hollow Village—"

"We can't have children." May's statement is soft, like a sigh of wind slipping in through the partially opened window. The room stills as everyone looks at May.

May, though, looks only at Neil—not with a plea for support or love. Nor with faith or confidence that he would provide either. With something colder than hate, which is at least a passion of the moment. With disdain.

Lily bites her lower lip. She'd had moments of anger, of even thinking she hated Daniel, especially during their tumultuous courting years. Even anger at him for dying. But disdain—never that. Disdain is a coldness that kills love. From the flatness of May's voice, her disdain for Neil became deeply rooted some time ago.

"We can't have children, so how do you know what kind of mother I would be?"

"Of course you'd stay." Neil is shocked at his wife's reaction. He looks to George for support. "Mothers should stay with their children. Mine left, so why should I have done anything more than what I did? I gave her more than she deserved. I did the best I could. I paid for the boarding room—"

"That was your best?" George's voice is like ice. His habitual amused smile, as if everything is a game, drops from his face. In its absence, there is no new expression. Only hardness, like a stone statue. "You could have found help for her here. If she needed the care of an asylum, you could have had her at the Cincinnati Sanitarium. Instead, you abandoned her."

Neil recoils back into his chair as if he's being snipped to pieces, one syllable at a time—snip, snip.

What is driving George? There is a story here—random compassion for others or empathy is not a George Vogel trait. Nor is sympathy for old women. Everything with George is calculated, hard, for his own purposes and gain.

It has never occurred to Lily to think of George having a past, to be driven by haunts, as she herself is driven. To her, he has always been simply a terrifying force, swooping in and out of her life, a raptor seeking its prey.

Whatever his reason, whatever his background, George for some reason is fully on Lily's side. She hadn't read it in his face last night, but something about the story of an ailing elderly mother, left behind by her son, struck a chord in George. Does it connect to his past—or to his own mother?

"Perhaps," George concludes, "she was attempting to follow you, Professor Leitel."

The air sucks out of the room at the import of this possibility— the elderly woman, alone, in the cold, ultimately barefoot, stumbling along, looking for her son. Her death a random happenstance, after all. Falling from the top of the tunnel, onto the train.

Her death having nothing to do with her connection to Hildy's family or the past in which Thea had witnessed—and been partial cause of—the hanging execution of one of her father's wards on the Underground Railroad. Nothing to do with the rise of the WKKK. Nothing to do with her past at the farm.

Simply a mother, looking for her boy.

The memory of the shadowy silver boy, flitting through the woods— an act of her own imagination—grasps Lily.

"No." May's voice is like a handkerchief clenched in a hard fist. "No. Thea was not looking for Neil. She was looking for a baby."

Neil laughs, a high-pitched trill. "That was delusion. Her delusion, probably guilt—over being a neglectful mother! Why would she care about another baby?"

Lily shakes her head. Was Neil really jealous over his mother's concern about a baby—real or imagined—after all of these years?

"She was so certain," May says. "So sure. She mentioned it several times to us. There was a baby that she needed to find, to save—"

"The ramblings of a delusional old—"

"Enough!" George's voice cuts through the room like thunder.

Abe steps in the room, stands behind Neil's chair, drapes his hand casually over the back of the chair, his fingertips a wisp away from Neil's neck. If Neil turns his head in the slightest, his collar, the tips of his hair, will touch Abe's hand. Sensing Abe's presence, Neil has stilled and stiffened.

George looks back at May. It is enough for her to go on.

"I don't think she was delusional. I think she was remembering something—someone—important to her. Maybe important enough to search for. Maybe she wrote about it in the autobiography she was working on—before we left her at the rooming house."

Lily leans forward on the couch, tingles dancing over her skin. *Thea Kincaide had been writing an autobiography?*

Neil rolls his eyes, presumably at the ludicrousness of an old woman wanting, at the end of her life, to capture as much of it as possible on paper. Who would want to read that?

Well, Lily would. Most assuredly.

Neil clears his throat and says softly, reasonably, as he might in explaining a concept to one of his students, "Unfortunately, we had to get rid of that box of papers, you know, to make moving here easier, so—"

"I didn't get rid of that box," May says.

Neil's gaze strikes at her, but May sits up straighter, stiffening her spine, emboldened by George. She looks at Lily. "They are in a trunk. In the attic. You can come see them—"

"Just let her have them." Neil's voice twists bitterly. "I will never read them. And May, if you were going to, you would have by now. So this sheriff can have them"—he looks at George; his expression turns pleading, his voice soft and rotten with fear—"and then, we can forget that this happened?"

George's smile returns, small, thin, slithering up his face, one-sided. "That is up to Sheriff Ross here, and what she finds in them—"

The butler rushes into the room, holding a piece of paper. He looks directly at Lily. "This telegram came to the Sinton Hotel, where the concierge had the wherewithal to send it here with a delivery boy."

Lily jumps up, rushes to the butler. *Oh God. Something about the WKKK? Jolene or Micah? Mama, Caleb Jr.?*

Lily snatches the telegram from him, scans it hurriedly, barely able to breathe, her heart pounding. Then she reads it again. It's from Mama.

Hildy taken to Hollows Asylum.

CHAPTER 32

※

HILDY

Friday, October 1—7:00 p.m.

Hildy stirs to wakefulness. Her stomach grumbles. She's alone in the windowless room she shares with three other women.

The dose they—for already the nurses and orderlies blur into "they"—had given her after dragging her from Thea's old room is wearing off, but her mind is still foggy. She feels too light, as if she might float away.

She must force herself to focus, to calculate. That's what Lily would do.

Tears spring forth at the thought of her friend. Hildy dashes her hand across her eyes. *Focus. Calculate.*

Stomach grumbling: it's past dinner.

Alone in the room: not yet bedtime. The other women must be at activity hour.

Hildy pushes her mind back: She'd been dosed for being out of her room, at the cottage. But she'd spotted the nurse's aide Helen, who seemed sympathetic to Thea.

Hildy groans, wishing to roll over, let her mind drift back into a numbing mist. Instead, she makes herself sit up. Then carefully, she climbs down the metal ladder from the top bunk.

She's out of the room before she realizes that she's barefoot, wearing only a nightgown. A morbid laugh starts to rise, but—though the hallway is empty—Hildy claps her hands to her mouth. She moves swiftly down the hallway, back to the wall, then finds the exit.

Hildy stops outside, stares up at the dark sky. The moon is a sliver, a waning crescent. There would be no light to guide her as it had Thea. Hildy shivers in the cold, wishing already for a sweater. But the cold also helps her head to clear.

Focus. Calculate.

The darkness will give her cover. She's much younger, far more fit, than Thea. All she has to do is make her way to the cottage where Thea had lived, where Helen worked, and hope to find her. Or, if she's not still there, hide away, wait until Helen came back to her room. And there—there's the flickering coal-oil light at the back step of the cottage.

Gingerly yet swiftly, Hildy walks across the damp lawn, her vision focused on the lamp. A rock pierces the sole of her foot and she stumbles but keeps from falling. Swallows back the urge to cry out. *Keep going.* One step. Another. Another.

At last, she is at the cottage. Hildy looks around. She appears to still be alone. She runs up the steps to the door. *Dammit!* It's locked.

Focus. Calculate.

If she waits, others will come back. Maybe she can blend in with them somehow. . . .

A hand claps down on her shoulder, spins her around. A security guard. He looks annoyed at first, but then a lascivious grin takes over his face. Hildy's blood runs cold.

"Well, little miss, what are you doing out, all by yourself?" He licks his lips. Hildy looks down. *Ah*—a ring of keys hangs from his belt loop. If she can steel herself for another second . . .

"I'll help you, sweetheart," the guard says. "Come on down."

Hildy remains stock-still on the top step.

The guard frowns. "I told you, get down here!"

She gives him a taunting smile.

He grabs for her, at the same time as he starts to step up. In the split second that he's standing one-legged, Hildy kicks him as hard as she can in his groin. The guard curses, falls backward, and knocks himself out cold on the ground.

For a moment, Hildy stares at him. *Oh God.* Had she killed him? No, he's breathing—just unconscious for the moment. Her hands tremble as she unclips the key ring from his belt.

The first and second keys don't fit. By the time she's on the third, the guard moans, coming around. *Focus!* The fourth, no . . . *Ah.* The fifth key slides in. Hildy turns it. The door creaks open.

"Get back here, you bitch—" the guard yells, struggling to his feet.

Hildy gets in the cottage door, slams it shut, locks it.

As he starts pounding on the door, Hildy runs down the hall, past a few bewildered residents, and into the common bathroom.

For a moment, she sinks to the floor, catching her breath. *Helen.* The resident aide. Where would she stay?

Then she remembers that earlier Helen had come out of the room across from Thea's.

Hildy runs down the hall to the room across from Thea's. A few residents gather as Hildy bangs on Helen's door. Helen opens the door, looks alarmed at seeing Hildy, but the door is open far enough that Hildy can shove Helen back, slip in, shut the door. Hildy locks the door, then grabs a chair and shoves it in front of the door. That should hold off the guard and whoever else for at least a few minutes.

"Please don't hurt me," Helen whimpers. She rushes to a wardrobe, opens it, starts pawing through. "I'll give back the brooches, and the shoes. They didn't fit anyway—"

Hildy grabs the slight girl's arms. Her head is pounding, but she has to know, has to ask before her brain is again dosed beyond thinking. "Why did Thea want to leave? Why was she so desperate?"

Helen begins crying. "There are some nurses here, in some crazy group. They want me to join, but I won't. Miss Thea—I liked her, I did, and she trusted me. She'd heard two nurses talking about going to kill a Negro—a man—except they'd used a mean term for him, in the mines up in Rossville. They never said his name. Poor Miss Thea—she made a fuss, and she was put in solitary until she calmed down. Bound her wrists and everything. She behaved, got sent back to her nice room on probation, but she was desperate to go. She seemed to think she knew him—a fellow named John."

Oh—those marks on poor Thea's wrists. Fury rises in Hildy. She gives Helen a fierce shake. "Why didn't you report this?"

"I didn't know how many there are! Or if I'd be reporting to someone in the group with them. They were scary—I was scared—but I wanted to help Miss Thea—"

"So you helped her escape. But not without taking possessions from her."

Helen looks down. Her voice turns sour with defensiveness. "She was prideful. Wanted to pay me. So I took the brooches—someone would have anyway sooner or later—"

"And her shoes!" Hildy screams, shaking the girl even harder.

"Please, please, stop—" the girl whimpers.

Hildy wants to, but she is so angry, angry with this girl who is so weak—weak from desire to please everyone, weak from wanting to have everything without consequence.

The shadow of the old-fashioned woman comes to the corner of Hildy's vision. Whispers . . . *Stop.*

Suddenly Hildy does. *Oh, Thea.* She lets go of the girl, who stumbles backward to her bed. Hildy sobs, drops to her knees. She thought she was shaking Helen. She'd really been shaking herself.

The door bursts open; the chair goes flying. The guard who Hildy had earlier kicked stands in the doorway, red-faced and seething.

Hildy looks desperately at Helen, silently begging for help.

But Helen looks aside and steps out of the way of the shattered door.

A scream rises in Hildy's throat, but she swallows it back and stares evenly at the guard, even as he charges through splintered wood toward her.

Whatever fate awaits her, she refuses to face it with whimpering acquiescence.

CHAPTER 33

꧁

LILY

Friday, October 1—8:00 p.m.

Abe had chosen his route well—the old Main Market Route 45, re-named State Route 7 a few years ago, east out of Cincinnati, then State Route 27 to Milford, and State Route 26 to Athens. The automobile he's driving—George procured only the newest models—runs much smoother and faster than the automobile Lily had inherited from Daniel. There is no train tonight from Cincinnati to Athens that can hurtle her fast enough to Hildy.

Still, there are curves and bumps aplenty on this modern, new two-lane road, and Abe is pushing the automobile to go its speediest.

As he hits a bump, Lily's hat flies off of her head. She yelps, staring at the pages rattling in her hand, under the beam of her flashlight.

"You all right back there?" Abe asks. His voice holds no concern. It simply would not do for Lily to foul his boss's automobile by throwing up in the back seat.

"I'm fine!" Lily snaps. "This has nothing to do with your driving. Matter of fact, if you could pick it up, I'd be much obliged."

She's already more than fully obliged to George—first for bring-ing Neil to her, then for sending one of his men to retrieve Thea's autobiography, and now for Abe driving Lily as speedily as possible through the night to the Hollows. George, with a flat smile, had even promised to send along a telegram on Lily's behalf to the institution.

But none of this—or Abe's tire-tilting driving style—is what inspired Lily's yelp.

It's Thea's writing. Lily has quickly skimmed the first sheath of pages—long, overwrought descriptions of Thea's time on the stage, sights she'd seen in various locations, lovers she'd had. Now, finally, fifty pages in, Thea's writing turns to her childhood, as if she had to work through the gloss to finally have the courage to turn to the root of who she was.

And what she had to say—riveting.

THEA'S HANDWRITTEN AUTOBIOGRAPHY, PAGES 42–58

My father gave me his compass that last night.

I believe it was meant to placate and comfort me, for I had been begging and crying all day to go with him to see off John and Garnet—who were, Mama said, to be the last of the escaped slaves we'd help along the Underground Railroad, for Daddy's activities over the past few years in this regard made her nervous for our own safety.

I had taken a particular liking to them, I suppose because they stayed with us the longest. I'd brought them food for weeks where they'd hidden, far back in a cave known only to us and a few others, down a windy path on the other side of the crick that ran behind our cabin, up the hill from the Stanehart Hollow Friends Meeting House.

Chicken and corn pone and soup beans and sometimes I'd take extra biscuits for myself, but hold them back, and make a mash of butter and sorghum to spread in the middle—as much a sweet treat as breakfast.

I'd been hearing Mama and Daddy fighting more of late. Mama thought it was too dangerous to go on offering asylum to the escaped slaves. More and more bounty hunters were coming through, looking for escaped slaves who had made it across the Ohio River and into the deep hilly forests of southeastern Ohio— into freedom, if they avoided bounty hunters, who, by law, could return the escaped slaves to their owners and receive good payment for doing so.

Plenty did not sanction helping men and women on the road to freedom—even those in our Friends gathering, who thought it would be best to receive enlightenment and blessing for ourselves alone as true stewards of the Word. Daddy grumbled that listening for the "still small voice" was for more than that, for us to help those in our community, and that didn't mean just the Friends. That meant anyone whose path we came across.

Still, Mama argued that it would be better to follow the law, to keep our heads down.

Daddy said he had been keeping his head down in prayer, and the law of the Lord was above the law of Man, and what good comes from enlightenment if not applied to right action?

Mama snapped back that he wouldn't ask that if he had grown up as she had—poor, hungry, in the deepest hollers. Daddy, who had moved to Kinship with his family soon after the town's establishment, came from wealthier beginnings—his father, my granddaddy, was a blacksmith, after all. My uncle Claude had stayed in Kinship, but Daddy, always restlessly seeking the divine, had joined the Friends group, and he became a farmer— preferring even a hardscrabble life in nature to the busyness of a town like Kinship.

I longed for happier days, when Mama and Daddy mostly got along—though truth be told, I don't remember Mama being happy often, and after Daddy's death, well, she never was happy, even when she found relative ease with my stepfather, Mr. Adam Dyer.

I'm getting ahead of myself.

Tired of hearing them argue, I tucked the compass in my pocket, and took big slices of ham and green tomato pie—with Mama's seasonings and some sweetening, it tasted close to apple—out to the cave. Plenty for John, a big man, and for Garnet. I was only seven, but I knew what the big bulge in her belly meant, even if I didn't fathom yet how it came to be. She was going to have a baby—any minute.

That's why Daddy wanted to keep them hidden for a while longer—so Garnet could have her baby safely with us, and be tended to by Mama and some of the other women. And she'd need John—though he was not the father—to protect her. That kept them with us longer than previous runaways, and so besides bringing them food, I tried to get them to tell me stories of their lives on the run. They wouldn't—and now I don't blame them. So I brought a book to read to them, because I didn't have stories of my own, and from there started to teach them a little bit about reading.

Garnet never said who was the father—but now, with knowledge and experience I certainly didn't have at seven—I can guess that her master or one of the men who worked for him was the father. John and Garnet, unrelated, had come up from Charleston, South Carolina, at roughly the same time. They didn't get on. Quarreled worse than Mama and Daddy. Still, John felt obliged to watch out for her. That's the kind of man he was.

Me, I hoped Garnet would have the baby while still with us. I knew Mama had lost several babies before and since having me— her only live birth—and I thought maybe seeing the hope of a new baby, even under such circumstances, would make her happy.

Once, out hunting with Daddy, I asked him why he thought the Good Lord had seen fit to spare me, separate from all those siblings whose lives had ended before they could begin. Daddy said I was a rare rose, a blessing to him and Mama.

Now I think that instead of being a blessing to Mama, I was a reminder of the others she'd lost. Maybe that was why she wanted Garnet and John to move on—so she wouldn't have to see a baby born.

I wish I could say I remember what I talked about with John and Garnet, at the back of the cave, that night. Maybe Garnet sang, soft and low. She had a beautiful voice. Or John might have sounded out words from the Bible, as he liked to do. Somehow, the tragedies that followed, and all the places I have been, have blurred those specific memories. I don't think it's just because I've been losing track of memories and ideas of late. I think, maybe, all these years I've been forever moving—seeking asylum somewhere, refuge from my guilt, because it's too hard to remember. It's better to blot out specifics.

But I've never been able to blot out that last night. After I came back to the house, we had our own dinner, ham and corn and what was left of the green tomato pie. Mama lit the candle on the table and the light from it and the fireplace caused shadows to dance on my parents' heads, and I peeked from over the tops of my clasped hands to watch those shadows as Daddy led us in prayer, same prayer as every night—"We thank thee, Lord, for our many blessings and humbly ask for your strength to do your will on behalf of those made less fortunate by the wickedness of men. Bless this food to our bodies and our bodies to your use. Amen."

Even though I'd heard that prayer so often I could recite it word for word at age seven, for the first time I must have really *heard* it, for I was struck by the notion: it was God's will I go along with Daddy on this last run. I heard that still small voice, and I was determined to obey it. I understood, at some level I couldn't put in words until years later, that no matter how it might test or break us, we should do what is right—and that what is right might not fit what wicked men would tell us is right. It was an understanding I'd be forced to put aside later, to sacrifice John, to save Daddy's true killer.

We ate in silence until I clutched my stomach, feigning pain. My first bit of acting.

"Whatever is the problem, child?" Mama asked.

"It's all those damned green tomatoes!" Daddy snapped, and we both looked at him in shock. He rarely raised his voice, never cursed, but he had been particularly tense all day. He'd been to Kinship on some business, and probably visited his brother, Uncle Claude, who was a blacksmith. Daddy always came back from visits with him unhappy. Uncle Claude was strictly on the other side of Daddy on the topic of abolition.

Uncle Claude never came to our cabin, but we visited once, the year before, when my grandmother died, and even at the funeral service, Daddy and Uncle argued over the topic.

Because of my "stomachache," I was allowed to sleep that night in the front room, closer to the door and therefore to the outhouse. I waited for a while, after my parents went to bed, and then I made my pillow look like a lump under the quilt on the bench where I'd been sleeping.

I snuck out to the wagon in the barn, and hid in the false bottom, wrapped in a blanket.

There I did fall asleep, until I jolted awake and realized that in the wagon with me were John and Garnet, tucked close.

We jolted and rattled along, until my stomach really did hurt. Suddenly we stopped, and then we were tumbling, the wagon turning, turning, turning.

John and Garnet and I spilled from the wagon, then into a ravine. We crawled out. Garnet's face was gashed and both of us were crying. John checked us—miraculously, though we were cut and scratched, nothing was broken on any of us.

But up on the road, lit by tar-dipped torches, my daddy was surrounded by angry men, pushing and prodding him.

Bounty hunters. One in particular was shouting into Daddy's face.

I thought I recognized him, and when he turned and looked down the ravine at us, in those bright lights, I did. Uncle Claude.

That's when John looked at Garnet and me, shouted at us, "Run!" and ran, himself, up the hill toward Daddy.

Garnet and I went the opposite way, stumbling and crying, running as best we could, until we no longer heard the jeering voices of the men or the howling of the hounds.

Somehow, we got back to the cave. Garnet's face was pinched with pain.

I fetched Mama, and, after all, she delivered a baby. A healthy boy.

Garnet did not make it.

Mama studied the baby for a long time, even after she cleaned him up.

And then she thrust him at me.

"Take him to the Dyer household," Mama said. And for the first time in a long while—and, as it would turn out, for the last time ever—Mama's voice was firm. Strong.

We went sometimes to Joyce and Adam Dyer's house to do laundry and household chores, because Joyce was sickly, but her husband had leased land to the B&R Railroad, and made a fair penny from it.

Mama continued, working things out for herself, out loud. "Babies are left on the doorsteps of their fathers from time to time. No one will question that Adam would step out on Joyce—she's always so sickly. And Joyce wants a baby more than anything." She looked then at the baby boy, smoothed back the fine reddish hair on his head. Studied him for another minute. "He can pass," she said.

I took the baby gently, and tried to keep my eyes from looking at his poor mother. I couldn't resist a glance—maybe I was wrong? Maybe she was just tired? Still alive?

I yelped as I looked at her. She was dead, and already shrinking in on herself.

Yelped again as Mama grabbed my arm, pinched hard. "I will take care of her! You do as I say. Take the boy; leave him at the back door. Throw a rock through the kitchen window. Then run down the train track back this way—it's the fastest, and no train is running this late. When you're back, you do as your daddy and I say—whatever it is—to keep us safe!"

I stared at her, eyes wide.

She gave me a shake. "If'n you don't, this baby'll die, too!"

So I stumbled through the woods with the baby, holding him close lest he cry out, praying I wouldn't smother him, holding him so tight. I got to the Dyers' place quick as I could, and left the baby as Mama said, and threw the rock, and then stumbled down to the train track and ran, and ran, and ran.

Until I saw him, hanging.

Daddy.

His body swaying, outlined in the moonlight.

I went back to the Dyers to ask for help, though I knew Daddy was far beyond helping.

Later, though I knew in my bones it had to be my uncle Claude, that it couldn't be poor John, who'd killed him, I went on the witness stand and said it was.

I listened—I did—for the still small voice to tell me something else to say or do than what Mama told me I must. But I couldn't hear it. I reckoned that no matter what I said, someone would find a way to pin the blame on John. And I wanted that baby to live. Garnet's baby.

Murphy.

By the time of the trial, the Dyers had named him Murphy.

Acted like he was theirs. Like he'd been theirs for a year. And no one questioned it, because the Dyers had so much money and the people of Moonvale relied on them.

I did as Mama said I must—testified, as Uncle Claude

wanted, that I saw John take Daddy's life. I never said a word about Garnet or the truth of how Murphy came into this world.

There was no still small voice telling me to do any different.

I've listened for it, ever since, and never heard it, no matter where I went, or how I tried.

Until lately—and maybe it's just the foolishness of an old woman—but I hear a voice in my head telling me, Now, Thea.

Now is the time to get your truth written down.

CHAPTER 34

LILY AND HILDY

Hildy
Saturday, October 2—2:00 a.m.

Hildy again stirs to wakefulness.

Angry voices.

She tries to lift her hand to rub her gummy eyes, but her hands are bound behind her. She vaguely recalls something about the binding being necessary for her to not hurt herself or others.

Bound—just as Thea had been, shortly before her escape.

But she *had* escaped. Hildy shakes her head to clear it. She must also find a way.

Then, as her vision clears, she sees etched in the plaster wall across from her the message: *I never was crazy.*

Well. Could Hildy say that? She'd feigned being crazy to get in here—but in some ways she'd acted crazy of late. Not about Tom and Merle. About her jealousy of Lily and Marvena's friendship. And yet, she realizes in a flash of clarity, what she'd really been jealous of was not their relationship, but their independence. Their courage. They respected each other for those traits—and Hildy had wanted to be like that, too.

So, she'd tried. And look where it had gotten her.

Angry voices. One is foggily familiar. A nurse who had tried to force a foul-tasting liquid down her throat, while guards held her.

Hildy had fought. Yes, fought and bit. Even now, as her head pounds with stabbing pain, a slight smile cracks Hildy's lips. She'd *fought*. But when they couldn't make her swallow, they'd injected the liquid into her.

Still even as the needle slipped into her vein, she'd repeated the important information she'd gotten out of Helen over and over to herself, until it became a gruesome lullaby. She had to remember what she'd learned, so she could tell Lily.

Lily.

That is Lily, outside this door, shouting, "God Almighty, I will take her out of here. Jurisdiction be damned! I'll deal with that later!"

As Hildy starts to weep, the door opens, and Lily rushes in.

LILY

Saturday, October 2—4:00 a.m.

"Hildy will be fine."

Lily, suddenly light-headed, leans against the doorframe in the bedroom at Mrs. Gottschalk's house. Abe had brought both Lily and Hildy here from the asylum. On the drive, Lily had tried to keep her friend calm and quiet, but Hildy insisted on telling her what she'd learned from Helen.

Every word struggling from Hildy's lips had wrenched Lily's heart—not just for the content, but for the effort. Why had she ever discounted Hildy as anything less than brave?

At the house, while Mama and Mrs. Gottschalk settled Hildy into bed, Lily told Abe, "I need one more favor. Get Dr. Goshen from Kinship. If he drives here on his own, follow him to make sure he really comes."

Abe, who'd said nothing on the drive back from the Hollows, glanced at Hildy, an expression approximating a smidge of sympathy crossing his face. Then he'd nodded, left, and forty-five minutes later Dr. Goshen was knocking on the door.

Now, in the next room, Mama and Mrs. Gottschalk are settling the children—rightfully stirred and upset by the night's commotion—as

Dr. Goshen stares at Lily with concern. "What about you? Are you all right?"

"I'm fine." Lily barely keeps her tone patient. "Tell me about Hildy."

"She was given too much potassium bromide at the Hollows. More than any doctor should sanction—even for the most severe psychiatric cases. Fortunately, she is stronger than she appears. With rest and time, it will work itself out of her system. She should have only light liquids for now, until she can hold down food. The bromide will keep her nauseous for a while."

After a long moment, Lily nods. *Thank God.* "And you have the paperwork?"

Dr. Goshen's eyes darken, but he nods. "She should never have been taken there in the first place. I'll take it to the director today."

Lily exhales, relieved. The doctor's letter would assure the Hollows has no hold on Hildy. Just as Abe—somehow—had made sure that there would be no ramifications for Lily overstepping her jurisdiction in Athens County. George now has a deeper hold on Lily, if he wants it. But the moment she saw Hildy in that solitary holding cell, where Lily herself had been for a few hours earlier in the week, Lily knew she'd pay any price to get her out.

The doctor says, "If you need me, send for me. But you don't need to have your friend follow me!"

"He's not a friend. And I'm guessing he drove on after you pulled in?" Lily pulls back the curtain, glances out the window, but it's impossible to see what automobiles are in the gravel drive on this dark, nearly moonless night.

"He did," Dr. Goshen says abruptly.

"Would you mind giving me a ride back to town? I need to return to the Hollows—"

"I said I'd take the paperwork!"

"I know—and thank you. I need to interrogate a nurse's aide there."

Dr. Goshen nods and swiftly leaves the bedroom.

For a moment, Lily gazes at Hildy. She gently pulls the quilt up to cover Hildy's shoulders. *Rest and heal quickly, my dear friend.*

"Lily?"

She turns to Olive, sitting up in the twin bed on the other side of the room. Olive had observed the comings and goings with Hildy with wide-eyed alarm.

Now Olive stares at Hildy. "Do you think Margaret had anything to do with this?"

"Not directly. She is still being held in the jail." Lily considers. Olive remains fragile, recovering. "But she's retracted her admission of beating you, and I can't hold her more than another day without official charges." She pauses, calculates. Actually, enough time had passed that she should have released Margaret—but with the need to rescue Hildy, she'd gotten back to the area later than expected. No need to upset Olive with this fact, though. "Anyway, Hildy was able to tell me on the way over that a nurse's aide confessed she helped Thea leave the asylum. Thea was upset because she'd overheard two nurses talk about a plot to lynch Clarence—though they just referred to him as a Negro working to integrate the mines. In Thea's mind, that meant John."

Olive looks confused at this last reference. "Explain that to me later." As she glances at Hildy, a mix of sorrow and anger flashes across her face. Then she looks resolutely at Lily. "I'm ready to press official charges against Margaret."

LILY
Saturday, October 2—8:00 a.m.

"I don't know who the nurses are!" Helen says. She looks from Dr. Harkins to Chief Warren. Her chin trembles, and her eyes well up.

Lily turns her gaze to the window behind Dr. Harkins, watches a hawk swooping past. They've gathered at Lily's insistence—though both the location and the presence of the police chief are Dr. Harkins's preference. When Lily looks back at Helen, the young woman shrinks back as if struck.

"Hildy swears you told her that Thea said she overheard two nurses talking over plans to murder a man," Lily says. "Did she share the names with you, or if not, who do you suspect—"

"She's already answered! Kincaide didn't say, and furthermore, her comments were the ramblings of an old woman with dementia!"

Dr. Harkins snaps. "Certainly no one in our employ here would be conspiring murder. We hire only the finest people—"

"People who would administer a deadly dose of bromide to Hildy—a sworn officer of the law, by the way, here undercover"—never mind that Lily did not know of Hildy's choice, and would never have sanctioned it—"to find out why Miss Kincaide was so determined to leave."

Helen inhales sharply and starts to cry. "Is she all right?"

Lily ignores the question as Dr. Harkins says, "Bromide was administered because Miss Cooper, who was brought here willingly by her mother and fiancé, attacked one of our guards!"

Chief Warren clears his throat. "If you were going to send an officer in to conduct undercover investigations, you should have cleared it with myself and Dr. Harkins."

"That would hardly have been undercover," Lily says. "And who knows how many of your fine people are part of the WKKK, or the KKK for that matter, and part of a conspiracy to murder an employee of the United Mine Workers."

"Are you making an accusation, Sheriff Ross, beyond these two alleged nurses?" Dr. Harkins's tone is cool.

Lily sighs. She's gone too far. "No. I'm trying to find out the names of the nurses. If they confirm they were talking about this conspiracy in a location where Miss Kincaide could have overheard, then I have proof—"

"That her fears weren't delusions?" Dr. Harkins steeples his fingertips.

"That she had—or felt she had—justifiable fears, though jumbled with a tragic past murder in her mind, to leave the grounds. If she really feared this, and then stumbled into a WKKK meeting, and shared her fears, then someone at that meeting would have had motive to murder her." Lily looks sharply at Helen. "As it was, the poor old woman was willing to trade her jewelry, and even her shoes, for your assistance in leaving, wasn't she?"

Helen sobs. "Yes, and I know I shouldn't have, but I didn't think she'd get far, figured she'd come back—"

Dr. Harkins frowns. "Taking advantage of a patient in this way is cause for dismissal."

"It might even be considered thievery." Lily looks to Chief Warren for confirmation. He nods.

"I can give them back; I told Hildy that—" Helen claps her hand to her mouth.

"That doesn't undo the original thievery," Lily says. "Though if you would tell us who the nurses are, I'm guessing Chief here wouldn't press charges"—he opens his mouth as if to protest, and shuts it again at Lily's hard look—"and Dr. Harkins might be persuaded to let you keep your job—"

"Well, on probation," Dr. Harkins says. "We do have our reputation to consider."

For a moment, Helen stops sobbing. She's thinking about it. Lily's heart lifts: if she can talk to those two, find out if they can tell what happened that night at the meeting to Thea—

Helen looks down. Shakes her head. "I—I can't."

It's not that Helen *can't,* Lily realizes. She won't. She is so afraid of these two nurses, of the hate that might push them and other WKKK members to take revenge on Helen, that she'd rather lose her job and go to jail for theft.

Lily stands up, pushing her chair from behind her so hard that it scrapes the wood floor. She'll have to accept never finding out who those two nurses are. She strides to the door.

"Sheriff Ross," Chief Warren says.

She turns and looks at him.

His expression is surprisingly sympathetic and concerned. "You can still rule Miss Kincaide's death accidental."

Lily stares at him until he looks down. Then she says, "Not until I'm sure it was."

In the old garden, Lily stares at the moss-specked, chipped statue of the woman with the urn in the fountain. Lily'd swept leaves off a bench, the back half of it covered by overgrowing bushes, so she could sit. Let the cool October breeze refresh and calm her. Think.

She will have to find another way to prove that, though suffering from dementia, Thea Kincaide had motivation to make the trek to the WKKK meeting at the former Dyer farm.

There's Helen's confession to Hildy—the threat against Clarence.

The attack on Olive.

Thea's own writings in her autobiography—but she'd written her memories later in life, so the argument could be made that her writings, as articulate as they are, were also the "delusions of an old woman."

But if her writings were correct, then with everything else Lily's learned, two interesting facts stand out.

Thea believed her uncle had killed her father, besetting his wagon with a gang of thugs, sending the escaped, pregnant slave Garnet scrambling away with Thea. If that was the case—and Thea had in a moment of clarity recognized and confronted Mrs. Cooper at the WKKK meeting—then would Mrs. Cooper have motivation to attack, even kill, Thea?

Just as intriguing, Thea's writings revealed that she'd taken Garnet's baby to the Dyer house after Garnet died, then maneuvered to work at the Dyer household and watch over that baby. Lily had already noted that the dates on the Dyer gravestones—Murphy born in 1856, to a mother who was sickly, never had children, and yet had given birth at fifty-one.

That would make Murphy either fully Negro or half Negro and half Caucasian. Which would make Murphy's son—Perry—of mixed race as well.

If Thea had revealed this at the WKKK meeting, would it have enraged Margaret—or, for that matter, Perry—enough to kill her?

Lily needs more support for these possibilities than Thea's writings and her own conjecture.

She needs to find the remains of Garnet.

LILY

Saturday, October 2—11:30 a.m.

"I need to see the cave on your property." Lily keeps her voice as close to honey as she can.

Anna Faye shakes her head. "I don't know what you're talking about." She starts to shut the door to her house.

Lily catches the door in her hand, forces it to stay open. Anna Faye peers at her, fearful. So much for honey. "At one time, this house was occupied by Rupert Kincaide and his wife and daughter, Thea. I've come across some of Thea's writing, in which she claims there's a cave nearby where those coming through on the Underground Railroad would hide. She states a woman died in the cave—and if it is true, this corroborates her story."

"I don't know of any such cave—"

"I do," her grandfather, Harold, pipes up behind her. "Move out of my way, child!" he fusses at his granddaughter.

Anna Faye steps aside, and Harold gives Lily a long, studying look. Finally, she must pass muster, for he steps out onto the porch. "I can take you there."

An hour later, Harold is out of breath. Lily had wanted to walk slowly, even claimed that her skirt made it hard to trek the rocky hill, but Harold had shaken his head at her—he knew better. Finally, they are at the cave, one of many such natural crevices embedded in the hills in this part of the county.

Lily looks at Harold. "How are you sure this is the cave Thea wrote about?"

"There were specific places only a few of us knew about. This was one of them." Harold sits down on a flat rock. Behind it, another rock fallen long ago, no doubt before white men came through, forms a back. Harold sighs, leans back like he's sitting on the most comfortable seat in a lush parlor. "This here is Bench Cave. If you don't mind, I'm going to sit here a spell. I don't cotton to walking stooped over. I may never straighten back up."

Lily starts toward the mouth of the cave, but Harold's voice stops her again. "Just so you know—after Rupert's death, this area's efforts for freedom died, too. Far as I know, no one's been in the cave since." He pulls out a ball of twine. "Here. Take the end. Hang on. Give a tug if you get in trouble. Bats and all—"

Lily smiles. "I'm not afraid of bats. I thought you don't want to go in, all stooped over?"

"I don't. But I can make it down this hill a darn sight faster than we walked up it, and get help for you. If you need it." Then he smiles back at her. "I reckon you won't."

Lily follows the beam of her flashlight into the cave, ducking, then stooping, and finally walking half-hunkered down. If the cave gets much narrower, she'll turn around and go back. She knows better than to crawl through narrow passages in caves—and surely, if this was where humans had hidden, she must nearly be in as far as any adult would go.

At last, something glints in her flashlight's beam. A tin cup, left on a pile of rocks. In the cup, more rocks. Lily shines her light into the cup, spots something metal. Gently, she lifts it out. It is a copper tag, embossed with: *Charleston. 612. Laundress. 18560.*

Lily isn't sure what this means, but carefully she folds the tag into a handkerchief and tucks it into her pocket. Then she kneels by the mound, puts down her flashlight and the remaining bit of twine, careful not to give it a tug and send a false signal for help.

She begins pulling off rocks at one end, her hands quivering, but not at the effort. At knowing what she will likely find.

A few more minutes, a few more rocks set aside—and there, in her flashlight beam, she sees the bones. Thea's mother hadn't been able to dig a proper grave. So she'd done the best she could with rocks over the body, and the marker of the cup and the tag. The burial site for Garnet.

LILY
Saturday, October 2—2:30 p.m.

"Is this about Hildy?" Mrs. Cooper looks worried, but Lily thinks the expression is for show.

"In a way," Lily says. "We ought to talk inside." She glances meaningfully at the townspeople walking past them, then nods at the Presbyterian church. She'd gone to the Coopers' house earlier and then was reminded by a neighbor that the church was holding a reception for the retiring organist and decided that bought her a little time with which to find Seth, the newspaper reporter, and show him the tag she'd found and ask him to do some research. He already thought he knew what the tag meant—though he promised to go to the library in Columbus as soon as he could to do some research to verify. Then Lily had returned to the church, waiting outside until people started coming out.

The first woman out rushed over to tell her, *I'm so sorry.* At first Lily thought she somehow knew about Hildy, but then she went on to say, *About your vinegar pie. Didn't even place in the pie competition!* Oh—the fair is this weekend, Lily thought, breaking away as she spotted Mrs. Cooper, wearing all black as if Hildy had died yet also managing to walk with a bit of preening as Merle accompanied her. Lily had stepped in front of them.

Now Merle says, "We've been so worried about Hildy."

Lily swallows back her distaste. *God. Merle is closer in age to Mrs. Cooper than to Hildy—is it possible he will end up courting her? That is probably how it should have been all along. They'd be well suited to each other.*

"I'm sure." Lily doesn't bother to keep the sarcasm out of her voice, but they follow her—breaking apart momentarily so Mrs. Cooper can follow Lily through the women's door and Merle can enter through the men's.

Mrs. Cooper settles into a back pew, hands on her lap, as if awaiting dire news. Lily sits next to her, uncomfortably aware of Merle hovering behind both of them.

Lily takes a moment to look at the front of the church, at the simple wooden cross hanging in the apse, directly behind the pulpit and between two small stained-glass windows, one depicting Jesus and the miracle of the fishes and loaves, the other Jesus as a shepherd. She takes it all in, wanting the image to douse that of the other night's burning cross, prays that someday this cross—which for all her doubts has always represented grace and transformation—is the only one she sees in her mind's eye.

For now, she turns her gaze back to Mrs. Cooper. "What happened at the WKKK meeting at the old Dyer place the other night?"

"You have no business asking me—"

"Do you want to know how Hildy is doing?"

Merle grabs Mrs. Cooper's shoulder, makes the woman gasp. Lily should tell him to let Mrs. Cooper go, but she watches as Merle snarls, "Tell her, so we can find out about Hildy!"

"All right . . . you already know I was there. What more do you need?"

"Did you see your cousin, Thea Kincaide, there?"

"I did, but I didn't do anything to her, I swear! I was shocked to see her after all these years, to recognize her—" She stops, sniffles. "She recognized me, too. Started screaming that my father had a gang attack her father—that they were responsible for killing her father! I told her to shut up, that her father was a dirty abolitionist, and deserved whatever he got—"

Merle inhales sharply, giving Mrs. Cooper a withering look. Well, as harsh as he could be, he's at least not as monstrous as Hildy's mother has become over the years.

"So what did you do, Mrs. Cooper, after you saw her?" Lily asks.

"I told Margaret Dyer that she was there. That her father had been an Underground Railroad operator. That Thea could be up to no good at our meeting."

Lily considers. If Mrs. Cooper had murdered Thea, why admit this much so easily? She'd only done so hoping to stay in Merle's good graces—likely holding out hope that Merle and Hildy would still marry and take care of her in her old age. But she could have admitted being at the vile gathering without implicating Margaret.

"One more question, Mrs. Cooper. Why have you held on to such hatred for Thea all these years? She seems at most . . . eccentric."

"Didn't you hear me?" Mrs. Cooper snaps. "The other night, or today? She came to my father's funeral to gloat that he'd died! She said—even then—that she believed my father and his friends had actually murdered her father! As if he could do such a thing!"

"You don't believe he could?" Lily casts a meaningful glance at the cross at the front of the sanctuary, to remind Mrs. Cooper of where they are.

By the time she looks back, Mrs. Cooper's face has blanched. "No—no—of course not."

But in Mrs. Cooper's eyes, Lily sees the truth. She does believe it. Has always believed it, ever since Thea's visit all those years ago. And fighting that possibility, rather than reckoning with it, has soured her very soul.

Lily stands, starts to the church door. Merle rushes after her.

"What about Hildy?" Merle calls after her.

Lily pauses. Mrs. Cooper hasn't even asked. "She'll be fine."

With that, Lily exits the church and walks briskly toward the jail-house. Thank goodness Margaret is still locked up. It will be easy enough to confront her while she's in a cell.

HILDY
Saturday, October 2—3:30 p.m.

"Now let her be!" Mama fusses.

Hildy smiles, sips on the bone broth that Mrs. Gottschalk has poured for her. A half hour before, Hildy had finally stirred to wake-fulness and quietly come down to the kitchen. She looks at Mama with gratitude—she knows it's due to her and Mrs. Gottschalk's ministra-tions that she is clean, in a fresh gown, and well rested.

She keeps her voice gentle. "I can play a simple game of checkers." She smiles at Jolene, who brightens. "I've been sick, though, so are you going to let me win?"

"No!"

Hildy laughs. "That's the way."

Jolene hasn't quite finished setting up the checkerboard, though, when there is a commotion in the parlor.

Merle. Talking over top of Mrs. Gottschalk. Hildy looks, stricken, at Mama. Anger flashes over Mama's face—and Hildy knows that Lily has told her everything.

Mama starts toward the door to the parlor.

"I can handle this." Hildy stands, pulls her robe tightly around her, and smiles at Jolene. "Play a practice game with your mamaw—I bet she has some clever moves to teach you!"

In the parlor, Merle and Mrs. Gottschalk fall silent and look at Hildy.

"I'm sorry," Mrs. Gottschalk says. "I told him he needs to leave my property. I'm not sure how he got past the deputies, or found us—"

"Because I'm her fiancé!" Merle hollers. "And one of the deputies' wives told me."

Hildy stiffens her spine and squares her shoulders. "No," she says firmly. "You're not my fiancé. Not any longer."

Merle's face crumbles. "Hildy . . . what am I to do? . . . I need your help at the store, and you need a firm hand to guide you—"

Hildy silences him with a hard look. "No. I do not. Hire help if you need it—"

"Hildy, you may be out of that asylum, but we all know you're prone to hysteria—"

"Prone to hysteria?" Hildy's voice filets the question. "Here's some hysteria. Go to hell, Merle."

LILY

Saturday, October 2—3:30 p.m.

Lily stands on the Dyer porch, fuming. *Dammit!* Margaret wasn't in the jailhouse after all. The deputy on duty explained that she'd been released earlier—her hold time more than exceeded without actual charges.

Which left Lily with a choice—wait until Monday, when the court opened, to have Olive formally file charges and to get a warrant for Margaret's arrest. And risk Margaret fleeing, if she senses, or receives word from someone at the asylum—one of those unnamed, cowardly nurses—that Lily is closing in.

Or come today, risk overstepping legal rights, thus nullifying any hold she'd have on Margaret.

She'd come. She'd have to speak, and move, carefully.

Lily removes her hand from her holstered revolver. Forces a smile to her face. And knocks on the door.

To her surprise, the door opens quickly. Missy, her pale face tear streaked yet eager, gazes out. When she spots Lily, she quickly turns crestfallen. "Oh. Oh, I was hoping . . ." Then she looks anxious. "Are you coming with word of my boy?" She clutches Lily's arm. "Junior? Has something happened to him?"

Lily, though alarmed, takes gentle advantage of Missy's distress. "Why don't you let me in and we can talk?"

Missy throws the door open, and Lily enters swiftly. In the parlor,

Lily sits in the same spot she'd selected days before at the Woman's Club meeting, while Missy hovers in the arched entry to the room.

"Junior? Is he all right? Did something happen to him?"

Then it hits Lily—Junior is not here with Missy. If she is so concerned, why is she still here? Why isn't she out looking for him?

"Please, take a deep breath," Lily says. "Tell me what happened."

"He ran off this morning, been itching to get back to his father, and this morning he was gone, and . . . and—Oh." Missy comes to an abrupt stop and sinks to her knees. Her next words are bitter. "You're not here with news about Junior, are you?"

Margaret and Perry appear in the hall behind Missy. Margaret kicks Missy. "Get up!"

Lily's jaw drops. *My God.*

"Go clean up the kitchen!" Margaret snaps.

Missy staggers to her feet, starts to leave, but Perry says, "For God's sake, Margaret, she's had a shock. Let her rest!"

"We all have." Margaret's words snarl and tangle. "Losing our boy!"

Our boy?

Missy puts her face to her hands, crying. Lily stares from one to the other. Perry stares, crestfallen and with tender worry, at his wife. Those three children's plots in the Dyer cemetery . . . Margaret has, in her mind, taken over Junior as if he's her son. Margaret's hatefulness notwithstanding, the whole scenario is simply tragic.

"Please," Lily says, rancor gone from her voice. "Come sit down, talk with me—"

Margaret's nostrils flare. "Who are you to tell us what to do in our own home?"

"She's still sheriff, honey." Perry gives his wife a gentle nudge into the parlor.

"Very well." Margaret enters her parlor as if a queen taking her spot in her court. "I hope you've come with news about the boy? Perhaps found him on his way back to that miserable farm?" Margaret sits down on the sofa, and Perry takes an uneasy seat next to her—but not too close, Lily notes. Missy remains trembling in the entryway. "Perry and I had hoped to rear him to be a fine young man."

Missy's face convulses with sorrow—and something else. Fear. She does not want to be with the Dyers. Yearns to go back to the farm—which surely can't be any more miserable than this household. Yet she stays. Why?

Lily clears her throat. "Thea Kincaide came upon your gathering at your old house. The poor woman was haunted by a choice she was forced into as a child—and she was trying to set it right. She'd overheard two nurses at the Hollows Asylum talk of the WKKK's plot to attack and kill Clarence Broward—referring to him by how he looks, rather than by name, and assuming any nearby residents wouldn't understand, or care, what they were saying. That is what prompted Thea's desperate plan to leave the Hollows—not that she knew Clarence. Just that a man was in danger, and she had her own reasons—"

Margaret gives a dismissive wave of her hand. "Haven't we been over all this?"

"I just came from talking with Mrs. Cooper," Lily goes on as if she hadn't been interrupted. "She admits recognizing her cousin, and says Thea became upset, accusing Mrs. Cooper's father's gang of attacking Thea's father's wagon and killing him. She says that she brought Thea to you."

The room goes still as Margaret stiffens. A snake almost caught. A snake wishing to strike. "Indeed, she did."

"Then what happened?" Lily asks.

"I told her she should deal with the woman—who was her cousin, after all." Margaret smiles thinly. "Apparently she did."

Lily shakes her head. "I don't think so. If she had 'dealt' with her, why admit to me that she'd even seen Thea there? I think she did bring her to you—but I think Thea's ravings confirmed something you might have suspected all along, living in the Dyer farmhouse. Seeing the gravestones. Wondering, as I did, about Perry's father, Murphy, being born to a sickly woman who'd never been able to have children, but who suddenly was able to give birth at fifty-one. Hearing tidbits about Perry's stepmother and stepaunt—Thea herself—coming to live at the house so soon after Murphy was born. And now I have writings by Thea claiming that Murphy really was born to another slave on that wagon—a woman named Garnet."

Lily takes a quick glance at Perry—and sees from the shocked look on his face that he has just figured out his actual lineage.

Margaret laughs. "You have it in writing? When, exactly, did Thea write this? Near the end of her life? The delusions—"

"I know, I know." Lily finally loses patience. "The delusions of an old woman with dementia. Except I found the burial site of Garnet—right where Thea's writings placed her. I'll have the remains exhumed—and buried properly, with respect. Even after all this time, the coroner should be able to approximate age and gender. Plus, at the site is a slave tag, likely used in hiring out slaves as part-time labor in Charleston, which is where Thea's writings say Garnet and John came from. Who knows why Garnet would have kept it—perhaps as a reminder of what she was hoping to escape." She looks at Perry. "Hoping to keep her descendants from experiencing."

Margaret gives Perry a look of distaste. "Well. How awkward for you. Perfect motivation for killing your great-aunt Thea—"

"No." Lily studies Perry's shell-shocked expression. "This is news to him. But not to you. A perfect motivation to kill Thea—lest word got out. You couldn't stand the notion of being married, all this time, to someone of mixed race. Especially as the leader of the WKKK. And you knew that if word got out, you'd not only lose that position; Perry's chances of getting votes from the prejudiced members of our community would put his election as sheriff in jeopardy."

Perry jumps up, fists clenched. "My God, Margaret. My God. I didn't want to run, I didn't want to move, I did this for you, trying to make you happy for once in our miserable lives—"

Margaret laughs. The out-of-place trill shocks Perry and Lily but not, she notes, Missy. "Oh please," Margaret says. "I didn't kill that old woman." She cuts her sharp eyes to Missy. "If you ever want to see your boy again—even from behind the bars of a prison cell—"

Missy drops back to her knees, sobbing. "She told that poor woman that we were going to go find the baby. She made me come with them and help get Thea to the top of the tunnel."

Lily's blood goes cold. Thea wouldn't have been strong enough to make that climb by herself. It had nearly bested Lily. As tiny as Thea had been, carrying her corpse up the ravine had been a challenge. Getting the confused but wiry and determined old woman to the top of the tunnel would be hard, even for a strong woman such as Margaret.

So she'd picked Missy to help her. Missy—vulnerable, and foolish, and no doubt caught up in the moment. Just like the Klanswomen who had put the burning cross in Lily's yard.

The truth finally hits Lily, why Missy had stayed working as a servant for Margaret, even as Missy gasps out the confession between ragged sobbing breaths: "She told me I had to. That it was . . . it was an initiation rite I had to do . . . that if I gave the old woman a little push, I'd be putting her out of her confused misery, and she'd, she'd get Ralf to stop hitting me, so I could go back and be happy with him, and I know I shouldna done it, but it was like something took over me, and I was finally going to be free and part of something big, and I wanted to do it, and so . . . so I did." Missy stares up at Lily, shivering at the awfulness of what she's confessed—but more than that, at relief, as if finally expelling the sick that had roiled within her ever since. "I killed Thea Kincaide."

Margaret's smile widens, even as Perry stares at her in horror. "Well, there you go, Lily. You have your confession." She looks at Perry. "And now that word will get out—well, perhaps we should dissolve our marriage. I could run for office as sheriff in my own right. I'd have plenty of supporters, voters I'd turned out for you, but—"

Missy hurls herself at Margaret, spitting, scratching, clawing. Perry pulls the sobbing woman back. "Stop," he says. "Stop. She's not worth it."

Lily stands. "I'll take in Missy. But I'm taking in you, too."

Margaret snorts. "Weren't you listening? *She* just confessed." She gives another dismissive wave. "And I'll vow in court that everything she said is true."

Lily looks at Perry. "Will you swear to what your wife just said?"

Perry nods. Even as he holds the sobbing Missy, tears course down his cheeks. "I knew about the meetings Margaret has been going to and having this past year. I didn't approve, asked her to stop. I found her notes about the initiation ceremony that was to happen at our old farm and finally forbade it, but when I got back home after work, Margaret was gone. I knew she'd found someone to drive or take a mule and wagon to the access path we used to get to Moonvale. I went after her, but once I got to the village I—I just couldn't bring myself to go to the old house. I knew if I did, our marriage would get even more troubled. Now I wish I had gone."

Lily returns her gaze to Margaret, who suddenly looks confused as to the undercurrents about what had just happened. Lily smiles grimly. "You've just admitted to being an accessory to murder. Olive is filing charges against you for assault. I'm guessing we can convince Missy to testify you coerced her, then held her against her will with blackmail—that should reduce her sentence. And if I put word out that I won't stop digging until I find out who was the ringleader behind the attack on me, my family, and my home—and by now, I think everyone knows I won't stop—one of your supporters will step forth and point the finger at you. Even if it all doesn't stick, enough will for you to spend a good long time in prison."

HILDY
Saturday, October 2—4:00 p.m.

Hildy sits on a kitchen chair down by the Kinship Tree. Mama and Mrs. Gottschalk had fussed at her that she should be inside, in bed, but when she told them she'd had enough of being cooped up inside, they'd look first struck and then understanding.

They'd insisted on carrying out the chair for her and only left her alone after she was cozily secure under a double layer of quilts. For a long time she'd looked around, poking her gaze under bushes and between trees, hoping to catch a glint of the old-fashioned lady—*Thea*—in the corner of her eyes. But she knew she never would again.

So now her eyes are closed, her face tilted up toward the sky. Though a bright blue day, it is cold, and a stiff wind clips along with the thrumming creek. But the fresh wind and air feels like a sweet caress of freedom. Hildy breathes deeply, savoring the hum of the creek but most especially the musty scent of autumn, which foretells the dying of leaves and the barrenness of fields and gardens—but to her, it is not a hollow season. The scents and riotous colors of leaves in their last glory, of goldenrods at last blazing like their name, also foretell the spring to come after winter. After a period of rest, new life comes after the old one is shed.

Hildy hears the tread of footsteps and knows it is him.

But she keeps her eyes closed even as his tread grows closer, then stops. There's his scent—earth and tobacco. *Tom.*

When at last she opens her eyes and turns to look at him, she sees him before her, hands clasped on one knee as if in prayer, though he is staring up, wide-eyed. She knows he would have waited as long as need be, even forever, for her to open her eyes.

Giving her time. At last.

She smiles, and that is all it takes for the tears to start coursing down his cheeks.

"Hildy. Oh, Hildy. I came to check on Olive, to give her the news that the union voted yesterday. It was close—but for integration."

Hildy nods. *Good. That is good.*

"Mrs. McArthur and Mrs. Gottschalk told me—" Tom's voice breaks, like rock under pickaxe. "Told me what happened."

"I will be fine," Hildy says. "I just need . . . time."

"Yes, all the time you need. Hildy—I couldn't take it if something bad happened to you. If I lost you. I mean from this world. If'n you don't want me, I understand, and I'll be glad to know you're all right, but if'n you'll have me . . . Hildy? Will you marry me?"

For a long moment, Hildy gazes into her beloved's eyes, as far and deep as she can, savors his gaze entering hers. Slowly, she untucks her warm hands from the quilt and cups them around his cold, whiskery, dear face. Then she puts her forehead to his and whispers.

"Oh, Tom. Yes. But first I have something I need to do." It's an idea that just struck her, in the first few minutes she'd been sitting out here. Suddenly she is sure. "I want to get my teaching certificate and maybe, if I'm lucky, teach in Rossville."

Tom gently strokes Hildy's hair. "Take all the time you need, my love."

LILY

Saturday, November 6—1:00 p.m.

A brisk wind bearing the promise of snow sweeps across the Kinship Cemetery and swirls the last of the leaves from the cedar's boughs around the gray headstones.

Lily walks quickly, Jolene on one side and Micah on the other, their mittened hands in hers. Micah stops, jerking Lily's arm.

She looks down at him, sees fear puckering his little face, and doubt douses her heart. Maybe bringing the children here, for the first time since their father's burial, was a bad idea.

Jolene pulls away from Lily and runs around to Micah, pulling him to her in a hug.

Jolene's soft voice barely reaches Lily over the wind and scuttling leaves. "Mama wouldn't bring us anywhere that isn't all right."

Jolene's confident proclamation goads Lily's heart into a sharp flip. Lily wants to believe her daughter is right—not just about this cemetery visit, but about their upcoming move to the Gottschalk farm.

Now their farm.

When Mama had first broached the idea, Lily had started to reject it out of hand.

Then the statement Harold had made at the Quaker meeting weeks before echoed across her mind—the wisdom he'd intoned, seemingly directed right at her.

Find the wisdom in your grief.

She thought, would it really be wise to move herself—her children, her mama, her little brother—here?

It's the sight of the Kinship Tree, where she has so many happy memories of Roger. Where she and Marvena had bonded their friendship a year before.

Yet across the way is the house where Daniel had spent a miserable childhood—and so much drama had played out after his murder a year ago.

But that's also where she'd met Daniel, years ago. Where they'd fallen in love. She'd never trade a moment of her life with him for anything—or the memories.

Find the wisdom in your grief.

Maybe the wisdom is finding a way to hold both sorrow and joy, tragic and blissful memories, in your heart without breaking it.

A new family lives in Daniel's childhood home. Life goes on.

Maybe Mama and the old Quaker man were on to something.

Maybe her and her family's life should go on in Widow Gottschalk's house.

So Lily had bought the house the day after the election on November 2, going from the courthouse after voting across the street to the Kinship Trust Savings & Loan to sign paperwork with Mrs. Gottschalk. Moving out of the town, into the countryside, on the land with the Kinship Tree felt right whether she won the election as sheriff or not. She's calculated—she can drive her children, and several others along the way, into town for school and if she wins the election, go into the new office in the courthouse. If she doesn't win, well, she'll have to figure that out. Maybe instead of leasing out the land for buckwheat farming, she'll farm it herself.

Now Lily says gently to Micah and Jolene, "We don't have to go look today."

Micah looks from Lily to Jolene, eyes wide as he stares up at the big sister with whom he usually tussles and quarrels. Jolene gives a small nod.

Micah looks up at Lily. "I'm ready, Mama. I can do it."

Lily hesitates. Should she really trust the judgment of her small children?

Go on, her own mama had said that morning. *Go on, and take them. It's not going to get easier. Your young'uns—they're strong, Lily. But they need you to help them get on with life.* Then Mama had looked away, back to the clothes she was folding for her and Caleb Jr.'s own move. Mama has sold her house, and they are going to move in with Lily and her children. *Just like you're helping me. This house . . . it's full of too many sorrows. Too many haunts.* Mama meant Daddy and Roger, and Lily wondered if they ever came to life for her in the shadows, the way Daniel sometimes did for her.

Now Lily scoops up Micah in one arm and holds Jolene's hand. They continue on across the cemetery. Lily glances at a fresh grave—the new burial site for Garnet. Seth had confirmed the information about the slave tag. Lily doesn't pause, for this will be too much to explain to the children, but she knows she'll come back after the marker she's ordered is in, to properly pay her respects.

Finally, they come to Daddy's and Roger's markers, side by side, labeled *In Memory Of,* for Daddy's physical remains are under the coal mine cave in where he'd died trying to save others and Roger's body never came home from France.

And next to Roger—Daniel's grave.

Lily had received word last week that Daniel's headstone had finally been engraved and installed.

Slowly, still holding Micah in her arm and Jolene's hand in hers, Lily sinks to her knees before the grave. Micah wiggles and Lily gently releases him. Lily blinks, hard, swipes the back of her hand across her eyes, stinging as the wind pulls forth the tears she's trying to hold back.

"'Here rests Daniel T. Ross,'" Jolene reads the engraved words. "'Loving husband and father. February 11, 1892–March 25, 1925.' Did I get it right, Mama?"

Lily clears her throat. "That's right, sweet pea. That's what Daddy's marker says."

"This is where Daddy is, now?" Micah asks.

"No, silly," Jolene says. "Mama said he's in our hearts and smiles and eyes, that one night. Don't you remember?"

Micah gives Jolene a little shove. "I'm not silly! You are!"

"Children!"

They both look at Lily, afraid of getting in trouble. But Lily laughs. Life goes on. Life does go on, in all its troublesome, petty, wonderful, detailed, glory.

Lily pulls her children to her. "I wanted you to see that your daddy's marker is all complete. And Jolene's right—your daddy's remains are here, but he's not here. The spirit of him." He lived now only in the memories of everyone who'd known or loved him. "He's in our memories and hearts. But sometimes it's good to come to the cemetery where someone's remains were laid to rest. To remember them. Talk to them, in your heart, even."

"Do they hear us?" Micah asks.

"I don't know," Lily says. "I think what's important is that we pay attention to what we want to say."

Micah wiggles free and goes to the headstone. He presses his forefinger into the lettering, tracing it, and then he rests his head on top of the stone. "I miss you, Daddy," he says.

Oh! How Lily misses him, too. And will always miss him, no matter what else—or even who else—life brings her.

As Jolene goes to stand with her brother, Lily looks beyond the headstone and the fence, into the woods. And there he is—the shimmery, silvery boy. Lily draws back as he grins at her. All along she'd thought she'd been envisioning a child from a future they'd never had.

Perhaps it was a young Daniel—Daniel from before the weight of his own father's anger and pain, from before life was so brutal.

At the very notion, Lily quivers. Why would she see, all along, this young version of Daniel she'd never known—carefree and unfettered as he chased after whatever it was that had caught his attention and desire.

"Lily?"

She jumps, then realizes it's Hildy, come up quietly behind her.

Lily stands, turns, looks at her friend. *Dear Hildy.* The bruises and marks on her face have faded. Light has returned to her eyes, and a soft rose to her cheeks. Since both Clarence and Olive have left the area—separately but, Lily hopes, finding each other again in a new location—Hildy has taken on Olive's job as a substitute school teacher in Rossville while making plans to eventually get her official teaching certificate. She's excelling at it—as well as at living life independent of her mother, who whines at anyone who will listen, which are few people. Merle has started courting another young woman in Kinship. Junior, Lily has verified, did run back home to his father, Ralf, and so far, there has been no trouble between Junior and Jolene.

"The results are in," Hildy says. After the stunning news about Margaret—and a speedy trial for both her and Missy, in which both women were convicted and sent to the women's penitentiary in Ohio—Perry had withdrawn from the race. He'd disavowed any knowledge of or support for either the men's or women's Klans, and, fortunately, there have been no other WKKK gatherings that Lily knows of. It seems the snake has, at least for a time, returned to the hole in hell from which it had slithered.

Meanwhile, in Perry's stead, Leroy—the guard Lily had fired—had started a petition to run as the Republican candidate for sheriff in Perry's place, though it was too late to be officially added to the ballot. Yet enough people had written in Leroy's name that the count was close and had required a recount.

Lily can't breathe. For suddenly, with all her heart, with every bit of her being, she wants to have won. She wants to be sheriff, in her own right. Wants it, even though such a close count means she'll have to keep working hard for all the people of her county, no matter who they'd voted for, while still staying true to her values. Wants it, even though she knows the opportunity would never have come to her had Daniel lived.

That life is gone. She has to find a new path forward. Her path. Free of guilt. She glances back into the woods and sees only bare tree branches shivering in the wind. Maybe that's what the silvery, shimmering boy has been trying to show her all along—whoever he is.

She looks back at Hildy. Nods. *Tell me.*

"It was close, but it is official," Hildy says. Then a grin breaks free on her face, wordlessly delivering the news, but still, Lily holds her breath, until Hildy says, "You won!"

As she breathes again, Lily feels her own grin breaking free. She grabs Hildy in a hug so hard that her friend squeals. "Oh, Hildy! I'm going to have a dinner to celebrate! You have to come, and Tom, and Marvena and Jurgis—"

Hildy laughs, then pulls back a little. "All right, all right! I'll help you with it—but first I need to finish some writing."

FULL MEMORIAL OF THEA WRITTEN BY HILDY

November 14, 1926

Submitted by Miss Hildy Cooper

Thea Kincaide Leitel Tyler Javitz, age 76, went to be with the Lord on September 21, 1926.

The circumstances of her gruesome death have already been well documented in this newspaper and become a story that gained international attention in publications as far away as New York

City and Paris, France, and London, England—all places that Thea once lived.

What I wish to share here is the story of her long life, which I have pieced together from postcards, articles, detective work, and a partial autobiography, which she did not live to finish.

Thea was my first cousin, once removed, on my mother's side. My mother, Mabel Kincaide Cooper, and Thea were first cousins. Their fathers were brothers—Rupert Kincaide being Thea's beloved father and Claude Kincaide being my mother's father.

Thea was born in 1850 to Rupert and Cleo Kincaide and was their only child. She grew up on a modest farm in Stanehart Hollow, a small spot situated southeast of Moonvale Hollow Village and northwest of Athens and the Kinship River. Her parents were members of the Stanehart Hollow Friends Assembly, and her father was particularly devout. It was his strongly held belief that all humans are created equal, and that none should be held in forced servitude to another. His devotion to this belief and his faith emboldened him to serve as a "conductor" on the Underground Railroad—helping to escort escaped slaves to freedom from bondage in the southern region of our country, at a time when doing so ran afoul of the law.

This law gave rise to bounty hunters for runaway slaves— earning a reward for returning them to their owners. It is a fact, embarrassing though it is to me to aver, that my own grandfather Claude was one such bounty hunter—putting him in direct conflict with the convictions of his brother: my great-uncle, and Thea's father, Rupert Kincaid.

By Thea's own testimony in her partial autobiography, she preferred the company of her father to that of her depressed and often harsh mother and wished to help him escort escaped slaves along to freedom. Wisely, he would not allow her to accompany him, for he knew the treks were too dangerous for a young child.

But Thea took a particular liking to one pair of escapees from Charleston, South Carolina—a young, pregnant woman named

Garnet and a young man, unrelated and unattached to Garnet, named John. And so, Thea snuck into the back of her father's wagon one fateful night in September 1857, a night of a full moon just like the full moon on the night on which Thea died.

On that night, Rupert's wagon was beset by bounty hunters— including his own brother, Claude. Rupert died in the accident, and John, Garnet, and Thea escaped. John became separated from them, and Garnet went into early labor, delivered a son, and tragically died in childbirth. Thea took the baby to a prosperous yet childless couple, a couple her mother had done laundry and mending for, and that Thea knew longed for a child—Joyce and Adam Dyer—and left the baby there on the back doorstep of their farmhouse in Moonvale Hollow Village.

I will not make too much of what ensued—John was accused of killing Rupert, and partly based on young Thea identifying him, and partly due to bias against him, was hanged to death in our very own town square. Again, these details have been sufficiently covered in the reportage on the solving of Thea's murder, by our own Sheriff Lily Ross, who I am grateful to call my dearest friend.

After the trial and death of John, Thea and her mother were turned away from any help by Rupert's brother, my grand-father Claude, perhaps out of fear that familiarity would lead to contempt and Thea realizing that her own uncle—a realization she came to later as an adult—was part of the gang that attacked the wagon, killed her father, and set up John as a suspect. Thea and her mother were even shamed by some members of their assembly, and so, per her partial autobiography, Thea managed to connive so that she and her mother went to work for Joyce and Adam, allowing Thea to tend to Murphy Dyer—the very child she'd sacrificed so much, even as a child herself, to save. Not long after, Joyce passed away, and Adam married Cleo, making Thea his stepdaughter, and Murphy's older stepsister.

Again according to Thea's partial autobiography, Adam resented Thea, for she alone, besides him and Cleo, knew that Murphy was not really his and Joyce's son. And so Adam treated Thea cruelly, even beating her. For a time, she took the beatings without question, for her own mother would not defend her lest she lose the only position of relative wealth she'd ever enjoyed or was ever likely to achieve—an admittedly logical choice for a woman of her time. What's more, young Thea believed that the beatings were punishment from God for her choosing to let an innocent man— John—hang for the brutal murder of her own father.

Yet did she so choose? She was only seven years old, undoubtedly terrified, and easily manipulated by all the adults around her to do as they wished her to do—point at John as the attacker. More than that—imagine the horror, as a mere girl, of knowing that if she told the truth, she was unlikely to be believed and Murphy's care would be in jeopardy and John still just as likely to be scapegoated for her own father's death. Perhaps not knowing, at age seven, but sensing it. Eventually knowing. Carrying that for a lifetime.

No doubt she had reasoned it out by the time she ran away at 17 with a pots-and-pans traveling salesman. Some may call that scandalous, but her own mother had been dead for 5 years by then and according to Thea's diary, her mother Cleo's marriage to Adam Dyer had been so bitterly unhappy, Adam had Cleo Kincaide Dyer buried in a graveyard in Athens rather than in the Dyer family plot. Without her mother to protect her, from age twelve Thea had been worked as a servant and as she grew older, was brutishly taken advantage of by Adam Dyer. By the time Thea was 17, Murphy, who she had saved and doted on, was himself 10, and sufficiently strong to take care of himself.

The salesman—Thea only refers to him as "Clyde" in her journals— was perhaps only a means of travel for Thea, for once she alighted in New York, she became a dancer in gentleman's clubs.

Some tender readers may find Thea's choice of work condemnable. But I ask you, what would you have Thea do? She had no family, no community here in Kinship that would give her a shoulder to lean on. Should she have simply fallen down in a pitiable heap to allow herself to wither away, spiritually and perhaps physically, all in the name of propriety? I say—nay. The instinct for survival runs deep in all humans, and in this we are no different from beasts of burden or wild animals foraging and hunting.

But we are different in that we have spirits, and in Thea the spirit of our Creator, I would contend, ran particularly strong.

She worked her way to the still scandalous but more acceptable entertainment form of burlesque, and indeed found joy in her performances. They became, she wrote in her journals, less for the audiences of men who cheered her on—she could almost forget about them beyond the glare of the footlights—and more about the woman she wanted to present to the world, a woman who was free and in ownership of her own body and mind. A freedom of self-possession not unlike the freedom her father fought and died for, for others.

In 1880, Thea met a handsome businessman, Scott Leitel. Perhaps she was in love with him—she never stated so in her journals. Or perhaps a part of her longed-for security—like the security her own mother had sought with Adam Dyer. In any case, Scott was fascinated with her, and they married in 1880, and a year later had a son, Neil.

But restlessness, perhaps born of her own guilt and haunts from her childhood, beset Thea and she was unable to remain faithful, by her own admission, and seven years after having her son, upon being divorced, left her son in his father's care. Again, some may judge her decision—but I do not. According to her writings, she realized that her son would be better off with his father, that not every woman, simply by virtue of being female, is called to motherhood, and this was the case with her.

So Thea pursued her dancing career, took various lovers, and lived what many would judge as a salacious life. But to Thea, it was free and exciting.

In 1905, my grandfather Claude Kincaide passed away, and though by now Thea planned to move to Europe, she came back to Bronwyn County for the first time since she'd run away from the area—and for the last time until her death.

This was the only time I met her. After that, I received three postcards from her, one a year. My father made sure I saw them. I don't know if she sent more that my mother may have destroyed in an effort to protect me from overly worldly ideas.

Once Thea was in Europe, she lived in Paris and London, returned for a brief stint as a typist in New York, saved enough money to journey to Oslo, married Joseph Tyler, another businessman, divorced again, married again, and was widowed. From her autobiography, she truly loved her last husband, Oscar Javitz, a poor but happy painter, and through and with him at last found contentment and peace. She studied art and gardened and entertained. She laughed and loved. It is at this point that her autobiography trails off.

After she was widowed, at age 74, she developed dementia. A concerned friend tracked down her son, Neil, who brought her back to the United States—ironically, to Athens, Ohio, where he was a professor at Ohio University. But he abandoned her there, in a lodging house, finding her antics—she loved to dance, it seemed, at the most inopportune times—embarrassing, leaving money for the lodging house owner to cover expenses, and instructions for his mother to be committed to the Hollows Asylum for the Insane if she became too much of a problem. Well, of course she soon became a "problem," for what better way to capitalize on this sum of money than to keep it, and have Thea committed, and then rent her room out to someone else?

At the asylum, her haunts became stronger and stronger, and as has been reported, she soon set out on a night with a full moon, much like the night her father died nearly 70 years before, desperately searching for John and Garnet, hoping against hope to somehow save them after all.

The Bible and Shakespeare both claim that in old age, should we live so long, we return to a childlike state. And so it was with Thea. At the end, though she was 76 in years, she was but 7 in her mind, and came full circle to the haunts that never fully departed her mind and soul.

Perhaps those who have continued to read this far are wondering: Why does a cousin once removed who I met once, from whom I received only three postcards, hold such fascination for me that I should write this special obituary?

This is a question I will long ponder. The easy answer is that it is caused by the shock of learning my own grandfather's role in the tragedy of Thea's youth and in the horrific misjustice brought to the man named John.

I think it is more than that. The memory of Thea's visit—such a disturbing, shocking moment in my seemingly proper and bland childhood home—came further and further into bright relief, the more I pondered. I eventually realized what a blazing bright light Thea was. Her spirit for adventure, for curiosity, for enjoying— dare I say—all that is sumptuous and surprising and tender about life.

And there is this, too.

In the brief time she knew them, even as a child, while they were hidden with her family, Thea wanted to teach John and Garnet how to read. I too am teaching those who have been deprived of education simply by the draw of their birth and station in life. I believe she sensed, through even a slim book, how much wider and more wondrous the world is than any of us can ever fully know. I believe she was in awe of that and wanted to share that awe.

For it is in sharing our stories and journeys, without reservation but with only an open and honest heart, that we might find, as Thea sought on the dancing stage, freedom.

I wish to give Thea that justice, at last. The freedom of her story, told as honestly and openly as I can.

And in so doing, find at last the start to my own true story, my own freedom.

I conclude, finally, by saying to my first cousin once removed, Thea Kincaide Leitel Tyler Javitz, do not rest in peace.

Instead, dance across the heavens, forgiven and accepted in God's true grace.

EPILOGUE

⟫

LILY

Saturday, December 4—4:00 p.m.

"Mama, please stop being fussy and come on!"

Lily glares at the four-tiered wedding cake as if a long, hard stare will put its lopsidedness to rights. She'd added extra cream frosting on the leaning side, but in her nervous hurry she'd pressed too hard with the spatula, and now the top tier looks close to plopping right off the top. By the time the damned ceremony is done, she won't have to worry about how she'll get it out to the barn. The whole thing will more'n likely have crumpled, right here in the kitchen. This disorganized kitchen.

It's tempting to blame the kitchen. The oven rack is definitely warped, and the oven doesn't heat evenly like the one at the old sheriff's house. And she doesn't have essential items—mixing bowls, and her hand beater, and her wooden spoons—properly sorted and settled, either. Why had she thought she could make a decent cake while still settling into her new house?

"Mama!"

Lily whirls with irritation, but as soon as she sees Jolene standing in the doorway, clutching a basket filled with fragrant dried rose petals and lavender, her heart softens at the sight of Jolene, hair in perfect curls, in a new navy blue dress Mama had sewn for just this occasion, with the lace trim Jolene had picked out at the notions store.

Lily laughs, for Jolene also has one hand on her hip and her head tilted to the side. She looks and sounds like Lily did as a child, when frustrated with her own mama. Indeed, Mama stands behind Jolene, smiling at Lily over the top of the child's head—*yes, I see the resemblance, too.*

Lily holds out the frosting-covered spatula. "Want to lick off the spatula?"

Jolene purses her lips and shakes her head. "The wedding is supposed to already be starting! I can't get my new dress messy!"

In the next instant, Jolene's eyes widen and she licks her lips—a child again, who would love a treat of leftover frosting. *Ah. She's already too old for her age. Let her be a child every moment she can.* "I'll save it back for you, all right?"

Jolene looks relieved and nods. Lily quickly wraps the spatula in a bit of waxed paper and gives the cake one more rueful glance as she follows her mama and daughter out of the kitchen, out the back door, and to the barn.

The frozen ground crunches under their hurried steps, and the abrupt cold, blowing through the trees and off the river, across Lily's farmland, snatches their breaths. Nearby, she hears the tiny chirp of the white-breasted nuthatch couple, nesting in the hollow of a redbud tree. She will have to get in the habit this winter of leaving out suet and seed.

Mama and Jolene keep their heads bowed against the wind, but Lily looks around across the barren stretch of her land, looking. Looking. She's been looking ever since she and Mama and her children and her little brother had moved into this house, claimed it as their own, three weeks before. But all she sees, as the wind stings her eyes and pricks forth tears, is snow slowly sifting down from the sodden sky—white upon gray upon darker gray. The only spot of color is the red barn, and even that is drab, like a dab of rouge that's lost its luster.

Next spring, she will paint the barn. Widen the gravel path from the road to the barn, add a parking shed to the side for her automobile.

Over there, expand the garden. There will be plenty of peas and corn and green beans and tomatoes for eating and canning. Shimmering next to the barn, as if it's already there and not a promise she's made to Micah, a new chicken coop, filled with the fussy clucks of hens. So many new plans. She's already made good on the promise of getting a dog, purchasing, at a steep price, Sadie, the tracking hound.

They are at the barn now, entering. Inside the barn, kitchen chairs and hay bales have been arranged into makeshift pews. Some of the seats are hers, but most have been brought by the wedding guests. And still, at the back, many people stand, some townspeople, but mostly miners dressed in their finest. Lily inhales sharply at the sight of so many people filling the space. Then she nearly laughs. There is certainly not enough cake in her kitchen for everyone here—and it will not matter if it has fallen into gooey crumbs. A makeshift table is laden with a wedding feast—cakes and pies and hams and potato salads. The old smells of the barn that Lily had worried about have for now been replaced with the good, warm scents of the small offerings of individual families, brought together to create a bounty.

Someone has thought to bring in a portable coal-fired oven to heat the space—though truth be told, there is also the warmth of body heat. Many of the people here had worked with Lily to clean out the barn for this wedding and to help her and her family move in. Though there was plenty left to unpack, they'd moved furniture and household goods from the old sheriff's house out to the Gottschalks' old farm. To Lily Ross's new farm.

All except for Daniel's old chair. By her request, she'd asked that it stay out here, for seating for the wedding. She'd move it in herself. Later. When she is ready.

She'd expected that one of the older people would be settled comfortably in the chair, but it sits empty at the front of the makeshift pews. Did no one wish to sit in his chair?

Then she feels a soft grasp on her arm and turns. It's Tom. He smiles gently, and she realizes then, as people stand aside and let them through, that everyone has saved the chair for her. Then he pauses, gives her a small nudge, nods his head to indicate—*look over there.*

Benjamin Russo. She is surprised—yet not—that he had come. She'd heard he'd already moved to the area. Of course he'd get to know Tom and other miners and know of this wedding. *Benjamin.* He looks handsome, in his neatly pressed suit, his carefully parted dark hair. His amber eyes, focusing on her.

For a moment, Lily hesitates. Then she nods at Benjamin, offers him a tremulous smile, which, though expressing only the most proprietary emotion, shows that the door to her life, if not fully thrown open, is at least not latched shut forever. He smiles back.

Lily and Tom continue on. She searches for Mama and finds her, settling into a kitchen chair that a man has vacated for her. From somewhere, Caleb Jr. has broken free from the watchful eye of another mother in the community and has scrambled up into his mother's lap. Even as Mama shushes her young boy, she's giving her grown daughter a stern stare and nodding at her. *Go on, Lily!*

At the back of the barn, by the open doors, Jolene waits.

Finally, Lily sits, sinking into the warm, broad embrace of the leather chair. *Welcome, Sheriff Ross. It's fine, Lily. You're fine.*

Tom heads to the back of the crowd, and Lily slowly inhales and exhales, telling herself to focus on the wedding at hand. It's not the one she'd expected to be planning and holding in her barn. Someone takes her hand, squeezes. She looks to her right—it's Hildy, who is holding little Micah and smiling at her, and Lily sees all that her friend needs to say in that smile: *It's fine, Lily. I'm fine. This isn't my day. It will be soon enough.*

Lily looks back, past all the people gathered behind her. Some directly invited. Some coming by word of mouth. This is truly a community wedding. Finally, flower girl Jolene starts down the makeshift aisle—right step, pause; left step, pause. With each pause, she strews a bit of the rose potpourri in the aisle, marking the path for the new bride.

The crowd rises to its feet. As Lily stands, Micah takes her hand.

Then a voice, as clear and simple as the strum of a single fiddle string, rises. Fiddles and banjos and foot stomping will fill the barn later, after the ceremony, after the feast. There will probably be moonshine that Lily will have to ignore, and she smiles at that.

But for now, it is Frankie at the front, facing the gathering, singing a hymn solo, and as Lily lowers Micah, then stands and takes his hand, she lets the words wash over her, carried by Frankie's simple, rustic voice: "O perfect Love, all human thought transcending . . ."

A feeling overtakes Lily of the endless beauty that can at times fill a single moment. Jurgis nervously comes to the front of the gathering, handsome in an old but still-well-fitting suit. The preacher stands on a hay bale and opens a Bible.

"O perfect Life, be Thou their full assurance, Of tender charity and steadfast faith . . ."

Marvena, escorted by Tom, comes down the makeshift aisle behind Jolene. Lily's grin widens at how beautiful Marvena is in the dress she's sewn from soft white satin—the cloth a gift sent from Olive and Clarence now settled together in Boston—at how she would growl at being called anything so soft as *beautiful*. Yet she is. Radiantly beautiful.

"Grant them the joy which brightens earthly sorrow . . ."

A few people at the back of the gathering gasp, as a whoosh of wind blows in.

There, at the back of the crowd, stands Perry Dyer.

His expression is ravaged with sadness yet holds a boyish expression of hope that he might yet be part of this community.

He rushes to the sliding barn door, eager to help, and starts to close it. Perry catches Lily's eye. Stops. Somehow knows that she is looking for something. Someone.

Lily takes a moment to look. All she sees is swirling snow, the cold white bright day. She will not see him again, the silvery smiling boy, chasing his ball. Or his dog. She never had quite decided which. She will not see him again, nor try to.

Hildy squeezes her arm. Lily scoops up Micah, hugs him tight, feels his warmth, his fine hair tickling the bottom of her chin, his soft breath on her forearm. She presses the back of her legs hard against the chair. *It's fine, Lily. You're fine.*

Lily gives a slight nod to Perry, who slides the barn door closed. He disappears into the crowd, and Lily at last turns her full attention to the wedding, to Marvena, who smiles at Lily as she walks past, before turning her gaze back on Jurgis; to Tom, who winks as he passes at Hildy, who in turn giggles; to Jolene, who takes her place beside Frankie and looks nervously at Lily.

Lily nods at her daughter. Smiles. *You're fine.*

Then, as Marvena and Tom reach the front, Lily sits, along with the rest of the gathered community. Jurgis's smile is atremble as his gaze settles like a sigh on Marvena. Tom releases her elbow and Marvena steps beside Jurgis. Her grown-up duties over, Jolene clambers into Lily's lap. Lily wraps her arms around both of her children, pulls them close, as Frankie sings:

"Grant them the peace which calms all earthly strife."

AUTHOR'S NOTE

When I completed my first novel in the Kinship Historical Mystery Series, I had a firm idea about where I wanted to go next, emotionally and in character development, with Lily, Marvena, Hildy, and the other regular inhabitants of Bronwyn County.

However, I wasn't sure right away about how to ground my next novel in actual history.

So I started poking around in my stacks of research and notes about Appalachian Ohio, and came across Moonville and Moonville Tunnel. Because I take fictional liberties with events set in the town and on the train line, I renamed these locations Moonvale Hollow Village and Moonvale Hollow Tunnel. But it is true that by legend Moonville is considered a haunted area, based on the number of accidents on the twisty-turning train track that once ran through the holler and the tunnel. It's also true that Moonville was only accessible by train or mule path, even though it was occupied through the 1940s. The track remained in use until 1988. What remains of the track, deep in the Zaleski State Forest, has been turned into, or is in the process of becoming, a rail-trail. My husband and I found the Moonville Tunnel by following increasingly remote roads in southeastern Ohio, until we were on a road so infrequently used that butterflies and birds alight in the middle of the road, fluttering away as automobiles approach. When we could drive no farther, we parked and hiked to the tunnel. I even walked the old trails barefoot, just for a bit, to test out the opening scene. Though my feet were sore for a few hours, no husbands, birds, or butterflies were hurt in the researching of this novel.

After that experience, I knew I had the right setting for *The Hollows*. You can learn more about the lore of Moonville and its tunnel at www .moonvilletunnel.net.

Another fascinating setting is the old Athens Lunatic Asylum, as it was called. The "mental hospital" went by a variety of names in its existence from 1874 until 1993, and was also nicknamed "The Ridges." Now, The Ridges is part of Ohio University. Though much of the structure is closed off, it houses the university's beautiful Kennedy Museum of Art as well as offices, classrooms, and storage. I'm indebted to the book, *Asylum on the Hill: History of a Healing Landscape*, by Katherine Ziff, as well as to a terrific walking tour I took of the exterior of the facility, sponsored by the Southeast Ohio History Center (www.athenshistory.org) and led by George Eberts, a longtime Asylum employee and local expert in the asylum's history. I so appreciate the respectful, detailed, and non-sensational approach Mr. Eberts took in sharing the institution's history. He brought the asylum's history to life—in a good way.

I chose to rename The Ridges as The Hollows, again because of fictional prerogatives I took with the location and events. Characters employed at The Hollows are strictly from my imagination. I also liked the play on the word "hollows," both as the "formal" word hollers, a synonym for valleys; additionally, many roads in the area are named after hollows, as are several in my novel.

I will confess to rearranging the topography a bit for my purposes. In real life, a river runs in front of The Ridges, not behind it. But I liked the images of Lily and Marvena coming upon the asylum, and Lily having to cross a swinging bridge—mostly because I'm terrified of swinging bridges, and have only crossed a few, and then under duress.

Sometimes, writers are compelled to apply our own fears to our characters. (My apologies, Lily.)

As I developed *The Hollows,* I poked around in my history books for anything unusual or interesting about 1926. I'm not sure, honestly, how I ran across it, but I do remember my complete shock when I stumbled upon the WKKK. As I read and researched, I learned that the WKKK has a complex history, growing out of numerous women's groups that advocated for the supremacy of white, Protestant, non-immigrant women. These groups, which grew out of a subset of the suffrage and temperance movements, ended up coalescing into the WKKK, which started in 1923 and collapsed at the end of the decade. In the 1926 timeframe, the WKKK had chapters in all U.S. states in existence at that time. I found no direct evidence of chapters in southeastern Ohio, but the WKKK's strongest chapters were in Ohio, Pennsylvania, Indiana, and Arkansas, so it is certainly possible. The history of the role of women in this group and in white supremacy in general is complex, and I only touched the surface of one way it could potentially have manifested in a community. Though members of the WKKK tended to favor psychological warfare over physical assault, both types of events occurred, as portrayed in *The Hollows.* For my research, I first read "Women in the 1920s Ku Klux Clan Movement," by Kathleen M. Blee, published in *Feminist Studies,* Vol. 17, No. 1, Spring of 1991. I also read her excellent, well-researched—and chilling—book *Women of the Klan.*

Shockingly, Daisy Douglas Barr, a Quaker evangelist and KKK/WKKK leader, is also pulled directly from history. I quote her poem, which I discovered in an article on *Timeline.com,* "One woman's effort to mix Klan-style hatred with wholesome Christian values," by Laura Smith.

Yet, the Quakers were, of course, part of the Underground Railroad, and it was fascinating to me to have both views represented in the same group.

And though the WKKK existed in Ohio, so too did true-life hero Richard L. Davis, an African-American man who was a mine labor organizer in the Hocking Valley area of southeastern Ohio in the late

1800s, and who worked hard to help found the United Mine Workers of America. His fascinating life is well-documented in *Richard L. Davis and the Color Line in Ohio Coal,* by Frans H. Doppen.

I'm grateful for the National Underground Railroad Freedom Center in Cincinnati, Ohio. I've visited several times over the years, both for my own edification and more recently for researching *The Hollows,* and follow in my own work the museum's policy in using terminology true to the time they're documenting in historical displays. To quote the museum's introductory panel to its detailed, moving exhibit on slavery and the Underground Railroad: "Over generations, people of African descent have changed how they refer to themselves . . . In this exhibition, we will use any and all of these terms when they are historically appropriate." I have followed the accurate terms as documented in the museum to fit the various contexts and time frames of *The Hollows.*

In addition to its exhibit on slavery and the Underground Railroad, the museum also has exhibits on more recent history, and current issues. I highly recommend a visit; learn more at www.freedomcenter .org.

Finally, on a more light-hearted note, I must mention Guibo, the mule. Neither I nor my daughter Gwen have any idea where that name came from, but she worked for a time on a ranch in southern California, where there was a miniature donkey named Guibo. I've always thought that if I have a spirit animal it would be a mule or donkey. (I like to think that that's because I'm stubborn and a hard worker . . . though I probably have other mule-like attributes.) When my husband and I visited Gwen at the ranch, I was instantly taken with Guibo and his hilarious and heartfelt whinnying, and knew he'd find a role in a future novel. In the midst of a novel with such serious and often dark themes and history, it's good for both writer and reader to encounter a loveable, intrepid being like Guibo.

ACKNOWLEDGMENTS

Thank you to:

- First and always, the joyous lights of my life: my husband, David, and our daughters, Katherine and Gwen.

- My writer friends who are also friend-friends: Heather, Katrina, Jessica, Kristina, Jeffrey, Marti, and Cyndi. This writing journey would be impossible without you, and you enrich my life beyond the realm of writing.

- The Book Group and Minotaur Books—I am grateful in spades to work with such amazing professionals: Elisabeth, for your thoughtful guidance; Catherine, for your inspiring editorial wisdom; Sarah and Joe, for your passion in getting the word out to readers; Nettie and Hallie, for patiently and promptly answering questions (even when I sometimes ask the same ones twice).

- Readers and book clubs, who've given me the greatest honor a writer can receive—welcoming the creations of my imagination into your own. You complete the magic of storytelling, and I'm ever grateful.

1. The Hollows asylum is a key setting for both the novel and its namesake. On first sighting the place with Marvena, Lily says, "if one didn't know they were in a state-run asylum, the scenes would be idyllic" and notes that "Asylum, after all, means a refuge." How do these statements line up with your own understanding of asylums at that time? How does your view—and perhaps the views of the characters—of *The Hollows* change throughout the novel?

2. The night the action begins, "the full moon ladles light into the deep, clear night." The moon is used as a tie between the different perspectives introduced in the first few chapters. Can you think of other examples of how the moon plays a role in this story?

3. Before reading *The Hollows*, were you aware of the Women's Ku Klux Klan? Does the knowledge that there was a women's branch of this heinous organization change the way you view the women of the time period?

4. The postcards that a young Hildy had received and a present-day Hildy rediscovers are our only firsthand look at Thea's character, at least until the discovery of her unfinished autobiography. Why do you think the author chose to reveal more of Thea to the reader via her writing? Does Thea's characterization and story differ from what you expected when Lily was first called to the elderly woman's body?

5. In Chapter 20 of *The Hollows* an elderly Quaker man says, "Find the wisdom in your grief," to which Lily can't help but internally respond: "What nonsense!" In what way does grief shape Lily's journey in *The Hollows*? Thea's? Hildy's?

6. "I defend the rule of law" says Lily during her debate with Perry in Chapter 26. She is speaking specifically about Margaret Dyer beating Olive Harding in this case, but how does this statement work alongside other threads in *The Hollows*? Do you feel this statement could be used to define Lily herself?

7. In Chapter 17, Lily comes across two women chatting over a baby in a baby carriage—normally a heartwarming scene. And yet, she wonders if perhaps these women, her neighbors, might be in the WKKK, and thinks to herself "Can anyone really know their neighbors—what's more,

their neighbors' hearts?" How might knowing your own neighbors' views change how you feel about them? Is this unsettling? Difficult? Or is it helpful to reconsider our assumptions that those around us view the world in the same way as we do?

8. Though good friends, Hildy and Lily are very different kinds of women, which leads to them sometimes misunderstanding or misreading the other. How do the way these two women view each other impede the growth of their friendship? Are there instances where it aids them?

9. Did you relate to Hildy's or Lily's point of view more throughout the story? Why?

10. Men and misogyny play a part in this novel, but in many cases our female protagonists are pitted against other women: Hildy against her mother, Margaret Dyer against Olive Harding, and of course, the majority of the WKKK against Lily's reelection campaign. What do you think this adds to the story? What does it say about women during this time period, and even our own?

11. Kinship and family are an important thread throughout in *The Hollows*, from the discovery of Dyer's real family, to Hildy's relationship with her mother and with Thea, to Lily's worry for her children, to the novel's last scene, of Jurgis and Marvena's wedding. How is family celebrated in the novel? Are there times when the ties that bind get a bit too tight for some of these characters?

Turn the page for a sneak peek at the
next book in the Kinship series

Available Winter 2021

JESS MONTGOMERY
THE STILLS

PROLOGUE

Wednesday, November 23, 1927
Thanksgiving Eve
8:42 a.m.

Week before last, cold shooed warmth into a wish and a memory, then rattled tree limbs to leaflessness with one gnarly hand, while gripping the earth with the other.

Now on this cold earth Zebediah Harkins lies belly down in the shaggy brush line by an old clearing, as if he had crawled here through the forest itself. Truth be told, this morning, as on every morning for the past two weeks, he'd turned off just a mile into the three-mile trek down Forbidden Creek Run, the dirt road between his home and the Rossville schoolhouse, then traced his way to his post along nearly-hidden, almost-forgotten paths once cleared to make way for the iron works business—itself now all but gone.

A not-yet-sticking snow teases Zebediah's face with quick melting licks. With his right eye squeezed shut, he focuses the other over the top of his Hamilton single-shot rifle—the only gun Pa will let him have, though he's hoping for a new Winchester repeating shotgun for Christmas—and aims at a squirrel, over there by the old stone iron blast furnace, stout as the hill against which it was built back in his grandpa's youth, and where his grandpa, so the old man told him, had once worked. Now the furnace—as cold as the earth since the industry had left the region two decades back—stands in uncrumbling defiance against time and vines and brush and twenty-year-old trees growing where the old ones had been clear cut, burned to charcoal, and fed along with coal into the hot smelting fires of the furnace.

All that's left of iron works in the Appalachian hills of Bronwyn and nearby counties are old furnaces like this, bits of glassy slag littered in amongst the natural rocks and dirt, and stories like his Papaw's. But those stories now just live in Zebediah's memory—the old man had passed on the year before—and are fading fast.

Zebediah has learned, of late, the value of focusing on whatever's going on in the moment as a way to secure the immediate future—like that unwary squirrel, shoveling acorns into its cheeks. The critter would be good in a stew, and wouldn't Ruthie be right pleased if he brought it home? It'd proffer savory bits to chew, alongside the greens and biscuits she'd likely serve up for supper yet again.

But he hears his sister's weary voice, as if she's just knelt beside him to whisper in his ear: *Where'd you get that, Zeb?*

Where you been all day, if'n not the schoolhouse?

And he can see her suspicious pinched expression as she eyes the dark smears on his jacket—dirt she'll have to scrub out on the washboard—and as she notes the flashing quickness of his looking away. Somehow, though it's not for want of trying, Ruthie is the one person he can't lie to. And Zebediah doesn't want her to know that he's been skipping school.

Zebediah impatiently swipes the snow from his face, and when he refocuses, the squirrel has skittered to the other side of the makeshift ledge of plank on stone, on which sit bottles of moonshine. God forbid he shoots one of them. Boss would have his hide.

It's his job to keep an eye on these bottles, and on the bigger swigging jug, always set out when he gets here, and stowed away, he reckons, in some hidey-hole after he leaves. He doesn't know where the moonshiner's still is—probably not too far off, but surely in a cave or crevice or deeper woods. Out here, in the thinner new woods, it would be too easy to find. But that's none of his business—boss had made sure to tell him that, along with plenty of other admonishments:

Better you not know. All you need do to earn your coin is stay quiet. Just watch. Make note if someone don't leave money for their bottle or swig, or overly-guzzles from the jug, or pockets the coins left on the plank.

Zebediah tried to gather up the money between customers, but sometimes the customers came too close, or overlapped, always looking startled to spot someone they normally saw in the fine town of Kinship, Bronwyn's county seat, then laughing at being caught out: *you won't tell Mary? Not if you don't tell Sue!* Never led to trouble, but anyway, the moonshiner had told him, if there *was* trouble, *Just run, boy! You report any deceptions to me. I'll mete out any needed retribution.*

Several men have already been by this morning and stuck to the honor system. After each man was out of sight, Zebediah gathered their coins in the pouch he keeps in his pocket.

He will only get a small portion—five cents for every dollar collected. But plenty of men are coming by—not just because it's the day before Thanksgiving, but because in winter's bone-jarring cold, making shine at small, personal stills will be harder, and with smoke rising twixt bare-limbed trees, hiding stills' locations will be tougher too. 'Sides, talk is that revenuers—the federal agents that work for the Bureau of Prohibition, *men of God,* his pa said, will soon beset the land like ill-timed locusts.

The boy rolls to his side, sits up. Suddenly his vision speckles, grey spots waltzing with snowflakes. He closes his eyes, leans his head against a rough tree trunk. His head throbs, and his stomach roils. As Zebediah reaches into his pocket, his hand shakes, but he manages to grab the hard biscuit that he'd nabbed on his way out this morning from the remnants of last night's supper still out in the kitchen. Usually, Ruthie cleans everything nice and proper at night, rises early to make a good hot breakfast and fills his dinner pail for school, but she's been so preoccupied of late. It's too early for a mid-day meal, but he skipped breakfast and suddenly he's ravenous and wobbly. Though the biscuit has dried overnight to the toughness of hard tack, he snaps off a bite. His mouth waters for want of the squirrel, and that's enough to soften the biscuit.

Mayhap it's just as well if he doesn't bring home squirrel. Besides, when he'd complained about the sameness of Ruth's suppers evening afore last, Pa had backhanded him so hard that his vision blacked out for several moments. From the other side of this inflicted darkness, he'd heard Pa growl: *Don't go making work for your sister! She's got enough.*

By which Pa means—tending to Ma, dying.

'Course Pa don't call it *dying*. He calls it: *taking a bad spell*. As if Ma just has a touch of fever, and Pa—with all his prayers and acts of faith—can force God to make her whole again.

But Ma knows. Ruthie knows.

Zebediah knew before even they did. There'd been that day back in early September, when the last breath of summer taunted red-tinged leaves loosening on high limbs, and made the Rossville schoolhouse so suffocatingly warm that Miss Cooper, the schoolmarm, had let everyone tote their dinner pails outside when the mine's noon bell rang. Zebediah had kept right on toting, down to the creek and up a winding way into the hills west of the coal town, then up Forbidden Creek Run. Once he reached the turn off to their farm, he heard a terrible crackling sound coming from the direction of their house, though it was yet far off enough to be out of sight. And so he'd broken into a full run to the house, dropping his pail as he realized, with a frisson of foreboding, that the sound came from Ma, coughing so fierce that by the time he reached her, she was bent near double on the side porch and holding her stomach.

Yet it wasn't seeing her in this *bad spell* that made him know it was something more. It was the glassy, begging terror of her gaze as she looked up at him.

Since then, Ma has taken to her bed. Ruth, who is in the eighth grade and loves school so much she has pretensions toward high school, has dropped out to tend to Ma and the twins, not yet school age, while Pa works as a laborer for Sheriff Lily Ross and others in Bronwyn County, and spent all the rest of his time at River Rock Holiness Church, looking for a miracle. 'Til recently. After church one Sunday a month or so ago, he proclaimed it was *good for nothin'*. And at least twice since, Zebediah's thought he smelled liquor on Pa's breath, like when he was backhanded. Like before he got all church-if-ied and said the Holy Ghost had cured him of the bottle.

Now, it both terrifies and amuses Zebediah to consider the possibility of Pa himself showing up here at the still as a customer.

But Zebediah—well, they expect him to just keep on going to school, even though he's the opposite of Ruthie. Reading is tricky. No matter how hard he tries to focus, it seems the letters lift off the page and swim around nonsensically. Why, he ought to be the one dropped out, tending to Ma, but Ruthie is older, and a girl.

Or at least he ought to be allowed to take up some of Pa's work, or go hunting in Pa's stead. But last week, when they went hunting for a Thanksgiving wild turkey, Zebediah's hands got to quivering, and Pa thought it was because he didn't have the stomach to shoot a critter. Ridiculous. Zebediah is twelve, plenty old to be hunting alongside his daddy, and he knows of boys, farther up in the hills from where they live, who lay claim to hunting since age four. Zebediah had tried to explain that he doesn't know why sometimes his body trembles and his sight blurs. Pa had shaken his head in disgust, muttered, *you ain't ready yet*, and threatened to take away his hunting rifle.

A snapping sound startles Zebediah to wide-eyed alertness, in time to see that it's just a small branch, wind-flicked from a treetop down to the ground near the bottles of 'shine. But the bottles are fine, lined up side-by-side, as if the plank is a proper store shelf.

Zebediah shifts on the hard ground, trying to find a comfortable divot. He feels the pouch of coins, digging through his pocket into his hip. His stomach roils. That hard biscuit won't stave off hunger for long.

And yet he grins, thinking about the fanciful books Ruthie covets at the Kinship General Store—most especially one that's been in the store for nearly a year, *The Blue Castle*. Since Pa had found church, the Bible was the only book allowed in their house, and he'd surely not allow a title so worldly. But with these coins, Zebediah could go back, buy that book for Ruthie for Christmas—he'd memorized the cover with its goldenrod yellow binding and, on the front, the outline of a grand castle impossibly built into rocks and clouds—and sneak it to her. Maybe getting the book would remind Ruthie of who she was before Ma took sick. Who Ruthie still is, deep down, below the weariness and sorrow.

Suddenly, footsteps crunch the frozen spikes of grass on the other side of the old iron furnace.

Zebediah quickly goes back down on his belly, makes himself a creature of the forest, hidden but still able to see who approaches. Like a sneaky snake, he thinks, and grins at the notion.

The men who emerge into view are not ones he recognizes, nor are they the sort he expects—farmers, coal miners, hunters. One man is in a fine wool coat and boots, the other in just a suit and two-toned leather lace up dress shoes. Both wear fedora hats.

Zebediah frowns. There's a speakeasy in Kinship for men like this—everyone knows that. Even the ladies and children at his church know, because the preacher, Brother Stiles, likes to rail at length against such big town dens of iniquity.

"Here it is," the man in the coat says, gesturing at the makeshift shelf of bottled 'shine.

Zebediah's frown deepens. This man's voice has the sound of the hills and the hollers, each word jangling into the next, like beads on a string, but something makes him seem an outsider even more than the younger man, coatless and in fancy shoes too fragile for backwoods hiking. The older man takes off his fedora, nervously slicking back his hair. What are these fancy men doing here? Are they the *revenuers* people have been talking about?

The coatless younger man shivers so hard that his voice crackles as he asks, "This is it? You were supposed to lead me to George Vogel's main operation!"

Vogel? Who in the world is that, Zebediah wonders.

"Well, now, one small operation leads to the bigger ones." The older man grins, drawing his mouth back tight as if trying to appear clever, but he looks more like a rat baring its teeth.

Zebediah's heart pounds. Something is not right. He wants to yell at the younger man: *run!*

Through chattering teeth, the younger man says: "It had better. We're paying you enough—"

The older man frowns. "No. The pay isn't what I'm after. You promised—"

"You'd better not be toying with the bureau," the younger man says. "We're deadly serious—"

The younger man pulls out a revolver, but it shakes in his hand. *Damn mister*, thinks Zebediah—he's already rooting for him, whether he's a revenuer or not—*stop shaking!* But maybe he can't help it, just like Zebediah can't.

The older man's expression stiffens. "Here—let me show you some markings on the jug that will help you believe me—a symbol that leads straight to Vogel. But put away the damn gun first."

Markings? No, no . . . the only marking on the jug was three Xs, to signify that the whiskey was triple-distilled. That wouldn't lead to whoever this Vogel is.

Zebediah wants to cry out, *don't be a fool!* but already, the younger man is putting away his gun. Something blue and gold pinned to his vest flashes in the spare morning sun. Then his jacket closes over his vest again, as he steps toward the plank holding the bottles of moonshine.

Suddenly, the older man pulls out a pistol from inside his overcoat, holds it out steady, and shoots twice—once, missing the revenuer and grazing the stone furnace. At the cracking sound, the revenuer starts to whirl around, just as the older man shoots again, hitting him in the head. Blood spurts as the revenuer goes down to his knees, grabbing at his head, knocking his fedora to the ground. But then his eyes roll back, his bloody hands drop, and he falls forward. The older man puts away his pistol, strides to the younger man, kicks him over to his back.

For a long moment, he stares, as if regarding nothing more than a fallen tree limb.

Run. The moonshiner had told Zebediah to run if there was trouble—and this is the greatest mess he's ever seen. But Zebediah freezes, and all he can do is stare, transfixed.

Then the older man's mouth curls, just the slightest self-congratulatory smile

Zebediah gasps, startled by the odd, cold reaction. The man looks around, his eyes small and glassy, and stares into the woods in Zebediah's direction. He holds his breath.

A chipmunk darts out from the old iron furnace, making the man jump, look away. Then he laughs—startled and relieved—and shakes his head. He pulls a flask from his hip pocket, starts to drink. Frowns, apparently discovering that it's empty. He moves toward the plank of moonshine, opens the sipping jug, takes a swig, then sloppily pours some into his flask, which he caps and pockets as he walks away. Shortly after he's out of sight, he starts whistling some merry up-tempo tune, off-key and wheezy.

Tears fall down Zebediah's face, but the boy carefully gulps back his sobs.

Finally, the man's wretched whistling fades, and the only sounds are a thin hum of breeze, occasional bird song, creaking bare-limbed trees.

For a long time, Zebediah lays where he is, staring at the younger man's body. What to do, what to do? Wait for someone else to come along? Run to find the moonshiner?

The man's hand twitches.

Zebediah swallows back a whimper. Surely that was just the man's body shutting down. He'd seen that with deer and pheasant out on hunts with Pa—the post-death twitch.

But then there's a soft moan. Zebediah closes his eyes. Just the wind . . . just the wind. The moan grows louder.

Slowly, Zebediah rises stiffly, as if he's aged decades in the last minutes. His mouth is sticky, parched. He opens the sipping jug, wipes the top with his jacket sleeve. The jug is so heavy he nearly drops it. But he manages to take three long gulps. The liquid burns like fire down his throat, in his chest, in his stomach. He gasps.

The man moans again.

Zebediah finally finds the strength to walk over to him, moving so slowly it feels like he's trying to run in the muddy bottom of a creek.

The man's eyes are open, glassy, staring up at him in shock. His mouth is agape. He does not appear to be breathing. Had Zebediah only imagined the man's moans?

The man's jacket has fallen open, revealing a pin on his vest. The item that had flashed, moments ago. The pin dangles, knocked loose by the man's fall. It's beautiful, in the shape of a shield, with a bright royal blue background, and gold letters, a U. and an S. on either side of an insignia that looks like a gold coin. But the other letters seem to rise off the shield, float around, like they do in his schoolbooks. Ruthie would know right away what the letters say.

Ruthie.

Zebediah starts crying again. He wants his big sister.

Another moan. The man's eyes flutter.

Zebediah stares at him.

"Mister?"

JESS MONTGOMERY is the "Literary Life" columnist for the *Dayton Daily News* and Executive Director of the renowned Antioch Writers' Workshop in Yellow Springs, Ohio. Based on early chapters of the first in the Kinship Series, *The Widows,* Jess was awarded an Ohio Arts Council individual artist's grant for literary arts and named the John E. Nance Writer-in-Residence at Thurber House in Columbus. She lives in her native state of Ohio.